THE DESIGNATED VIRGIN

A Novel of the Movies

JOHN W. HARDING

Pulp Hero Press publishes its books in a variety of print and electronic formats. Some content that appears in one format may not appear in another.

Editor: Bob McLain
Layout: Artisanal Text

ISBN 978-1-68390-211-9
Printed in the United States of America

Pulp Hero Press | www.PulpHeroPress.com
Address queries to bob@pulpheropress.com

Contents

To the Reader

Few accounts remain to us today of life inside the legendary American Mutoscope and Biograph Co. during its early New York City years. This novel is not intended to be the final word on the subject. Let film historians continue to dig and sift. The goal throughout my research was to provoke interest, not provide documentation. However, when dealing with facts such as timelines and biographies, central players and other pieces of the historical puzzle, I have tried to remain faithful to what is known or has been accepted as known.

In the early 1900s David Wark Griffith performed as an actor in stage companies under the name Lawrence Griffith, wishing to spare his family any embarrassment. He used his real name on a published poem and a full-length play in 1907. But it wasn't until August 1910 that he used his own name again professionally. While renewing his contract as a motion picture director at Biograph he crossed out "Lawrence" and wrote "David" in ink above it.

Something had changed for him. He had accepted his destiny and was announcing that from that point forward he would take full responsibility for his work as a "picture maker." Soon afterward he traded New York for Hollywood, where he would help lay the groundwork of an industry and leave his lasting mark on world cinema as D.W. Griffith.

Our story is set in 1909, however, before Griffith was at all sure about his future in motion pictures. He was just 34 years old and still known to one and all as Lawrence.

—JWH

Note: All chapter titles are taken from Griffith's Biograph releases of the period.

PART I

ONE
"The Girl and the Outlaw"

"Why not just lie there, darlin', and let me look at you?"

"Mind your manners, mister."

"I don't get it. Women spend all their time fixin' themselves up so men'll pay notice. Then when we get you home and naked, you won't let us look."

"What you want to look at? My *eyes*?"

"You know my favorite part of a woman's body?"

"Prob'ly."

"No. It's not that. Not that at all. I'm thirty years old, darlin'. Way beyond an infatuation with Br'er Rabbit's briar patch."

"Whose what?"

"I've had lots of favorites since then. Back of the ear, just below the hairline. Loved that spot for a time. ... That whatdayacallit vein, up side of the neck? ... Back of the knees. That's a sweet spot, too. Refill?"

She held up the cup he had given her. "Still got some." He clearly had something more on his mind. He was just looking for the time to bring it up.

"You tellin' me," he said with a furled brow, "a Southern gal never heard no one refer to it as Br'er Rabbit's briar patch?"

"Why, Mr. Trawley," she replied in her most coquettish drawl, "whatever do you mean?"

"Your fur. Your bunny thatch. ... Your *beaver*."

"What is your obsession with animals?" she asked. "You some sort of botanist?"

"*Botan*—?" Deward stopped. "You know, I'm starting to have a new understanding of riverboat educations."

Augusta couldn't restrain a naughty smile.

He picked up on it at once. "Ah, I knew you were joshing me."

"Were you by any chance referring to 'our little secret'?"

"What's that?"

"That's what the gentlemen on the river call it."

"Well, I hate to tell you, darlin', but your secret's out," he chortled.

"And what do your fine lady friends here call it?"

"A cunt."

Augusta reeled back in half-feigned shock. "Excuse me?"

"Don't blame me. That's what Willie Shakespeare called it. That makes it okeedoke with Deward Trawley."

"Shakespeare never used such a word."

"Sure he did. 'Henry Five.' The French court scene. Look it up." He took another drink and smacked his lips. "I played in it once."

"Were you Henry?"

"No, not exactly."

"Well, I guess they don't do that scene on the showboats. *Not exactly.*"

She took a quick sip from her cup. "So, you didn't tell me. What's your favorite part these days?"

"In Shakespeare?"

"No. You were sayin' what's your favorite parts of a woman's body."

"Oh." His grin returned as he laid there in deliberation. "Today I'd have to say feet."

"Feet?" She pulled her right foot out from the covers and wiggled her toes like a pink caterpillar crawling on a twig. "You don't think they're dirty?"

"Dirty? Not to me," he said. "Those canoes of yours—that's the first thing I noticed about you. I said to myself, this gal could be a champion swimmer. Or a runner."

She tucked her foot back under the sheet. "I should've run when I saw you, that's for sure."

He took another sip. "Who said they were dirty?"

"Never mind."

"What else you learn about on those showboats?"

"Ever heard of a bunny show?"

"No. But sounds intriguing."

"You dock in some new town and there's already someone hanging up your posters. Everyone gets dressed up in their parade clothes and next thing you're marchin' down Main Street with your banners and drums. They got your handbills sitting in stacks in shop windows. But show time comes and the seats are empty. Maybe an old farmer there with his wife. Two young ones sittin' down front by themselves. *That's* your bunny show. In the morning the hired men go out with gunnysacks for rabbit stew."

Deward smiled. "Maybe they should call 'em *bunny sacks*."

She pretended like she didn't hear him. "You know how to catch a bear without a gun?"

"Wait. They don't have guns on them showboats?"

"Sure, they got guns. But little towns have little sheriffs and little judges. They keep their ears out for poachers. So you got to go about it quietly."

"Bow and arrow?"

"They're river folk, Deward, not Indians."

He tossed back a final gulp and brought his glass down hard upon the lamp table.

"What they do is," she went on, "they make a loop in a rope and tie one end to a short log by the water. Then when a bear steps in the loop, the log drags him in and pulls him along until he drowns."

"Bears drown? Who told you that?"

"I've seen it. Deers, too. But it's harder to catch a deer by its leg."

Augusta downed what was left in her cup and let her head sink back on the pillow. The feathers came up over her ears and she couldn't tell if Deward was talking now or not. That ceiling was a marvel. She could only imagine waking up with that long braid of molding hanging over her with that bulge in its center like the snake digesting a fox.

"What do you do with so much space?" she asked.

He gave the room a glance around before shrugging. "I got an active imagination."

"How much do they want for a room like this?"

"Six and a half clams."

"A month?"

"That's per week, sweetie."

"Oh."

"There's some for four without the steam heat." He reached up to tip his glass and have another peek inside. "Where'd I put that bottle?" he asked.

"Table, next to the kitchen."

"Oh, yeah." He swung his legs off the mattress and sat upright on the edge.

"I don't suppose I need a residence in town," she said.

He looked back at her in disbelief. "A residence in—" he began and then stopped. "Listen, if you're going to work in this city you got to live here. There's no 'supposeds' about that." He stood up and wavered a bit before starting off bare-assed across the rug.

Augusta scooted herself higher against the headboard to wait. She wondered if she could get by without a radiator. It was colder here, that was for darn sure. But winter would be done in another month or two. Where was that radiator he was paying an extra two-fifty a week for? Was it over behind that sad old saddle-seat Windsor, or hidden away in back of the armoire?

She turned her head to the lone window with its chintz drapes. Passing headlamps in the street below left delicate angel-hair etchings on the glass. An icy lick of air ran up her neck. She shivered and tugged the sheet higher around her shoulders. Yes, two-fifty more for a radiator was probably a good idea.

The mattress fell with a sudden dip and Deward was back, perched on the edge holding the dark bottle with no label. He tilted it over his glass and watched the amber liquid slosh inside. When it reached the brim he looked back at her and saw she was holding out her cup.

They shared a silent drink and this time Augusta ended by smacking her lips. Deward smiled. "How do you like our uptown moonshine?"

"I was thinking you both must've been drawn from the same creek."

"How's that?"

"You start off rough but grow smooth over time."

"What was the first thing you noticed about me?"

"Honestly, it was your eyes. They were so dramatic."

"Thanks."

"In a sad sort of way."

"Hunh?"

"I remember thinking, that poor man. He's just like me. Bet he doesn't know a soul here in New York."

Deward scoffed. "Well, you were wrong. I've known plenty of souls here. I've been in their homes, their offices, even in their plays. What passes for a soul in this city isn't hardly worth a thimble full of candle wax."

"What stage plays you been in?"

"Well, 'Aunt Lettie's Salad Days', for one. That's the one everyone remembers." He paused for her reaction. "Oh, come on! That was a hit play. Ran forever. You never heard of it?"

"Sorry. What role did you play?"

"The nephew. The whole story was about me, really—how I have to stop my kindly widowed aunt from making a fool of herself with some huckster. After that, I had two agents *and* a manager. Stocked my closet full with tailored suits."

"So, what happened?"

"No one plays juveniles forever. Couldn't get a decent role to save my life. Sold off the suits one after the other. I had some tips but nothing worked out. I figured I might as well try the flickers until something come along."

"You mean those peep shows? With the crank?"

"No, not that arcade garbage. Boxers and hula girls? Nah. Not them. I'm talking about the ones they got now, in the nickel theaters."

"Oh."

"It's not real acting, of course. There's no lines to learn. No elocution. Most of the time you're not even on a stage. Everyone goes outside or up on a roof, because they take lots of light. So basically you're out in the open, pulling your cap on and off like a monkey for some stuck-up hurdy-gurdy man."

"I think I know what you mean. I did some modeling once."

"The last fellow I worked for—now there was a real stuck-up phony. He was from the South, too. No offense."

"What part?"

"Kentucky, I think. I heard an actor slip up once and call him '*Kain-tuck*.' He got his liberty handed to him in a hurry. Everyone was supposed to address him as *Mister* Griffith.' 'Yes, sir, whatever you say, Mr. Griffith.' ... We were all expected to dance to his tune."

"The man I did modeling for, he didn't care what you called him. He was the one dishing out the names."

"What'd he call you?"

"'Dirty Feet.' "

"Oh, *he's* the one." Deward took another gulp and thought a second. "How'd they get dirty?"

"That studio was a pig sty! I don't believe he ever had that floor washed, not once. You walk across it barefoot and the bottoms of your feet were darker than Uncle Remus. Like that." She tried to snap her fingers, but they wouldn't make a sound. "Humiliating," she said.

"You should've known better than to wave 'em in the air."

"Yeah."

"How'd you get mixed up with him?"

"Oh, it was November. On the Monongahek."

"Sounds pretty. Like the sheet music on a parlor piano."

"Well, it wasn't like it sounds. They were about to put the boat up for winter, and I needed to get some new photos taken. I didn't much look like the ones I had any more. I heard about this fellow who'd do 'em cheap. He had all sorts of painted backdrops, elegant ones, and a big room in the back."

"Naturally."

"When he heard my resources were limited, he proposed an arrangement. He was a godsend."

"What did God's emissary want in return?"

"Mostly pose around some potted plants. If I never see another fern or holly tree, it'll be fine with me. Or lacy shawls. Or men in masks."

"So, that was his game."

"That—that was it. For starters."

"What else?"

"It never come to that."

"You run away?"

"Someone tipped the local sheriff. They came and got the photographs and tossed him in the pokey."

"You, too?"

"I didn't wait to find out."

Deward gave her a reassuring nod. "Well, you've come to the right city to get lost in. I can vouch for that. You going to try more modeling?"

"No, thanks."

"Kitchen work?"

"Nothing to do with food. I swear. I'm never going to peel another spud."

"Well, how you plan to make your rent? They don't have bunny shows in New York."

"No."

Deward shifted his weight to stare squarely in her eyes. "You want to make some money fast?"

"Maybe."

"I don't mean pocket change. I'm talking about a real stake."

"What do I have to do?"

"You know that stuck-up picture director?"

"*Kain-tuck?*"

Deward nodded. "I got an idea while you were talking. You and him being fellow Southerners, I think he might go for you."

"Is he married?"

"No, I don't think so. But so much the better if he is. Fact is, this bastard's rolling in Yankee dollars. He hands out stacks of vouchers at the end of each day—five dollars per actor, maybe more for regulars. And he rents the costumes and buys whatever he needs for the pictures. So at the end of the week he's sittin' on a lot of cash. I figure there's a few thousand there or more, just waiting. You know how to play a sucker?"

"I know some angles."

"I knew you and me was going to hit it off. Listen, tomorrow's the start of the week. How about I take you down there? Introduce you around."

"Where is this place?"

"Back past the train station a bit. Not far at all. Down on East Fourteenth."

"You think he'll like me?"

"Don't worry. I'll give you some pointers. He don't go for vulgar talk, that's for starters. Not that he's a country parson, by any means. He's been on stage himself out west. He's like most of the men in this town. They don't care that much for a real woman. They go for the 'hometown sweetheart' type. Youth and purity—that's what gets their juices flowing. Innocence. What you call an *aphrodisiac.*"

"What's that?"

"Aphrodisiac?"

"Hunh-uh," said Augusta with her naughtiest smirk. "Innocence."

Deward broke into his biggest grin yet. "Darlin'," he said, "you're a natural."

TWO
"A Woman's Way"

Maybe God was punishing her. That had to be it. There was no other way to explain how she ended up dressed like this.

All through breakfast she had told herself it would be okay, that somehow it would work itself out. But her last shred of optimism vanished in the glass of a department store window.

She had only meant to take a quick peek. Deward was off in a mob of pedestrians waiting on a traffic cop when the display caught her eye. It showed a sunny beach, as happy and open as the blue painted backdrop. Standing there scattered around on a buttery sand dune were a half-dozen mannequins. The women were dressed in a lively gingham material, and two had on those modern eyeglasses with the darkened lenses. The male dummies stood farther back sporting lightweight suits with crushed ribbon ties. Their blank faces were the very mask of serenity and contentment, ready to absorb the coming colors of spring.

But there was a movement in the glass and Augusta's vision pulled back to its surface. A brownish-red smear stood at the center wearing the squashed, plump face of a blonde schoolgirl. Her bonnet was not too different from her own but she was holding tightly to the two sides of a dusky horse blanket.

How sad, she thought. *Some absent-minded old soldier must have marched off and left his half-witted little daught—*

Then came a mule's kick to her gut. That was her reflection up there. That was her lumpy blue bonnet and her stiff-as-hay curls wrapped in the folds of that faded rag of an overcoat.

It was mortifying! Any smart director worth a teaspoon of salt would demand a closer look. He would wait for her to take off her coat and then her bonnet in front of everybody. The snickering would start at the sight of her wig. They would probably not even bother to hide their amusement. And there she would stand exposed to the world in her horrid *Nancy* costume, that blue calico horror with its puffed sleeves and doily-white pinafore. There would be nothing left to hide behind.

Deward thought it would make the perfect impression on his stuck-up Southern director. He said it was sure to put him in mind of some ancient "Alice" drawings by a man named Tenniel.

Lord! Why didn't she have the sense to leave the whole get-up back on the *Water Queen*? Better yet, why didn't she toss it overboard? It had been years since anyone thought she was cute in it. All she could do now was brace herself for titters and ridicule in the greatest fashion capitol this side of Paris.

Deward's face ballooned behind her in the glass. "What's so interest—?" he began. His words were stolen by the shriek of a whistle. The pedestrians were on the move again, stepping off the curb with their level stares. It was time for little Alice to hop down from her looking glass.

She took her place in the sluice of strangers. Tin boxes careened along beside them on rubber band wheels, bouncing off across shiny streetcar rails and dodging the occasional clip-clopping carriage.

All of Manhattan seemed to her powered by a giant blast furnace that leaked at every seam. Vapors spewed from mouths and tailpipes and rose from cast iron plugs in the road.

Augusta saw Deward break from the pack and go barreling along the curbstone. She skipped and hustled to catch up, frantic with the thought she might lose him. He was her only hope now of finding a path back.

"Jesus, Deward, what's your hurry?" she asked as she fell in next to him again.

He must have taken it as a scolding because he frowned and did not speak until they rounded the next corner. He led the way down a mostly deserted block. "Tell me more about that cameraman of yours."

"I told you what there was to tell."

"The local sheriff—you think he put out a warrant on you?"

"A warrant? No. I don't think so." She couldn't understand why he was bringing all this up again now.

"A circular, maybe?"

"Maybe."

He gave a single nod. "You're probably okay, then. Warrants, though, they're different. A judge issued one of those on me once."

"What happened?"

"Nothing. It was up Yonkers way, anyhow. Different jurisdiction. It wasn't even on me, really. It was for this fellow *Longacre*. ... Deward Longacre." He gave a lopsided smile, clearly pleased with his cleverness.

"What did you do?"

Deward's face fell in a scowl. "It wasn't me, I told you!" he snapped. "Had nothing at all to do with me."

"What did *Mr. Longacre* do?"

"It should have been a simple business deal. Strictly legit. It didn't have to go like it did, you know?"

"Not really."

"Once lawyers get in on a thing like that, well..."

They came to a corner standing in a wedge of sunlight and Deward paused to get his bearings. In an instant he was striding away up an alley that howled like a wind tunnel in a sudden arctic blast. Deward didn't try to speak again until he got to the end of the block and came to an abrupt halt.

Augusta did not see he was stopped until it was too late. She rammed hard against his back.

"Hey, careful!" he grumbled. "That's it up ahead. Looks like something's going on."

"What? What is it?" She clutched his sleeve to peek around, not sure what to expect.

Halfway along a string of sooty brownstones marched a dozen ladies in a line wearing long winter coats and hats the size of washtubs. Some had white banners draped across their chests and others held placards on sticks. Even at this distance Augusta could tell they meant business.

"That's the studio," said Deward. "Can't make out the words. Looks like some sort of boycott."

"A *boy*—"

"Damn! ... One of them signs is calling on Governor Hughes!"

"What? What do they want?"

"Damned bitches! What a load of... First the bookies, and now this." He turned to face her. "I had a piece of the pony action for a time. It was sweet. Then that old Canon Chase stuck his nose in and got everyone riled up." He looked back at the picket line. "Governor Hughes saw the light. He got religion. Before we knew what for, he was signing a law. Off-site betting was outlawed. Numbers games done for. ... Looks to me like this could be part of that same pack. Coming after the flickers now. Damn!... Well, we're here. Might as well go see."

Augusta grabbed his sleeve. "No, Deward. ... We should wait. We can come back tomorr—"

"Forget that!" he said with a yank. "Are you with me or not?"

"Of course I am."

"'Cause I'm doing this for you, ya know."

"I appreciate it, I do. It's only... I don't want any trouble with the governor."

"Look, this could be a blessing in disguise. They'll all be distracted. Just remember, you're a sweet, shy little daughter of the South. Leave all the talking to me."

A prune-faced woman stepped from the line as they drew close and came forward as if to greet them. Across her chest a banner read "Break the Chains of Bondage!" She clutched a sheaf of leaflets under her elbow, peeling one off the top to hand to Deward before pivoting sharply to rejoin the line.

Augusta leaned in to read over Deward's shoulder. "On Temperance and Public Morals" it said in large printed type across the top.

"Holy—" blurted Deward in a whisper. "Temperance Leaguers!"

"What do you mean?"

"Anti-saloon gals. It's worse than I thought." He scowled and nudged her arm with his. "Just keep walking."

As they hewed close to a wrought-iron handrail, Augusta stole sideway peeks at the other placards. *Down with Demon Rum ... Join the Cause of Suffering Humanity! ... Boycott Immorality and Vice.*

Deward headed up a flight of cement steps to a solid oak door bearing the brass number 11 and gave it a rap. Then as Augusta stepped up beside him he grabbed the round metal knob.

The door swung into an empty marble foyer reverberating with the sound of sawing and hammering. As he stepped inside, Deward pinched his nose and frowned." Whew," he said over the din, "it stinks."

Augusta's nostrils flared with the musky smell of fresh-cut lumbers and turpentine. She understood instantly what it meant. A new show was in the works. Production days on the river were always her favorite days, when even the most miserable among them put aside their unhappiness and pitched in.

There was a birdlike rustle at the front window and a thin woman dashed off across the chilly marble. She took up her station at a folding table before a flight of stairs that circled as it ascended to a sunny third-story corridor. The high ceiling and curved banister gave the little foyer the open, airy feeling of a rotunda.

"Stay put," said Deward. "I'll see what's going on."

Augusta drifted over to the wall. The construction noise was coming from the rear, behind two tall, decorative doors tucked under the staircase. She pictured a room with dozens of elegantly dressed couples swirling in a mirrored ballroom. It was harder to imagine a sweaty stage crew working on sets.

A whoosh of air from the front brought a sudden aroma of pastries and butter. A thin boy of fourteen or so stood at the door dressed in a knit sweater and knee-britches. He was holding two large, grease-stained paper sacks.

"Hey, Miss Bratt," he called happily to the bird lady. "They had the apple ones today!" He clicked his tongue then scurried off toward the tall rear doors and vanished in the darkness.

Deward gave a short whistle and was already on the move toward that same dark chamber. He motioned for her to come.

The room beyond the tall doors turned out to be as chilly as it was dark. Augusta wrapped her arms around her and waited for her eyes to adjust.

"Donuts! … nuts … nuts …" echoed the delivery boy's voice off the curved inner walls. "Get 'em while they're HOT! … hot … hot …"

The noise of saws and hammers dropped off and all she heard was the shuffling of feet and the creaking of floorboards. High above her was a dome rigged with catwalks and black cords that ran from housings to banks of unlit bulbs. From the back somewhere came the soft strumming of a ukulele and the tentative sound of a female voice traipsing lightly up and down a minor scale.

Two men came from nowhere with a long sofa and argued over where to set it on a wood platform at the center of the floor. A plump lady in a hair scarf hurried past them on the stage with hangered garments laid across her forearms.

"Here's your rural constable, Mr. Griffith," she said, lowering one arm to lift the next, "and this is your town judge."

"Fine, fine," came a distracted reply.

Deward leaned in to whisper in her ear. "That's him."

Across the floor sat a thin man in a tweed suit on an unusually tall stool. He wore a torn straw hat with a brim that extended out over his long, arched nose. As he leaned forward in the dark he kept one heel of a leather boot hooked over a cross-brace and listened calmly to the unheard concerns of an older man in shirtsleeves.

"Which one's *Kain-tuck*?" whispered Augusta.

"That's him with the nose. That other one must be an accountant by the looks of him."

Shifting to get a better view, Augusta instantly felt her bonnet being lifted from her head. "Hey!" she cried. Deward had pushed in close and was fumbling to remove her coat.

"Hold on, there are buttons!" she said. "I can do it!"

"May I be of help?" boomed out a voice behind them. Augusta turned into the toothy grin of a large, unkempt man with rounded shoulders and a thick jaw. "Who do you two kids want to see?" he asked, batting two unruly patches of eyelash.

"You know me, Mack," said Deward, peeling Augusta's coat away with one fluid tug. "It's Deward Trawley."

The stranger leaned back and looped his thumbs in his vest pockets. "Oh, right," he said, then nodded toward Augusta. "What about little Alice here? Is Wonderland closed?"

"We're together," said Deward. "She's my friend."

"Why, Deward Trawley!" spurted Augusta. "I am truly shocked and mortified. How can you tell the nice man such a bald-faced fib? The truth, sir, is that I am Mr. Trawley's cousin on my very first visit to your *fair* city."

Deward managed a smile. "I wasn't done introducing you, *Cousin*. I was going to say this is my *friendly* cousin Augusta."

"Well, hello, friendly cousin Augusta. I'm friendly, too. You can just call me Mack." He gave an awkward curtsy. "We've got to be careful. We've been getting a lot of curiosity-seekers this morning."

"We passed some mighty curious specimens out front," said Deward.

"That's one boodle of biddies, ain't it? Temperance gals."

"What do they want?"

"They're tryin' to drive us to drink, is my theory."

"You hiding a saloon in here?"

"Nah. Someone said it might've been our 'Jonesy' pictures. They might have set 'em off."

"I guess I missed 'em," said Deward.

"The first was kind of fun, about how Mrs. Jones invites the local temperance gals to tea, you know, hoping to do some social-climbing. She ends up serving them spiked tea by accident. The whole group ends up feeling no pain and making fools of themselves. The audience loved it, so we did a follow-up. *Mr. Jones Has a Card Party.* Jonesy and the other husbands throw a little party while the wives are out of town. But the ladies miss their train and come home to find the men all three sheets to the wind."

Mack fell into a sort of braying laughter that ended with a snort. Augusta had to smile. "I can't imagine anyone taking offense at such charming tales."

"You're right, ma'am. Nothing offensive about 'em. But there they were out front this morning, all mad as hell. Excuse the expression."

"Bunch of silly bitches," said Deward.

"They scared me, all right. I told Mr. Griffith we should send Billy out to get some footage of them. We could put it in our next picture. Charge folks a nickel to get in and three bucks to get out."

Augusta felt ashamed for chuckling. "That's awful," she said.

Mack's hunched shoulders gave another shake. "Just my opinion, ma'am. Of course, my opinions are all one hundred percent accurate—unlike my directions."

"Any chance you can get us a word with the man?"

Mack grinned. "You got any royal blood?"

"Who's that with him, anyway—the bun in the shirtsleeves?"

"It's *Mr. Bun* to you. That's Arthur Marvin."

Deward's lips knitted and his head bobbed. "You don't say?"

Augusta saw he was impressed. "Who is he?"

"Arthur Marvin. Him and his older brother Henry started this studio. I never saw him around here before."

"Well, two things catch his attention," said Mack. "One's a bunch of picketers demanding a boycott. That's bad for business. The other's a new director that needs replacing."

"Oh, oh."

"Like I said, your timing ain't up to Swiss standards."

The man in the shirtsleeves suddenly stopped speaking and gave a final nod before heading for the rear doors.

"Okay, there he goes," said Mack. "I better check in, see what the old man needs."

"Just mention I brought someone with me he should meet."

"Good luck," said Mack, giving them both a nod before loping away toward the director.

"Criminy," said Deward in a more confidential manner. "Couldn't that guy's voice melt the wax in your ears?"

"What would you call that accent? It's sort of funny."

"I know he's from Canada originally, but there's nothing funny about him. His name was Michael when he first come. He was just your stock heavy. Any time they needed someone to play a thug or a cop for a strong-arm bit, they used him. A couple months ago Griffith put him in a comedy. He played a crazy Frenchman, running around town, knocking people over with a curtain pole. Silly stuff. But audiences loved it and the laughs went to his head. Now he only wants to do comedy. Changed his name to Mack, Mack Sennett. But it didn't change a thing," ended Deward with a shake of his head. "There's still not a damn thing funny about the guy."

The odd stranger who called himself Mack Sennett wound up his talk with the gentleman in tweed. With a final nod he raised an arm and gestured for them to come.

"Okay, it's our turn," said Deward, grabbing hold of Augusta's wrist. "Remember—I do the talking."

The director was busy thumbing through papers on a clipboard as they stepped up behind his stool. He did not look around until he heard Deward say, "Mr. Griffith, could I have a word?"

He craned his neck to study Deward's face a moment. "I know you," he said. "Your name ... I've forgotten it."

"It's Trawley, sir. Deward Trawley."

"Yes, Mr. *Trawley*. But the others—they called you something else, something amusing."

"Yes, sir."

The dapper man waited, watching.

"Clang-Clang," admitted Deward with a pale wince.

"That's it!" blurted Griffith in delight. His chuckle was mostly internal, causing his shoulders to rock. "*Clang-Clang* Trawley," he repeated to himself, enjoying the sound of it.

As he shifted on his stool a shaft of light fell on his face, giving Augusta her first good look at the man. His thin mouth and the edges of his eyes drooped a bit, giving even his smiles a slightly woebegone air. He wasn't as old as Deward had made out, though it was probably true he never looked young. His gaunt cheeks combined with that arched bridge gave him an almost imperial visage. She knew actors like him back on the river. They might appear gracious in a social gathering but when they happened upon you in town they could stride right past without so much as a nod.

"Uh, Mr. Griffith, I'd like to—" began Deward but the director stopped him with a raised hand as if shooing away a fly.

"Thank you," he said, doubling over to wipe at a scuff on the polished toe of his boot. "There'll be no further casting today."

"Actually, sir, I would like the honor of introducing my young cousin. Uh, she is also an actor."

"We don't use *actors* here, Mr. Trawley. We employ *artists*."

"Yes, sir. But her being from the South and this being her first trip to the city—" Deward reached back blindly for Augusta's hand. "She was inquiring how we make our motion pictures here."

Deward gave her no time to object. He tugged her forward and pushed her at the director.

Griffith looked up grudgingly and his expression instantly softened. "Oh, my dear," he said, slipping off his stool to unfold himself before her like a great gray stork.

She kept her eyes lowered until he was facing her full on, then offered a proscribed curtsy and raised her gaze to his.

"It's Little Nell," he proclaimed loudly. "Come closer, young lady." He held out an open palm so that she might lay her fingers in it. He was not really taller than the average man but appeared to hold himself in a higher esteem. "Please forgive me, it has been a long, trying morning. I apologize truly for being abrupt."

"I do understand, Mr. Griffith," she answered. "It must exhaust the mind to be responsible for such an establishment."

In the time it took for a real smile to register on his face, Augusta had gotten a flash of the man's true story. He was no stuck-up bully of a taskmaster after all. He was actually quite shy in that way grown men have of being shy when they believe themselves ugly in the sight of women. And Deward was wrong about something else: He loved the ladies. There was no question about that. In that instant the one thing she was absolutely sure of was that if he could be granted just one wish it would be for the gift of exciting the true interest of a beautiful woman.

"What is your name, child?"

Augusta pressed on her bottom lip and waited for a formal introduction.

"Mr. Griffith," interjected Deward Trawley. "Allow me to introduce Augusta. She is my oldest niece's daughter—from Kentucky."

"Augusta. A lovely name for a lovely girl. But, surely, not from Kentucky."

"No, sir. My people are all from Georgia. Once upon a time, as they say. Mother and Father were actors together on the river."

"Showboat actors?"

She gave a slight dip of her chin. "Artists, sir, I am proud to say."

"And your family name?"

"Lee, Mr. Griffith. Just like the beloved general."

"Miss Augusta Lee. It has a pleasing sound to it. Tell me, are your parents still practicing their art?"

"Sadly, sir, they have passed."

"My condolences. I played on tour with many gentlemen from the showboats. They are a special breed. I remember at the end of a season one of our riverboat gentlemen took gravely ill. I visited him on his deathbed and I asked him, 'What do you hope to find waiting for you in Heaven?' He did not have to think a moment. 'An audience, sir,' he said, 'an audience.'"

Griffith chuckled and there were scatterings of laughter from beyond the stage. It was the first time Augusta was aware she was being watched by others in the dark.

"Well, Miss Lee, thank you for coming. I would love to spend more time with you. Unfortunately, we've fallen behind our schedule, due to circumstances. ... Bobby!" he called out suddenly.

"Yes, sir," answered a high voice, and a body came hurtling onto the stage. It was the delivery boy from earlier with the donut sacks.

"Bobby, you may gather our cast now. Tell them we will start in five minutes."

"Sure thing, Griff!"

The director turned back, half-startled to find Augusta still there. "Thank you again. It was a pleasure. I do hope your stay here is—"

Augusta knew she was being dismissed and that whatever happened next would be up to her. "Mr. Griffith," she said, waiting for him to look at her. She reached up without hesitation and yanked the netting of blond curls off her head. Gasps rose in the shadows, followed by snickers of laughter, as she fluffed up her matted auburn hair. "Sir, I have no desire to deceive you."

"I can see that."

"As for your current circumstance, I take it you are referring to the ladies out front. I think I know how you should deal with that."

A hush fell over everything. The director's eyebrows dipped as he considered her words. "I plan to ignore them, Miss Lee. I think that's usually the wisest course."

"With respect, sir, we found a better way. On the river."

She heard Deward shifting nervously behind her. He cleared his throat and reached for her hand. "Come along now, cousin. We've taken up enough of Mr. Griffith's time."

The director lifted three fingers and held them up until Deward backed off. "Perhaps you will tell us, Miss Lee. Just what would river folk do in a situation like this?"

"We would join them."

"*Join* them?"

"We would paint our own signs and banners and go marching along beside them. People of the theater can also deplore coarse and ungodly behavior. We would remind them we are all good Christian people, and we would announce a free public performance of 'The Drunkard' or 'Trust Be Not Forsworn'—some tried and true piece that left them no doubt we stood on the side of virtue. We usually found that after that they would leave us free to perform the plays we had come to do."

Griffith nodded in thought all the while Augusta spoke, and when she finished he looked at her with a twinkle in his eye. "Miss Lee, I had forgotten. We used a similar tactic in my tours out west. It never occurred to me until now. Bless you, my girl. ... Mr. Sennett!" he hollered.

"Yes, sir," said the man with the bushy eyebrows, slipping out of the shadows.

"Mr. Sennett, see what you can do about digging up one of those moldy chestnuts. You know the sort—a real snorter about a drunkard dragging down the family bloodline."

"Landlord at the window! Sheriff pounding at the door!"

"That's the idea. We'll give it a twist, of course. Some modern touch. Let's get it in the works right away."

"You got it, Mr. Griffith," said Mack, turning at once to leave.

"Whether audiences will buy such a thing or not ..." said the direc
tor under his breath. He gave Augusta a gracious smile. "Thank you,
my dear. If you're still interested, come back tomorrow. First thing in
the morning. We'll see how you register on film. I suspect the camera
might favor you. Yes, it might favor you strongly."

"Thank you, Mr. Griffith."

"Five dollars a day is what we pay. ... Where's *Clang*—uh, Mr.
Trawley?"

"Here, Mr. Griffith."

"Thank you for bringing your cousin in today. Fate may have
guided you to me. We must talk at length later. For now, please
excuse me as I do need to get back on schedule."

Deward barely waited until he had Augusta in the foyer before
lashing out at her. "You mind telling me what you were doing
in there?"

"What do you mean?"

"I said *I'd* do the talking."

"But you didn't."

"Because I couldn't get a scat-blasted word in!" he hollered. He
glanced at the receptionist listening from her table and fell silent,
holding up the red coat as Augusta slipped her arms in.

They were out the front door and on the top step before Deward
addressed her again. "I'm just saying you were laying it on thick."

"I don't think I'd have been any better standing there on display."

He struck a mocking stance with his fist against his hip. "The name
is Lee, sir," he said in a loud falsetto, "just like our beloved general!"

Augusta felt her temper stirring. "I thought you were supposed to
be his favorite actor or something."

"I never said that."

"Seemed to me he hardly knew you at all, *Clang-Clang*." It felt good
to be dishing it back at him for a change.

"All right, lay off, hear?"

She stuffed the wig into her purse and gave the clasp a snap, then
started down the steps and pushed through the line of picketers.

Deward bumped and shuffled along behind her, skipping and
snorting until he managed to catch up. "Makes me wonder ... what
sort of line you been handin' me!" he said.

"Why'd you make me dress like this, Deward? It was humiliatin'."

He smiled. "That old goat sure as Hades liked it."

"I don't think he was such a goat at all. Nor a scarecrow. Nor a pelican, nor any of those names you called him. And he *loves* the ladies."

Deward cocked his head at that. "Yes, ma'am, you were sure a fresh saucer of milk to that mangy tomcat. Now, what's next is we got to get him off alone. He has to think it's his idea, though, get it? He can't be expecting me to come popping in on his little love nest. I'll have a witness, too, of course. Can't just be our word against his. And whoever it is, we'll send him off for the police."

Augusta came to a sudden halt. "Police!"

Deward turned to see why she stopped.

"You never mentioned calling the police," she said.

"Relax. We got to get his attention, that's all. He won't let it get to that."

She started to walk again, picking up speed quickly.

"With all that's going on," said Deward from back of her, "I figure he'll pay extra to make us go away."

"I'm not so sure I want to go away just yet."

"Wait!" he said, grabbing her arm. "What?"

She stopped to face him. "Weren't you listening? He said he might have a real job for me."

"*In flickers!*"

"So? What's so awful about that?"

"That's the rube in you showin' through. Don't you know it's all just a scam? The whole thing. Motion pictures. It's just another huckster game. Strain your eyes—and what for? Most of the time they don't even make sense. Just silly shadows doing silly things. No one with a brain pays them any notice."

She turned to start away again. "Temperance ladies pay them some notice," she said.

Deward hurried up beside her. "Well, temperance gals don't buy tickets," he said. "You know who goes to those things? Immigrants! People who don't even speak the damn language. I tell you, the novelty's gonna wear thin. It can't hardly last another—"

She heard him come to a stop behind her.

"Hey, hold on," he said, swiveling his head in all directions. "We're going the wrong way."

"I'm not going back now."

"You're not?"

"There's something I want to see."

"What're you talking about?"

"An older gentleman on the train said I should visit the Statue of Liberty."

"You mean that Frenchie thing out on Bedloe's Island?"

"I ought to at least have a look."

"I've seen it. There's nothing to it."

"We'll split up then," she said. "I'll find my way back."

"Suits me. There's a couple of fellows I need to see anyway."

"Tell me your address again."

"East Eighteenth and Second Avenue."

"What number?"

"Two-twelve."

"Two-twelve, Eighteenth Street."

"*East* Eighteenth."

"East Eighteenth. Okay. I'll remember," she said.

"And don't go getting lost." It was clearly meant to be a warning.

"Thanks for the concern."

He reached out for her upper arm and yanked her to him. "You don't have any more surprises, do you? Because I got your clothes and things at my place." Then with a scowl he shoved her away. "So go on. See you're back in an hour or two."

Augusta watched him stomp away up the block and breathed a small sigh. What got him so riled all at once, anyway? Where did he get the idea he could just order her about? It wasn't like she owed him anything. Somehow he had gotten her mixed up with someone primed and eager to do whatever he asked.

But things were different now. Things changed that moment she got the urge to pull off that dumb wig. Her whole outlook shifted. Even the city looked different to her. The sidewalks were sunnier and less hostile, with less traffic competing for space on the road. The people she passed were out for a pleasant stroll, following signposts that pointed to places with intriguing names like Madison Square and Battery Park.

Was there steady work in these new motion pictures? Maybe it was a scam like Deward said, and maybe his Mr. Griffith was only pulling the wool over folks' eyes. But wasn't that what all directors did in one way or another? That was show business in a nutshell. At least he showed he could get the job done. Whether the whole business was washed up in a year or two or something longer, he had issued her a personal invitation to tag along.

The Statue of Liberty did not disappoint. The robed lady stood boldly off across the water on a rock, holding aloft freedom's flame with dignity and confidence. She had been keeping that vigil for two decades now, diverting the eyes of newcomers to the prospect of a better life.

Down below the railings the choppy harbor water lapped against the rocks with hypnotic urgency. She slipped into a reverie and absently rubbed the smooth clasp on her purse like it was Aladdin's lamp.

Whatever was coming next she deserved sole credit. She was the one who had taken a chance and walked away from all she knew. She was the one who put her life savings down on some unknown X on the map.

The folks from the Water Queen would be signing aboard soon, wondering whatever became of that sweet orphan girl. They all had their plans and dreams, but that's all they were. The current carried them along. While they acted out their parts and nursed their squabbles and drank too much, they were actually hiding from the truth. No bolt from the blue was going to change their lives. How could people be so clever at learning their lines yet so inept at reading between them?

After a time Augusta heard a low, lascivious whistle. A couple of muscular dockworkers were walking by with their lunch pails, and they had their eyes trained on her.

"Hey," she called impulsively, "either of you know where a person might find a telephone around here?"

"Harbormaster's office," answered the taller one, indicating a narrow carriage road paved with cobblestones.

A secretary in a high-collared work blouse sat tucked behind a frosted green glass door, drowning in boredom. She told Augusta she was happy to let her use the new "candlestick" telephone on her desk, especially after learning it was needed to report a robbery.

Getting through to a switchboard operator proved no problem, and Augusta was soon connected to a police station in Yonkers. While the secretary made a show of shuffling her paperwork around, Augusta knew she was eavesdropping. It didn't matter to her at all as their paths weren't likely to cross again.

Eventually the proper sergeant came on the line and asked her to repeat the name Longacre several times until he was satisfied he had it right. He asked her to hold on, and when he returned next he wanted the address of the Union Square hotel.

"Two-twelve, Eighteenth Street," she said, then corrected herself, "*East* Eighteenth Street."

By now the secretary had her eyes fastened on every clue in Augusta's face. Occasionally she would glance down at the purse lying flat and empty upon her desk, then look to Augusta again with another nod of encouragement. She almost certainly expected the visitor to burst into tears when the call was through. But instead she saw the woman place the telephone in its cradle and gather her purse with a breezy smile.

"Thank you for your hospitality," she chirped to the secretary as she swept out the door.

She could hardly believe the sense of calm and optimism that came over her now. There was no need for her to hurry, nothing at all to be done. Some casual exploring and a bit of window-shopping would round out her morning most pleasantly.

She spent some time in a small hat shop, and then browsed through the unclaimed shoes in a bin outside a repair store. Later she paused at the window of a steamship company and imagined herself in its photos and posters of faraway places.

By the time she returned to Deward's block there was a paddy wagon parked at number 212. After a flash of activity through the lobby door the glass began to revolve and out came two burly policemen in loose-fitting uniforms with little Deward Trawley squeezed between them. His hands were pinned behind him in shackles.

He didn't spot Augusta until after he was helped into the rear of the wagon and the iron latch was dropped. Then his eyes locked on hers and he pushed his face to the bars as if she might be able to free him. But the wagon lurched forward and Deward's wide eyes grew smaller until they were consumed in one bite by the midday dust.

Augusta held her hankie to her nose and asked the front desk clerk to summon the manager. She fought back tears as she explained how she had come all the way from Georgia to stay with her cousin. Only that morning she had been offered a job in the city. Now her cousin had some horrid misunderstanding with the law and she did not know where to turn.

Would it be possible for her to take over the payment on Mr. Trawley's room—room number 306—until he straightened things out with the police? It was a larger room than she needed, she sobbed, but her trunk and all her things were already there. ... Yes, she would be quite happy to pay the next week's rent in advance.

She spent the whole afternoon transferring Deward's belongings to her trunk, then scrubbed the grease-spattered hotplate and changed the bedding. By early evening she felt exhausted and settled back in her very own quarters in her newly adopted city and fell instantly asleep under the grandest bedroom ceiling the world had ever known.

THREE
"An Awful Moment"

The number of picketers had tripled overnight. The line of dour faces outside the studio reached in both directions, packing the sidewalk from entry steps to curbstone. Surprised businessmen with no time for such nonsense grumbled as they stepped in the street to get by.

Augusta noted her distance from the brownstone, lowered her eyes and pushed ahead.

She watched the pendulum passes of her shoes over the pavement and felt better prepared for the jostlings of the crowd. Someone called a name that might have been hers but she did not look up. It was clearly not possible. Who would know her here? It could only have been an odd trick of the blood pounding in her ears.

At the first glimpse of a cement step she shot out an arm and caught hold of the iron handrail, using it to pull herself to safety. For the first time she saw there were men in the crowd. Most looked well tailored, though others wore badly rumpled suits with mismatched trousers or topcoats flecked with dust. They were dead giveaways of actors wearing costumes straight off the wardrobe racks.

Some of the morning's placards glistened with wet paint. Many had obvious errors. *Defense the Rights of Artsists* urged one long white banner tied by corner ribbons to the iron fencing.

"Miss Lee!" shouted a voice. This time it could not be explained away.

A dark-haired young man in a brown checked suit was working his way toward her. He wore a straw boater pushed back on his head like a college boy at a spring picnic. "You do know, Miss Lee," he said, "that you are responsible for all this? Isn't it amazing? It's your doing."

The way he carved out each syllable reminded her of a bit player making the most of his few lines of dialogue. "How do you know my name? Have me met?"

He lifted the boater by its brim and gave a shallow bow. "Arthur Johnson, Miss Lee," he said. "It is truly a joy to meet you. I have been an ardent admirer—it seems for an eternity. Well, since yesterday, anyway."

"You were there? You're an actor."

Arthur Johnson nodded toward a sandwich board outside the step-down basement. "Mr. Griffith has asked me to play the young father."

The first thing she saw was the studio's monogram at the top—the large white letters AB inside a black circle. Below it was a flow of words painted with a calligrapher's sure hand:

American Biograph—The Studio

Known for Wholesome

Motion Picture Entertainment—

Announces

The Most Powerful

Temperance Lecture

Ever Filmed—

**The Drunkard's
Reformation**

Coming to a Mutual Exchange

Theatre This Month!!

"My, they work fast here," said Augusta.

"I'd rather it were Falstaff, understand," said the young man, batting his dark lashes at her. "But *c'est la guerre,* as the saying goes on distant shores. A *bard* in the hand is worth two ... in the bush leagues."

"Thank you, Mr. Johnson," she said dismissively. Playful or not, his manner was tiresome. "I have an appointment to keep. If you will excuse me."

"I will not wish you luck—" he started, and waited for her to pause with curiosity to look at him again—"because you won't need any. You have a most capable and attractive head on your shoulders."

"Not one to be turned by you, Mr. Johnson," came a commanding voice from amid the ranks of picketers.

A handsome woman approached in a large flowered hat, resting her placard on a stick upon a broad shoulder. She certainly knew how to command attention. She was clearly younger than the other women. Augusta guessed she was probably still in her early thirties. Instead of the usual winter overcoat of somber ash or brown she wore a colorful theater coat aswirl with prickly holly leaves and berry clusters presented in the thick nappy weave of an antebellum carpetbag.

"Perhaps you would honor us with an introduction, Mr. Johnson," she said, smiling upon Augusta.

Arthur Johnson had lost his flamboyance and was visibly withering in place. "Miss Augusta Lee, may I introduce Miss Linda Arvidson, one of our company's most esteemed actors. "

The two women traded nods.

"I was attempting to express to Miss Lee my measure of regard ... for the impression she made on all of us yesterday."

"Perhaps you should retain a small measure of regard for your wife and child, Mr. Johnson," said the actress. As she spoke she tilted the wooden stick away from her shoulder and twisted the sign forward as she brought it down to rest against her boot. *Biograph Believes in the Sanctity of Marriage* was painted on its face.

The young actor gave a dip of surrender and returned the straw hat to his head with a tap. "Ladies," he said, retreating back into the crowd.

"Some people see a new female member as a challenge," said Linda Arvidson. "We have a word for them. Do you know what it is? ... *Men*," she harrumphed. "And where is your dear Mr. Trawley?"

"I'm all on my own today."

"Oh? Well, in that case we shall have to keep a close eye on you ourselves, shan't we?"

Augusta thought it an odd thing to say, more warning than favor. But she responded with her most sociable smile. "A pleasure meeting you, Miss Arvidson," she said, turning to hurry up the steps.

It wasn't until she shut the door behind her that she felt free of the woman's eyes.

The marble foyer was chilly and still like a family crypt. "Hello?" she called. Her voice echoed off the walls as she unbuckled her coat and took a deep breath. Yesterday's sweet aromas of sawdust and turpentine were gone, replaced with a nose-stinging wash of ammonia and wood rot.

Passing a partly opened door on her left she heard someone speak her name. "Miss Lee?" it called softly.

Lawrence Griffith sat almost buried behind a desk stacked high with opened envelopes and papers. "I thought it might be you," he said, slipping a pair of wire-rimmed spectacles off his nose to rise. He seemed taller than she had remembered and without a hat to cover his thinning hair he appeared years older as well. "Do please enter."

Behind him hung an oil painting of horses grazing in a field. Its display of open space and an unfenced horizon was more than offset by the boxy wooden desk and a cracked-leather sofa taking up the entire left wall. "I fear I've come too early," she said.

"Your timing is splendid. I was just poring through yesterday's mail."

"Mercy. Is all that yours?"

His eyes skidded over the stacks and stopped on one unfolded piece of stationery. "This one's mine," he said, lifting it with a shy grin. "Mother's weekly report from home. Some are invoices. All the others came addressed to our 'Biograph girl.' That's Miss Lawrence. Florence Lawrence. Her fans don't know her rightful name or address. But somehow the postmaster knows to bring them all here."

"Like Santa Claus."

Griffith gave a knowing grin. "We do get a bracing North Pole breeze here from time to time."

Augusta let the belt of her coat fall loose and started to unhook the buttons.

"Let me help you with that," said the director, dashing out around the desk. "Of course, that's only what the postman left. There's more from the exchanges." He pointed to the wall in back of her.

Behind the door three tall canvas mailbags leaned against one another, each packed to the brim.

"I am speechless," she said.

"I've worked with the theatrical greats in my day. They might get ten, fifteen letters in a week. Maybe one or two from different cities, from someone who passed through town and caught a performance. But it was nothing like this—not sent from four continents and written in a half-dozen languages."

He lifted her coat from her shoulders and took it over to a rack by the door. "Marriage proposals. Offers of ranches. It's hard to know what to think of it all—all this ... *adoration*." He turned to study her simple striped dress and figure. "Most attractive, my dear."

"Thank you."

"Did you see our announcement out front?"

"'The Drunkard's Reformation?' It was quite a surprise."

"Really? In what way?"

"I guess I don't … I don't expect to be taken so seriously."

He came close to her again, frowning as he examined every detail of her face. "We take good ideas very seriously here," he said. "That's all that we have to sell." He reached for her chin and raised it to the light. "What are you wearing?"

"Just a little stage makeup."

"Stuff from the showboat?"

She nodded. "I have tubs left."

"Well, throw them out, please."

"Really?"

"You'll find that all those pinks and rouges show on film as a mostly unflattering gray. Shades of red appear black and hollow—suitable only for ghouls and cadavers. Do you know where our name Biograph comes from? It is Latin meaning *life story*. That's what we're about here. Stories of life."

He smiled at her and his eyes seemed to dance with excitement. "The old ways are over, Miss Lee," he said. "The old ways and the rules of the past no longer apply." He pointed her toward the door. "What say we go and greet our new world?"

"Billy!" called Griffith as they breezed through the darkness.

A floor lamp on a pole crackled and spit, then burst into a noisy shower of blue-green sparks, as though some rare jungle bird was roasting alive in its cage.

Augusta tried to bury her eyes in Griffith's shoulder.

"It's all right, Miss Lee," he told her with a pat. "Don't be frightened. Ah, there. … I wish you to meet our Mr. Bitzer."

A small, squarish man with a bushy mustache stood under the still-sizzling lamp. He was dressed in a common woolen coat with a knotted ribbon tie, like a country doctor invited to a weekly council meeting.

"This is Mr. G.W. Bitzer—"

"Please, call me Billy," said the man, adding quickly, "*Hallo*, Miss Lee." His diction was precise but bore a tinge of some foreign influence.

"Billy is the only one around here who is truly indispensable. Have you a fresh reel loaded for us, Billy?"

"All set, Mr. *Griffitt*," he said, ducking back into the shadows.

"Whenever I'm not sure what I am doing, I count on Billy to set me straight."

SCHWACK! A second warm slap of air hit Augusta's cheek as another lamp surged to life.

"We want to try a little test first," said Griffith, holding out a hand.

She reached to take his fingers. "Whatever you wish."

He led her to some makeshift plank steps and waited as she climbed up on the stage. Then she watched him disappear and raised a hand over her eyes to see beyond the blinding towers. From the darkness came more sounds of creaking and of wooden legs being scraped across the floor.

"Can I be of any use?" asked a new male voice from back at the doors.

"Later, perhaps," said the director. "Tommy!"

"Ready here, Mr. Griffith," answered a man from the rafters. There was another electric surge and a bank of overhead bulbs snapped to life.

Now she could see a varnished wooden box on three tilted stilts standing a yard from the stage. A single polished mound of glass twinkled at her with its dozen pinpoints of light.

"All right, Billy," said Griffith holding his arm over his head. "When you're ready."

A hand reached from behind the box and took hold of a crank. Suddenly the quiet studio was infused with the pulsing screech and ratcheting of gears.

"Enough, Billy!" cried the director. The noise dwindled again to an eerie silence. "Now, Miss Lee, I need some reaction from you. Listen only to me. Pay no attention to anything else. Respond only as you believe you might in the given situation. Do you understand?"

"I don't know. Respond to what?"

"To *me*, Miss Lee. To what I say. If I say it's cold, I need to see a shiver. You may shake as much as humanly possible. Just convince me you are cold. Is that clear?"

"Yes, sir." She held her shoulders taut and tried to look composed.

"Now, Miss Lee, you are the daughter of a man who works for a living. ... Camera, Billy."

The ratcheting picked up again as Griffith raised his voice to be heard. "You love your father, because you are his own sweet daughter. Yes, good. You are trusting. But you live in fear of the times he goes drinking. Now you hear something. Look to the door! Are those footsteps? Is that your father fumbling with a key? Maybe he has been drinking. He will come in slurring his words, bullying you! There's the door! It's opening, opening. No, no! Stop, Billy."

Again the studio withdrew into silence.

"What were you trying to show us, Miss Lee?"

"I was listening to the door open."

"Listening is *not* an emotion. The audience needs to see your *feelings*. Now, again, Billy. ... Begin!"

Griffith launched into the scenario again, and this time Augusta widened her eyes in the direction of the door, recoiling and bringing her fingertips to her cheeks.

"*Stop! Billy! Stop, stop, stop.* Miss Lee, if I were to come over there and raise my fist to you, what would you do?"

"I'm not sure—"

"We wish the audience to feel your peril, Miss Lee. Imagine them sitting on the edge of our stage here. Would you give them some silly pantomime solely for their benefit? Of course not. You want them to believe what they are watching. And they are all watching you. Mr. Bitzer's camera there captures everything you feel and think. ... Well, let's try something else. Mr. Moore, are you still here?"

"Yes, sir, Mr. Griffith."

There was a steady beat of footsteps on the boards and then the contours of a man appeared. At first she saw only a trim figure in a suit and then a great swell of black hair. Even in the dimness she had a sense of the man's presence and saw the glimmer of his eyes. An alert intelligence was at play there under that daunting jut of a brow.

"This is Owen Moore, Miss Lee. He is what we commonly call a leading man. Mr. Moore, would you be so kind as to join Miss Lee?"

In just a few hops he was at the stage and up the steps, standing close beside her. Yes, now she was sure. This Owen Moore was possibly the single most attractive man in the entire world, and she knew she would be his. With just his eyes he had scooped her in his dice cup and given her a shake. Now the game was decided. Even without a tumble there was no doubting the outcome.

"Let's imagine," said the director, "that Mr. Moore here is your sweetheart. ... You may start the camera, Billy. ... Move in, Mr. Moore. Let your presence be felt. Place an arm around her waist. Yes, just like that. Now take her hand. Look into one another's eyes. Say something to him, Miss Lee."

"What shoud I say?"

"Good, that's fine."

She couldn't stop a quavering twitch of her top lip. She prayed that no one could see it.

"Lean closer, Mr. Moore. Bend toward her. Closer. Yes. He wants to make love to you, Miss Lee. Allow yourself to be taken."

His voice was like a pebble dropped in a cavern. As it receded she fell toward the emerald shimmer of a flame. She was Haley's Comet, plucked from a clockwork orbit by a more powerful gravity of arms and lips, sent spinning out into the deepest reaches of heaven.

Then the ratcheting returned with a deafening machine gun rattle that quickly faded to an echo.

"What do you think, Billy?"

"I think we got it, Mr. *Griffitt*."

"Good. Thank you, Miss Lee, Mr. Moore."

Owen let her drop loose a bit and then lifted away. There was a series of pops as the bulbs overhead went dark row by row. They were quickly followed by the floor lamps as Owen stepped to the platform's edge and disappeared.

"Bobby! ... Is Bobby here?"

"Yeah, Griff!" called out a high voice. Instantly the same donut boy in knee socks from the day before came shooting down a ladder and landed on the stage with a thud. "Here I be!"

"Bobby, would you show Miss Lee upstairs? Ask Miss Nina to please start a card on her."

"You got it. This way, Miss Lee," said the boy.

Augusta did not want to leave. She wanted to run after the mysterious man with the emerald eyes who had caused such havoc in her universe. "Will I be doing more acting today?" she managed to ask.

"No, not today," answered the director from behind his clipboard, then lowered it to give her a reassuring smile. "I'll have a look at it all. Perhaps tonight. Check back tomorrow. Now run along. Bobby'll show you the way."

Bobby had waited at the studio doors as long as humanly possible. Now before she could get to him he was skipping off across the marble floor to grab hold of the banister and sling himself up to the fourth row of steps. In a split-second his skinny knees were pumping madly on the stairs up to the third-story landing, where he ducked through an open archway.

She found a large and deep room flooded in sunlight from a wide row of windows facing the street. "Ah-ha!" shouted Bobby as he leapt out at her from behind a cork figure-dummy. He had found a blue cavalry cap and stood slashing the air between them with a cutlass.

"Don't go scaring the lady," scolded a woman's voice. "Mercy's sake."

She looked for the source of the voice. Across the room was a lone electric floor fan whose blurred blades were directed down at a plump seamstress seated on a stool by the cutting table.

"Hello," said Augusta.

Bobby rested the cutlass tip on the wood floor and tossed his cap into a canvas hamper. "This is her, Nina," he said. "This is Miss Lee. She's kin to *Clang-Clang*." He pronounced the name with exaggerated disdain.

The seamstress seemed intent on passing an invisible needle through a bunched fold of fabric in her lap. It was the woman Augusta had seen the day before on stage with the costumes. She barely paused for a quick glance up. "You feeling ill, dear?"

"I don't believe I was prepared for the heat. I got a bit tuckered, that's all."

"Bobby, fetch the lady some water."

The boy scraped the tip of his sword across the floor.

"No," blurted Augusta. "Don't bother, please. I'm fine."

"You think it's hot now, wait 'til August," said the seamstress. She yanked an unseen thread. "So, wha'choo need now, hon?"

Bobby tossed his saber on a shelf with many others. "Griff wants you to gather her particulars," he said, then clicked his tongue at her and added, "See ya." With that he disappeared out the door.

"Thanks, dear," called Nina after him.

A loud thumping down the stairs ended with the inevitable thud of a very long leap. Augusta couldn't help smiling. "That boy's a fire-cracker," she said.

"You ain't tellin' me nothin'," said the woman. "Whatever it is you need, Bobby's the one can get it."

"Mr. Griffith doesn't mind being called 'Griff'?"

"Bobby can get away with it. He was here long 'fore Mr. Griffith come," said Nina, pulling her needle up to her shoulder and giving it a tug. "Mr. Marvin made him a star of a picture once—one of them 'boy detective' stories. Turned out he was a darn good little actor."

Augusta watched as she sent the needle swooping back into the fabric and pushed it through. "Are you an actor, too?"

She gave a snort. "I give all that up when I left Bal'imore. I was just a slip of a thing in them days. Now I'm the whole darn harbor."

"May I call you Nina?"

"Best you do. Elsewise, how'd I know who you're talking to?"

"How long have you been here, Nina?"

"You mean the Biograph? Let me see, must be a couple months now—that is, if it's still 1907."

"It's 1909. February."

"In that case, make it a year and a half. No one tells me nothin' up here." She cut the thread with her teeth and held up the seam for a final inspection. "Ever go to the Brooklyn Theatre? I was head of costumes there. Found out I liked it better than acting. But it caught fire and burned to the ground."

She straightened out the fabric on her lap and started to carefully fold it. "Let's see, I went to the old Casino Theatre from there." She stopped to look up as if at a loss to explain it. "That one burned down, too."

"Gracious."

"It was always a problem in them days. Fires. What with gas lamps and oil rags and drunks wavin' their cigars around at the chorus gals." Nina struggled to her feet and motioned to a worn wooden riser next to a full-length mirror. "Step up there while I find my pencil."

She pulled out a blank card and rummaged around in a woven basket. "Let's see, after that I worked for a time at the Broadway. That's where they had 'Ben-Hur' all those years. That was before I got there. They called it the safest theater in New York. Took a lot of pride in that. 'Thirty-four exits,' it said, printed right there across the front of their programs."

"Did it burn down, too?"

"No, not that one. But the manager was a first class ass, so I made use of one of them exits."

Augusta had to smile.

"Anyway, electricity come along and made the theaters safer. Of course, we still got more than our share of drunks." She pulled a yellow measuring tape from around her neck. "What are you, five foot three or four?"

"Four, I think."

"That's good. My, what I wouldn't do now with a figure like yours!" She began to take measurements and scribble the numbers on her card.

"May I ask you something, Nina? In confidence?"

"What's on your mind, hon?"

"What do you know about ... Mr. Moore?"

"Owen Moore?" She rolled her eyes. "Oh—to be twenty years thinner! The man's a charmer, no doubt about it. His brother's an actor, as well. But it's Owen the ladies all go for. You like him, too, don't ya?"

"He's awfully sure of himself."

"Yeah, you like him." She roped the measuring tape around her neck. "That's all I need now. You can step down."

"What sort of parts you think I'd be good for?"

"All depends what the camera thinks. Cameras don't care beans about actin'. You might've been making a good livin' on Broadway for years playing Indians. But if that camera don't think you're an Indian, the job's gonna go to some other fella. It don't matter if he's ever acted a day in his life."

"Hardly seems fair."

"Nothin' fair about the picture business. You got anything special in your trunks?"

"Just the usual things."

"I always ask, 'cause the right clothes can make the difference. Ask your friend, Clang-Cla—." She caught herself and broke into a guilty smile. "I meant to say *Mr. Trawley*."

"What about him?"

"Well, he come lookin' for work one day. And Mr. Griffith was set to shoot a dinner party and saw him sittin' on the bench. I'm sure Mr. Trawley thought he got the job because he did such-and-such a play or worked for Mr. So-and-So Big Time Producer. Truth was, he was wearing a nice tweed suit that day—and that saved us the cost of a rental. Not that Mr. Griffith is the most frugal producer I ever worked for. But even he will keep an eye on making his budget go farther. Anyhow, that's your picture business in a nutshell."

"Why do people call him *'Clang-Clang'*?"

The seamstress grinned broadly. "Well, it ain't what you think. And he has no one to blame but hisself. He was up here, killin' time and flirtin' with the girlies—you know the way he is. No one was payin' much attention. He was chattin' up this new gal, telling her about this play he was in that used this naughty word. He always used to tell that story to get a rise from the gals. Anyway, we all knew what he was up to."

"Was it from Shakespeare?"

Nina smiled. "I guess he told you, too."

"Henry Five."

"That's the one! Well, he's talkin' and talkin', buildin' up to the point where he's about to blurt out this naughty word, and just when he gets to it this streetcar goes passin' by and rings its bell loud. *Clang clang!* Like that. Well, everyone giggles, 'cause we all know what he said except for this new gal, and she probably didn't want to hear the darn word anyway. But the name stuck, and that's what the girls called him ever since."

Somewhere in the middle of Nina's story a commotion broke out below. It was just a muffled distraction at first but it grew as the voices got more heated until Augusta could hardly ignore the uproar below. Echoes of bodies flailing and arms lashing about rose from the foyer, and then a door slammed and everything fell into a deathly silence. Moments later there was a storm of footsteps coming up the stairs.

Even Nina stopped and her brow furrowed. Whatever was coming was not some everyday occurrence. Nina edged back behind the cutting table.

In the archway loomed the darkly disheveled figure of Linda Arvidson. Her flushed cheeks glistened where they had been scraped, and her feathered hat hung broken off the side of her head.

"Miss Arvidson!" exclaimed Nina in alarm.

Dazed and unsure of where she was, the actress's eyes flitted around for the source of the voice. Then her bewilderment shifted and reformed into a burst of fury. "Damn the man! Damn that miserable, backward little fool! What was he even thinking? Didn't he see what was going on in front of his own eyes?"

"Lord save us," sputtered Nina. "What happened to you, hon?"

Linda took a few more steps into the room. "Tell me you were not a party to this."

"Why—whatever? ... Party to what?"

"Tell me you did not give that little troll those ... those ridiculous things?"

"Who are you talking about?"

"Poe! Edgar Allan Poe!"

"*Edgar Allan*—" she started to repeat.

"Someone must have given them to him. He couldn't possess anything so ... so preposterous! That ludicrous opera cape!" As she spoke she paced toward the standing mirror and now she looked at herself and gasped. "Oh, no! My lovely coat! What's become of you? All the way from San Francisco, ruined!" Her anger fed into a tidal wave of self-pity. "Oh, my hat, my poor hat. ... Look what they have done."

Augusta kept looking to Nina for some clue as to what had happened. But Nina appeared only baffled until a tiny flicker of understanding showed in her eyes.

There was another stomping of feet up the stairs and a short, odd-looking man with a mustache came to a halt in the doorway. To Augusta he was dressed like a melodrama villain in a gambler's ruffled shirt and red vest. He sported a dandy's black cape but was anything but handsome with his deep-set eyes and ballooning forehead.

He addressed the actress with horror. "Miss Arvidson, are you all right? Please allow me to apologize," he said, taking a hesitant step forward.

"You stay away from me!" she screamed. "You silly puffed up little snail of a creature. You are a stain against our whole profession!"

The small man rubbed his hands in dismay. "I am s-so dreadfully, so very, *very* deeply ashamed," he stammered. "Please—"

"What was in that empty, sordid little brain of yours? Did you think I was playing with you?"

"I am truly mortified. So, so sorry. Never once did I dream—"

"No. How could you stop even for a second to consider anything but your own selfish desires?"

He ventured another foot forward.

"I'm warning you!" she yelled. "Do not come any nearer! I shall thrash you. ... Were you not able to discern the difference between reality and make-believe?"

"Miss Arvidson!" called out a mature-sounding voice. Lawrence Griffith was standing in the doorway now, his brow a jumble of questions and concern.

As soon as she saw him she seemed to withdraw. She slumped into a seated posture on the fitting platform.

"My dear, Linda," he blurted, rushing to kneel beside her. He grabbed for her hand. "What on Earth has happened? What did they do to you?"

"It was horrid. I could not breathe. I thought I was dying."

Griffith rubbed the actress's hand, stopping only to sweep a lock of hair from her forehead. "Are you hurt? What is this about an attack?"

"They pulled at me, and lashed out at me with their placards."

"They hit you?"

"I feared ... I felt like I was suffocating."

Griffith looked around the room. "For God's sake, can no one tell me what happened?"

Linda glared scornfully at the man in the cape. "Why don't you ask *Mr. Poe?*"

Griffith recognized the actor for the first time. "Mr. Yost," he said, scanning him up and down. "Why are you dressed like that?"

"I assure you, Mr. Griffith," he sputtered, lifting a hand to peel the mustache from his upper lip. "It was—I mean, never for an instant did I foresee such a thing as this. You must believe me. Really. I meant to be sly. I thought it was a clever thing—you know, to capitalize on the situation. I am so, so ashamed."

Augusta kept looking back to Nina through all this. She was clearly growing more dismayed by the second. Now suddenly she had to speak out. "It was me, Mr. Griffith! I did it. When he came asking me for the Poe get-up, I didn't know no better. He didn't say what he was up to!"

The caped actor continued to mumble. "I thought it would get us a mention somewhere, a little notice in the trades, that's all. Some publicity. That's all I was thinking."

"I thought you sent him, Mr. Griffith," added Nina. "I thought you wanted him like that. If I done something wrong—"

"Nina," said Griffith, "I'm sure no one blames you."

"I wouldn't have done it if I'd knowed."

"It was his doing," shrieked Linda, pointing with fury at the guilty actor. "He started everything, then scurried away like a rat."

"I thought you would be in … a better position … if I slipped off."

Griffith tensed and held up his hands. "All of you, please take a breath and calm yourselves." His eyes brushed over Augusta to the far wall. More office employees were arriving from downstairs and taking up positions for themselves. Their faces were masks of anxiety and alarm.

"Did any of you witness what happened?" asked the director.

The onlookers traded blank stares and rocked silently on their feet.

Finally Griffith sighed and slapped his hands on his knees to stand. "Does anyone know who was responsible?"

Linda Arvidson was looking at her image in the mirror, making a futile bid at repairing the damage. Suddenly she yanked off her cockeyed hat. "Ultimately, Mr. Griffith, I'm afraid the responsibility is all yours," she scolded.

Griffith blinked. "Well, yes, as the studio's ambassador—" he began but stopped abruptly when she pitched her hat at his feet.

"It was *your* choice," she shouted. "You were the one who insisted on it, a tribute to that horrid man. We warned you. We all told you it was not a good idea. But you went right ahead anyway."

So the truth began to come out in dribs and drabs. Augusta would not put all the pieces together until that night in her room, when she found a stack of Deward Trawley's Biograph circulars. What was soon clear was that people had been wrong about those picket ladies. They weren't there to protest any disrespectful jabs taken by the Mr. and Mrs. Jones comedies.

A few weeks earlier the studio released a split-reel film honoring the centenary of Edgar Allan Poe. Griffith wanted to mark the January 1809 birth of his favorite American poet with a drama about his writing of "The Raven." Biograph's front office did not share his enthusiasm, however. Eventually they released it with a cavalier misspelling of Poe's family name in the very title—"Edgar *Allen* Poe."

The caped actor was engaged to play Poe. Under the stage name Barry O'Moore he had won critical acclaim for his 1906 Broadway performance in "The Measure of a Man." But roles suited to his talents were not forthcoming and he was working sporadically in motion pictures as Herbert Yost. Linda Arvidson was cast to play opposite him in the role of Virginia, Poe's dying bride.

Griffith presented Poe as nearly delirious with worry over the stricken Virginia. Late at night he has a vision of a raven above his writing desk repeating the single word—"Nevermore." Inspired, he pens "The Raven," and then races around town in hopes of selling it to buy medicine for his beloved. A publisher at last gives him money for it but it's too late. Poe returns to his garret to find Virginia's lifeless body. When will the artist find true love and redemption in such an uncaring world? A final title card holds the answer: "Nevermore."

Linda Arvidson expected to reduce audiences to torrents of sobbing as the doomed Virginia. Herbert Yost thought his Poe would make him the talk of the town. But nothing of the sort happened. The public was largely unmoved by what they saw as a commonplace tale of consumption and death in the big city. After playing out their allotment of bookings, all remaining prints were sent to Europe and the film was forgotten. One group that had taken a serious interest in the film, however, was the leadership of the local temperance society.

Linda Arvidson learned only that morning that the Poe film was the real reason for the boycott. To moralists there was no more depraved figure in all of American letters than Edgar Allan Poe. He was a public drunk and possibly a drug fiend, and he had married his own cousin when she was thirteen years old. Clergymen and reformers joined with leaders of the anti-saloon movement to put motion picture makers on notice. They could no longer solicit public sympathy for such a thoroughly despicable character as Edgar Allan Poe.

It was as Linda Arvidson was digesting this information that Herbert Yost came strolling down the sidewalk. Without his costume and mustache, the actor did not so greatly resemble the sad-eyed author widely depicted in illustrations. Still, she rushed to warn him so that a public scene could be avoided.

Yost must have seen this as his overdue moment in the limelight. A short time after ducking inside the studio he re-appeared in his full Poe get-up to take his bows. Linda could hardly believe her eyes.

Shouts of "Shameful!" and "Disgraceful!" mounted as the picketers grew aware of his presence. A portion of the mob surged forward and Linda tried to shield the actor using her own body. Then someone called her a Biograph spy and the crowd's anger transferred to her.

They hit at her with their signs and tore her clothes as Herbert Yost slipped away, leaving the actress to fight her way to safety.

As the last account of this was heard, Nina's wardrobe shop fell hushed and frozen. Griffith nodded his head in deep thought and started off toward the front windows.

Finally Herbert Yost broke the silence. "I wish to go on record, Mr. Griffith," he began. "What happened was an outrage. I accept the guilt for my responsibility in it all. But just as certain am I that it's the studios themselves that must share in the blame."

"Please, clarify your thoughts for me, Mr. Yost," responded the director.

"Those Christian ladies out front were acting on ignorance, doing what they believed to be true. They know nothing of actors and the make-believe of motion pictures. It's the studio owners that keep them uninformed. They choose to keep the public in the dark. Film actors do not command the respect of Broadway because audiences don't even know we have names. How can the public at large appreciate the distinction between role and actor if they are not informed of it? How can we hold them in contempt for reacting in such planned ignorance?"

Griffith pulled himself upright to see over the heads of the growing crowd. "Thank you, Mr. Yost. You are speaking to a policy matter, of course. I will raise it again for you in our next policy meeting."

"I'm saying this for the good of the studio."

"Of course. You have nothing to gain. I will remember to tell them that. ... Does anyone else have any thoughts?"

"We've put up with enough of this picket-line nonsense," groused one of the stagehands.

"That's it!" called out a slim, deeply tanned actor with a heavy Cockney accent. "What're we waitin' for? Let's give 'em a bit of their own back!"

"Yeah," brayed a bandy-legged man with yellow teeth. He flashed a lopsided grin and raised a dark bottle over his head. "What say we go down and wet the old biddies with some of our special brew!"

A ruddy-cheeked fat man with a penciled mustache raised his finger. "Mind if we pass it through our kidneys first?" he cracked.

When the laughter died down an older, level-headed woman said, "We can't let an attack on us go unaddressed, Mr. Griffith."

"It'll only encourage worse," nodded a man next to the Cockney gent.

Augusta studied Griffith's face as other shouts were followed by ever more fierce cries of agreement. What was he thinking? He was losing control of the group and had better say something to quell the calls for violent retaliation.

At last he held up an opened hand to call for order. "Everybody, please. A little civility here." The angry voices trailed away to a mumble and Griffith went to the bank of windows. He stood gazing down in the street for a while, and soon the only sounds were the rumblings of motors and a dull clicking of hooves.

When he was ready to speak he heaved a small sigh and licked his lips. "I remember when my first poem was published. The magazine peaked from the racks amid scores of others. But I knew. There inside it somewhere was my verse."

He raised a hand as if reaching out to touch the hem of an angel that only he could see. He began to recite from memory.

> Look, look, above the hilltops,
> With eyes turned back to the mainland,
> And tired wings wearily beating, but vainly,
> For the wind blows out to sea in the evening.
> Poor little wild duck! Poor little wild duck!
> In the evening,
> For the wind ... it blows out to the sea.

"It was not 'The Raven,' not by any means. But ravens, ducks ... you know what they say about birds of a feather."

From her angle Augusta could see his cheek rise into a smile. She smiled too, telling herself it was his attempt at relieving the tensions. He must have come in a hurry for he had forgotten his hat. Sunlight glanced off the exposed strips of his scalp, and he seemed to her frail and needy.

His hand fished around inside his jacket, and when he turned around to face the room he held a folded square of paper. "Soon after that my first full play was accepted for production. It would open in our nation's capital, and it would mark the return to the American stage of the legendary Fannie Ward. I believed it worthy of her. It was a very modern play, a look at youth and folly and the triumph of love."

He had been fumbling for his reading glasses and now he opened them and balanced them on the bridge of his nose. "Opening night was the happiest of my life," he was saying. "The audience enjoyed it and gave it a warm ovation. It was gratifying to have this public acceptance of my vision."

Now he unfolded the yellowed square of paper and held it up to read. He gave no introduction but clearly it was a review cut from a newspaper. Augusta found it hard to concentrate on the stiff, self-important words, and her eyes strayed to the entryway.

A constant stream of stragglers still appeared from the hall. Actors and carpenters and tidy account secretaries from the front office were finding places against the wall to stand as they strained to hear the director's soft voice.

When she finally looked back Griffith had come to the bottom of his clipping. The critic was saying how offensive it was to watch a play depicting a young woman sharing alcoholic beverages in public with young men not of her acquaintance. The reviewer had saved his harshest condemnation for the immorality of the playwright.

"'It may be that the dramatist wanted to show where his hero's feet strayed,'" intoned Griffith grandly, " 'and where he found the girl he was afterwards to make his wife. But if one wants to tell the old and beautiful story of redemption of man or woman through love it is not necessary to portray the gutters from which they are redeemed.'"

At this point Griffith looked up and began to fold his clipping back into a square. He recited the final words by heart. " 'If this be art, it is the art of Zola—and Washington wants none of it.' "

He tucked the paper into an inside pocket and removed his reading glasses to rub his eyes. "I wonder if it's too late to send a 'thank you' note to that critic," he said. "He turned me into an ardent fan of Monsieur Zola."

Laughter rippled uneasily through the costume shop. Some onlookers nodded knowingly while others appeared as puzzled as Augusta. Why did he waste everyone's time with an old clipping? What did it have to do with the violence at their doorstep?

"Most of our other notices, by the way, were good," he said as he slid his glasses into his coat. "Nevertheless, my play closed at the end of the week."

He turned to pace before the windows. "Why should anyone read an unhappy book, or buy a ticket to an immoral play? What good can come of exposing oneself to the work of some upstart playwright named David Wark Griffith?"

David Griffith? Was that his pen name? she wondered. Or could it be his real name? She would have to find out. Right now she was still hoping he would get to his point.

"Artists are put on Earth for a purpose. If writers like Zola or Edgar Allan Poe wish to reflect on the conditions of an imperfect world, they must by no means be silenced. When their voices are mocked or censored or suppressed it is the duty of other artists to defend them."

The director stopped to let his eyes roam from face to face. "I know what some of you are thinking. I see your concern. This is your livelihood. Some in the front office are not happy with my decisions. None of us wishes to see Biograph fail. In times like these, it's not good news to be out of a job.

"To be an artist is to be constantly reminded of the wolf at the door. But we have a responsibility above all others. To stay faithful to our gift, and show the truth. We must never lose sight of that over fear of the mob."

Augusta looked around her. She wondered if the others felt as abandoned as she did. Maybe Deward had been right all along. What sort of stuck-up phony would have such little concern for the lives of others? Lofty speeches were fine but they would sound pretty empty if the studio was allowed to fail.

"We're through seeking common ground with these people," said Griffith, stiffening with defiance. "We will not sit by while our rights are threatened. We offered a truce and they responded with violence. It is clear now that if they win, we lose. It is as stark as that."

He signaled for Linda Arvidson to come closer and then slipped his arm over her shoulder. "I am going to ask Miss Arvidson here to come with me to the police station. We shall lodge a formal complaint against the actions of those occupying our doorstep. After that I shall meet with lawyers from the trust to seek an injunction. We shall go all the way to the governor if necessary. I promise you to do whatever it takes to break the will of these boycotters and defend our rights as artists."

Griffith thanked them for their hard work and loyalty, and it was clear that the meeting was over. There was a round of light applause as the director whispered something in Linda Arvidson's ear and gave her a comforting hug. Then the crowd broke into lines and filed from the room with a general murmur of approval.

Augusta had been counting on Griffith and his promise to give her work. But even though she had a place to stay, her life now seemed as unsettled as ever. Her fate rested on the actions of a failed, arrogant playwright whose loyalties seemed to shift with the winds. Once he had mocked the anti-saloon people but now was readying "temperance lectures." His pictures denounced the injustices to the noble redman and the plight of low-paid workers, yet where was that great social conscience when it came to his own employees?

Maybe she expected too much stability from a clearly unstable leader. Right now he seemed to her like just another vain Southern dilettante, in way over his head. Or was he about to lead her to the promised land? That was the great unknown that was guiding her fate. What had she signed up for—and who in the world was the real Lawrence "David" Griffith?

FOUR
"The Honor of His Family"

Hop yards! Holy Mother of Jesus!

Wait. What time is it? No dawn's early light here. No crowing cocks, no restless paddock. Just icy cement and brick and—

Four-fifteen!

Holy Mother of Jesus!

Why on Earth was he dreaming about *that*? Hops! ... Hops for the beer masters, for the suds lovers. All so vivid. And the gloves! Those worn, soiled hop-picker's gloves meant to preserve his soft and delicate hands. When was the last time he had given them a thought?

Set the watch down quietly. It's still way too early. Pillow's warm and shouldn't take long ...

Maybe I should get up, go and find my notebook.

No, that was much too much effort. Better to turn on his side and try to get a few more minutes of rest.

Yesterday was quite stressful. Emotions took a toll. Today there would be more time wasted with policemen and lawyers. Or everything could change. There was no telling with the Marvins. If they concluded it was best he move on—well, maybe he should think about that. Where would he go? Back to acting? Tryouts and waiting around for news. Or maybe go back to old Mr. Porter or someone worse, someone who didn't care half as much for what he was doing? ... How could he put himself through all that again?

Where could the Marvins find a replacement? Maybe they had someone in mind. There were plenty of old stage directors around. Some would be willing to give the flickers a try. It wouldn't be hard finding another fool like him—someone who didn't think there was much to the job until he actually took it on. Glorious. What a surprise awaited the next poor fool.

Oh, well. Forget about scribbling down any notes. ... Not even a poetic muse gets up this early. Just close the old eyes and get a few more winks.

But hop yards? Lord almighty! Didn't he empty himself of all there was to say about that? The play should have been the end of it. *Wait.* ... There it was. That explained it. The play was on his mind because he had been talking about it. He even chose to read that damned review aloud once again. No wonder it came back in his dreams. Still, never in so much detail. ... The fuzzy clusters of cones swaying in the breeze. The row after row of trellis and wire. Everything stretching off with no end in sight, not even if one balanced himself on the topmost step of his—

Really ought to get up and fetch a notebook. Might be a poem in it.

Sunshine settling like dust on the parched leaves. The mottled shadows of afternoon spreading its gray shawl in the dead Ukiah air.

Not bad. No, it still meant turning on lights. It didn't warrant disturbing the whole house.

But the dream brought it all back. He was present in every sense of the word, standing by a tall ladder, smelling the baked sod as it soaked up the morning's bucket dousings. He could hear the murmuring of passersby as they stole a second look at him. "Who's the lost *gringo*, the big-city hombre with a nose like a basket handle?" Laughter. "Never mind that one. That's only Larry. He's all right. Keeps to himself." "Some say he was once on the stage. ... Of course. An actor. In town they call him Lawrence. But here among the *vaqueros* and the poor students on summer break, he says to call him Larry. Just Larry will do."

It was a part he could play to the hilt. He recalled some homeless old Texan with no front teeth sidling up close to him. "Fella told me you was from *Kain-tuckee*," he says, his words whistling past. "Ain't that where all the good Bourbon comes *outa*?"

"Not quite *all*, *maw* friend," he answered. "We like to keep a small amount for *ah-se'ves*."

The work felt so good in the beginning, those uninterrupted hours out in the field. The mindless, repetitive tasks. After so many weary months of histrionics on the road, the disturbing arguments and fights with that *crazy woman*—this is what he needed. He welcomed every physical strain. Stretching up for a wheated top, then bending it to him for a careful snip. Watching the plant snap back to attention as he stooped to stuff another prized sprig down in his burlap.

Every so often he would give the sack a lift and guess: *A hundred pounds? No, not yet. Not by another half-hour, maybe.* So he would move on to a fatter row of sprays, dragging his bounty and trying not to knock down the chubby-legged toddlers in the way.

This was what it was like for them, too, those field hands back in Father's day. Those poor souls, denied education, denied even a seat at the table in this land of plenty. All due to an accident of birth. The death, the sacrifices—the end of slavery came at a terrible cost. But it was worth the suffering it took to end that fetid institution. ... Sorry, Colonel, we both know that it did.

His work was so different. He had chosen it, for one thing. And in the beginning it was bliss. No one depending on him. No lines to learn or trains to run for. When the sun went down his sole value to a living soul was set by how wonderfully soft the mattress felt and how quickly sleep would come.

Oh, for more such nights! These days the sun never set, not really. There was always a need to produce more. To top himself. To come up with even better stories. People constantly were judging him against his peers. There were still scales here, too, though not the kind that could be seen. They waited invisibly for him to step up and be weighed so that others could estimate his worth.

Much of the work at Biograph was satisfying. For the first time in his life he was in full artistic control. Any story he chose might end up before an audience. But that was also a trap. With the exchanges expecting two or three finished features each week, there had to be always more in the pipeline. What would be the settings, who should be cast, how would they be dressed? The conferences were endless, as were the budget meetings, the business lunches. No breaks, no vacations, just the constant search for new situations, understandable motivations.

Why wasn't he dreaming about *that?* That would make greater sense now. What was it about that handful of weeks in the fields of Sonoma?

There was a doctor in Vienna—some fellow with a book about what he termed the subconscious. Freud. Yes, that was his name. He argued that our dreams say a good deal about us. Like Joseph in the book of Genesis. He also knew the messages of dreams. Not that it helped him much.

What did it mean that he should dream of events from so many years ago? It wasn't the only time he was stranded on the road. He had seen it coming and put aside enough money for a train ticket back to San Francisco. It was safe to return by then. That crazy woman was off to destinations unknown with some new, unsuspecting lover. The poor fellow. And there was an actress there he was thinking of making his wife. She had arrived at just the right moment and appeared receptive to his overtures.

But with the nightmare of what happened with Mary still fresh in his mind, he was not eager for another entanglement. He yearned for change—a life free of content and career responsibility.

He considered joining the military, and for a time it was an appealing idea to him. But it was far too much of a commitment. There were jobs harvesting hops in a section of Indian territory known by *gringos* as Ukiah. California breweries were said to be offering workers food and lodging, requiring a minimal commitment in return. That intrigued him. Living as a simple field laborer could be his path back to health and sanity. The more he thought about it, the more it looked like the sort of healing he needed. And the harder he worked, the faster he would have his fare back to New York and the heart of the theater world.

In any case, he could never go home the way he was. Mama. His sisters. Dear old Aunt Easter with her great chocolate face as loving and righteous as the holiday she was named after. They could not have understood how he got involved with that woman. They had brought him up to be smarter than that, and deserved a better outcome.

Thankfully, they never read the trade papers. Some details had leaked into the public record, but the whole story was so much more depraved. Not even other troupe members knew of the indignities he tolerated. A few months at hard labor was not too harsh a sentence for his years of dishonor.

The reality, of course, was different than he imagined. The notion of purification gave way soon enough to new doubts. What would old "Roaring Jake" have said if he had seen his son there, his head wrapped in a dirty bandana? No medals of valor were bestowed in the hops fields. His father would have been aghast at his hop-picker's gloves. Those thin canvas sleathes with their slapdash stitching were not even a distant cousin to the tanned and oiled gauntlets of a Confederate officer.

Those Ukiah field generals hid in their tents until the sun fell and the purple shadows stretched from the mountains. Then "Day's done!" would come the cry, and some foreman would respond, "Sacks up!" The enlisted men and women would thank the heavens for the time of reckoning was at hand.

Even *Roaring Jake*'s son would breathe with relief and take stock of his day. How many sacks did he have to show? It would not do to lose a dime of what was owed him.

"Hey, *Kain-tuck*! How'd ya do?"

"Three hundred pounds, I guess. Fair 'nuff for a day's work."

Next would come the rattling of wagons as the metal scales were rolled around. Tired workers dragged their sacks out to the clearing. The married men among them stood guard over the family's pickings because they knew there were thieves in the ranks.

"Don't leave your burlap out of your sight," was the warning for newcomers. "Turn your back a minute and you'll lose half your hops. You never did see such people."

After the weigh-ins and the auditing, the tired pickers traipsed back to their tents and the "hoppers' huts," only to reappear after dusk satisfied with food. They set their beveled-glass lanterns on planks around a make-do stage and waited for the Mexicans to come with their guitars. Then the younger folks would lie back and study the night sky like it was a mystery to be solved. The children zigzagged through the rows of hops, giggling in a game of tag to the twangs and rhythms of Old Spain under that low-pitched canopy of stars.

There was a stage play in this, he thought. Road companies were in dire need of fresh dramas. Costs on the road went up each year but producers kept hoping to attract new moths with the same old flames. Victorian chestnuts like "Ramona" with their dishwater lather about stoic savages and the tyranny of heathen *Americanos*—that just wouldn't do for this generation.

It was 1905, for Lord's sake. Sons and daughters of farmers wanted what the big cities offered. Young bachelors traveled in automobiles now and drank lighter brews and wore sportier fashions. They danced to fast songs filled with nonsense and spoke in a clipped and sassy tongue known as slang. It was small wonder that stage companies were going broke right and left.

He saw he had a contribution to make. He would write a play that cast light on what was really going on. It would contain the age-old intrigues and reversals but presented with up-to-date ideas of fearlessness and liberation. He would use the wonderful folk music of Mexico, and there would be songs and dancing that would bring audiences all the romance of "Ramona" but with greater abandon and a rawer passion.

Audiences would come to see his play, and when it was a success he could go back to his home and his family would be so proud of him. Even the snootiest philanthropist in Louisville would be talking up the local lad who had made such a success of himself. David Wark Griffith would assume his place in the cultural affairs of his state and become an important force in New York theater.

But "A Fool and a Girl" closed after one week. And now even his days in motion pictures appeared to be numbered. In the silence before dawn he could hear the ghosts of his future slamming doors. No one was too thrilled with his work of late—not even *Roaring Jake's little boy.*

He couldn't quite shake the symbol of those worn canvas gloves, all shiny and slick with dirt and sap. Maybe they were telling him something. Maybe his dream was warning him to prepare for another failure. If some sign of victory at Biograph was not forthcoming he could only pray that his family would not hear of it. They did not need to know how he had again diminished the name of Griffith.

What time now?

The pitch of traffic is picking up. Vendors are on the move. Must be after five, then. Forget sleep. Might as well get to it.

Oh, well. He had given it his best try.

He swung his legs off the mattress and sat up straight on the edge.

Whatever might happen today, he could make it through. He could hang on another week or so, most likely. He would see how things were going then. If all was lost he might still sign with a booking agent somewhere.

Light filtered in through the curtain. He could see to find his notebook now, perhaps scribble a few thoughts and phrases before he forgot them. *Oh, well, what's the point of that?*

He eased himself off the mattress, moving deliberately at first and taking pains not to disturb his sleeping wife.

Let the next fellow have the worries, if he wants them. Let him find out for himself how much fun it is calling all the shots.

FIVE
"Two Memories"

"Poor Mr. Griffith," said Mrs. Mulgreevey. "I suspect it's his liberty he'll be handed soon."

Her husband's head bobbed like a towboat caught in the wake of a battleship. "I told you he wouldn't last."

"Tends to happen to the directors here, heaven knows."

"I did like some of his pictures, though. The early ones at least." He scowled bitterly. "But nothing in 'em to appeal to the common man."

"Ooh, Eddie," said Mrs. Mulgreevey, her eyes growing bigger, "that one about the stolen baby! Remember? Sealed up in a keg, poor thing, and carried off by gypsy heathens in a wagon."

Her husband's smile widened. "Then the barrel ups and slips off the back—*splash!*, in the river. That's something you can't put on a stage, no sir!" He chortled, then stopped short as if caught telling a joke in a funeral parlor. "Anyway, it's sad I am to see him go."

Both Mulgreeveys sighed and their wizened heads bobbed in a comical unison that made Augusta smile.

Matilda Mulgreevey was a large-framed woman with exaggerated brows and rosy rouged cheeks. She was dressed in a lacy-sleeved apron with a blue bonnet that made her look like a life-size rag doll. Edmonton Mulgreevey appeared normal by comparison. His tall stretch of scalp was fringed with the final tufts of brown hair. He wore a high collar with a Dickensian topcoat and a vest that strained against each of its leather-covered buttons.

Augusta had barely noticed the couple in the dark when she took a seat on their bench. She was mad at herself for wasting all morning on an Irishman who refused to show up. Mr. Griffith sent word he would see her after lunch. Now he was embroiled in another animated meeting with Arthur Marvin. It was when she settled back against the wall and shut her eyes that she felt a tug on her sleeve.

"You here for work today, dearie?" whispered the rag-doll lady.

"I'm not sure. I was told I should wait."

The woman stuck out a sympathetic bottom lip. "Oh," she muttered, and looked away.

"You too?"

It turned out the woman and her husband were a vaudeville team "between engagements." It was their routine to rise at dawn and pore over the trades for casting calls, personnel changes, and anything else to do with the entertainment business. That morning they had come across a curious item about the troubles at American Biograph.

"Protests up and down Fourteenth Street? Temperance ladies calling for a boycott?" Mrs. Mulgreevey's eyes grew wider and wider until she had to shake her head. They had decided then and there to make Biograph their first stop of the day.

What they found was something like a political rally.

An open-topped 1906 American Berliet made the grand centerpiece, rolling down the street next to the curb in full patriotic bunting. American flags were stuck in every crack. When it came to the corner it made a sharp turn and headed back. Meanwhile a man behind the driver would raise a large brown funnel to his mouth from time to time and shout toward pedestrians like a midway barker:

"Yes, ladies and gentlemen, American Biograph finishes today its production of 'The Drunkard's Reformation.' Prepare yourselves for the most profound story of repentance and salvation in the long history of the animated picture. American Biograph produces only the most wholesome of family entertainments. Our pictures are famous the world over for extolling sobriety and virtue and good citizenship. Watch for our upcoming production of 'The Drunkard's Reformation,' soon to play at a Mutual exchange theater near you. ... God bless America!"

Edmonton Mulgreevey scowled and shook his head. "I've seen sideshow hoopla in my day, but this one takes the cake."

"It just don't make sense, puttin' on such a show," said his wife. "And why was the police there, jottin' down names?"

Augusta never liked involving herself in backstage gossip. But the Mulgreeveys reminded her of actors she had met and had grown fond of. She wanted to share with them what she knew.

"The police were here doing a follow-up, I suspect. On a report that was filed."

"Didn't I tell ya, Mattie?" said Edmonton, giving his wife a thump on her shoulder. "It's because of them sourpusses, I bet."

Matilda looked too perplexed to respond. "A *police* report? Are you sure?"

"Mr. Griffith went down to the station himself."

"What was it about?"

"An assault. On one of the older ladies of the company. A Miss Arvidson."

The husband shook his head. "Don't know her."

"I think I know who she means," said Matilda. "Come here not long after Mr. Griffith arrived."

"Apparently the picket ladies found one of her pictures offensive."

"I've seen some stinkers but none that made me want to assault anyone," said Edmonton.

Mrs. Mulgreevey gave him a sharp look. "Temperance ladies got a right to be put-out."

"Oh, here we go again," he said, rolling his eyes.

"Drink's a curse on womenfolk. That's the sad truth of it. When a husband runs off with demon rum, it's the wife and young 'uns foot the bill. We don't get to vote and we don't have a fair shake in the courts, either, when you come down to it."

A loud crack sounded at the studio entrance and all three heads swiveled toward the tall double doors.

"Oh, oh, watch yourselves," said the husband.

An older, gray-haired man in a blue suit and tie was storming straight for Griffith's private meeting.

"Looks a bit riled, don't he?" said the wife.

"Who is that?" asked Augusta.

"Why, that's Arthur's older brother, old Henry hisself," exclaimed Edmonton.

"Lord if it ain't," agreed Matilda. "Haven't seen him around in a month of Sundays."

According to the Mulgreeveys, Henry Marvin was the one who really ran Biograph. He had founded the company over a decade before in 1895, the same year the Mulgreeveys were getting into vaudeville. They had taken a special interest in him and his company ever since.

In the early years, Henry and Arthur Marvin and their associate J. J. Kennedy brought aboard a fourth partner named William K. L. Dickson. Dickson had been a cameraman for Thomas Edison and was something of an inventor, so after his falling out with the notoriously stingy "Wizard of Menlo Park," Dickson brought the Marvins his own contraption for producing moving pictures. It was a peep-show gizmo that flipped a succession of stiff picture cards under an optical lens. He dubbed it the *Mutoscope*, and since it did not violate any Edison patents it became the cornerstone of the Marvins' new business. They renamed their studio the American Mutoscope and Biograph Company. Dickson's box was mostly used as a sales tool at first. Salesmen would carry it with them to show prospective buyers how a piece of machinery worked in action. The company branched out into what was known as "railroad scenics" and "news happenings," and when the patent wars ended the whole business switched over to projected film strips.

"Now Mr. Griffith's got himself in a pickle, if you ask me," said Mrs. Mulgreevey. "Word is he's become a bit too free with the Marvins' money."

Her husband nodded. "Two hundred dollars for a one-reeler? Unheard of! And there's more competition these days. The studio hasn't had much to point at in terms of box office lately."

"His one-year contract has got to be ending soon. It's not a good time to be filing criminal complaints."

Mr. Mulgreevey frowned. "A court trial's always a roll of the dice. Don't matter who you are. And the Marvins are businessmen, not gamblers."

"Love to be a fly on that wall," said his wife.

They watched the three men talk and wave their arms around a while. Then suddenly Mrs. Mulgreevey seemed to inflate with excitement. "Eddie! The McClellan Massacre!"

Her husband stopped to deliberate a moment. "You know, you might have something there, Mattie. It would explain the hoopla out front with the flags!"

"What about a massacre?"

"You weren't here for the McClellan Christmas Eve Massacre?" said the wife. "You see, Eddie? Last night—didn't I tell you? I heard voices. From far out in the heavens, they came. 'Be at Biograph in the morning,' they whispered!"

Her husband's face scrunched in dismay. "For cryin' out loud. You can't even hear me talking to you in the next *room*."

"It all began with the sort of protest you got here," said Matilda. "Clergy and civic groups claimed pictures were a bad influence. They finally got to the mayor and last Christmas he shut 'em down."

"You got to follow the money," said her husband. "It wasn't just the bluenoses. Who was hurtin' most because of the flickers? One nickel for a whole evening's entertainment? Not even vaudeville can compete with that."

"Vaudeville folks wasn't responsible," scolded his wife. "Weren't they first to put the flicks on their bills?" She looked at Augusta. "The comedies bring whole families back to the houses, which is a joy to see."

"I didn't say it was all vaudeville's doing," said Mr. Mulgreevey. "But the theater owners and Broadway bosses sure got the mayor in their pocket. They had to do something to protect their profits."

"Well, whoever was behind it," said Matilda, "this past Christmas Eve Mayor McClellan ordered all the business licenses pulled on the nickelodeons in the city. They all went dark just at the busiest time of year."

"And then the mayor skedaddled out of town," added her husband.

"Didn't go on too long, though. Picture people got their own lawyers and filed an injunction against the mayor's action."

"But it sure made people in the picture business skittish," said Mr. Mulgreevey.

"No one wants another shutdown, that's a fact," said his wife.

"Whoops, there they go," announced her husband.

Both Henry Marvin and his younger brother Arthur had broken away from the meeting and were on their way to the exit doors.

"Whatever it was about, looks like it's settled for now," said Mrs. Mulgreevey.

Lawrence Griffith sat upright on his stool, thumbing through his papers a moment. Then he slipped forward and went hurrying off behind the stage. A bank of lights popped on overhead, providing the cue for studio carpenters to start their hammering and sawing again.

"One thing's for sure," said Edmonton Mulgreevey, "they weren't here just to swap tales of the Biograph ghost."

"Ghost?" said Augusta.

Mr. Mulgreevey grasped his wife's wrist. His eyebrows lifted as he continued to stare at Augusta. "You mean to say no one's told you yet about the Biograph ghost?"

"No. ... No, they have not," she repeated, as if the subject had been kept from her on purpose. "Is there a ghost?"

"As sure as I'm sitting here looking at you," he answered.

His wife also warmed to the topic. "A horrible visage, he has, and peeks up at you from about knee-high 'cause he's bent in half!"

"Bent in half?"

"Sure thing," said Mr. Mulgreevey. "A broken back, you see. Scuttles along like a crab, he does, all doubled over with just his knuckles to keep his balance."

"I don't believe I've ever heard of a crippled ghost," said Augusta.

"It's due to his having been stuffed in a trunk," said Matilda. "He was like that for most of a decade before they found him."

"Imagine going through eternity like that," said her husband. "I'd be seeking vengeance on the living myself."

"Just be warned if you ever have to go in the basement, dear," said the wife. "It's there he appears to this very day. Wandering in the darkness, all folded over. Just before he appears they say you'll catch a whiff of mothballs and mildew."

"From bein' in a trunk," explained the husband.

There was a sudden flurry of activity down on the stage. "Little child!" hollered a tweedy production aid with a clipboard. "All those on call for 'Little Child,' please stand by. Included are the following: Miss Marion Leonard, Mr. Arthur Johnson, Mr. Mack Sennett, Mr. David Miles, and Adele DeGarde. ... Please make sure you've been checked for wardrobe and makeup. Technicians, please be ready. Mr. Griffith wishes to commence in five minutes. Thank you!"

"Well," said Mr. Mulgreevey, rising to his feet. "They won't be needing us today."

"I'm still glad we come," said his wife, reaching to grasp Augusta's hand. "It was a joy meetin' you, dear." Then a twist of pity laced her lips. "God bless you and your poor Mr. Griffith," she said.

"I did enjoy his pictures, though," added her husband before ushering her away toward the exit.

Augusta maintained some hope that Owen Moore would yet make an appearance. Each time the tall doors parted she whipped her head around, and each time she turned back to the stage in disappointment.

Mack Sennett entered at one point followed by Arthur Johnson, the young dandy in the boater from the day before. More actors collected on stage and Billy Bitzer came out to feed a spool of film into his mounted box. Finally it was Lawrence Griffith's turn, sweeping from the shadows to settle on his high stool.

"Gather closer, everyone," he called. "So much was going on here yesterday, I fear we did not do justice to the story we aim to tell. The title is 'And a Little Child Shall Lead Them.' The role of Mother, of course, will be played by our own Miss Marion Leonard."

He waited as a stocky, operatic-looking woman tipped her head a few times to a scattering of applause.

"Mr. Arthur Johnson will play the role of Father. Everyone here knows Mr. Johnson, of course. ... Now recall that our Father and Mother have lost their only child. The death of their young girl has left them in grief, as you will appreciate. They have little to remind them now of her happy youth but a favorite toy, the carved figure of a dog."

Here Griffith consulted his notes then looked up to glance about the stage. "Where is our carved dog? Has anyone seen it? ... Bobby?"

"Back here, Griff," called Bobby from the rear, waving something in his fist from side to side.

"Bring it to me, please."

Bobby ran up to lay a small object in the director's hand.

Griffith flipped it over and smiled. "I had one much like this as a boy. Not made of wood, of course." Titters rolled through the cast. "Just an old yellow hunting dog with a long snout. I don't think anyone knew his breed. Perhaps his beauty was not evident to the world. To me there was no finer animal or more loyal friend. After school, we would go off exploring he and I. As the school years added up, he grew slower and finally only wished to pass his days lying on the porch. My father thought the time had come to take him for a walk. The crack of a rifle out in the field ended my youth. ... Maybe today as you play your parts you can think back to a thing you loved and lost."

The director signaled for a young girl standing at the front of the group to come forward. He said something in her ear and placed the carved dog in her hand. "Do you all know Miss Adele DeGarde? She has a key role in the second part of our drama today. We find that seven years have passed, and Father and Mother now have a second daughter, a child of six. That shall be Miss DeGarde."

Augusta watched as the girl gave a rapid scrubbing motion to the others. Griffith's child of six was more likely nine or ten.

"As too often happens in their situation, our husband has been neglecting the needs of his wife. Their marriage is in the process of dissolving and they are agreed on a divorce. We meet them as they divide their household possessions. 'This is yours, and that is mine.' Then little Adele finds the carved dog and brings it up to her parents. 'Mama,' she asks, 'who gets this?' ... End title."

Marion Leonard cleared her throat and slowly raised a hand. "Mr. Griffith?"

"Yes, Miss Leonard, you have a question?"

"Is Adele—I mean, regarding the title—is Adele to be taken as the little child 'who leads them?' Is that the idea? I recognize the Biblical quotation, of course. But is it here a hopeful indication of the couple's reconciliation? The child leads them back to their marriage vows?"

"Miss Leonard knows Scriptures," teased the director. "Yes, Miss Leonard, it's both, I suppose. An echo from Isaiah. A world of peace awaits those whose sins are lifted."

Arthur Johnson shifted from leg to leg, clearly uncomfortable with this. "But what exactly was their sin?"

"What was that, Mr. Johnson?" said the director. "Speak up."

"I just asked ... it seems to me—What was the sin? I mean, they *were* married. And they didn't *murder* their first-born."

"It's original sin, Mr. Johnson. Read your Bible," he said. "All right, everyone, let's get to work! Billy!"

Augusta saw Bobby coming her way and she gestured for him to stop. "Would you do something for me, Bobby? Can you ask Mr. Griffith if he'll be using me at all today?"

Soon Bobby came running back to her with the word. Yes, Griffith wanted her up in Nina's wardrobe shop after lunch. Bobby couldn't say what the director had in mind, but he was pretty insistent.

She waited around a bit longer and watched the filming. But by eleven-thirty she was ready to call off her vigil. Even if Owen showed up looking for her now, it was too late. She no longer felt she could tolerate his excuses.

As for Lawrence "David" Griffith—it hardly seemed to matter anymore what roles he had in mind for her to play. In a day or two he was likely to be gone. He was hardly in a position to offer her much work.

SIX

"Mrs. Jones Entertains"

Every actor loved basking in the spell of Nina's wardrobe shop. It was an afterschool playhouse for flirty games of dress-up and gossip, a sunny place to put off life's demands and lose oneself in a whirligig of make-believe.

At present, though, Augusta was not so much interested in fantasy as in answers. Did she have a job here or not? She had to decide on her own next move. And that made what she found waiting on the third floor almost as annoying as it was surprising.

It was the Statue of Liberty.

Well, no, it wasn't *that* statue, it turned out, or any statue at all. It was the statuesque figure of some mortal goddess draped in iridescent folds of mint. Harvested sprays of wheat rested like a tiara in her dark brunette hair, and nature had provided the perfect cleft in the center of her porcelain chin to mark the pride of workmanship.

"*Rmm, mmbar, dmmsk,*" came a growling mumble near the goddess's ankles. It was Nina, crouched on the floor with a mouthful of pins and a stub of chalk. She scooted about on her knees like a schoolboy shooting marbles as she struggled to define the proper hemline length for an immortal.

"Sorry," stammered Augusta, "I don't wish to intrude."

Nina grunted something in reply.

"She's too much of a lady to talk with her mouth full, sweetie," said the woman in the green robe. Her voice sounded surprisingly down-to-earth for a goddess. "Pull up a pedestal if you'd like to be next."

Augusta looked about for a place to leave her coat. She was standing at a row of coat hooks on the wall when Linda Arvidson came bursting through the door like she was about to miss her cue. "Have you seen Mr. Griffith? Did he come—?" She stopped short when she saw Augusta. "Oh, hello," she said.

"No sightings today," answered the beauty on the riser. "You two have met, I take it."

Augusta nodded. "We have. Nice to see you've recovered, Miss Arvidson."

The actress gave a thin smile. "I try to carry on. I thought I saw Mr. Griffith coming this way."

"You're welcome to search the room, dear," said the woman on the fitting platform.

"I guess I was mistaken," she said, spinning to hurry out. "Thank you, Florence."

So the goddess had a name. Suddenly it made sense. "You must be Florence Lawrence," said Augusta.

"Well, if I must be."

"I saw your sacks of mail. In Mr. Griffith's office."

"It's a game we like to play. He keeps my fan letters and I don't ask him for more money."

"If people wrote me I'd want to read every one."

"No, you wouldn't. It's just sad. You have no idea how many lonely people there are in the world."

"*Vat'll* do it," muttered the seamstress, straightening up to spit the pins into her hand. "What was Miss Arvidson in such a state about?"

Augusta looked to the door to make sure she was gone. "She's been following me," she whispered.

"No-o-o," drawled Nina. "Why would she want to do that?"

"I'm not sure. But she's been watching me like I'm an enemy spy or something."

Nina fanned herself with the bottom of her apron. "Poor thing. That was a nasty business she went through."

"Are we done here, Nina?" asked Florence.

The seamstress nodded. "Have a look."

She gathered together the train of her robe and stepped carefully off the riser, heading straight for the full-length mirror.

Nina stood and looked at Augusta. "Now what do you need, love?"

"Mr. Griffith asked me to wait. Do you know if—is he planning to use me or what?"

"I can look at the schedule."

"Thank you."

"Oh, Nina," said Florence Lawrence as she swished back and forth before the mirror. "It is divine."

"Yes, it's lovely," said Augusta.

Nina was trying to make out a typewritten carbon copy on her clipboard. "Here we are. *A Little Child Shall Lead Them.* ... Let's see ... Mr. Arthur Johnson, Father—'Respectable but unkempt.' ... Miss Linda Arvidson, Mother—'Respectable but neglected.' ... And Adele DeGarde, The Daughter—"

"Respectable but only nine," interjected Florence.

"That's all I have for today."

Augusta tried to smile. "Nothing for me. Well, thank you for checking."

"Sorry, dear," said Nina. "There's always tomorrow."

"Spoken like a true Christian," said Florence. "The robe is really lovely, Nina. I simply adore the material."

"Is it for your next picture?" asked Augusta.

"That's right. The next 'Jonesy' comedy. Mrs. Jones and I are destined to live out our days together. *Mrs. Jones Has Driving Lessons. Mrs. Jones Goes Flying.* ... Some day I expect it will be *Mrs. Jones Takes the Cure.*"

Augusta chuckled as a sing-songy voice chimed in from the hallway: *"Mrs. Jones has visitors."*

Arthur Johnson peeked through the archway with a mischievous smirk. "Are you all decent?"

"Not since last century," chirped Florence.

"See, Mack, I told you we were running late," said Arthur. He strolled quite casually toward the front windows followed by Mack Sennett. The larger man took deliberate strides, pitched forward in his shoes as if pushing into a hard wind.

Next at the doorway stood a stout, middle-aged man in an impeccable brown suit with a white boutonniere. "What's all this about?" he paused to ask, then drifted back to join the other men. Augusta had met him earlier. He was John Cumpson, the actor who played Mr. Jones in Florence's comedy series.

A handsome man with a straight, aristocratic nose arrived next. "What does he want us all for?" he asked.

"A new parlor game is my guess," said Arthur Johnson. "It's called 'Where will you go from here?' Mack will have a shovel in his hand by morning, I expect."

Mack grinned. "And Arthur tried to get a job making taffy. Turns out he didn't have the pull."

Florence gathered up her own clothes to take them behind a modesty screen. "I don't know about pull," she said as she disappeared, "but you'd be surprised what a little tug will get you."

Another group of young men showed up in the hall, curious to see what the laughter was about. Some were stagehands in paint-spattered overalls with rags trailing from their rear pockets. Others were clearly freelancing actors in natty sport jackets or untailored suits.

The rustle of a new round of footsteps in the corridor came accompanied by the youthful titters of office girls. All eyes turned to watch their happy faces fall one by one into a tar pit of self-consciousness.

"What is this?" asked Nina. "Is it someone's birthday?"

Sennett twitched his rounded shoulders. "All we were told was Mr. Griffith wants to talk to everyone at once."

"Where's Bobby?" said Nina. "If anyone knows what's up, it's him."

"God," exclaimed Florence from behind the screen. She was pulling a blouse down over her pile of hair. "I hope it's not another 'old West' picture! It's a sin what passes for horses in this town."

"All right, everybody," announced Linda Arvidson as she swept in from the corridor. "He's on his way."

"Cue the Berlioz funeral march," muttered the man with the handsome nose. He had lit a cigarette and held it pinched tightly between two fingers.

"I refuse to appear glum prematurely," said Florence. She came around from the screen fastening the final buttons of a flouncy, cream-colored top. "I need to know my motivation first."

"Come now, people," said Linda Arvidson. "Change can be healthy."

"I'll pay my way, thank you," said Mack. "You can keep the change."

There was a new smattering of nervous laughter.

"Enjoy your merriment," barked John Cumpson, "but this business shall have a sad outcome."

"There are no sad outcomes in art," came a sonorous voice from the hallway. Lawrence Griffith stopped under the archway and took a look around before heading for the center. "I do apologize for the inconvenience," he said, nodding and smiling at the faces he passed. "But I wanted as many of you here as possible."

Augusta thought it a brave smile, worthy of a leader with a bit of confidence remaining. How long could he keep up that act?

"Oh, good, Florence, you're here," said the director, "and Mr.

Cumpson." He nodded to the stout man with the boutonniere. "We shall be taking up with the Joneses as soon we finish here."

Another group of office girls entered and stationed themselves at the rear. Augusta was struck by how young they looked. Some were hardly more than high school girls, yet here they were holding down jobs in the big city. She could only hope things turned out as well for her.

"Let's see, who is missing?" said Griffith, rising on his toes to see to the back. "Miss Arvidson, thank you for coming. ... Mr. John—" He halted to look down.

Augusta had pushed a wooden riser at him to stand on. It was lighter than she thought and had slammed against his boot. "Sorry," she muttered. "I thought it would help."

"Thank you." He stepped up and looked out across the crowd. "Yes, that's better. Can you all see me now? ... I see Mr. Johnson is here. Thank you for coming. ... And Bobby? Where is Bobby?"

Bobby Harron jumped up at the door and waved his arm over his head. "Here. Griff!"

"Bobby, would you mind taking a look downstairs to see if anyone else is coming?"

"Sure thing," answered the boy, vanishing in a blur.

Augusta saw the top of another head settle into Bobby's spot.

"Is that Mr. Yost back there?" called out Griffith with a grin. "Do you all know our Mr. Poe? Thank you for joining us, Mr. Poe. Is anyone else out there?"

"Just a few old hens with picket signs," he cracked.

Griffith waited for the nervous laughter to die down. "So, thank you again, everyone, for coming. ... I learned yesterday that I rather enjoy these talks. ... Some of you know I have been in meetings with Mr. Marvin and Mr. Kennedy. We have not always seen eye-to-eye. But today I'm happy to say we're in agreement about a big change here."

Augusta's cheeks were starting to twitch from maintaining her smile. She braced herself now for a sentimental farewell.

"Many of you have asked me about the name American Mutoscope and Biograph Company. Why do we keep it when we are out of the Mutoscope business? The exchanges know us simply as American Biograph, or even The Biograph Company. That's what is seen on our circulars and press releases, as well. Today I can announce that henceforth we will be legally known as American Biograph."

There was a flurry of approval and some applause, but Augusta sensed people were holding something back for the real announcement.

"Anyway, we wished to share the news with you. You are among the first to know. We are out of the arcade racket for good. From now on we will concentrate solely on the nickelodeons. ... Two additional items I need to share. Before I do that, do any of you have questions?"

Linda Arvidson's hand rose.

"Yes? ... Everyone, of course, knows Miss Arvidson."

She traded smiles with a few of the women standing near her. "Mr. Griffith, I would like to hear from you how things are going with the police. Will they be making arrests soon?"

Murmurs and frowns of concern passed from face to face.

"Miss Arvidson is referring to an incident yesterday on our front steps. We have filed papers and our lawyers are moving ahead with the next phase. When we have something to report, we will make an announcement." He looked to the back where Herbert Yost's hand had suddenly shot up. "Yes, Mr. Yost?"

"About the question I raised yesterday. I gave it more thought. We all know Broadway advertizes its players. The legitimate stage doesn't have a problem with actors' names. Even vaudeville actors get mention in the billing out front, while the actors appearing on screen do not."

"With a name comes a following," said a voice in the back.

"Yeah. Bigger names mean bigger business," shouted another.

"And bigger salaries!"

"I understand your concerns, believe me," said Griffith. "I know how a name on a marquee can boost ticket sales. But keep in mind, not every actor here wishes it to be known what he's doing."

"Yeah," bellowed a man from the rear, "like ladies of the night!"

That prompted a raucous wave of laughter and more comments.

"But those are our faces up there," continued Herbert Yost, striking a more contrarian tone. "We cannot hide our faces. Artists deserve recognition for their work."

There was a new round of comments and a bobbing of heads as Griffith held up his hand for order. "In my book, right now, all of you are stars. I'm sure in due course the studio will modify its policy. And I promise you again, I will take up that cause when the time comes."

He gave a nervous pull on his tie before proceeding. "Are there any other concerns? ... Well, I do have one more announcement. ... I have spoken with Mr. Marvin and we have received permission for a brief outing to the Palisades. We will take the ferry in the morning, as usual. So those of you on the schedule, please arrive early for your tickets."

"You mean tomorrow?" asked a man.

"Yeah," seconded another. "What's the haste, Mr. Griffith?"

Young Bobby had slipped back in the room and was standing in the back on a chair. "To get away from those wacky picket dames, right Griff?"

Everyone laughed.

"I think that will benefit us all, Bobby," said Griffith. "It just so happens we need a snowy backdrop before winter is gone. So please, check with me if you are not sure about your schedule. One last announcement," he said, growing serious again.

Augusta braced her back against the cutting table.

"As you may have heard, we have a new arrival. Mr. Bitzer exposed some footage and last night we had a chance to look at it. I was quite pleased by what we saw. I want to ask you all to join me in welcoming to our little family the lovely Miss Augusta Lee."

Why was everyone smiling and clapping and looking at her? Wasn't Griffith telling them he was leaving? Wasn't she out of a job? What sort of joke was going on?

The director was standing on the riser, smiling down at her. "Billy and I have big plans for you, Miss Lee," he said.

She looked quickly around her, jumping from face to face, certain there was some mistake. Broad smiles and nods of congratulations met her from every corner.

Abruptly her eyes landed on one unhappy frown and the brooding, wounded features of Linda Arvidson. In a flash she had spun around and was hurrying out the door.

"That's all, then," Griffith was telling the crowd. "Thank you all for your hard work. I am delighted to have you aboard as we embark on more adventures under the flag of American Biograph."

The applause continued a moment before dying off as people began filing for the door.

Lawrence Griffith stepped down from his platform to hold out a hand to Augusta. "May I have a moment with you, my dear?"

"Of course."

He led her away to a private spot under the windows and motioned for her to take a seat on a work stool. "It is true what I said about your test," he said. "You have an unusual quality. The camera loves you."

"I know I can do much better."

"Oh, I am convinced of that. You have a great deal to learn. But I can help you." He reached into his coat and pulled out an envelope. "This is yours. It's a voucher for fifteen dollars."

"Why, whatever on Earth *for*?"

"'The Drunkard's Reformation.' That *was* your idea."

She took it and held it to her heart. It was her first pay in New York. "Thank you."

"Tell me, are you comfortable here?"

"People have been very kind."

"I meant—with me?"

She looked down and found it easy to raise her eyes and smile. "Yes."

"Good. Delighted to hear it. ... I want you to come tomorrow, to the Palisades. The weather looks favorable."

"Sounds wonderful."

"Like I said, Billy and I have an idea for using you. ... So, we leave Union Station at 7:45. Meet us here or uptown at the ferry station. Naturally, Biograph will provide tickets for yourself and, um, Mr. Trawley."

"I will only need one ticket."

Griffith appeared confused. "Surely he wouldn't allow his young ward to go off without a chaperone?"

"I can assure you, I am used to being on my own."

"No. It would not be right."

"Then I am afraid it's a problem."

"A problem?"

"Mr. Trawley is not ... available."

"Oh? May I ask why?"

"Well, he's come down with a condition. A health condition."

"Oh, Lord. I hope nothing serious."

"The doctors say it could be, yes. It's an old condition, you see."

"Recurrent?"

"Yes. He thought it was gone ... but it flared up again."

"I see."

"They had to take him to a sanitarium. They say he needs lots of bed rest."

"How are you managing?"

"I am fine. I promised to look after his belongings and sundries—you know, until he is well enough to return."

"We'll send him flowers."

"That is very kind. But it would embarrass him."

"Maybe a visit ... to raise his spirits."

"No. I mean, that's very thoughtful, Mr. Griffith. But they do not allow visitors. They only let me come on Sundays, when he's feeling up to it."

"Well, then, I guess we can provide you a chaperone."

"That's not nec—"

"No, no. I insist on that."

"Very well."

"Let me ask Miss Arvidson."

Augusta's eyes must have widened in alarm.

"Something wrong?"

"I'd hate to bother Miss Arvidson. She is so busy, and she has been through so much."

"That's exactly why it will be good for her to get away. I'm sure she will agree."

"If you insist."

He rubbed his hands together and straightened up. "Excellent."

"Who else will be coming?"

"Just a few of us this time. Mr. Sennett. *Mack*. He is the one responsible for the story. And Mr. John Cumpson—he was just here—he will play our lead. Then Billy Bitzer, of course. And his wife usually likes to come on our outings. ... Charles Inslee is coming, and little Bobby. ... Oh, and Mr. Moore has volunteered to help."

"Owen Moore?"

A look of concern passed through Griffith's eyes. "You've met, haven't you? Oh, that's right. He helped with your test. ... We'll have a nice time, you'll see."

Augusta found it easy to return an eager smile. "I simply cannot wait. Look at me ... shaking all over."

SEVEN

"The Winning Coat"

The Hudson Palisades, rising craggy and tall upon the water, were once described to a Spanish mapmaker as a "fence of stakes," and the name had stuck.

The crevices still bore long streaks of ice where the shade was strong, and trees down on the shoreline stood heavy with snow. Any morning gust might set the branches bobbing again. In the mist it looked to Augusta like some grand, enchanted waterfall feeding a frothy trough.

Nature's magic paled, though, in comparison to the thrill of watching Owen Moore striding along 125th Street.

In his charcoal coat and ribboned fedora he could have been any well-tailored businessman with a newspaper folded at his elbow. But Augusta knew better. Their kiss had planted something within her that refused to let her go.

So it stunned her more than a slap to the face when Owen gave the gateman a cocky salute and went straight for the gangway without even a sideways glance at her. The nearby blast of the steam whistle did not faze her. It wasn't until she heard the rattling of a chain as it was pulled through the gatepost that she sighed and went to find a seat aboard the rusted ferryboat.

Lawrence Griffith had led the others to the deckhouse. Through a fogged porthole she could see them inside, lit by the flames of a cast-iron stove. Griffith was unmistakable in his fuzzy brimmed hat and knitted scarf. He sat leaning forward to speak with Billy Bitzer. The matronly Mrs. Bitzer ignored them both, holding up her knitting needles as she untangled yarn from a floppy quilted bag. Toward the front stood Owen Moore, uncoiling his scarf from his neck and standing over two studio men Augusta had first seen on the train.

Most everyone was holding up the morning edition like a fortress wall. Linda Arvidson sat a bit off from the rest with an open book. So much for the great, conscientious chaperone, she thought.

A seat on the open deck was more to her liking anyway. She had been lying to herself, pretending that she didn't care at all if she never set foot on a boat again. But the caws of unseen gulls in the fog and the moaning of the boards underfoot worked their dreamy magic. She found a bench at the fore behind a windbreak and let her heavy lids sag and sag until finally they fell closed.

The engines started with a growl and an old man in a uniform and a faded cap climbed backwards down the ladder to begin his ticket rounds. Augusta imagined a dockman at the aft hurling the last hawser from the pilings. Then with another blast of the whistle the ferryboat shuddered and began to ease itself from its slip.

Little Bobby came barreling from the deckhouse like a demon. He wore a large man's winter coat and as he ran its hem dragged and swished behind him. Suddenly he stopped and gave his shoulders a shake, and instantly his coat was flying across a capstan.

Augusta watched him balance on a handrail with the toes of his shoes buried in the wire mesh guard. When he was through watching the silt churned up from the river bottom he made a breathtaking leap backward and was off to the pilothouse as if summoned for a chat with the skipper.

Why did no one think of Bobby as the one needing the chaperone?

Linda Arvidson. That was quite a laugh. The idea that a woman like her could shield her from anything was an outrage in itself. But everything about her manner rubbed Augusta the wrong way.

Who was to say she hadn't engineered that confrontation on the front steps herself? One thing could be said about actors: Never take their calamities at face value. Manipulating audiences to their own ends was their gift, after all. Most of them discovered the knack for drumming up sympathy at a very young age. A mature leading lady might easily dream up an incident like that if she felt she was losing her advantage.

There was no overestimating how devious an insecure actor could be. She had seen how her mother was when a younger, more attractive woman signed aboard for a season. She became capable of doing just about anything to keep from being ignored.

In the end, even dying fit her needs. No, that was unfair. Whatever had happened between them, the dying act grew real enough in time. It was painful to see her like that, lying helpless in her stuffy cabin, her long dark hair in matted strands across the pillow. Even the narrow wooden cradle of her bunk looked too spacious for her. Everyone walked by on eggshells. The last thing even the toughest of crewmen wanted was to set her off now.

But the dragon lady didn't have much fire left in her by then. All that she had were two accusative eyes and those sweat-soaked curls.

The two of them hadn't really gotten along well since—when, exactly? Some time in her thirteenth year. Maybe earlier. Certainly before the business with Mr. John Gillette. John's brother might have been the celebrated one on Broadway, but the younger Gillette boy was just as handsome, and certainly behaved like the real star of the family. It was puzzling to see how he bragged about his famous brother in public but spoke so badly of him in private.

The ladies on the river took notice of him, that was sure. They would parade by him, sending out glances and signals—especially the married ones. Why was that? At one time she thought even her mother was caught in his spell. Then out of the blue one day she dismissed him with absolute scorn. People said they must have had a falling out, though none of the explanations ever made much sense to Augusta.

Mostly it was trivial matters and gossip. *He shouldn't have said this or shouldn't have forgotten that.* What did any of that matter? Actors were petty people. But nothing could account for her mother's change of heart, and relations between them got progressively tense.

John was the first to show any real interest in her acting. Maybe that sparked the friction. One day her mother insisted she must never be caught alone with the man again. Augusta took her words quite literally, and always did her utmost to never be *caught.*

They did not discuss the matter, either, even after John bid the company farewell. Some accused her mother of having a hand in the cancellation of his contract. There were innuendos and she noticed the curious silences when she entered a room. Whatever had happened, things never got back to the way they were.

There was no room on a riverboat for hurt feelings. Quarters were too tight. There wasn't even space for modesty, and no one tried to protect her or any of the other juveniles from the facts of life. When it came to making the most of a sultry summer's day, when the boat was out of dock and no matinee was in the offing, actors might try the cool waters over the side and get both bath and exercise with unequaled efficiency. Likely as not, that meant skinny-dipping for the men and the young ones, while the ladies would defer to a sponging in their private chambers.

From the time she was seven or eight, Augusta knew about the physical differences between the sexes. For a while around age ten she began to take an active interest in those differences. She tried not to be seen staring because she sensed the boys didn't like being appraised, while some of the older men liked it a bit too much.

It was while performing the role of Nancy one season that some of the men took to calling her "Nary-a-stitch Nancy." It did not bother her at first. She was even flattered by the attention. But then her mother got wind of it. After that it was strictly bathing in her own quarters, just like the grown-ups.

Thud!

Out of nowhere young Bobby landed with both feet on the deck next to her. He shot rapid looks around like a hunted fugitive, then took off at full speed and ducked under a *No Entry* sign on the door to the engine room.

God, the engine room. No one needed to tell her about the allure of engine rooms. The noise of the pistons and the feel of the steam on her body. Wedging herself into a warm, tight spot to let the vibrations roll through her. How much of her youth was spent in the hold of one tug or another? Engine rooms behaved exactly as they were designed. No unwelcomed adult ever ventured into such a place to impose a beer-soured nuzzle.

She always felt safe with her mother, though. Reading aloud to her in those last days, it seemed they were on the verge of a reconciliation. Time passed in an unreal blur of Jane Austen and Dickens and James Fenimore Cooper. Her mother would open her eyes from time to time to look at her with tenderness and affection.

Love alone could not lift her above the pain. But her mother appeared almost happy one day, and managed a smile. She asked her daughter to come nearer.

"You're so much like me," she said between her labored breaths. She loved to stroke Augusta's hair. "You're such a lovely girl. And so ... needy." Then a cough forced her to stop and she waited for the strength to go on.

"Yes, Mama?"

"It was never John Gillette, you know," she said. "He was river trash. Everyone could see that. ... But you and me, we were always so much alike, baby girl. You and your mama. I'm sorry. We tried our best. I know. But nothing can stop a person from being what she is. I knew ... because we were the same. I hoped to save you. Because I could see ... you're a trollop too, just like your mama." A few hours later, her mother drew a final breath.

"Hello," came a nearby voice.

Oh, God. It was that peculiar Mack Sennett, standing over her. He must have seen her sitting alone with her eyes closed and thought she needed company.

Crammed into an off-the-rack coat with cuffs that ended above the wrist, he looked out of place and uncomfortable—like a sideshow primitive escaped from the midway and sentenced by a judge to do a long stretch at hard civilization.

"Mind if we talk?" he asked.

She smiled and slid over to give him lots of space.

"Thanks."

She watched him square himself on the bench and lean back with a sigh. He did not speak and after a moment she felt she had to say something. "I thought no one actually talked on these trips."

"That's New York," he answered. "No one gives away nothin' for free."

"Does that include your story?"

He gave her an open-mouthed stare.

"The one we're going to film. Mr. Griffith said you wrote it."

"I doubt he said I wrote it. He knows I stole it."

"Oh."

"What else did he tell you about today?"

"Not much, really."

"What part does he want you to play?"

Augusta shook her head.

"Hunh." Mack filled his cheeks with air and his cold steel eyes bulged a bit. He exhaled and sat staring straight ahead. "The reason I ask is, that story I sold him didn't have any women in it. Not even one."

"Well, I guess we'll find out."

"I like the old man. I call him 'the old man' but he's really not much older than me. I respect him. But in a lot of ways, we're mysteries to each other."

"Mr. Trawley said you are Canadian. Did you come here to make motion pictures?"

"Me? Hardly. No. I was going to be an opera singer."

Augusta chuckled, thinking it was one of his jokes.

He gave her an earnest wag. "I'm not kiddin'. I have a good voice. Bass, of course. The glory notes, they call 'em. I read music, everything. Hand me a sheet of music and I'll sing you to sleep. I found a good coach here. Professor Waldemar. He's got a studio in Carnegie Hall. He told me I had great equipment. No diction, no control, but good, loud equipment."

He turned to see her smile. "You have a nice face."

"What made you stop?"

"Oh, the lessons, I guess. They were expensive. I found some stage work down on the Bowery. I sang some, played the back end of a horse for a couple years. That gave me a fresh perspective, you could say."

He gazed off across the deck. "Anyway, the more I learned of opera singers, the more I preferred the Bowery."

He told her how everything changed for him one day when he bought a ticket to a nickelodeon. It was a short French comedy, and the comic was doing a lot of the same stuff he was doing on the Bowery. No one in the theater understood French, but the pictures told them everything that was necessary.

"That's what I wanted," he said. "You get it right once and people all over the world are entertained. So I told my pals goodbye. None of them saw it as a step forward. Being a horse's rear end was better to them than being in flickers. They give me a send-off that was more like a funeral than a party."

Augusta couldn't tell if Mack was flirting with her or not. If he was, he had a peculiar notion of how to go about it. At least he didn't just start with a lot of dirty talk like other men. She liked him, and would not have liked to hurt him. "Your friends must have been sad to lose you."

"Maybe. I left some big pants to fill, that's for sure. But I like what I'm doing now. No butterflies. Nights free, more or less. And every day's a challenge. We learn as we go. There aren't many rules." He breathed a heavy sigh. "I have to say, though, it just wouldn't be the same without the old man."

"You think that's likely?"

"Did you hear his Zola speech?"

"Yes."

Mack shook his head. "All that literary stuff—Poe, Zola, Shakespeare—none of that will fill any seats on the Bowery. Maybe your Broadway types will buy a ticket or two, just for the novelty. But it's not what most folks go to nickelodeons for. Thing is, he keeps expecting them to come around to his way of seeing things."

A sudden ear-piercing blast announced their arrival at the docks of Edgewater.

"Look, I got to run," said Mack, slapping his big hands on his knees. "They asked me to help with the bags. Just do one thing for me."

"What's that?"

"I know he likes you. He was like a puppy dog begging for a scratch that day you came in the studio."

"That's not exactly how—"

"I think you might be able to talk some sense to him—before it's too late."

"What could I say?"

Mack clamped his jaw and grew serious. "Ever seen a soup line? There's a big difference between servin' up what folks want and giving 'em what you think they ought to eat. Maybe he's a genius and I don't have nothing to worry about. But he either winds up in a suite at the Ritz or livin' out of a bottle on the skids. I don't see no middle way for a man like him. We just could be his best chance. Promise me you'll think about it."

"I'll try."

"That's it. That was my curtain speech."

The ferry creaked and rocked as it scraped against the baffles. Mack stood to stretch his long arms over his head. "Thanks for listenin', Sis. See ya on dry land."

As he wandered off toward the stern Bobby galloped past him in a frenzy to be the first off the ship. She watched in amazement as he slipped past two deckhands and leapt over a low-hanging chain to go bouncing down the gangplank. He was on the dock in a flash and scampering along an unpaved road leading up to an imposing, three-story barn of a building on the crest of the hill.

That would have to be the Edgewater Ferry House. It was a large structure, big enough to accommodate a constant stream of travelers. It had a two-story portico in front for the carriage trade and tall windows all around on three separate levels.

Up on top was a bell tower that no doubt commanded a panoramic view of the whole Hudson valley. That seemed to be where Bobby was headed. She smiled at the spectacle of his skinny legs whipping up big clouds of dust. But, wait! ... *Oh, Bobby!* ... He didn't have his coat, and his arms swung back and forth freely at his sides.

Sure enough, there was his long coat, still hanging from the capstan where he left it. She wagged her head and went to retrieve it. What that boy really needed, she told herself, was a mother.

Most of the studio folk were gathered at the edge of the dock, bundled against the cold and waiting for their instructions. Only Owen Moore was off by himself, reading his newspaper and smoking a pipe. He did not look up when Augusta arrived to take her place with the others.

"Has everyone made it?" asked Lawrence Griffith, appearing out of nowhere in a chipper mood.

"We have," responded Linda Arvidson with a nod.

"Where's the snow?" called out the muscular man standing behind her. His question provoked smiles and a few snickers.

The director simply smiled at him. "They have it in safe keeping for us at Rambo's, Mr. Inslee."

Augusta had met Charles Inslee at the train station and was impressed by his physique and bearing. She made a point of asking about him. It turned out he had played the gypsy villain in Griffith's first film at Biograph, "The Adventures of Dollie." His round face and broad nose made him a natural for all sorts of ethnic parts. He provided female audiences especially a thrill playing half-naked Indians. Most recently he had been off freelancing with a maverick company known as Bison, spending weeks in upstate New Jersey to elude Edison's patent thugs.

Griffith took a quick head count and frowned. "Where is Mr. Sennett?"

"He's helping with the wagons," said one of the players.

"Very good. And ... Bobby? ... Now where's Bobby gotten off to?"

Augusta raised her hand. "I saw him going up the hill," she said. "To the ferry house."

"To the belfry, more likely," cracked the jovial John Cumpson.

Griffith brushed aside the unkind titters. "Splendid," he said. "We have two cars waiting for us. Let's see, we are twelve, by my count.

Ten will fit in the two vehicles, so we'll need two volunteers to ride with the luggage. All right. What say we enjoy a morning constitutional and make our way to the ferry house?"

They started as a group up the dirt road as Griffith laid out the day's schedule. The cars would take them three miles along the river road by the treeline and then up the steep climb to the Palisades. At the crest they would pass through Fort Lee, and a mile or so beyond that would be Rambo's Hotel, the country inn that served as their home-away-from-home.

Charles Inslee waited until he finished and raised his famous "Indian" head above the pack. "I am most anxious to hear about the story we will be telling."

"Of course," said the director. "It was brought to us by Mr. Sennett, who is not here so I will explain it as best I can. It centers on a colorful town character whose choice of career is remaining unemployed. … Yes, he is a hobo."

The ferryboat whistle sounded in the distance, signaling the return trip across the Hudson. In a moment Bobby appeared over the rise of the hill, racing toward them in his latest emergency to be somewhere else. He did not slow down as he passed by the group, causing a few smirks and headshakes.

"Our lead today," continued Griffith, "is Mr. John Cumpson. Mr. Cumpson, please raise your hand."

The portly character actor raised a fist and smiled.

"Mr. Cumpson today will be playing our upaithric hero. Now normally this man finds himself—" Griffith stopped when he saw Cumpson's hand waving about in the air.

"Yes, Mr. Cumpson. You appear vexed."

"My character—what did you call him? Operatic?"

"*Upaithric*, Mr. Cumpson. From the Latin, meaning 'without roof.' Your character is a hobo. He lives outdoors, unencumbered by domicile, so to speak."

"Oh, a bum," said the actor with a nod, provoking general laughter.

"If you insist," said Griffith. "Normally the man sleeps on a bench in the park. But it being late December, he does not fancy those icy fingers on his toes. So he has it in mind to break the law and earn himself a warm jail cell. Try as he might, though, he can't seem to run afoul of the town constable. Our title for Mr. Sennett's story is to the point. We call it 'Trying to Get Arrested.'"

"I'm sorry, Mr. Griffith," intoned Charles Inslee. "That story sounds familiar. I think I read it in a magazine."

"Possibly, Mr. Inslee. Mr. Sennett had the good luck to be paid for his idea before we learned that little detail. A local writer who signs himself O. Henry should get the credit. ... But we are adding our own touches. I am giving our hobo a buddy, a poor orphan and outcast of society." Here Griffith paused dramatically and waited for the others to stop and turn to watch. "This waif will be played by our newest member, Miss Augusta Lee."

Griffith had moved up behind Augusta and now grasped her by both shoulders. "Miss Lee plays a generous soul who understands her friend's need of warmth."

Augusta squirmed but he was not ready to let her go yet. All eyes were on her except for Owen Moore's. He was still paying no attention to the others from behind his newspaper. As for Linda Arvidson, whatever she might have been thinking, she was already turned and heading up the hill alone.

"I'm the town constable, I take it," said Mr. Inslee.

"You are. On the right side of society's laws for a change!"

"But still the villain," he snapped.

Griffith smiled. "The soul of Christian charity, Mr. Inslee. For each time our hero breaks a law you are there in the spirit of the season to forgive his transgression."

Mr. Inslee nodded, apparently satisfied with the part.

"Let me tell you, we have a little topper to Mr. O'Henry's story," said Griffith. "At the end our hobo succeeds in getting himself arrested. We see him snug in his cell, laying out his socks on the bars to dry. Outside his tiny window the snow is falling. Lights down. But that is not quite the end. Lights up! We find ourselves outside with a final tableau. It is of our little friend here," he said, giving Augusta another shake. "She is sitting alone on the mountain ledge, wiping her nose as she watches the snowflakes tumble on the distant town. The plight of the homeless goes on, unseen by a cold and uncharitable world. Lights down, and title card up. The end."

The actors gave a round of applause as Augusta managed to finally break free of the director's grip.

There was a shout from down at the river and a distant voice called, "Hey! Help!" It was quickly followed by other shouts. "Help! There's someone in the water!"

Off in the choppy gray Hudson a dark figure struggled in the expanding wake of the ferryboat.

"Oh, Lord," muttered Lawrence Griffith. "Some poor soul has fallen in."

"Must've fallen overboard," someone added.

Two men broke off to start down the slope as Mack Sennett appeared at the slip. He funneled his mouth with his hands. "Mr. Griffith!" he called up, then made a slashing motion with his arms and shouted again. "It's Bobby! ... He's in the river!"

"What?" said Owen Moore, dropping his paper to look around.

"I think he said it's Bobby," answered Charles Inslee.

Augusta strained to make out the dark object there bobbing and splashing on the waves. It couldn't be!

"Our Bobby?" cried Billy Bitzer, his eyes filled with alarm.

"Oh, no!" blurted the director and took off in a trot, soon breaking into a full run down the road. The others followed, one after another, each yelling in turn "Bobby! Bobby!" as they hurried for the landing.

Griffith arrived at the dock first and began demanding that the workers do something. "He's fallen in! Help him!" The men pointed to a rowboat that had just launched and was beating hard against the current.

A wild-haired ferryman sneered at the uptown stranger in his fur coat and fancy hat. "He didn't fall in," spat the dockworker. "I watched what he was doin'. He jes' throwed himself in and swam off."

"Bobby, hold on!" screamed Owen Moore.

"Oh, this is awful," said the director. "That boy is my responsibility. What can we do?"

People fell into a bout of yelling in unison until at last the boy stopped flailing long enough to turn towards them and wave an arm. "I'll be back," he hollered, coughing and spitting before shouting to them something that sounded like, "My goat! Gotta get my goat!"

"What did he say?" asked Griffith.

"Something about a coat," said Owen.

Augusta was standing paralyzed in the presence of danger. But now this mention of a coat snapped her out of her trance. She looked down to make sure it was still there in her arms. "He doesn't mean this, does he?" she said to no one in particular. She raised it up a bit for all to see.

"Is that his coat?" demanded Owen Moore.

"Yes. He left it on the ferry."

"It's Bobby's?"

She nodded. "I picked it up for—"

The actor snatched it from her hands and cracked it back and forth like a flag. "Hey, Bobby! Here's your coat! We found it! It's here!"

The others took up the cry. Augusta watched as the boy's eyes fixed on them and then his jaw fell slack. He slapped his forehead with the palm of a hand and grinned. Instantly he was swimming back to meet the rowboat.

"T'ank God," said Billy Bitzer.

"Poor fellow," exclaimed Inslee when a new man came out of the gatehouse with an armful of blankets. Suddenly everyone was wound up and trying to speak at once.

"Mother's alone with eight kids."

"Got to be hard.

"With a brood like that?"

"Lucky to have one good coat among them."

"Didn't dare go home without it!"

"Such a good son."

Augusta's heart was booming like a parade drum. She watched Bobby scoop and flail against the waves until the rowboat was within reach. He grabbed for an outstretched oar but missed, then tried again and caught hold. No one dared breathe until the two rowers had pulled him close and lifted him by his shirt to safety.

"Hooray!" shouted onlookers with broad grins and a raucous round of hand clapping.

"Well done, all," murmured Griffith several times, looking immensely pleased.

In the midst of it all Owen sidled up next to Augusta and wrapped his arm around her waist. "You're my hero, Miss Lee," he said with a squeeze. "For Bobby and for myself, my heart-felt gratitude."

He let Bobby's coat unfurl and gave it a shake. "I'll get this to him."

"We'll wait for you," said Griffith.

"No," said Owen. "You all go ahead. I'll bring Bobby along in the carriage when he's had a chance to dry out." With that he set off walking towards the waterfront.

No one appeared more deeply relieved than Lawrence Griffith. Augusta had never seen his face so full of happiness and optimism. He mingled with his small band and shared in the communal sense of deliverance and gratitude. Finally, though, it was time to raise an arm and gather everyone around.

"All right, all right," said the director "We have gotten our Bobby back safely."

"Praise the Lord!" shouted John Cumpson. Others seemed to offer their own silent prayers.

"Now before we lose the sun there's much to do. Warm rooms and food awaits us up at Rambo's. There's work to be done. So, everyone, please, to the cars!"

EIGHT
"Fools of Fate"

"Luke! A *bay-er*!" shouted Billy Bitzer.

Mack Sennett scooted forward in the rear to look out the windshield. Whatever Billy saw was already gone, escaped into the trees. "What did you see, Billy?"

"A *bay-er!* It was a *bay-er.*"

Mack traded knowing grins with John Cumpson, seated beside him in the back. Not much excited Billy, but they knew that when it did his vowels took on all manner of exotic colorations, the legacy of being raised by German immigrant parents.

"What was it?" asked Charles Inslee, coming to life at the far end of the seat.

"Mr. Bitzer said he saw a bear," said Linda Arvidson, squeezed into the back between Inslee and Cumpson. It was the first time she had spoken since they left the station. She reached forward to give Griffith a tap on the shoulder. "Did you see it?"

"I'm afraid I was daydreaming," he answered.

Mack snorted skeptically. "You sure, Billy? Where would anyone get a bear suit way out here?"

"Maybe it was an oilcloth horse," teased Inslee. "What do you think, Mack?"

"No, it was a *bay-er,*" insisted Billy again. "A *ree-al* one."

"Perhaps our driver saw it?" suggested Mack.

The driver shook his head. "No, sir. I was watching the road."

"What sort of bear was it, do you suppose?" asked John Cumpson in a pompous, professorial manner.

"A black *bay-er,*" said Billy.

"I think what John meant was, was it male or female?" said Inslee.

Billy was clearly out of patience with their foolishness. "Who can say—male, female?"

"Well, the bear had better figure it out," replied Cumpson.

Mack's mind was suddenly reeling with possibilities. "Hey, there's a story idea. This bear wanders into a mountain cabin and climbs in this fellow's bed. It's too dark to see—maybe the wind from the open door blew out the candle. So the man comes to bed and slips under the covers. He figures his wife needs to borrow his razor—"

Mack stopped to savor the chuckles. Only Griffith remained silent and unmoving. But his reflection in the passenger window appeared to have sprouted an impish half-smile.

"Find me a bear, Mr. Sennett," he said, "and I will direct it for you."

"Sure," said Inslee, "we've had dumber animals in the studio."

"No offense, of course, Mack," interjected John Cumpson.

Mack ignored them. "I tell you, it would be a howl with the right comic."

"Who's the right comic? You?"

The portly Mr. Cumpson shivered with disgust. "I would not relish crawling in a bed with any wild beast."

"I'm sure those feelings would be mutual," quipped Miss Arvidson.

"*Lats out!*" shouted Charles Inslee all at once in an exaggerated Southern drawl. "The two *poh* creatures snuggled there in the same bed. Then *lats up*—one year later. We see the man rockin' and drawin' on his pipe, bouncing a little fuzzy cub upon his knee."

The car filled with laughter again but it quickly came to a halt when everyone realized Inslee was as much as mocking the director to his face. Guilty glances were traded in the back seat and Mack watched for any trace of a smile to form on Griffith's thin lips. When it came, Mack led the others in more laughter and generous sighs of relief.

Everyone breathed easier again. But Charles Inslee was not ready to let it go. He started carrying on in the same burlesque drawl.

"Of course, the sorrowful *plat* of *poh*, unwed forest creatures everywhere goes on," he said, his face becoming a mask of tragedy. "*Lats out*. End title."

This time the actor had gone too far. Griffith's smile vanished and he turned to stare impassively through the glass. Ribbing the man's Southern heritage was one thing. Making sport of his social convictions was another. Mack knew that Inslee had just plunged his future career with Biograph into extreme peril.

No one dared speak again now. The hired driver turned off River Road and sent them tossing and bumping along an unpaved patch of highway before straightening out for a steep climb.

Mack was pinned back in his seat, feeling oddly isolated. He had felt so totally drained by Bobby's brush with drowning that he had given little of his attention to anything else. Maybe it wasn't smart to have spoken so frankly to the new girl. What if she took his misgivings to Griffith now? That could almost sound like disloyalty to him. It would only serve to further divide them. There was still much he needed to learn about the picture business, and he sensed Griffith was the one to teach him. They were learning together, in a way. Any suspicion raised between them would just be an unwanted hindrance.

But he was confident his instincts about Augusta Lee were correct. She was a smart girl and would be a good ally. What mattered more was that she had Griffith's trust. If anyone could influence him, it was someone young and naive like her, someone without an ounce of guile and all but incapable of deceit.

Florence Lawrence and one or two others could be trusted, but only so far as they were doing what was best for themselves. Most of the attractive women he knew would trade on any advantage to get ahead. He was smart enough to stay on his toes around them. They were like champagne for the eyes—fizzy spirits designed to make a man say and do foolish things.

He had never really been much of a challenge for that sort of woman. Throw him off a train in the middle of any strange city and odds were good he would feel at home there by nightfall. Lock him in a holding cell with a dozen hairy-fisted thugs and he wouldn't break a sweat. But stand him up against some budding prime example of feminine perfection and his spine would take on all the structural integrity of a soda cracker in a bowl of chowder.

It wasn't so bad in his younger years. Back when he was stomping with the fellas through the flowerbeds of old Quebec there were always lovelies around. And they usually had fair sisters and the fair sisters had fairer friends. So he got the pick of the best-looking gals, whether they came from the homes of hotshots or hod carriers just off the boats. There was Ethel and Martha and Dorothea—*God!* ... *Dorothea.* Now there was one pink vaporous whiff of freckle-faced intoxication!

In high school, nothing could hold him back. He would stride up to a gal bold as daybreak and tell her exactly what was on his mind. If what popped out of his mouth was any dumber than normal, it might still stack up against the best his tongue-tied rivals could offer. He and his dumb pride could move along intact to the next challenge.

But New York complicated things for him. All that was on the minds of most people here was work—and not honest work at that, but *careers*. Beautiful women didn't come to Manhattan to get wooed. They came because this was hands-down the best damn watering hole on the whole sun-baked continent. Most of them arrived parched and tuckered with their ribs poking through their slips. If a pretty gal hadn't already "gone Broadway" when he met her, she sure as hell was on her way. All she could offer him was the potential to turn his head and keep him from doing something important with his life.

A threat—that's all beautiful women seemed to represent to him now. He hadn't met many recently that were worth the time of a proper courtship. Augusta Lee might be something different, though. For good or ill, she didn't make him feel like running fast in the opposite direction.

Out of the blue John Cumpson blurted, "Hey, Mack, how about a traveling song?" as if he were asking a wizard for an incantation to calm the tempests.

"Only if Mr. Griffith gets it started," said Mack.

All eyes swiveled toward the director, but his severe face in the window showed no sign of softening. Everyone was ready to abandon hope and return to more private thoughts when Mack noticed the man's lip tremble and form a ring. Out tumbled a string of paramusical sounds, delivered with full-bodied Italian gusto in his barely passable parlor tenor.

"*Or muoio ... tran—quilo ...*"

Mack recognized it as an aria by Verdi. But which one? His mind raced to place it. The other passengers sat with pasted grins on their faces, well versed in the art of tolerating Griffith's passion for all things operatic and arty.

"*... Vi stringo ... al corio ... mi—o ...*"

Heads began to nod and sway in something akin to enjoyment. It was their form of blowing on a campfire ember. They all wished to encourage whatever small flame struggled in the darkness there of Griffith's black mood.

Mack suddenly had the aria pegged. It was the leading mens' duet from *La Forza del Destino*—the "force of destiny." Verdi's answering verse was about to come up, and Mack was ready now to jump in without hesitation. He hammered his long-neglected bass into the soft middle range of a creditable baritone:

"*Amico. … Fidate nel … ci—elo …*"

Mack saw Linda Arvidson wince as they crossed through the bumpier patch of their duet. What did it matter? There was really no one in the car that mattered anymore but the two unabashed music lovers sharing the maestro's perfect elegy to heartfelt sorrow:

"*… fidate … nel cielo. … Ad—dio.*"

They held the climactic note longer than written until the sound of applause from the others overtook them. Mack had to wonder what they would think if they understood that the passage was intended for the play's two masculine rivals, Don Carlo and Don Alvaro. Those romantic adversaries spent half the opera proclaiming their eternal devotion to one another and the rest of the time wishing for the other's demise.

Mack promised himself that when he spoke of this episode in the future he would dub their impromptu duet an escape from the trip's "*unbearable* silence." It was guaranteed to get some laughs.

In the meantime there was a far more pressing problem to solve: Where on Earth could he get hold of a real live bear?

NINE
"The Helping Hand"

All the way up from Edgewater the ladies went on and on about the charms of Rambo's Hotel—what a fun "away" treat it was for picture people. So when the driver pulled off the paved road and parked beside a wavering picket fence, Augusta stared from the back window in open-mouthed silence.

If ever a place deserved a ghost, she thought, it was Rambo's Hotel. Set deep in the tree line, the two-story clapboard house looked more like a highwayman's secret lair than a cozy rustic inn. With a tar papered overhang for a porch, its sole attempt at style was a simple pointed gable jutting from its roof like a dunce cap.

What waited for them inside was not an improvement. Sagging plank floorboards were partly covered in braided rag rugs meant to hide the cracks, while the forest green wallpaper could have looked faded back when Abe Lincoln first ran for office.

The front door led to a low-ceilinged parlor with water-stained wainscoting, and far to the left was a sliding wooden door sealed with a sign announcing "Saloon Opens at 10 a.m." A wide oak staircase off the parlor had a rough-hewn banister that was no doubt to blame for the inn being known in less charitable circles as "The Splinter Palace."

A plump, pleasant-seeming mountain woman in a hairnet hurried from the kitchen rubbing her hands on a damp apron. She introduced herself as Mrs. Rambo, explaining the spelling as an Americanized take on Rambeau, her Canadian husband's surname.

Mrs. Rambo was flushed with all the excitement of show business guests. She asked each lady in turn whether she preferred tea or coffee.

"Neither for me, thank you," said Augusta. "Could you tell me where I might freshen up?"

"First time here? I'll show you, dear. ... Anyone else? Then, please, everybody, make yourself right at home."

Upstairs a small bedroom at the front was set-aside as a dressing area for actors. There was a full-length mirror at the center, and in place of a bed was a stuffed sofa and chair in a matching floral ticking. Augusta laid her purse on the glass top of a small vanity that had a skirt tacked around its edges.

"There's a water closet at the end of the hall," said Mrs. Rambo. "You'll find clean towels there, too."

"Thank you very much." She began taking off her coat.

"If you don't see what you need, give a shout." Then with a sweet smile, the woman was backing away and closing the door behind her.

It was touching, really, how tickled Mrs. Rambo seemed to be by just an anonymous group of picture actors. Of course, she was running a business not likely to show up in vacation brochures. Maybe she thought motion pictures might really take off some day and leave her husband and her sitting on a gold mine.

A crunching of tires through gravel sounded in the front yard. Through the slats of a shutter she watched Griffith's noisy retinue pile out like it was New Year's Eve. Everyone was talking and chuckling, and Mack Sennett even appeared to be singing.

Why hadn't she been invited to ride with them? Here she was the featured player of Biograph's next production and all she merited was a back seat in the wives' hired car? It hardly made her feel valued.

Griffith was stretching next to the picket fence, bending his spine to the left, then the right. He stopped when he saw a tall, laced boot pop out of the rear door. A feathered hat appeared next and then Linda Arvidson was bending forward and scanning the icy mud for a spot to stand. Griffith jumped to take her hand as she scooted from the seat.

Why was she getting such preferential treatment? It just wasn't fair. The actress was only supposed to be there as her chaperone. Now she not only felt ignored but quite foolish, spying on her own guardian from an upstairs window!

Back on solid ground the actress mouthed "Thank you" to Griffith for his help, and then turned to pull a tied brown-paper parcel from the back.

Off in the distance was the luggage wagon with its two harnessed plow horses, and behind that was a buckboard with a black canvas hood. That's where Owen would be with the half-frozen Bobby Harron. Where had Linda been when all that was happening?

The actress was gone now and Griffith was shouting at one of the local men in the yard. Augusta leaned closer to the window to hear. He was saying something about snow—there wasn't enough of it. He had been led to believe there was still plenty of snow, but now he could see there was hardly any.

"You have wheelbarrows?" he said after a pause.

"Yes, sir," said the local man.

"Well, get all the wheelbarrows you have and fill them with snow. Understand? I need it here by the time we get back."

"Uh, what time would that be?"

"I don't know. Before lunchtime."

"Well, how much snow you want?"

"See this dirt? All this here, and there, clear up to the veranda? All of that must be covered, understand? I don't want to see any—" He stopped.

The worker was rubbing his neck, looking confused. "Wh—what was that? ... A *ver-anda*?"

Griffith rocked back in his boots with exasperation. "Oh, for heaven's sake. The porch! The porch! Do you understand? Now get going."

"Well!" barked a loud voice standing right behind her.

Augusta nearly jumped out the window.

"*There* you are." Linda Arvidson was standing inside the door. "I looked everywhere for you."

"That can't have taken long."

She had removed her hat and coat already but was still holding onto that wrapped parcel. "My, so pretty," she said, giving Augusta's dress a quick glance before shutting the door. "Was that something you brought with you from the river?"

"I haven't been able to do much shopping here yet."

"Well, I have something for you."

"For me?"

"Your costume. Here. Go ahead and open it."

She found the parcel was not heavy and came tied with a string bow. Augusta tugged one end of the string and the wrapper fell open. On top was a bulky woolen sweater. Under it lay a scruffy pair of Levi's.

"I don't know how it is with you, but I cannot begin to understand a character until I've put on her clothes."

For the second time that morning Augusta fell speechless. The garments looked torn and lightly soiled, like cast-offs in a charity bin.

"They're meant to look lived-in," said Linda. "You'll find a piece of rope there somewhere. That's the belt."

When Augusta lifted the sweater up a visored cap dropped to the floor. It was the sort of floppy newsboy's cap favored by back-alley ragamuffins. "This—it's a joke, right?"

The older actress bent to retrieve the cap. "It's what Mr. Griffith asked for. It's what he *wants*. Here, try this on." She set the cap over Augusta's hair.

She stood before the full-length mirror and fought the urge to cry. "He wants me in … this?"

"It makes you look even younger than you are."

"A younger *boy*," said Augusta, studying her reflection.

A scowl of disapproval showed on Linda Arvidson's face. "You're being silly. It's adorable." She reached out to tug the cap's visor sharply to the left. "There. See? Now a smudge of grease across your cheek …."

There was hardly a man on Earth who would find her attractive in this. What were they thinking? People laughed at plays where the girls tried to pass as boys. What would Owen Moore say? … No, there was no way she could let anyone see her in this!

Linda had picked up the sweater to hold at Augusta's shoulders. "You'll find a greatcoat in the trunk when it arrives. An old veteran's greatcoat. It makes the perfect final touch. All you need is a slingshot. Maybe we can find you one."

"I need to speak with Mr. Griffith. I'm not at all sure about—"

"Miss Lee, look at me," said the actress sternly. Her smile was gone now and her eyes were all business. "You're being foolish and stubborn. Do *not* cause a hold-up on your very first job. Understand? Once you get a reputation, no one will work with you again. Now, no more pouting. Trust me, you will capture every heart in the audience. Smile. That's better. Would you like me to help you get dressed?"

"I can button my own jeans."

"When you're ready then, come have a bite. Mrs. Rambo made sweetbreads, and there's fresh coffee in the parlor."

"I'm not hungry."

"What?"

Augusta squared her shoulders and prepared to stand her ground. "Please, inform everyone that I shall not be coming to tea."

"Suit yourself, dear," answered the actress, tossing up her hands and making a big show of hurrying out the door.

Augusta threw herself into the stuffed chair and tried to think of some way out of this. Soon two workmen arrived with the trunk and set it down by the wall. Augusta finally forced herself to have another look at the costume. She had just slipped out of her dress when there was a knock at the door. So she pulled on the jeans and pushed her head up through the sweater before going to answer it.

Lawrence Griffith peered at her sideways through the open crack. "I heard you were not feeling well."

"No. I mean, I am fine. I'm just not a bit hungry."

"We want to head up to the cliffs first thing, before the sun gets any higher. Billy thinks he can get what we need. It will just be the two of us. And Mr. Bitzer, of course. And Miss Arvidson. Did you get the costume?"

"I'm trying it on now."

"Good. It's not far. The cliffs. Just a bit up the road."

Augusta sighed. "Fine."

"The winds tend to pick up there at times. Wrap yourself in something warm."

That was it! Her way out! She would wrap herself from head to toe and no one would see what she was wearing. "Thank you."

"We'll meet out front—say, ten minutes?"

"Perfect," she ended.

There was no use in wasting more time. She fixed her hair in a bun and held it with pins, then tied the rope around her waist and went to rummage in the trunk. She found the soldier's greatcoat right away and was pleased to see it covered her entire body. A wool muffler near the bottom of the trunk could be wrapped above her nose, and a shapeless knit cap easily stretched to cover her head. All that remained of her when she was done were her eyes.

She made sure the hallway was clear before bolting for the stairs, then took the steps two at a time and landed at the bottom only long enough for her final hurtle out the door. She instantly collided full-bore into the side of Lawrence Griffith, nearly sending him off the side of the porch.

"Whoa!" he bellowed, tossing away his cigarette to grab her. "What's the hurry? ... Is that you, Miss Lee?" He pulled the muffler away from her mouth. "Are you all right in there?"

"Sorry," she sputtered.

"It's nice to see a young person so eager to get to work."

Suddenly he seemed very much the considerate older gentleman. Even getting run over by a crazy woman did not rattle his composure. He actually looked handsome today in his fluffy raccoon coat and dark brushed fedora. She took his offered hand and allowed him to lead her down the steps.

Her sense of being protected, though, was brief. Outside the fence waited the two-horse buggy with the black tarp hood. Billy Bitzer was around in back, fiddling with some straps on the storage boot, and Linda Arvidson was seated on the carriage's rear bench under the hood. Up front holding the reins in one leather glove was Owen Moore.

The handsome Irishman squeezed a cigarette between the fingers of his free hand. "Good day," he called. He sent out a white tuft of smoke, clearly taking a sudden interest in her.

Augusta's breath faltered. There was no doubt that Owen was dressed for the morning's first outing.

"We found ourselves short a driver," said Griffith. "Luckily, Mr. Moore can handle a team. Now I will ride up front. You and Billy can sit with Miss Arvidson." He hurried ahead to hold the gate open.

All at once Augusta was the condemned prisoner being force-marched to the firing squad. She could only play along for now and try not to appear like there was anything to hide.

At the gate, Griffith uttered the words she most dreaded: "Let us see your costume."

She re-adjusted her muffler, raising it and lowering it on her nose, stalling for the time to think. "You know, I did my own makeup this morning," she told him.

"Yes, very good."

"Just as you suggested."

"Looks fine, from what I can tell. But let's see the clothes." He waited and watched, then held up a hand and waited some more. Silence spread through the mud and oozed through the fence to her boots. Even Owen Moore looked away to the team, then swiveled back again to see what the hold-up was.

Slowly pulling the belt through its buckle, she reached up for the top button of the greatcoat and began working her way down.

"Let's get going," called Owen.

"Yes. We'll be there in a second, Mr. Moore," said Griffith.

No last minute reprieve was in the offing. At last she inhaled sharply and pulled the two flaps of the coat aside.

"Well," spurted Griffith. He pulled the muffler away from her nose and began to unwrap it, looking unsatisfied. "Something is missing. Wasn't there a cap?"

Augusta nodded and lifted off her bonnet. She dug into her coat pocket and gave the floppy cap a snap before laying it over her hair.

"I think we ought to find her a slingshot," called Linda Arvidson. "What do you think?" Her beaming smile from her seat in the carriage conveyed much more satisfaction than Augusta felt was justified.

"I don't think she needs one," said Griffith. "What do you think, Mr. Moore?"

The Irishman squeezed another drag out of his cigarette. "Well, I'd buy a newspaper from him. Uh, excuse me. Meaning to say *her*," he added with a smirk.

Augusta suddenly felt annoyed with everyone's amusement. "Mr. Griffith, don't you think it would be better if this were played by a real boy? Bobby could do it. I'm sure he would love to—"

"No, not Bobby. No, you are perfect."

"But, I don't feel right. People will laugh."

"Let me explain something." He reached to pull the greatcoat closed and then straightened out the lapels at her neck. "Our story, you see, it is what I call *pat*. Perhaps too pat. A hobo wants to get himself arrested. All right. On paper, it is cute. But visually, it says nothing. It needs a touch of mystery. We must ask ourselves, who are these people? What is this bond between them? Are they lovers? Perhaps they are father and daughter."

"Or maybe 'father and son'?" quipped Owen.

Griffith ignored him. "Whatever the explanation, we want to set the viewer thinking. *That* is the important thing—to get the audience involved. If they are intrigued and full of questions, they will be looking for answers." He smiled over at Linda Arvidson. "You knew all along, didn't you? I asked for something girlish but you insisted on this, this tomboy look. Right again, as always, my dear."

The older actress beamed and gave Augusta a small smirk of triumph. "Don't forget to rub dirt in that pretty face of yours," she said.

Augusta felt her stomach muscles clench with fury. She wanted to grab a handful of mud and sling it at the back-stabber. The costume had been her idea all along. She manipulated Griffith and everyone for the chance to see her humiliated. For all she knew, she had been laying her trap since that first day at the studio. She was just waiting for an opportunity to make her appear foolish. But no more, she vowed. From now on she would be on guard. She knew exactly what she could expect now. Never again would she accept anything that bitch had to say on face value.

A burst of footsteps by the hotel ended in a mushy slide. Young Bobby Harron stood panting next to the front porch. "Hey, Griff," he said between breaths, "you want me for something?"

"What's that, Bobby?"

"They said … you was asking for me."

"Not just now, Bobby. We're all set. Just find me some snow."

"Yes, sir. We come across some drifts under the trees back a ways. It'll take us some time."

"You need any more wheelbarrows?"

"More *wheelers* is what we need. Old Frank had chores to do. I don't know where that other guy went. It's just Mack and me now."

"I can help," said Owen Moore. "Get someone to drive your buggy and I'll give them a hand."

"You sure?"

"Glad to."

Billy Bitzer's head poked out from behind the wagon. "I'll drive it, Mr. *Griffitt.*"

"Really, Billy?"

"It's my equipment."

"Well, fine. Another problem solved. … Thank you, Mr. Moore. You know where to find us when you finish. Otherwise, we'll be back by lunch."

Billy Bitzer collected the reins from Owen and while they traded positions Griffith took Augusta's hand and guided her toward the back of the carriage.

"No, thanks," she said, yanking her hand away. "I'll ride up front with Mr. Bitzer."

"It's not so windy in back," advised Griffith.

"That's all right. I need some fresh air." Instantly she raised a boot to the running board and vaulted up onto the bench with a bounce. She straightened out her coat and scarf as Griffith climbed into the rear.

Billy gave the reins a light slap. The wheels lurched ahead and dropped into a rut that sent a jolt up through the springs.

"Careful, Mr. Bitzer," cried Griffith. "Remember you're carrying precious cargo."

"Hyah!" Billy hollered with another slap. "We go!"

"I am glad you came to sit with me," said Billy Bitzer after sitting in silence for a while. They had the uphill road all to themselves and Billy had let the horses set their own pace before turning to Augusta. "I have been wanting to tell you something."

There was a trilling of birdsong in the branches, and the air was spiced with fertile earth and conifer sap. "It's so lovely here," she said.

"Yes."

"What kinds of trees are those?"

"Oak-maple. Sweet gum. Tulips."

"Tulip trees? ... Really."

"It's difficult for them here. The topsoil is thin, with bedrock underneath. There's no protection. In a strong wind, tall trees are uprooted."

"You seem to know a lot about nature."

A boyishly innocent grin sparkled in his eyes. "I never liked this being in a studio. When I first come to work they would send me places. I loved being outdoors, the sense of adventure."

"Where did you go?"

"Cuba, for one. Twice to Cuba, actually—once right after the sinking of the Maine. Then back again when the war got going."

"Sounds dangerous."

"We needed to stay ahead of the competition. Wherever disaster struck I'd pack my gear and head off. 'News happenings,' is what we called them. The cameras were larger and much heavier." He gave a soft whistle of emphasis. "But we got them where we needed them."

Billy rode on with his own thoughts before speaking again. "I came down with malaria. Almost died. But Galveston, Texas—that was the end for me. September, 1900."

"The big hurricane? You were there?"

"Afterwards, yes. Four hours it battered the coast. The city swept away like a house of cards. Forty thousand people left with no homes, nothing to eat. Biograph wanted motion pictures of it. The train could only take us to the storm center at Texas City. All bridges and tracks after that were gone.

"The water was thick. Stinking. Piles of timber and rubble being pushed around, far as the eye could see. Bodies by the hundreds. ... Women, dogs, cows ... little babies. All of it one big black hell."

The horses had come to an unpaved stretch of road and were straining harder against their straps. "Hyah! Come on!" coaxed Billy, giving the reins a slap.

"Where did you learn to handle horses?"

"My papa was a blacksmith. That's how he survived when he came from Germany. I always helped him with the horses. He showed me how to make harnesses. That was his specialty. Beautiful leather harnesses. He bought swaths of cowhide, and I helped cut them into strips. I made loops for the buckles and fancy designs."

"He must have been proud of you."

Billy shrugged. "People of that generation, immigrants especially, all they want is for their sons to learn a trade. He tried to apprentice me to a silversmith. That's what he wanted for his son. It was an Old World solution to the challenge of the New World."

"What happened?"

"I didn't like it at all. What fascinated me was magic. Magic tricks. Stage illusions. I wanted to know how things worked. I took classes at night—electrical engineering. To my mind, electricity was the magic of our time. Silver, that was the stuff of goblets and dowries."

The road became Hudson Terrace and was paved again. A signpost pointed ahead to a place called Coytesville Park.

"Watch for a turn-off soon," said Griffith from the back. "It'll be on the right."

Billy nodded.

Augusta could not wait any longer. She leaned close in a confidential manner to whisper. "What was it you wanted to tell me?"

The blacksmith's son gave her a shy smile. "I wanted to thank you ... for the boy. For Bobby."

"He's your favorite, isn't he?"

"Bobby's everyone's favorite. Me, my wife Nora, he's like our own. His family lives near to us. In Greenwich Village. Bobby's daddy would bring everybody's milk. He drove a dairy truck, you know? Bobby was just one of ten children. Then one day, the father is gone. Disappeared. No one can say what happened. Our priest at St.

Joseph's—Father Bill—he asks everyone to pray for the family.

"Not long after that, Father Bill brings Bobby into the studio. He says to Mr. Marvin, 'Bobby's a good boy and he wants to help his mama.' Mr. Marvin has a big heart. So Bobby starts work there as property boy. The end of the week, he gives everything he makes to his mama. Never a penny for himself."

Billy Bitzer just stared ahead hard at the team as a touch of moisture gathered in his eye. "Losing him in that river—it would be worse to me than Galveston, worse than malaria. It's unthinkable."

Griffith slid up from behind to lay a hand on his shoulder. "This is it," he said, and pointed off to a coming clearing.

"I see it," said Billy. He turned his eyes from the team long enough to offer his companion a final nod of appreciation. "Just thank you again, from me and my wife. From all of us. Thank you for saving our Bobby."

The horses responded to a yank on their reins and the carriage dropped sharply to the right as it rolled from the pavement. It righted itself with a hard bounce and pulled onto a parcel of dirt at the tree line.

Billy had instantly tied off the reins and hopped down. As he went about unstrapping the boot Augusta tested her legs. Griffith lit a cigarette and took a few draws as he waited to help with the load.

Augusta and Linda were each given a woven basket and a canvas bag with leather straps. Griffith was assigned a bulky cowhide valise and a heavy pouch. Billy slung a belted tripod over his own head and grunted as he heaved a varnished wooden box from the carriage by a rough rope handle.

They followed along a trampled footpath in the trees until Augusta began to think they were lost. There was a glimmer of sky through the branches ahead, and the forest opened onto a wide patch of bare earth and a flat rock stretching to the precipice.

"No snow, Billy," said Griffith with obvious disappointment.

Billy indicated the snow in the shoreline trees below. "I think I can frame all that from a high angle. With luck and some overexposure, it might pass for winter."

The director looked skeptical. "Whatever you think. All we need is the suggestion of the snow." He turned to Augusta. "Do you think you can wiggle yourself out there?" His breath left small clouds in front of his mouth.

"To the edge?" she said.

"Not all the way. But close."

"Closer the better," said Billy.

Her head bobbed of its own volition while she was still trying to decide if she could do it. She might be all right. Heights had never been a particular problem for her. Even as a schoolgirl she was always the first in her class to go exploring to the tallest peaks and farthest reaches. "Shall I go now?"

"If you would," said Griffith. "It will only take us a second to get things set up."

She put down her bundles and loosened the belt of her greatcoat. Raising a foot to the edge of the rock she gave a firm shove. It did not give way or wobble. She could do this. Removing the knit bonnet she cast it aside then stepped up on the stone and took two small strides forward.

Now she could see over the cliff to the river below. It hardly looked like water at all from this height. It was a sluggish flow of diamonds tumbling in glittery ooze between canyon walls.

She took another step and reached up to unwind the scarf from her neck, feeling suddenly naked and frail. A sudden howling gust rose up and held the greatcoat plastered to her skin. She could not breathe. All she could do was lean into the wind and try to remain upright. The force died off quickly and she stumbled forward a step before catching herself up and shifting her weight back on her feet.

She had been foolish, over-confident, and turned to look back in alarm at Griffith and Billy. They seemed so far away and useless now—just two little boys going about their little boy games, unaware of her needs and fears.

How could she have put herself in this situation? Why was she risking her life, literally casting her fate to the wind for the sake of some silly motion picture? What could she possibly gain that was worth putting herself in such peril?

It didn't matter, she decided almost at once. This was where she was now and she was going to make the best of it. She took a deep breath and tried to re-establish her sense of focus and control. She let her scarf fall free and watched it settle gently upon the stone. The next couple feet of rock in front of her was all she had to concern herself with. She moved a shaky leg forward and brought the other up slowly beside it, hoping to be in position before another sudden gust of air.

"That's good. Keep going," called Griffith. "Yes. ... Farther."

A light breeze whipped at her hair, frightening her just enough that she stooped toward a crouch. She could dive down and hug the rock surface if necessary. But the air grew calm again and she found the confidence to take another half-step toward the edge.

"How's that, Billy?" she heard the director asking behind her.

Billy was busy giving a final few twists to a hand screw on his tripod. He stopped for a peek through the viewfinder. "I think we are almost there. One more meter maybe."

"Augusta," shouted Griffith, "can you go just a little farther? Just one more meter should do."

"How much is a meter?" she called back.

"About two feet or so."

She bit her lip and nodded. "Okay. But from here out, I'll be scooting." She lowered her haunches onto the stone and kicked one leg in front of her, then the other, digging her heels in like an oarsman. Inch by inch she pulled herself forward. "How's that?"

"More," said Billy.

Griffith nodded to him and turned back apologetically. "A bit more."

She leaned against her palms and pushed her feet forward. This time her heel slipped over the slope and dangled in the open air. She yelped and instantly drew back her legs.

"That's as far as—" she began, but a sudden gust slapped her full in the face and forced the words down in her throat.

Griffith was having another animated conversation with Billy. After a moment he stopped and nodded, turning to come toward her a few steps. "Billy thinks you're fine there. But we still haven't got the detail we want."

Augusta felt a lock of hair fall loose and flap against her forehead. She swept it away with the back of her hand. "Wha—what does he want?"

"We have to show it's winter. We want to try scattering snow closer around you on the rock."

"What snow?"

"We passed a patch in the shade—back a ways. Not far. Billy thinks we can use the tarp from the wagon. We can load it with snow and drag it back here like an Indian sled."

"A *travois*," shouted Billy.

"Yes. Li—like a *travois*," said Griffith. Even he appeared frightened now by what he was asking. "You're being very brave, Miss Lee. Can you stay put a bit?"

"I'm all right. I'll just sit here."

"We will only be a minute. … Where's Miss Arvidson?"

"Over here, Mr. Griffith," said the actress.

Augusta had managed to forget all about the woman. Now when she stepped from behind a tree, her arms hugging tightly to her heavy coat, Augusta was too filled with dread to feel anything else. Another sudden arctic howl arose and a fist of air rocked her to the side.

Griffith mumbled something privately to the actress, and when she nodded he returned to Augusta. "All right, Miss Lee," he called. "Miss Arvidson will stay with you. If you need something, she will be here. … Are you all right?"

She forced a grin and waved him on. The faster he got going the sooner the ordeal would be over.

The two men traipsed off into the forest and Linda waited until their footsteps melted in the wind. She made a small step toward the rock. "How is it out there?"

"Beautiful. You should come see."

"You're shivering."

"Just cold."

"You look so … awfully alone."

"I'm all right."

"I think it's my greatest fear in life."

"Heights?"

Linda raised a brow. "Ending up alone."

"Oh. Well, I have you. Remember how you're always offering to keep an eye on me." She couldn't help giving a small, private smile as she threw another glance toward the gorge.

"I knew from the start what you were up to. You are quite the cunning actor, you know that?"

"I'm not sure what—"

"Don't forget, I'm an actor myself."

Augusta gave a nonchalant shrug as if to signal she was done talking.

"Your innocent act is the oldest in the book. That ridiculous costume and wig. You made one mistake, though. I knew Deward Trawley before you did. I knew he had no family in the South."

Augusta turned calmly back to look at the woman. "He said he'd help me. To find me a job."

"That was very noble. … And that story about a medical condition?"

She could only have gotten that out of Mr. Griffith directly. What a two-faced viper she was. "That's what I was told," she said. "I happen to believe he's quite ill."

"This isn't such a big city, Miss Lee. You wouldn't know that, being new here. But actors make up quite a small community here. Men like Deward Trawley can't vanish without someone knowing the truth."

"He's in a sanitarium."

"That's a lie."

"Says you."

"Clang-Clang's not in any hospital. … He's in the clink."

"Clang-Clang … in the clink? Well, if that's so he has no one but himself to blame."

"That's not how he sees it. He's telling anyone who will listen that it was all a lady friend's doing. Some gal he picked up at the Union Square depot. She played him like a fiddle and put him in there to rot."

Augusta stopped to push another wayward strand of hair from her face.

"It's a solid booking," the actress continued. "He's looking at maybe a five-year contract."

"My, my, imagine that."

"I'm not so sure he'll ever forget the gal who made it possible."

"Things change. A lot could happen in five years."

"Don't count on it, sweetie. His attorney thinks it could be squared if a certain company gets its money back. Even Deward Trawley has friends, and you know what I hear? I hear they're out raising money right now. You know what that means?"

"Clang-Clang sprung?"

Linda smiled. "That's right. And maybe the one who did him wrong—maybe she doesn't know Deward like I do. You see, he's the sort that settles his scores."

"Why are you telling me?"

"You said so yourself. I promised I'd look out for you. You should just know … what's coming."

"You'd like to see me run, wouldn't you?"

"Some would say it is the most prudent thing."

"Why? You want Deward for yourself. You're in love with him and you want me gone. Well, you're welcome to him."

Linda let out a scornful snort. "What would I want with a louse like him?"

"If it's not Deward then … *is it Owen*? You're in love with Owen and you're afraid I'll steal him from you?"

"*Owen Moore*? That drunken Irishman?" She gave a theatrical bray of a laugh. "He doesn't hold any sway around here."

Augusta tried to think. What was she saying? The only one with any sway at Biograph was Lawrence Griffith. A mental curtain parted and she knew she understood at last. "You're carrying the torch for Mr. Griffith! That's it, isn't it? You're scared to death he'll favor me and drop you."

"He could never favor you!"

"It was always about him, right from the start."

"You don't know anything," she said, stepping forward. Absently she placed a foot on the rock. "You thought you could just ease in here, get yourself in tight. Then when you didn't need Clang-Clang any more, you flushed him away." She brought her other boot forward and took two more steps on the hard surface. "You believed your way was clear, that no one would see what you were up to. But you were wrong. I was watching every devious step of the way."

She could never hope to defend herself if she stayed sitting down. She placed a palm on the rock and eased herself up, steadying herself in a crouch before standing up straight to face off against the actress. "You're out of your mind. I never had any designs on David, never."

"Don't you call him that! You don't call him that!"

"Why? It's his name, isn't it? David Griffith. That's how he signs his plays and his poems. If there's anything between us, it's because of you. You're the one who manipulates him and bosses him around."

"You don't know anything."

Augusta wiped the sweat from her hands against the greatcoat and squared herself for an attack. She was cornered, backed to the edge of the precipice with nothing behind her but a drop. All she could do was keep Linda talking until an opportunity arose to get around her.

"I don't even know why you care now," she said. "Everyone knows David's influence at the studio is over. He won't even be there in another week or so. There'll be no one left there to protect you."

"You don't know what you're talking about!" The actress advanced another two steps. "Biograph could fold tomorrow and David would still be mine."

"Believe what you will," said Augusta, casting a quick glance behind her. All she could see was open air and a few thin black squiggles of boats on the river. "Why would any man want to stay with a two-faced old hag like you?"

"Because he married me! You stupid cow! We've been husband and wife for three full years now! And he would never, ever leave me for someone like you!" Her eyes were wild with rage and deep from within issued a banshee scream as she lunged forward, driving both fists hard at Augusta's chest.

She reeled from the blow, gasping for breath. But before she could say anything Linda was at her again like a battering ram, beating both fists against her body.

"None of you will have him. Never, never, never!"

Augusta struggled to stay on her feet. All she could think was that she dare not trip nor take a single step backward.

Off in the distance there was shouting. "Stop! Watch out! Both of you! Look where you are!"

Lawrence Griffith was standing petrified in the clearing, one arm rigid and pointed at them as if frozen there in a lightning flash.

Linda gave several blinks as a glaze of confusion descended over her. She appeared momentarily lost. "Oh. ... Oh, my," she said, lowering her arms. She did not look at Augusta at all, but turned, drained and weakened, to stagger in the direction of the voice.

In a few bounds Griffith was there to grab her and clutch her close to him. "Whatever came over you?" he said, guiding her down from the rock. The actress was whimpering in his arms like a wounded animal. "What did you think you were doing out there?" he asked more gently.

When they were back safely on dirt she threw her hands behind his neck and pulled his head to her in a full, hard kiss on the lips. "Linda, please," he managed to protest, squirming to be free of her. "There are *others*."

She instantly released him. "Others?" she said.

Augusta managed a few weak steps forward before light-headedness overtook her. That dizzying whoosh might have been the blood surging in her ears. But there was some new presence there, as well.

As soon as Lawrence mentioned others and Linda pulled from him, Augusta saw the two figures standing in the trees.

Billy Bitzer held tight to one corner of a black tarp piled high with dirty mounds of snow. He must not have seen what had happened for he was chirping gaily, "*Luke, luke* who it was we find in the woods!" Holding up the opposite corner of the tarp was Owen Moore, a cigarette dangling from his mouth, those two dark eyes of his fixed upon her.

Augusta wobbled and struggled to counteract the swaying of her legs. She wanted to signal to Owen, maybe reassure him with a smile to prove that she was fine. There was really nothing any more to worry about.

But someone snuck up behind and slipped a dark hood over her head. It had to be that rascal Billy, making her a part of his magic act. Because with her head covered the whole world vanished into deepest night with only flashes of shooting stars. Her knees buckled and would no longer support her. She was Tenniel's Alice once again, teetering at the rabbit's hole, letting go of all earthly care as her endless freefall began.

PART II

TEN
"A Smoked Husband"

Silence. Funny how little he had appreciated it before. Now his job as a motion picture director made him a student of silence. He was becoming an expert on the use of pantomime and facial expression, learning all the things that could be conveyed in the absence of sound.

He knew, for example, that when a dining room full of actors is seen indulging in highly selective silence after some grave disruption it meant something. It meant that off in private the whispering had begun.

By lunchtime he was sure everyone had heard some account of Linda Arvidson's catfight on the Palisades. It may have begun with Billy, who could not make sense of what had happened and would naturally turn to his wife for an explanation. Nora would have her theory, but that would not keep her from seeking the theories of others.

By the time he took his seat at a table, each member had learned enough to *not* bring the matter into the open. None wished to be remembered as the one who violated that particular silence.

Linda herself sat calmly with two of the wives, sipping hot chowder directly from the bowl while talking recipes and such. She was still too upset over what happened to appear the opposite.

It was another adept use of silence, befitting her years and years of professional practice and study.

Once the company had finished the sequences in the snow at Rambo's they all got busy packing for a speedy trip home. He would never say such a thing out loud, but thank God for Owen Moore. The actor had picked up the unconscious girl and carried her to the wagon, promising to see her safely back to her quarters in the city. That saved him from a train trip packed with the most oppressive sort of silence.

Seeing his own dear Linda out there on the precipice—literally on the edge and spiraling out of control—it made his stomach turn. What could have driven her to place herself in such peril? It was so uncharacteristic of her. She had always been the judicious one, the one with a steadying hand on the keel when it was needed most.

Mature women would always be an enigma to him. It was much easier dealing with young ladies. They were rarely anything but sunny and sweet.

Something dark must have taken hold of his wife to make her behave like that. At dinner he decided it best to let the subject be for now. Passions would settle and rationality would return in time. He had learned that the hard way.

But at bedtime Linda was still rummaging through drawers and rattling about in the clothes closet. She was furious with herself or someone. Perhaps even with *him*. It made him wonder.

Neither of them brought up the incident at breakfast. So he was pleasantly surprised late in the morning when the gentle, loving Linda he had married stopped at his office door and poked her head in.

"Busy?" she asked, beaming from ear to ear.

"Never for you, my dear."

She came in holding a torn envelope with an unfolded letter. "I need to share this," she said, stopping at his desk to raise the sheet of stationery closer. "'My Dear, Charming Miss Arvidson,'" she read, pausing an extra moment to let it sink in. "'I have only learned this day of your presence in the city. I send you my best wishes as always for continued success with your career. Yours devotedly, Enrico.'"

"*Caruso*?" he asked.

A tear of joy pooled in her eye. "Isn't it the most amazing note? And here I had begun to think ... that no one remembered." She lowered herself into the stiff office chair. "With everything on his mind, he thought of me."

"How long has it been?"

"Three years? ... Yes, almost exactly three. I saw him in early April. He was doing *Carmen,* and I went backstage to say hello. It was just a night or two ... before everything ended."

"I can only imagine his Don José."

"It was transporting. Such power, such control."

"I only saw him on stage once. It was right here. At the Met."

"Without me?"

"*Before* you. It was *Les Huguenots*. Not my favorite. Not *Carmen*. Even one ticket was a bit steep for me at the time. It was a foolish indulgence. But who knew if I'd have another chance?"

"Money … it really means nothing in the long run."

"Treasure his note, my dear. He is a great artist."

"But you know what this means? Others will remember, too. And the theaters are coming back." She saw his skepticism. "No, listen, David, I know they are. One re-opened just last month. The Orpheus, I think."

"But we're here now. That's all the way on the west coast." He watched her smile freeze and dim. "This is where we've always dreamed of being."

"Maybe. As part of the theater, yes. … But not this. Your contract ends this August—if not before."

"Why before?"

"No one's pleased with this situation, David. The horrid picket ladies. A possible boycott. I know I needn't mention ticket sales."

"Slumps never last. The Marvins have a realistic understanding. They want me to make pictures that matter to me."

"Edgar Allan Poe?"

He looked down at his desktop and grinned. "Yes, they made themselves quite clear about that."

"All they want is to sell tickets. They don't care about you. … Were you really so unhappy with our life before?"

He thought instantly of living again on weak soup, the indignity of trying to collect on salaries they were owed. It meant more auditions and contracts and being forced to embark on endless tours.

Her eyes meanwhile had drifted off, distracted and sad. She said, "In San Francisco, Mr. Caruso considered us his colleagues. I don't really know what he thinks of … of what we're doing now."

"I didn't know you felt this way."

"I had a star on my dressing room. And theater friends."

"You should have told me."

"That's the problem, isn't it, David? We don't talk anymore. We used to have things in common. Now all we talk about is next week's pictures. Grinding them out like sausages—or them grinding you out. … We never hear applause now, or take bows. I'm more likely to be beaten by maniacs in the street."

"I promise you, that won't happen again."

"I have to share dressing quarters now, with the same old faces." She stopped and sat up stiffly. "At least you have fresh new ones every day."

"You know how deeply I care."

"We used to be equals. Now you are the top dog with all the answers. Everyone wants a word with you. No one even knows who I am."

"It's all been grossly unfair for you, hasn't it?"

"I never asked for favoritism."

"I know that. And neither of us saw our positions changing. It's all because we chose to live a lie." He was thinking of her sitting behind him on the drive to Fort Lee. How long had he been forcing her to take a back seat in his life?

"It must be flattering—the daily stream of hopefuls. All those eager faces. Younger, prettier all the time. Waiting to see you. *Depending* on you."

"It hurts me to see you unhappy."

"Then take me home, David."

"Perhaps if we'd had a crystal ball," he said softly, "we would have done it differently."

"We'll leave together. We'll go back to the stage."

"That life is not for me anymore. Give me time. Let me put things right. I know I can earn your trust again."

Linda slowly rose from her chair. In her eyes was only hurt and anger. "Won't you listen to yourself? Your capacity for self-deceit is stunning," she said.

"We can wipe the ledger clean. It's not too late. I will call a meeting today ... for this afternoon. I will get everyone around. I'll announce we are husband and wife, that we have been so for three years. If they wish to question my casting decisions, let them. Better I lose them than you. Everything will be in the open from now on. I know I can earn your trust again."

Her voice was hardly more than a whisper. "Can't you stop your lies for one minute?"

"What can I—?"

"I've watched you, David. From the sides. You and these new girls. Florence. This Miss Lee—whatever her name might be. It was never a question of me trusting you. The question is ... can you trust yourself?"

"I don't—" he began, and then looked away. "I've never been unfaithful," he said firmly.

"What will it take? That's what you should be asking yourself." She was heading toward the exit, speaking as she moved. "How long will it be? How long before you fall under the spell of someone new? Maybe Augusta, maybe Florence. Who knows? Perhaps it will be someone more like … like *Mrs. Castle*."

It was the first time he had ever heard her say the name aloud. It took him off guard, hanging there between them with all its dark associations. It was the one thing remaining after she had gone through the door and closed it ever so firmly behind her.

Linda, poor Linda. It was torture to see her in agony. And all of it over nothing, really. A fantasy. Augusta Lee? Florence Lawrence? They were mere images, designed to enchant the eye. They could never begin to fill her place in his heart.

This was not the Linda he had fallen in love with. Even in her most irrational mood she had never expressed such insecurities before. Outbursts were unlike her. That was the very thing he most loved about her. She was the farthest thing possible from … well, from *what he had been through.*

He always suspected that she knew the sordid details. The notorious *Mrs. Neville Castle* had been an object of public gossip and scandal for a decade before they ever met. Linda and her even shared the same hometown. She had surely read about her in the San Francisco society columns. Any actress would have become instantly intrigued about the former Mary Scott.

The Scott family was wealthier, of course. Through all her early successes on the stage she was dubbed a "society actress." She had been raised a debutante and it was still a novelty for such well bred native daughters to become a player for hire. She had married a rising Bay Area attorney who was ten years older and tolerant of her theater ambitions. What he would not accept was seeing his wife's name linked again and again in the papers to eligible young bachelors.

He himself was no more than a boy when they met. How old had he been? Was he even twenty-five? Already he had been an actor on the road for two seasons, yet he was a babe in the woods when it came to the opposite sex.

There was a new play and he was hired to take over the role from another actor. He noticed her in rehearsals, that self-assured beauty with the dark hair. But it wasn't until after the evening's performance that he saw her in a truly flattering light. She was dressed in a tight velvet gown, vibrant purple, trimmed in white sable. Her creamy skin appeared flawless next to her shiny, tar-black hair. He knew to his marrow that she could easily become his dark-eyed Carmen.

She was introduced as Mary Scott but everyone knew she was also Mrs. Neville Castle. On her finger was a sparkling solitaire ring, though no wedding band. He learned she shared his Southern heritage, and that her father had also been a colonel in the Confederacy. Together they wondered at times if it wasn't that "gray stain" on their past that kept them out of the most desirable social circles.

Griffith could not be sure if he was the reason or not, but soon the esteemed Mr. Neville Castle himself was gone from the picture. He had walked out on his sham marriage and booked passage to the Klondike without even stopping to file for divorce.

Even if she knew all that, Linda never placed him in the position of having to lie about it. Maybe she did not want to know the details. It would not have been easy for her to hear how truly naïve her gentle husband had once been, nor how completely he had surrendered to that raven-headed strumpet.

Yes, he might have been an innocent Don José at the beginning but there was nothing innocent about what he became. It was clear that the actress had insatiable hungers. She was quite as good as any seasoned director at provoking the response she was after. She exulted in rough treatment from her lover, and adored being bitten on the neck—even *spanked*.

He remembered telling an actor friend how he planned to marry her some day. The friend called it right: "She must be a devil in the bedroom," he said, "to make a fellow want to saddle up a bronco like that for his first ride out the gate."

Soon afterward, the horror show began.

One night she threatened to kill a female co-star on stage in front of a packed audience. A theater manager had to throw a pitcher of water over her head to cool her down. The prospect arose of a long tour through the great Northwest. He thought the change of scene would do her good. But T.W. Robertson's three-act comedy "Home" proved a most ironic title for a period that brought nothing like cozy domesticity.

No doubt Linda Arvidson's theater colleagues followed the accounts of Mary's screaming demands in hotel lobbies, the claims filed against her for shattered bowls and broken lamps. Some might even have heard the slapping fights and shouting matches coming from the room next door. The room they knew was *hers*. The one she sometimes shared with *him*.

Other actors drank more, but Mrs. Neville Castle could be violent without even a nip of alcohol. Gradually he had to accept there was something wrong with her, something it would take a Viennese brain specialist to diagnose.

When they returned to the Bay Area he insisted they live apart. He took up quarters in a modest hotel and she went to live with her mother at an upscale boarding house. They saw each other at performances of "Home" but met infrequently outside. By August he wanted to make a clean break. That was the first time he took off alone for New York. It was the summer of 1900, and all he wanted was to start the new century fresh.

Instead, the old century ended in disaster.

While working in some stale vaudeville sketch called "Richelieu's Stratagem," he wrote a short play about life in early America. "In Washington's Time" had a spirited female lead that would be exactly right for Mary Scott. He could never adequately explain why, but he missed her. He sent off a quick letter asking her to come.

They gave the new play a tryout or two in Massachusetts and booked a trial New York run at one of the Keith vaudeville houses. But one evening after previews, Mary Scott rose from the dinner table and disappeared without a word. Days passed with no message from her, and even Mary's relatives began to fear the worst. They spoke of her "high-strung nature" and her unhealthy obsession with a stage career. Some became convinced that she had taken her own life.

In any case, her relatives turned to him. As her intended, it was up to him to file a missing person report with the police. He gave authorities his stage name but kept his real relation to the missing woman a secret. He said Mary Scott was his cousin and that her relatives were putting up a five hundred dollar reward for her return.

Next day he was appalled to read about the disappearance in the police blotter of *The New York Times*. A young "society actress," it said, had gone missing from her family's dinner party. The article referred to the man who reported the incident as "a vaudeville actor." For a seasoned stage actor, that amounted to a public humiliation. He was still smarting days later when Mary showed up out of the blue saying she had merely gone off for a prolonged stay with friends. She seemed to expect everything to return to normal.

The next few years were now a painful blur. Reporters grew more impertinent and emboldened as her notoriety spread. Their stage partnership dissolved. Society mentions and gossip items gave way to news articles about Mrs. Castle's frequent lawsuits and her court-ordered sanitarium stays.

One thing he could be thankful for—Mrs. Castle was now long gone. The last he heard of her was that she had quit the theater and was earning her living as an artist's model. He did not worry what would become of her. She would have no trouble at all finding other unsuspecting paramours.

Linda Arvidson had come along at the right time. She showed up in a play one day, wearing that easy, approachable smile. There was not an ounce of the coquette to her. She proved as bright at conversing as she was at listening. He had opened up to her about his ambitions as a writer. She flattered his poetry, and on top of everything else, she had stenographic skills. She could take dictation like a secretary and offered to help him with the typewriting of his next play.

When his contract was cancelled mid-tour and he found himself stranded in Northern California, it was Linda who answered his letters. Their correspondence was his lifeline back to sanity. His letters to her in San Francisco gradually took a more personal turn.

When he did at last propose to her she said she would have to think about it. Both of them knew the additional burden that marriage placed on an actor's employability. Perhaps when his play was a hit and he made a name for himself as a playwright, she would agree to become his wife.

In the end it was not his play or anything he said that changed her mind. It was the earthquake. He still liked to joke to friends that it took a cataclysmic earth upheaval to make Linda see him as a husband.

He was back east by then, trying to reconnect with the theater world. Linda had stayed behind to await some producer's decision. But on the morning of April sixteenth a non-stop rumble began and the ground gave a mighty heave. Enrico Caruso dashed from the Palace Hotel clutching a signed photograph of Teddy Roosevelt. And poor frightened Linda sought safety in an open field, stopping only long enough to collect a packet of letters sent by her new Southern beau, a sensitive poet-actor who billed himself as Lawrence Griffith.

What a shock it must have been for her, losing the city she was born in, watching it burn to the ground. That night in her tent city on Telegraph Hill she wrote to him, bending over a smelly kerosene lamp.

Yes, she would come east on the next train and be his wife, if he still wanted her. They would have to keep the marriage a secret, but it would be an adventure. She was always quick to see something good in an imperfect arrangement. And she had a most romantic heart. As proof there was a wavy spot on the paper next to her signature that he would always think of as the teardrop that sealed their love.

"You kept me sane, you know," he told her the day they wed. She never asked for any further explanation. She probably knew exactly what he meant.

Now everything was up in the air again. Things had changed between them. That scene on the Palisades brought it all home. Some of her intuitions were no doubt correct. Even he had to question his true motives at times. Whenever he went off alone to an interview with a beautiful lady he sensed his danger.

After all, Don José had also been a man of honor and of station, a dutiful leader of others. And yet Carmen turned his hard-won discipline to just so much window dressing. What man did not understand his story at some basic human level? All men knew instinctively how vulnerable they were, how soon their lives could end in the ruins of desire.

He could not imagine losing Linda now. She had been the right life partner for him once and she probably still was. He could not just let her walk away.

But something had come over her, and it filled him with fear. The levelheaded Linda he had married was not capable of tirades and violent confrontations on cliff tops. Some inner demons were clearly at work. They had twisted her into something he hardly recognized. And if that was true, who was to say she wasn't also capable of becoming ... another *Mary Scott*?

ELEVEN
"The Sealed Room"

She wasn't sure how it happened, but it was midnight and she was outside Rambo's again, standing in the stark moonlight. The bright stars blinked with fear as she stepped up under the tar-papered slope.

From the treetops came a metallic whisper like bottle caps rattling in a little boy's pocket.

Oh, Lord, just let me be, she mouthed, though words would not come.

She took the plank steps one by one and stopped at the half-opened screen. The hinges gave a squeal that set off an unseen flurry of movement within.

Again there was a jingling in the trees.

She struggled to risk a peek.

Oh. Too bright!

"Come on, sweetness," said a man's voice. "*Carpe diem.* ... What's left of it."

It was her Irishman. Owen Moore bent over her, swinging the room keys close to her head. She raised a hand and took a swipe but missed.

"Wha' time is it?" she managed to ask. Her lips felt swollen and parched.

"Nearly eleven."

She yanked up the bedding with a groan.

"Look. ... Look here, me lass," came the voice, following her back to that warm place. "I've a present."

She slipped down an edge. "What?" Now he was dangling a rumpled paper bag to and fro.

"You look terrible," he blurted.

"Charmer." She scooted up a bit on the pillow. "You brought me something? A gift?"

"You deserve one?"
"I recall nothing but good deeds."
"Been out today?"
"What day is it?"
"Tuesday."
"I was out yesterday."
"Any luck?"
"There's no one's hiring this month."
"Don't give up. Hey, does the name Borowski mean anything to you?"
"Hunh? Who?"
"Borowski, I think."
She swept her head back and forth. "Who is it?"
"A friend of Sennett's, I gather."
"That doesn't narrow it any."
"I heard him and Mr. G going 'round and 'round about this feller Borowski. Thought it might ring a bell."
The thought of Sennett's muscle-headed grin made her smile. "How is Mack?"
"Still can't find suits that fit him."
"Seriously. Is he all right?"
"Why not go ask him yourself?"
"You know I can't."
He sighed and looked disappointed. "It's been over a week."
"So?"
"No one's even blamin' you for what happened."
"That doesn't mean a thing. He doesn't want me there."
"Who said?"
"He did. You know his exact words. *'Tell her not to bother coming back.'* You told me that, remember?"
"Ah, blarney! He was talking about the next day or two. Just for that picture. That's what he meant. Not forever."
"I don't think so."
Owen got off the mattress and went to his sport jacket hanging on the spindle-backed chair by the kitchen. "People say all kinds of things. Especially when they're upset—which most people seem to be nowadays. Upset over one thing or the other." He pulled a pack of smokes from the top pocket and shook one loose for her.
"No. Thank you."

He laid the cigarette between his lips and patted his trousers for the rattle of matches. "You've been missing the excitement."

"What excitement?"

"We had quite the donnybrook yesterday."

There came a loud scratch and he was holding a flaming stick to the tip of his cigarette. He took a deep drag and watched the smoke escape.

"Fistfight," he said, shaking out the flame.

"Who was it? *Miss Arvidson*?"

"One of the new fellers—Kirkwood. Know him? Jimmy Kirkwood?"

"Don't think so."

"Ugly sort of mug, but nice enough guy. Hell of an actor. Jimmy was up on stage, standin' there and workin' out his moves. Billy had the Cooper-Hewitts juiced and everyone was waitin'. All at once a body hurtles out of the dark. Gives my boy Jim a full-on tackle and over they go. Rollin' and kickin' and wrestlin' some more."

"Who was it?"

He shrugged. "Turned out Griffith knew him from somewhere or another. I couldn't have told him from St. Patrick. No one wanted to jump in the middle of it, not without knowing what it was about. Finally it took a couple of stagehands to pull 'em apart. ... Walton ... Walterson ... No. ... Walthall, I think, maybe was his name. Anyway, Jimmy was the only one this Walthall character knew. They were in a play together somewhere. Someone had told him what Jimmy was up to and he come after him, spittin' mad."

Owen stopped and Augusta saw he was looking at her with an odd expression. Her nightdress had slipped down, exposing her naked ribs. "Lord, lass. You getting' enough to eat?"

"I'm fine. What happened with the man?"

He took another drag and shook his head. "Griffith told him he had been lookin' for just his type for this prison picture. Said it was worth a fiver to him. Before you could say 'jumpin' geehosefatz' this Walthall feller was dolled out in jailbird stripes and heavin' a shovel. Show me an actor who'll turn down a quick fiver—for principle."

Owen turned to snub out his cigarette in a saucer. "You want to see what I brought?"

"Depends."

He took a seat on the bed and brought up the bag. "Are you ready for this?" He held the sack closer and then yanked it back when she reached her hand too quickly. "How about a kiss first?" he said.

He suddenly had her by the arm and was hoisting her in his lap. It was like she had no weight at all and no will to resist him. He pulled her body across his legs and pressed his mouth to hers.

She had no space at all to breathe. She was suffocating and wiggling her arms, trying to break free. When he relaxed his grip she pulled away, overcome with the sour stench of beer.

"You been drinking?"

"I made a quick stop off at Luchow's on the way."

"Luchow's? I wouldn't call that on the way."

"It was. For me."

"Jesus, Owen, what time is it? Is it even noon?"

"Do you want what I brought or not?" He tossed the rumpled sack on the blanket before her.

"What is it?"

"I was thinking of you that first day. At the studio."

"You mean our kiss?"

"No, not then. Your first day. The day you come in with that *Clang Clang* feller."

"You were there?"

"I was."

"You never told me that."

"So?"

She pulled the bag a little closer. "I can explain about him."

"Nothing to explain," he said.

She unrolled the top and took a cautious peek inside. There was something wrapped up in straw. Must be sort of precious after all, she thought, pushing her fingers down through the spongy packing. "What on earth—" she muttered and pulled up a scratchy fistful of golden curls glued in a net.

She could not believe what she was looking at.

"Surprise!" he said.

"But, how did you—where did it come from?" She turned the old wig over, looking for any telltale traces of water damage or seaweed.

"We sons of *Arland* have mystic ways," he said as if invoking a spirit. Then he broke into an amused grin. "All right, nah. Nina had it tucked away in a box. I thought it was just like that one you had on."

"It was disgusting. I can't tell you how much I hated it."

"Nope. Couldn't tell. ... Put it on for me."

"What?"

"Let's see you in it."

She could not believe he was serious. He was actually asking her that now? He tried to make it sound like some casual lark, an offhand suggestion with no expectations attached. But the set of his eyes told a different story. There was nothing playful or impulsive in those smiling Irish eyes.

"It was dumb of me to wear it. I don't know why Deward insisted."

"I do."

"I guess he thought it made me look pretty."

"No. Had nothing to do with it." He took the wig from her hands and groomed it with his fingers. "You play chess?"

She gave him an impatient frown.

"You see, in chess each piece has a unique power. The pawn is on the lowest level. He's expendable, a worker. Then comes the knights, the bishops, the castles … right up to the queen. There's only one queen, and she's the most powerful piece on the board. She's the last line of defense for the king."

Augusta gave a shrug of indifference. "So?"

"Well, I'll tell you whoever it was invented that game was a fool. 'Cause he left out the most powerful player of all. She can brush aside pawns and knights, corrupt bishops, even bring down a castle without firing a shot. Know who it is?"

"No."

"The virgin. Yes, now the virgin poses a special risk for the queen. She knows how easy it is to turn the head of the king. … Ask Linda Arvidson. Old Clang-Clang Trawley knew what he was doing."

"But that's ridiculous."

"I agree. The threat is over-rated. But I think you're past that now. You lost your wig, right? I doubt if anyone views you as a threat anymore. But to someone with imagination, someone like me, a little dressing up in a wig from time to time can still hold some of its fascination."

Augusta instantly tore the wig out of Owen's fingers and glared at him. Then she hauled back and hurled it at his face. "You're disgusting!"

"Don't be that way."

"Just get out of here!" she screamed. "You don't want me! Get out! Leave me alone! Now!" She flipped on her side toward the window so he could not watch her surrender to a spasm of sobbing.

Some time later he must have slid off the mattress because she was aware of him fumbling with his coat at the chair. Then the room fell silent and she found herself back at Rambo's, only she was upstairs now, standing in the changing room. All the furniture was removed and only bands of moonlight stretched across the plank flooring. She went to a wall and let her body sink down against it, propping her sleepy head on an arm.

Out in the hall was a light swishing, as of a nervous actress pacing in her silk petticoats. Another sound joined it—a hard fluttering like small wings at a windowpane. *Mr. Poe's raven!* she told herself with some amusement. But she was overcome with a desire for sleep, and pulled up her collar to muffle any noise.

A whiff of old clothes and storage bags rolled silently across the floor. The room was not empty after all. The smell apparently was coming from a corner where a battered steamer trunk sat back in the shadows.

She knew that odor, and rushed to place it. ... Mothballs! Yes! That was it. Then the dread certainty of what it meant gnawed at her. She wanted to scream but the effort was too great and all she could manage was a low moan. It was just an old trunk, she told herself. Must have been there all along. It was probably stuffed full of dusty old clothes and costumes, which would explain the smell.

But the swishing grew and now it was not in the hallway. It was coming from inside the trunk. Perhaps a mother mouse was building a nest. Or something larger, like a squirrel or a sick cat.

She boosted herself on an elbow and pushed herself to her feet. No use trying to sleep until the mystery was solved. She moved closer, one foot after the other on the boards, hoping not to cause any loud creaks that might attract attention. When she was near enough to the metal clasp she reached out and gently sprung the latch. It popped open.

The lid lifted easily. Inside were folds of cloth, cool to the touch. She drove her fingers down through layers of wool and tweed to something with laced stitching and a leathery hide. A boot, perhaps. It was dislodged and landed with a thud against the bottom.

There was a flutter of movement inside, and something quivered, starting to physically force itself up.

Augusta whimpered and tried to step back. A sleeve rose over the edge and from it appeared the pink fingers of a hand. They took hold of the side as the piles of clothes parted and a bony spine emerged attached to shoulders hunched over a darkened chest cavity. Deep in the dark were two pink eyes that held her in their gaze. Suddenly it wore a face, the face of Deward Trawley, grinning with a ghastly pleasure.

She awoke to the sound of her scream. She groped in the dark for the light switch as her heart raced. The table lamp snapped on and she saw the twisted bedding lying around her but nothing more. She was alone in a silence spiced only with the pounding of her heart.

If any neighbors had heard the scream they probably rolled over and were back asleep already. It was just one more howl of terror in the night. The city was full of them. No investigation needed.

In the past Owen was there to hold her. Maybe he would come back. He wouldn't hold a grudge. Before long he would see she was just being silly, raising such a fuss over nothing. She climbed out of bed to straighten her blankets and her foot hit something on the floor. His paper sack. With the wig inside. Yet it felt heavier now, and there was the clink of something metal inside.

Her keys. They couldn't have slipped his notice. They weren't put in there by accident. It was a message. It meant his visits were over. There would be no more heroic rescues on cliffs, no more overnight stays or unannounced drop-ins. When it came to Augusta's room keys, it told her, try as Owen might he could not imagine ever needing them again.

TWELVE
"Confidence"

She was done living like this. She hadn't come to New York to turn over control of her life to jealous wives, or stunted Romeos, or two-bit thieves. At first light she was on her feet, gathering her tortured bedding in both arms and dragging it all off onto the floor.

It was high time to get out and shake free of what she had become.

There was still one egg in the icebox, and a heel of bread for toast. It was enough to get her going. After breakfast she would slip down the hall for a quick shower, then pick out a nice outfit and set off for some unknown corner of the city. New York was a big enough place for anyone, after all. Today she would find a job that suited her and reclaim her lost independence.

It was just as she reached out for the cut-glass knob to the washroom that it began to twist. She hopped back to keep from getting smacked.

"Oh, sorry," said a slender figure hidden in a cloud of steam. It was her neighbor from the end of the hall, emerging elegant in a purple kimono, her auburn tresses tucked under a headwrap. "All yours, dearie," she said, guiding a white slippered foot up over the frayed edge of the runner.

The woman was almost certainly a prostitute. In the morning when everyone else was hurrying for work she would show up in a beaded gown at the stairwell with a pricey fur bagged across her shoulders like a trophy.

Augusta had never been this close to her before. She was certainly no classic beauty. Her eyes were a bit wide-set and her forehead was too tall. But as Augusta watched her pump her hips down the carpet to her room she couldn't help feeling admiration. She was getting by on her own, playing by her own rules and making a hell of a go of it.

By the time she was freshly scrubbed and her makeup was done, Augusta had a plan. She would put on the gray dress with the ruffled shoulders and the blue shirtwaist. It was a practical choice for the morning's chill and went well with her good walking boots. If she took Seventh Avenue north she would not likely run into anyone from the studio.

The front desk clerk was distracted with the mail. That was good. She wouldn't have to make any excuses about the rent. In a flash she was across the lobby and out the revolving door.

Her reward was waiting. The morning air was spiced with delicious aromas of fresh bread and breakfast rolls from the bakery next door. It was just a small step-down shop off the sidewalk, but it was already packed with customers. Surely the place would need more help. A card taped in the door glass stopped her short: *Not Hiring*, it read.

Anyway, it was a joy to be out again. She visited a pet shop twitching with feathered dancers in tall cages, and chuckled at the somersaulting antics of the pot-bellied pups. For a while she stood outside a tobacconist's window filled with fancy smoking pipes, soaking up all the sweet, soddy fragrances of home.

The city no longer held any terror. She could find her way back when she was ready. Besides, she had a mission, even though it ended again and again with the inescapable entry notice: *No Help Needed*.

One store had a window full of hairbrushes. One expensive-looking set had a satiny finish and etched grips exactly like one her mother had owned. She couldn't think where it came from now, but it had been her mother's most prized personal possession. Augusta was scolded many times growing up for daring to touch it. "Imported from France" read an engraved card in the window, and yet the price seemed ridiculously low. The merchant explained it was made of a substance called *Ivorine*, a new celluloid material also used to glaze doll heads and make motion picture film. To find that her mother's most valued possession was nothing but hunks of cheap chemical junk made her sad.

In the next block her spirits lifted at the sight of a well-lit bridal shop. Inside were elegant white satin dresses with all their trimmings. She tried to imagine herself in a silk gown lifting a gauzy veil with immaculate linen gloves. Her father used to tease her about the day he could "give her away" to some stranger. The idea of giving her away always struck him as funny. Of course, by the time she reached marrying age he was well on his way to a drunkard's grave. Her daddy and Owen Moore would have been great drinking buddies.

Just as she was about to move along she noticed the reflection of someone behind her in the glass. A man had been standing off a ways and watching her. She only caught a glimpse and could not make out any details in the glare. When she turned all she could see was the usual parade of strangers, each of them oblivious to the tricks an over-tired mind could play.

Anyway, it wouldn't have been Deward. That news would have gotten to her somehow. Someone would have come to warn her about his release. Still, for the rest of the morning she could not entirely shake the feeling of being followed.

The city had not yet recovered from the panic of 1907. As she got to the area around Pennsylvania Station the sidewalks were piled here and there with open boxes of belongings and abandoned stacks of furniture. Vacancy signs and eviction notices popped up in nearly every boarding house window. Down one side street snaked a line of men in dusty overcoats leading to the steps of a soup kitchen.

"Mayor cracks down on child labor!" screamed a boy with a stack of newspapers on a busy street corner. He could hardly have been more than nine years old himself. Augusta's hopes of a job were fading.

At 28th Street she ducked inside an emporium that specialized in "tools and cutlery," drifting to a back wall hung with hunting knives and archery sets. A salesman with an inverted-V mustache watched her browse along a glass counter packed with pistols.

"Is madam in the market for self-protection?" he asked when she drew nearer.

"I had no idea there was such a variety."

"Something for every hand and budget. If madam has questions ..."

"What is the range?"

"Well, with these you will find performance is best at rather close range."

"I'm sorry. I meant the range of *prices*."

"Oh. Would this be for madam's personal use, or as a gift?"

"I haven't decided. I mean, it should suit me."

"A smaller grip, then, light to hold, with a gentle kick. That would be my recommendation."

"A kick?"

"Madame has used firearms before?"

"Naturally. ... Perhaps I could hold that cute little white one?"

"That is quite popular with the ladies. A single bullet derringer with inlaid pearl. Only twenty-four dollars."

"Oh? But only one bullet. What happens if, God forbid, one does not hit her target?"

The clerk showed her how the barrel could be broken open to reload the chamber.

"Well, maybe something more practical. I don't really need pearl trimming. I don't expect I'll be carrying it to the opera."

"Something lightweight but reliable? And from a reputable company, I assume."

"Please."

Augusta watched as the man patiently brought out one pistol after another and laid them on the glass. Each had its pros and cons, though none cost less than twenty dollars. Anything more than eight would eat into the week's rent. She made an excuse and hurried out.

The next blocks were filled with walk-up tenements and butcher shops. She did not stop again until she came to a pawnshop with windows full of tools and musical instruments. Off to one side was a display of pawned handguns for sale.

A wrinkled, ruddy-skinned man behind a barred window watched her enter the door and head to the firearms case.

There under the glass was a gun much like one she had looked at in the other store. "Excuse me. Could you give me a price on this small revolver?"

The pawnbroker did not look up. "Sixteen," he said.

"This small one right here."

"Everything in the case is sixteen."

"Does it work?"

"Firearms are tested and oiled before we put 'em out."

"Perhaps you have another case. Something more within a lady's household budget?"

"How much you want to spend?"

"Six or seven dollars?"

"We got nothing for that. You interested in a layaway?"

"How does that work, exactly?"

"Pay what you can. We hold it 'til it's paid off."

"I was hoping to take it with me."

"You a club member? Club members can take a purchase with 'em and pay it off in installments.

"How can a person become a member?"

He shuffled to the case with a key and began fumbling with the lock. "I'll need some information."

"What information?"

"Address, date of birth, husband's full name, his date of birth ..."

"I'm not married."

"Your father's name will do."

"My father has passed, unfortunately."

"Look, lady, just a man's name, any man. A legal property owner who lives and votes in the state of New York."

"Oh," she said.

"You still want it?"

"No. I will be sure to come back the minute we women have the right to vote." She forced her sweetest smile and continued on her way.

A few grocery items and a new dress at a reasonable price were all she had to show for her outing. And yet after dinner she was feeling quite pleased with herself. She had found out some things on her own, and knew more about the city. Her new dress also turned out to look even better on her at home. With the right hat and shoes she was sure to impress a prospective employer.

As she went to hang it up in her closet she heard a light tapping at the door.

"Miss Lee?" called a scratchy male voice.

It had to be someone from the hotel. "Who's there?"

"It's Garrigan. From the desk?"

One of the bellboys. Probably the goofy one with the skin eruptions. She slipped into her robe and tied off the sash before cracking open the door. No, it was the older one, the one with the bedroom eyes. He gave her body a fast once-over to see if she was dressed.

"Yes? What is it?"

"Sorry to disturb you, ma'am. Mr. Childs said for me to run up."

"I'm really very busy."

"There's a guy here asking for you."

That eliminated Owen. He wouldn't wait around for anyone's permission. She feared the worst. "Well, who is it at this hour?"

A small head leapt up behind the employee, then fell and sprung up again. All she could make out was an uncombed mop of hair.

"It's me, Miss Lee. It's Bobby!"

"Bobby?"

"Yeah," said a voice, and sure enough, there was Bobby poking his head around the bellboy's side.

"Are you alone?"

"Yes, ma'am."

"Thank you," she told the bellboy, clutching her robe tight as she swung back the door. "It's my nephew."

Bobby swept in, holding out in front of him a bundle of purple flowers wrapped in newspaper.

"Are those for me?"

"Yeah," he said. He was already past the kitchen table, giving the room a quick inspection.

"That was very thoughtful." She shut the door in the bellhop's face.

Bobby gave a long whistle. "*Whewww.* Ain't that ceiling a honey!"

"Why are you here?"

"Nina asked me to come."

"I didn't think anyone knew where I live."

"Mr. Moore told us. He took something, and Nina needs it back."

"A wig?"

He gave a jerk of his head. "You got it!"

"Nina should have made Mr. Moore fetch it himself."

"I didn't mind."

The bouquet now hung upside down at Bobby's side. Its delicate purple petals swept against the rug. "Why don't you let me put those in water?" she said.

"Sure." He followed into the small open kitchen and watched as she pulled a tall glass from the cupboard.

"Lilacs are my favorite," she said. "They must be in season. There are vases full of them all over the lobby."

He gave a sheepish grin. "Yeah," he said. "Mind if I ask you something?"

"No."

"What do ladies see in a guy like him?"

"Mr. Moore?"

He nodded.

"Do you have sisters, Bobby?"

"Yes, ma'am. Frances and Tess."

"Why don't you ask Frances and Tess?"

"They mostly just play with their dollies."

"Oh. ... Well, Mr. Moore appeals to a lady's romantic nature."

He mulled this over with a skeptical frown.

"Is that why you came? You want to save me from Mr. Moore?"

"You could do a lot better than that guy."

"You don't like him?"

"He offered me alcohol once."

"Really? Why did he do that?"

Bobby lifted his thin shoulders. "I guess he thought we was pals."

She guided the stems down in the water and fluffed the petals. "There. Isn't that better?"

"Great. ... I didn't, of course."

"You didn't?"

"Take his hootch."

"Good for you."

"I'm Catholic, you know. ... Are you?"

"Hunh-uh," she mumbled, bringing the glass to the entry table. "Flowers bring such cheer to a room."

Bobby smiled.

"Now let me find that wig."

He drifted along after her and watched as she rummaged in a nightstand drawer by the bed.

"Want to know why I really come?"

"Of course."

"Father Bill said I oughta. He said I should thank you in person."

"Thank me?"

"For—you know, at the ferry."

She smiled at his sudden seriousness. "Is Father Bill your family priest?"

"Yes, ma'am."

"And you told him what happened?"

"He said God was watching over me."

"Well, you could have drowned."

"He said God put you there. To save me."

"I don't know about—" She suddenly lifted up the wrinkled paper sack. "Found it," she said, opening the top to show him inside. "I'll put it by the door so we don't forget."

"It wasn't about the stupid coat anyhow. You know?"

"It wasn't?"

"Nah. It's what was in it."

"What was that?"

"My manual. My *scout's* manual. I brung it with me so I could practice my knots. I had it folded to the page I was on. I stuck it in one of them deep pockets. Safe, you know? Then like a dummy I run off and left it."

"It was very foolish, jumping in with the ice and all."

"No way was I going to let it get away. Scouting is the greatest thing ever. It started over in England, with Sherwood Forest and Robin Hood and them guys. They knew all about livin' in nature. People in cities have forgotten how to do it. The book's set up to teach you skills like pitchin' tents and tyin' knots and identifying birds. You never know when you'll need that stuff. It's very scientific. President Roosevelt was a big believer in nature. He ain't president no more."

"I heard."

"You want me to show you how to make a 'fireman's loop?'"

"Sure."

"You got a piece of rope?"

"Rope? No, I'm not—"

"Any old rope will do. Or braided twine?"

"Let's do it some other day, Bobby."

"No. *Please.* It won't take long. You're gonna love this. After that I'll go home."

She was growing fond of Bobby, and she was surprised how good it made her feel to see him happy. "I had some somewhere. Where did I put it?"

She remembered finding a coil of dark cord with Deward's things. She went to the closet and groped around on the top shelf. "Here it is," she said.

Bobby took it eagerly and gave it a tug. "Wow. This is good strong rope here. You been campin'? You could tie up a bank robber with this and keep him prisoner 'til the sheriff come. ... Okay, watch close. First, you gotta make big loops like this. See how I got it here?"

Taking a seat next to him on the floor, Augusta tried to pay attention but her mind wandered back to a boy she knew on the river named Toby. He had freckles and a space between his front teeth. She had let him kiss her and later they planned to run away together. But his parents did not sign on again for the new season and she never heard exactly where he winded up.

"Now, you take this end here and you make a smaller loop—like this, okay? Now bring this one around and under the circle, through the top like so, and ... pull!" Suddenly he was holding the whole coil by a loop at the top. "Now you can hang it like this until you need it. And then ..." He reached up to a dangling end and gave it a yank. The coil came loose and unraveled in a pile at his shoes. Bobby beamed in satisfaction. "And that's what they call a fireman's knot."

Augusta wanted to smile but her eyes had become pools of sorrow. Bobby's youthful happiness drove home all the day's regrets at once. The reminders of her mother's rebukes and her father's drunken abandonment left her heart feeling heavy. She drew up her knees and wrapped them in her arms as tears began to run.

"Hey," said Bobby. "Don't be sad. Miss Lee? ... Please stop. You'll be okay. No one's sore about you takin' that wig."

She spoke with great effort. "I've made ... so many mistakes," she said. "I want to be a better person. Really, I do. I want—"

He looked for anything he could give her to stop the flow, finally grabbing a folded shirt from the top drawer of the trunk. "Here," he said. "Use this."

She wiped her nose and blotted her eyes, struggling to regain composure. When she glanced at Bobby again he was sitting quite still, transfixed by the sight of her opened robe and the exposed smoothness of her breasts. She discretely raised a hand to close the gaping neckline.

Bobby looked in her eyes with a smirk of contrition that instantly twisted into a mask of horror. "Oh, gosh. I'm sorry."

"It's all right."

"I don't know—I mean, I didn't mean to—What come over me?"

"You're a boy."

"But I know better."

"It's not a sin."

His head pumped up and down. "Yes, it is. We're responsible for what we think. It's called 'impure thoughts.' ... How can I ever tell Father Bill?"

He told her again about being a Catholic and how that meant going regularly to confession. It always made him feel better, he said, after being absolved for his failings.

"Do you think Father Bill would agree to see—a stranger?"

"Sure, he would."

"Even if she was … not of his faith?"

"I don't know. I could ask him for ya."

"Never mind."

"He's a really good man."

"It's all right."

Bobby frowned again and looked away. He was clearly still bothered a good deal by what he had done. "I never had to go confess," he started, "… nothing like this."

"Why don't we just say you've made your confession."

"What do you mean?"

"You confessed it to me."

"I don't think that counts."

"Jesus said to forgive those who wrong you. Well, I forgive you. There." She slapped her hands together. "Done."

A little color returned to the boy's face and he gave a weak smile.

She suddenly saw him as an answer to her own problems. "See that," she said, dabbing at her eyes with the shirt again. "I feel better, too. The truth is, Bobby, I haven't been sleeping well lately. I've been very troubled. You could help me."

"I can?"

"Nina said you were good at … finding things."

"I got my sources. You gotta be fast on your feet these days, otherwise someone just off a boat'll get there first."

"You must promise to keep this a secret. Can you do that?"

"You can trust me."

"When I first got here, to the city, I didn't know a soul. I was so lost and alone. Just trying to get by. I met a few people, some of them weren't so good."

"Mr. Moore?"

"Worse, Bobby. One man—I found out he was a criminal. A very bad man. He threatened to hurt me."

"The coward. Threatening a lady. Who was it?"

"It doesn't matter. The truth is, he's in jail now. And I'm … partly responsible."

"You should be proud. That's where bad people belong."

"But I've heard—he could be released."

"How come?"

"I don't know. Some legality."

"You think he'll come after you?"

"It's possible."

"I get it. So that's how come you hung around Mr. Moore. You hoped he would scare off the bad guys."

Augusta couldn't stop a sudden smile. "You're wise beyond your years."

"Can't you tell the coppers?"

"The police can't do anything. I have to protect myself. This morning I tried to buy a gun. They wouldn't sell it to me. Is there any way, do you think … you could get me one?"

"A gun?"

She watched him frown. "I mean, I don't want to hurt anybody, Bobby. But if he should come for me …"

"But a gun. … My people—technically we're immigrants still. We're not supposed to go near any firearms." He lit with a sudden thought. "Hey, Nina's got ones that look just like the real thing."

"No. No stage props. It's got to be real. I might have to fire it in the air to show him … I mean business."

"It's a tall order. What the hay—I can try. I'll get to work on it first thing in the morning."

"Thank you, Bobby. That's a big relief. But you have to promise. You can't tell a soul, not even Father Bill."

Bobby held up two fingers. "Scout's honor." Then he nodded meekly in the direction of her robe. "And the same … ?"

She made the sign of an X over her heart. "Our secret forever."

At the door she handed him the sack with the wig and bent quickly to give him a peck on the cheek. His face turned light red and he beamed up at her before skipping away down the carpet, sputtering and sparking like a lit fuse all the way to the stairs.

She sighed as she shut the door and twisted the key in the lock. Bobby would not say a word now, not even to Father Bill. A boy like that could soften in time and confess to stealing a handgun. But he would never admit anything so shameful as casting his eyes upon naked female flesh.

THIRTEEN
"A Change of Heart"

For such a strong man, Mack Sennett never found it easy to hold his tongue. Each morning when he passed through the appraising faces of the temperance ladies it seemed just a tad less likely he would make it through the day without exploding.

The Marvins were free to set their own policies, of course. And far be it from him to violate or contradict an executive decision. But if he were running Biograph, things would be different. For one thing, he wouldn't kowtow to a bunch of old scolds who reeked to high heaven from their own self-importance.

Another thing. If he ran a studio he would put all its resources behind making raucous comedies that kidded the starched bejeesus out of their brand of pomposity.

"This it?" he asked Nina, fingering a deep cardboard box that had his name scribbled on it.

"That's what they give us, yes, sir," said the seamstress without looking away from her stitching.

Mack accepted it as a warning not to expect much. "Thanks." He carried the box over to the cutting table.

Yes, his studio would do more farces like "The Curtain Pole." That should have shown everyone the way. It only cost a relative pittance, shooting the whole thing in two days outdoors at Fort Lee. Yet that one split-reel comedy already sold more tickets than any dozen prestige pictures and history yarns whipped up by the old man.

"Holy Jesus!"

"That's what they give us," repeated Nina in her told-you-so tone.

"I've seen better hairpieces on Methodist ministers."

"That's it. Take it or leave it," she said.

So he gave out a deep sigh of resignation and headed for the stairs with a heart as heavy as the special delivery package he now had to submit for Griffith's approval.

It was still unclear what the old man thought of the project. He claimed to like it, but then again he wasn't always easy to read. When he first heard the idea for "The Curtain Pole" he nodded after each sentence like he was digesting the plot of a Greek tragedy.

"It's the old bull in the china shop gag," Mack had said. "It's about this snooty Frenchman with a softness for hard drink. He's called in to decorate this rich home for some society bash. But just before the guests start to arrive he breaks a heavy drapery rod, so the owner sends him off to town for a new one. Naturally, Frenchie can't resist a stop to wet his whistle. So when he gets the curtain pole he can barely stand up straight. At every turn he whacks some fine lady in the rump or breaks some shopkeeper's window—until the whole town is chasing after him, screaming for his scalp!"

Griffith listened all the way to the end before betraying a small grin. Then he did something Mack did not expect at all. He laughed. Out loud. Not some dry flicker of amusement, but a big shoulder-rocking cackle that not even someone with his head up a burlesque horse's ass could have missed.

The old man wanted to put it into production right away and he even asked Mack to play the decorator. He was finally coming around to the idea that Mack might be more than an idea man or an assistant. It made him think there could be many more fruitful collaborations ahead for them.

So it was like being doused with a bucket of ice water later when he overheard Griffith telling the story to others. To him "The Curtain Pole" was not a farce about throwing a monkey wrench in the gears of the upper crust. It was about this clumsy servant who makes a spectacle of himself in town and brings disaster down on his employer. It was a way of ribbing the elites over the failings of their hired help.

Mack listened, dumbfounded. All he could think was, *Wait, maybe I didn't tell it right.*

It just highlighted the difference between the two of them. Griffith's people weren't any more a part of the social whirl than his were. The old man would mock the airs of the upper-class from time to time. But the truth was he still hoped to be accepted in some day. Only a handful of Southerners had made it to their high-tone soirees. Old General Lew Wallace was one. After his "Ben-Hur" novel was made into a Broadway phenomenon he found himself invited to all the best social functions. Maybe Griffith's move from actor to playwright was part of that push toward respectability. He couldn't be too happy now to be rising in a profession still viewed with such contempt by the city's elites.

Mack had given up trying to curry favor with their sort when he turned his back on opera. The pratfalling comics on the Bowery had things figured out. They didn't care a fig for what the civic set thought. All they wanted was to give poor working stiffs a bit of entertainment. The last thing they needed was a sketch that was morally uplifting.

Griffith had just finished his latest sermon, a little gem called "The Voice of the Violin." It was supposed to be a star-crossed romance about a music student and her teacher. But the old man turned the female student into a hoity-toity heiress and made the teacher a poverty-struck artist. Suddenly it became a treatise on class and social injustice in America, and it all ended with the planting of an anarchist's bomb under the rich girl's home. How plain nuts was that?

Now he was tinkering with "The Drunkard's Reformation." He took the old Victorian snorter Mack had given him and added elements from a novel by Emile Zola about the suffering poor of Paris. Griffith wanted to give his melodrama class, and this guy Zola was said to be lousy with it.

He would pay a high price some day if he loaded his releases with instructive messages.

Down on the studio floor the director sat in the dark on his favorite stool. His bony frame was pitched forward in an animated discussion with Billy Bitzer.

Well, he could wait until they were done. He was in no hurry to share what he had.

There was so much he admired about the man. No stage director he ever worked with gave more of himself to a project. None took half as much care to make his performers look good, either. He ran a tight set and was ready to physically confront anyone who dared to interfere. Those shadowboxing exhibitions were his reminder to everyone of who was in charge.

The one thing that nagged at him now was probably also keeping the Marvins up at night: Was there a ticket-buyer in all Manhattan who went to a nickelodeon in the hopes of finding art?

"Edgar Allen Poe" and other recent clinkers like "The Golden Lotus" and "The Politician's Love Story" were leaving Biograph on the outs with its own exchange repo. Griffith's recent pictures weren't likely to leave viewers happy to recommend them to others. And he had more in the pipeline. He was moving forward now with an adaptation of a Thomas Browning poem titled "Pippa Passes." ... Another poem! This time about a little girl!

The day before, Mack pulled Billy Bitzer aside for his own private talk. "What the hell, Billy? What's he thinking?"

Billy stared at him blankly a second before shrugging. "I'm a cameraman, Mr. Sennett, not an answer man."

It could be he was tired of the stress of two films a week. He might be looking for a release. With his one-year contract coming up for renewal in a couple months, this might all be the rational plan of someone hoping to get out of a bad situation.

On the other hand, if he wasn't consciously trying to fail he had better give the Marvins a box office winner—and soon. What he needed was another "Curtain Pole," and that's what Mack was determined to give him.

His eyes fell on the box in his hands, his smile soon after. Too bad this surefire comedy idea of his was already looking like a long shot.

"Mr. Sennett," called Griffith, signaling for him to come. He had finished with Billy Bitzer and was busy doing waist-twists in place beside his stool. He did not stop as Mack approached. "What do you have for me?"

"They sent us the suit," said Mack, fanning open the cardboard lid.

The director brought one knee up to his chest, held it a moment then brought up the other. The floorboards bounced and creaked with each move. He raised a suspicious brow. "What is this for again?"

"It's the bear. For our cabin comedy."

"Oh, yes."

Inside the box seemed to be one of those thick fur coats worn by prospectors in the Klondike. Mack lifted about a yard of animal hide from the box, exposing folds of visible stitches and bald patches. Two empty sleeves fell free and dangled over the edge of the box. The sets of white, curved claws clicked together like wind chimes.

"Oh, I see."

Mack had kept the facemask hidden under the box. He had to rally his courage before hoisting it up and holding it next to his cheek. Its shiny snout jutted out between two gaping eye sockets surrounded by a mess of matted hair. Mack smiled. "What ya think?"

Griffith recoiled and clicked his tongue a few times. "Is that the best they had?"

"That's what they told us. I can find out."

"Please do," he said, and then threw himself into more waist-bends as he shouted out, "Billy!"

Billy Bitzer's head popped up from behind the mounted camera. "Yes, Mr. Griffith?"

"We'll have to turn the lights low for this one. Very low. No one needs to get a clear look at Mr. Sennett's bear. ... Rodney!"

A voice up in the dark rafters yelled back. "Yes, Mr. G."

"You hear that?"

"Low lights. Check!"

"Good fellow," responded Griffith. He was bobbing and weaving around now, throwing short jabs in the air and starting to pant.

Mack was so busy struggling to get the costume back in the box that he nearly collided against a tall, dark man wearing a European duster.

"Excuse me. ... *Maestro Griffith*?" inquired the man. His naked finger poked up out of a dark palm glove.

"Over there," said Mack, nodding toward the invisible boxing ring.

The man gathered himself up with an imperious air. "*Tank you,* very much."

This is going to be rich, thought Mack, and stopped to watch.

"Maestro, please. *Scusa,*" said the stranger, wedging himself closer than comfortable to the director's face. He introduced himself with a flourish that Mack could not quite make out. "I hear very *mooch* about you violin picture. I wish to make my formal availability known." He claimed to be a tenor with the Metropolitan Opera and a personal friend of Caruso. He began reeling off the names of a long list of institutions and vocal coaches.

"Enough!" Griffith cried with an upright hand. "Sorry. We have nothing for you today."

"I would be willing to return tomorrow."

"Nothing then either. Next month, perhaps. You can try us then."

The singer from the Met pulled himself up with a great wounded pride. "It would not be convenient for me, as well. I have a performance tonight ... at Carnegie Hall!" he huffed, and turned to stomp away.

As much as Mack enjoyed a good brush-off, he felt pity for a fellow opera singer. When he swept by, Mack hustled to keep up. "Hey, I heard what you said. Just wanted to wish you good luck tonight ... at Carnegie. Break a leg."

The man stopped at the tall doors to pull on a floppy, wide-brimmed hat and then gave Mack a sharp look of disdain. "In my profession, we do not engage in superstitions like *theece* 'bah-reak a legg,'" he said.

"Fine," shrugged Mack. "Then break a *legato*."

He watched the singer wrap his duster around him and was instantly washed away in the blinding light of the foyer. There came a rustle as he hurried around a small figure blocking his path.

"Hello, Mack."

He squinted to make out the details of a soft female face. His chest suddenly inflated with delight. "Augusta!" he brayed, and juggled his box as he grabbed her in a big Bowery squeeze.

Her name echoed through the studio and a few actors and crew people stopped to shout their greetings.

"Hey, everyone," Mack called out happily. "Look who I found!"

Off by the stage, Griffith lifted a hand in a single wave of hello. "Welcome, Miss Lee. Don't rush away. I'd like a word with you at the break."

Bobby came swinging down from a scaffold and landed with a thud near them. "Good to see ya made it, Miss Lee," he said, bounding off at once and hollering, "Everyone on stage! We're ready to shoot!"

The pole lights sparked and hissed as overhead the battery of Hewitt-Coopers popped into service. Mack could make out the glistening highlights in Augusta's eyes.

"Wonderful to see you, Mack," she said.

"Back to you, kid. I was starting to think you were just a fixture of my imagination."

"Is this a bad time?"

"Nah." He hoisted the box on his hip. "I was just taking this up to Nina. Care to come?"

"Love to."

On the way up the stairs she asked how things had been.

"Couldn't be worse," he said. "Did you hear Florence is leaving?"

"Why would she do that?"

"Don't tell anyone. She thinks there's interest out there. She's got her own following."

"Is Mr. Griffith worried?"

"He knows the game. He's the one stole her away from Edison, after all. ... Mind if I ask, what happened to you?"

"It's a long story."

"I like long stories. Tell me later."

They found Nina at her cutting table, bending across a pattern with a pair of pinking shears. When she saw who it was she broke into a broad, toothy grin. "Mercy, where'd you turn up this one, Mack?"

"She was there under a clover leaf."

"Hello, Nina," said Augusta.

"Where'd you get to, hon?"

"I had a little business to attend to, that's all."

"I didn't even know you had a little business. They hiring seamstresses?"

Augusta laughed.

"You're stayin' this time, right?" said Mack.

"I'd like to. I haven't exactly been asked."

There was the distant clanging of a fire bell and Mack moseyed to the windows to let the girls get caught up. By the time he reached the glass the clanging had grown more loud and urgent. It could only mean another fire in the neighborhood. He pressed close to the pane and searched the sky for the trail of smoke.

The clatter turned into a muffled thundering of hooves and the rattling of a wagon. Even Nina stopped yakking to listen and wait for the racket to pass. But the fire bell sounded ever closer and Mack saw six horses round the corner with their fetters flying, strapped to the beam of a shiny hook and ladder. The driver hollered out and pulled the emergency wagon to a halt in the street down below.

"Fire wagon," said Mack. "She's a big one. Six horses."

"Where's the fire?" said Augusta, moving up to join him.

Mack pressed his cheek against the glass. "There's men jumping off."

"Oh, good Lord," exclaimed Nina. "You see any smoke?"

"Nothing. But they're coming in, shoving through the picket marchers. Good going, fellows!" he yelled, pounding at the window. "Give 'em one for me!"

Augusta felt the excitement. "They're coming here!" she shouted.

There was a crash of falling objects and when Mack looked back he saw Nina standing amidst rubbles of props. "This time I come prepared," she said. She had placed a dented red fire helmet over her head scarf and was lifting another from its shelf.

Mack would have laughed but he sensed the woman's fear. "If there's a fire," he said, "it's probably best we don't wait up here."

Nina hurried up to thrust the second fire helmet into Augusta's hands. "I only have two," she said. "Mack, hon, you're on your own."

"Let's go," he said.

Loud male voices echoed up from the foyer and he half expected to feel a whoosh of hot air in the hall. But nothing had changed, and they were halfway down the stairs and still had not caught a whiff of smoke.

The chorus of urgent voices continued below, tripping over one another.

"Did someone get the key?"

"See that it's turned off."

"You check the main?"

"Nothing there."

"All right. Someone look at the pipes."

"And tell him counterclockwise this time!"

Racing up the steps toward them came two fit young firemen in heavy canvas coats. They carried serious wood-handled axes but across their faces was only mild astonishment at coming upon Mack's female companions and their comically outmoded fire helmets.

"Mr. Marvin!" called out a voice from below the staircase.

Arthur Marvin was standing outside his office in a daze at the whirlwind of activity. "Griffith. Wh—what's going on," he muttered, starting across the marble floor. "What's all this about?"

Mack and the others reached the landing in time to see Griffith at the back wall with two fire officials. The more neatly shaven man wore a dark blue uniform and a visored cap trimmed in gold. Griffith introduced him to Arthur Marvin as Fire Captain O'Brien. The other fellow was dressed for action in a rugged fireman's coat and a flame-charred helmet. He was introduced as the precinct's Brigade Chief Odenton.

"Do we have a fire somewhere?" asked Arthur Marvin as he shook their hands.

"We're not sure," said Griffith. "They're still looking. Captain O'Brien here thinks it could be a false alarm."

"A what?"

"Someone pulled the lever in the street box," said the fire captain. "Anyone could've done that. But then someone also phoned the address into the station. I take it that was not you, sir?"

"Certainly not," said Mr. Marvin. "Mr. Griffith handles all studio alarms—I mean, the fire alarms and such."

The brigade chief frowned. "So this has happened before?"

"No, no," said Griffith. "This is our first."

The front door flew back and all heads turned to a burly stranger in the doorway. He was nattily dressed, looking like a Wall Street banker in his yellow felt overcoat and necktie. He had a full walrus-style mustache that stuck out well beyond his chubby red cheeks.

"What do we have here, Captain?" he said in a booming voice as he came toward the others.

"Could be a bad call. We're still waiting."

"Malicious prank?" asked the newcomer.

"Not likely. She was phoned in, as well."

"Well, I'll have a look around while I'm here."

"Excuse me," said Arthur Marvin suspiciously. "This is my establishment. May I ask what is your interest in this?"

"I'm sorry," said Fire Captain O'Brien. "This is the fire marshal—"

"*Assistant* fire marshal," interjected the man with the mustache. "E.T. Edwards," he said. "Nice to meet you." He offered each man his hand before stopping when he noticed Mack and the two ladies watching on the landing. He tipped his head slightly to Augusta.

"Look, how long is this going to take?" asked Griffith. "We've got a production schedule to meet."

"Yes, sir," said the fire chief. "As soon as we have our report, we'll be on our way."

"You know, there's a city fine for setting false alarms," said the brigade chief. He turned to address Arthur Marvin. "You have any idea who might have done it?"

The owner looked offended by the question.

"You might ask that of those protesters out front," said Griffith.

The chief raised an eyebrow. "Oh? Why's that?"

"They attacked one of our actors. We had to make a complaint. With the police."

"Mr. Griffith," said the fire captain, "are you suggesting someone might have been getting back at you?"

"I'm saying these people are doing whatever they can to stop us from conducting our business."

Mack saw the man with the mustache give another sidelong glance at Augusta. It was like they had met once and he was busy trying to remember where. He soon returned to address Griffith. "Sir, do you store any flammable substances on the premises?"

"We use chemicals in developing our film. Everything's kept sealed, if that's what you're getting at."

"Where are these chemicals kept, sir?"

"In our lab. Down in the basement."

"Could you have someone show me, please?"

"Of course," said Griffith. He looked up and signaled to Augusta. "Miss Lee, could you kindly take Mr. Edwards down to our lab?"

Augusta appeared taken by surprise. She glanced to Mack and then to Nina before looking back at Griffith. "Me?"

"Please. Just show him downstairs."

"The basement?" she asked.

"That's right. If you would."

Mack could see the fear in her eyes. She was clearly groping for any excuse not to go. "I'll do it," he said, stepping forward.

"No, no, Mr. Sennett. I want Miss Lee to handle this. I might need you here." He pointed to a small side door to the left of the studio. "Miss Lee, please take the fire marshal for his inspection."

"*Assistant* fire marshal," corrected the burly man.

Augusta removed her fire helmet and handed it to Nina with the air of a doomed soldier. She gave Mack a weak smile and then turned to the others. "This way, Mr. Edwards," she said.

Mack knew Augusta was in no position to answer his questions about the lab. She didn't even seem to know the way until it was pointed out to her. And yet Griffith had insisted and was watching them go with a hint of self-satisfaction.

In a flash Mack knew what he had done. He was falling back on one of the oldest gambits in show business, something known as the *designated virgin*. Theatrical troupes on tour in the provinces would use the ploy whenever a small-minded magistrate or hard-nosed local sheriff denied them permission to perform in their town. The company would send out its sweetest, most innocent-looking young flirt for a private meeting. It was her job to reassure the officer's fears and leave him more than happy to let the show go on.

Griffith had picked Augusta as his designated virgin. He must have noted the magnetic sway she held over the fire marshal. The old man hadn't had even a moment's doubt about her God-given instincts and ability, and was sure she would know what was expected of her. Mack was just as sure that Augusta would pull it off. Indeed, it would not surprise him if the two returned from making the inspection hand-in-hand to announce their betrothal.

The two young firemen they passed on the stairs now came strolling back down to proclaim the upper stories free of fire. However, they did find numerous code violations. In what appeared to be a dress shop or costume factory they noted high levels of flammable cotton dust in the air and ashtrays full of smoldering cigarette butts.

"We're going to have to cite you for that, Mr. Marvin," said Captain O'Brien, raising his pen and clipboard.

The owner looked distraught. "What does that mean—'cite' us?"

"I'm issuing you a ticket. Once you've attended to the violations, we'll return and clear you to re-open."

"Re-open?" exploded Arthur Marvin. "You mean you intend to shut us down?"

"Yes, sir. That's the procedure. We'll post a sign out front saying closed by order of the fire chief."

Furrows lined Griffith's brow as he listened to all this. "How long will this whole process take?"

"Shouldn't be long. Move your cotton goods and combustibles to a safer location. The walls downstairs are fireproof. You could have the whole thing cleared to open in, oh, thirty days."

The color drained from Arthur Marvin's face. "Thirty days!"

"Sir," said Griffith to the fire chief, "we are in a competitive market here. A setback like this—well, even two weeks without new product—that could be the end of us."

"Sorry, Mr. Griffiths. My department goes by the book." He ripped off a sheet from his board and gave it to Arthur Marvin. "I'm afraid my hands are tied."

"Is there anyone we could talk to about this?" asked Griffith.

The captain's lips puckered. He clearly did not like anyone going over his head. "There's Fire Chief Mullendore. He's the one sets the rules. Then again, you can take it up with his boss, Mayor McClellan." He smiled and tapped his shiny visor with two fingers, then gave a snap of his neck to his men.

Mack and the others watched the firemen file out before speaking again.

"It's an outrage," muttered Griffith. "This is exactly what our competition wants."

"It's that bastard Edison," agreed Arthur Marvin. "There's nothing he loves more than seeing us on the ropes."

"Well, whoever was responsible for this," said Griffith, "it could not have come at a worse time."

" 'Whoever was responsible?'" repeated Arthur Marvin in sheer disbelief. He spoke now in the hardest, most deliberate tone Mack had ever heard him use. "Mr. Griffith, you must fix this. You've had your way until now, and what has it gotten us? Boycotts and lawsuits and police reports! Now you've got us up to our neckties in red tape. I want this over, hear me? You get us back in business in two weeks time or you can begin looking for employment elsewhere."

The end of his tantrum coincided exactly with a sudden boom across the foyer. Everyone jumped a bit and turned to look. The basement door was pinned flat against the wall and Assistant Fire Marshal Edwards was leaning against it with a look of utter shock on his face. Across his outstretched arms lay the body, limp and unconscious, of Mr. Griffith's sweet and trustworthy *designated virgin*.

FOURTEEN

"Resurrection"

A cold leak of air whistled up the naked flesh of her leg. It came again. This time it couldn't be tolerated.

But—this wasn't her room. The framed pictures over her head were not familiar. The crack zigzagging down the plaster belonged to someone else.

At her feet a body shifted. Who was there? It was Bobby! Bobby was crouching over her feet with his lips puckered, about to blow again.

"Bobby?"

The boy grinned. "Oh, you woke up."

She reached to tug her skirt lower on her calf. "Where are we?" She twisted around and looked across the carpet to the fortress-like front of a desk. It was Griffith's office!

"They went to fetch you water. You feel better?"

She nodded, as if any of it made sense. Dizziness claimed her again as she attempted to rise. Her head flopped back with a hard bump against the leather arm.

"You clunked out. That fireman guy grabbed you before you hit. Good catch, if you ask me."

Yes, that stocky fire marshal with the odd mustache. ... He was taking her somewhere. No, she was taking him. To the basement! Yes, that dim, narrow corridor with the single lit bulb. She wanted to run. There was a noise. A thrashing at the end of the hall. Just the one open door there, surrounded in darkness. And then, an odor. Vinegar? No. It was mothballs!

She remembered seeing a movement, something sliding low on the cement floor. A bare scalp, pushing out through the door, turning. Those eyes! They gazed at her!

"I fainted?"

"Darned if you didn't," answered a booming baritone by the door. It was the burly fireman with the mustache, coming to her with a glass of water. He raised a large hand and nudged Bobby aside like he weighed nothing at all.

She felt his palm cushioning her head, lifting it up. The glass touched her lips and she managed to swallow.

"Thank you," she said.

His eyes were brown and set back under a wide brow like two wild raccoons nesting in an eave. He had ruddy cheeks, too fixed to be jolly. There were coffee stains along the bottom edge of his mustache.

"I must've caught a hundred fainters in my time," he was saying. "Never have I seen it done better, though. I think you were gone before your knees even noticed. Time enough for me. Yes, best job of fainting I think I ever saw."

"All the excitement ... the, the—"

"Sure, sure. Tell us about it in a minute. We aren't going no place. Let your blood get flowing again."

"Help me sit up."

"There you go. Easy now. ... Feel better?"

At least she could still bob her head. "Yes."

"Oh, I see you're back among the living," said Lawrence Griffith with a cheerful nonchalance at the door. He entered with a short, bald man who wore thick glasses and a tattered sweater vest. "Miss Lee, this is Mr. Shultz. He has something to tell you."

The bald man pushed his frames higher on his bridge. Its large round lenses revealed two dark, unkempt eyebrows. He appeared to be in pure agony standing before so many people. "I am sorry, Miss Lee. I did not mean to ... frighten you." He looked uncertainly back at Griffith.

Augusta could not make any sense of what he said.

"Mr. Shultz is the best film processor in the business," said the director. "That's his lab in the basement. Evidently, he dropped a pencil and was on his hands and knees when you saw him. He thought he might've scared you to death."

"I caught her as she fell," said the assistant fire marshal. "I couldn't miss the signs."

Everybody chuckled some from relief and Augusta assured the lab man he had done no lasting damage. He bent as if to show her the bald crown of his head, then straightened for a quick flash of a smile before darting out the door.

"Well, that ends that mystery," said Griffith. "I would like to talk with Miss Lee alone now, if you'll both excuse us."

"Sure thing, Griff," said Bobby, turning to make a quick exit.

The groomed and natty E.T. Edwards smoothed the outer edges of his mustache. "Miss Lee, when you are ready, it would be my honor to see you to your residence. My automobile stands at your disposal."

"That's sweet of you."

"Thank you, Mr. Edwards," said Griffith, taking his chair and sliding it closer to Augusta. "We won't be long."

He sat and examined her face while he waited for the door to shut. "Looks like your color has returned. Your skin is still very pale, though."

"I don't know what happened. You must think I'm the most feeble excuse for a young lady."

He raised a hand. "On the contrary. You're quite brave. Not many girls would have gone out on that cliff. I don't believe I got a chance to tell you that."

"Oh, don't remind me. My behavior that day—it was inexcusable. I was so rude."

"Miss Arvidson—Linda—I know she feels contrite as well."

"It's true, then? The two of you ... are man and wife?"

"Yes."

"That poor woman."

Griffith winced.

"No. I didn't mean because of you. I meant, the situation. It must be very hard for her."

"Generous of you to say so, my dear. Is it possible we can now put the whole episode behind us?"

"It's already forgotten. I wouldn't dream of betraying your confidence." She instantly blushed, knowing it was not true.

He gathered her hands in his and smiled in her eyes. "You know, I very much hoped you would come back. You haven't accepted a position elsewhere, have you?"

"No, sir."

"You see, I've been doing some thinking. I think you might be an enormous asset to us here. To Biograph."

"Me?"

"I am prepared to offer you a salary. Put you on the payroll as an employee."

"I'm sorry. You said something about ... an 'asset'?"

"I had an idea. I want to use you—your image—on our upcoming circulars. I want to see your picture all around the city, in every

nickelodeon. I want to put your face before the public alongside our
new name."

"Like a sort of circus act?"

He chuckled. "Hopefully a bit more respectable than that. It's what
advertisers call a brand. It's time we establish a new brand. When the
public thinks 'motion pictures,' we want them to think of you."

"What about Miss Lawrence? I thought she was *the Biograph Girl*."

"Florence has been good for us. But she is too experienced, I'm
afraid. She gives some men the idea she is laughing at them. Not that
we don't deserve it. ... You know she's married."

"Her too? No, I didn't."

"Harry Salter. He's her husband. Keep it in confidence. Harry's
a good friend. In fact, he helped us get her for Biograph in the first
place. But she is not right for what I have in mind. I'm looking for
someone fresh and unspoiled. I hadn't thought about you until
today, when I saw how that fire marshal was looking at you."

"What would I do?"

"Social functions, for one thing. We'll send you to dinners with
exhibitors and exchange reps. You will represent us and listen to
them brag and complain, mostly about their wives. The rest of the
time there'll be plenty to do. We'll keep you busy. You can keep my
calendar, remind me of my appointments."

"Will there be acting roles?"

"Oh, yes. We'll find parts for you from time to time. Only sweet
and wholesome ones, of course. Older sisters. Loyal sweethearts.
Nothing that might taint your image."

"You mentioned a salary?"

"Twenty dollars a week. Interested?"

"Twenty-five would be more interesting."

"Done," he said, slapping his long hands against his knees and
pushing himself to his feet. "Very well." He walked around the desk
to his oil painting of horses in a meadow, and swung it out, dodging
his head as it swept by. Seated in the wall behind it was a brass
cover on a thick hinge. He spun a central knob, rotating it back and
forth a few times before jerking down on a handle and pulling the
cover open.

He came back toward her holding a short stack of paper money
sealed with a band. "I want you to go shopping, pick yourself out
a new wardrobe. I want you to look like—I don't know—one of those

East Side wives. Attractive outfits, youthful but not too demure. Tasteful. Do you know what I mean?"

"Professional but fun?"

"Exactly. Miss Arvidson has volunteered to go with you."

"No. Tell her thank you, but I can manage."

"Fine. Here," he said, handing her the thin stack of bills. "There's two hundred dollars there. I know what you're thinking. My sisters in the South could get twenty new dresses for that. But this is New York. We want you to look your best, so shop around."

"I don't know when I can repay—"

"Oh, don't worry about that. This is an investment. If it goes well, the Marvins will get a good return on their money."

"When should I begin?"

"Unfortunately, the studio has been officially shut down by the fire people. Hopefully, it won't last long." He sat by her again and took her free hand. "I want you to go home. You need some rest after what you've been through. Check back next week. We'll see where we stand then."

He leaned close as if to share another secret. "Why don't you let that fire marshal fellow see you home? See if—if there's anything he can do to speed this business along. Never hurts to have a friend on the inside."

With that he gave her fingers a final rub. Then he hurried off to find Mr. Edwards to let him know she was ready.

"All set!?" bellowed Assistant Fire Marshal Edwards above the noisy putt-putting of his motorcar.

Augusta gathered the folds of her dress and tucked them under her legs. The tufted leather bench was vibrating hard beneath her. She saw the looks of envy and curiosity on the faces of passersby. Who was that young lady sitting up there amid such splendor like a queen on her throne? Who was that important mystery woman seated behind those arched golden fenders with her elegantly dressed driver?

Mr. Edwards worked up through a number of gears until he found the proper one and released a foot pedal. The vehicle jerked forward and emitted two rapid backfires before shunting to the street on a ball of black smoke.

"You sure you want to go to your hotel?" he half-shouted to her over the rumble.

"What are you suggesting?"

"I suppose I'm looking for an excuse for a drive."

"The day has been so eventful already."

"I understand. Your hotel, it is."

"I do appreciate your kindness."

"I want you to know, that wasn't my decision. Locking down your place of business."

"No?"

"Well, that is to say, I agreed with it. It's the rules."

"I don't think anyone blamed you."

"It was strictly the fire chief's call. He works for the city."

"Don't you?"

"What? Work for the city?"

She batted her lashes and smiled.

"No. Hunh-uh," he shook his head. "I'm employed by the National Board of Fire Underwriters. Good, conservative insurance men."

"Oh."

"A business owner buys a policy with us. After that I drop in from time to time, make sure there's no fire hazards. You might say my company pays me to make sure he never has to file a claim."

"I see. ... Is this your car?"

"It's the company's. Like it?"

"It's beautiful."

"Yes. She's usually reserved for the fire marshal. When he's out, though, I get to use her."

"What happened to him?"

"Who, ma'am?"

"The fire marshal."

"Oh, kidney troubles. He had an awful pain. I'm praying they can do something for him."

She nodded and looked ahead, tired of the effort it took to speak.

"It's fun to drive," he said after a pause.

She did not answer.

"Would you care to try it?"

"No. Thank you."

"It takes some getting used to." He negotiated a turn and waved back at a friendly pedestrian. "May I ask you a personal question?"

"Yes. If I can ask you one first."

He appeared tickled. "All right."

"What did you think of Mr. Griffith?"

"That your boss?"

"Yes, he is. In a way."

"Well, I'm not certain, but I got the impression he might be an atheist."

"Really? I wouldn't know. We've never discussed his beliefs."

"I don't take it on myself to judge, mind you. A man's relationship with his maker is something he has to sort out for himself. But I could tell your Mr. Griffith is a proud man."

"Is that bad?"

He shook his head. "I will say this: I have yet to meet a nonbeliever who had not filled that void meant for love of God with pride of self."

"I'll have to think about that, Mr. Edwards."

"So, my turn to ask a question?"

She gave a coquettish grin.

"Why did you faint? Was it seeing that little man?"

"He made me think of ... something I was told."

"What were you told?"

"It's silly. ... You'll laugh."

"No, I won't."

She could read the solemn sincerity in his eyes. She knew she could take him at his word. "All right, then. ... I heard there was a ghost in the basement." She searched his face for any sign of mockery but saw none. "I told you it was silly."

"It wasn't silly to you. It didn't seem the least bit silly to you ... until you went to tell me."

"That's true."

"I guess that's a good reason to tell your worries to someone. Just to see how silly they might be. ... This you?"

Augusta was surprised to see him stop in front of her hotel.

"My, that was quick."

He disengaged the motor and pulled up hard on the hand brake, then jumped down to run around and open her door.

She saw his large hand reach for her and she held it tightly as she got her footing on the running board. "Thank you," she said.

He did not let go until she was safely back on the sidewalk. "My pleasure."

"Mr.—? I'm sorry. I've forgotten your name."

"It's E. Tyler Edwards."

"What does the E stand for?"

"Ellis, ma'am. But I don't go by that at work."

"Thank you, Ellis. You are a gentleman."

She started toward the glass doors, feeling certain he was still standing there and watching her. At the door, she stopped to glance back. He appeared flummoxed, unsure of why he had waited. Behind his bushy mustache and rosy cheeks, she thought, he was every bit as proud as Mr. Griffith. He also seemed very lonely.

"Ellis?" she called, facing him fully. "I don't imagine you would be free tomorrow?"

His whole body straightened up then and he looked rock-solid and confident all at once. "Yes, ma'am, I believe I could be."

"Maybe I could have that ride?"

"Is there someplace you'd like to see?"

She thought a second. "Paris would be nice."

He looked confused again.

"I always dreamed of driving under the Eiffel Tower."

They traded easy smiles then and his cheeks stretched to the ends of his mustache. "Well, the roads don't reach to France at present. Anything closer do?"

"As the assistant fire marshal, how far do your duties extend?"

"Up through Queens. All the way."

"And beyond that?"

He shook his head. "That's Nassau County. They have their own company there."

"Why don't we drive up to Nassau County, then, and see what makes them so choosy? Say, ten o'clock?"

"I'll be here, fueled and ready."

All she could think as she sauntered through the lobby was how different men could be. Here was a man with a responsible job, nice clothes, and good manners. He was clearly someone who took care of himself and even found satisfaction helping others. What sane woman would not take a safe, reliable man like him over a girl-chasing cad like Owen Moore?

Climbing the stairs she thought of what life with Owen would be like. There would be uncertainty, tears and suspicion. She would never be happy with a husband who drank like he did. There would be constant bickering, always teetering on the edge of another fight. He shouldn't be gambling so much, or he should inform her when he intended staying out so late. She knew how couples bickered.

As she was thinking about this, his face gathered definition in her mind. By the time she arrived at her floor she was thinking of it with tenderness. She hoped to find him waiting for her in all his handsome masculine unworthiness. It was better than thinking of him in the arms of another woman. If grief and worry were what he had to offer, better her than someone else.

She went straight to the closet to remove her coat and when she looked around she saw signs that someone had been there. A kitchen chair was pulled out from the table, and the steamer trunk sat forward farther than before.

"Hello, baby."

She gasped and her eyes snapped to a dark silhouette by the window curtain.

"How you been? … Keeping your feet clean?"

"How'd you get in?"

"I still got a friend or two." He switched on the floor lamp and the harsh light drew tiny gravestone shadows from his chin stubble. "Not everyone's forgotten about old Deward Trawley."

"I didn't forget you, Deward."

"Well, it warms my heart to hear that."

"I always knew you'd be coming back." She indicated the trunk. "See, I kept all your things safe."

"You fixed the place up nice." He released the drape and it fell back over the window. "Who's the walrus-face?"

Augusta unfastened the last of her buttons. "Just an acquaintance."

"Got himself a nice car."

"It belongs to his company."

"She's a beauty." He watched as she hung her coat on a wooden hanger. "How good an acquaintance?"

"He offered me a ride, that's all. From the studio."

"Studio, huh? I heard you left there."

"No. They gave me a job."

"So, you got old *Kain-tuck* sweet on you? Good for you."

"I'm tired. I had a tough day. All I want is to soak in a tub a while."

"It's good that you got in tight there. We'll have to think this through. How should we handle this situation?" He flopped back on the bed with a bounce. "Ah. I forgot how soft the life is here." He fluffed a pillow under his head. "Inside, I thought I had it good. Had a nice bunk, held up with strong chains. I learned to sleep sound. It beat listening to the moans of a lot of gorillas."

He closed his eyes.

"You can't stay here, Deward."

"You going to stop me?"

"People come here. All the time."

"What people?"

"From the studio. Florence Lawrence for one."

He forced a burst of air through his teeth. *"Pffft!"*

"Some other gals. ... Nina! You remember Nina. If someone sees you here, they won't trust me anymore. I won't be able to help you."

"Relax," he said. "I have no intention of stayin' here."

In the silence they heard a squeal of brakes out front. Deward instantly swung his legs off the mattress and jumped to his feet by the window. He edged back the curtain to have a peek. "Oh. It's no one," he said. The curtain swung closed.

He was more relieved than he let on.

"You expecting company?" she asked

"A couple of old associates," he said with a look of scorn. "They might have got word I was out. ... How much money you have?"

"Haven't been paid yet."

He came around the bed, slowly walking toward her.

"You mad at me, Deward?"

"What's to be mad about?"

"You might've gotten a crazy idea I had something to do with ... what happened."

"Nah. That little vacation? I appreciated that. It retaught me an old lesson. Maybe I'll return the favor some time."

She felt an old lick of indignation rising. "As far as I'm concerned, we're even. You rescued me that day at the train station. Here I was a single girl, not knowing a soul in the city. But your heart went out to me. You saw I needed you. I'm sure it never crossed your mind that I might be able to help—"

Suddenly he was on her. His big hand clutched around her throat and he began to squeeze, pushing his face into hers. "You got one second to tell me where you got your money."

"What mon—?" she gasped before her breath was choked off.

She snaked a hand behind her and felt the way across the table, fumbling for her purse. When she had a grip on it she brought it forward and held it up.

Instantly he let go of her neck to grab at the purse. He rummaged inside and finally broke into a grin. "Well, what do you know?" he said, digging out the banded stack of ten-dollar bills. "Looks like payday, to me."

"Mr. Griffith ... gave me that," she blurted between breaths. "I'm supposed ... to buy some new clothes."

"This'll get me set up in my own place."

"That's all right, Deward. You take it. Take it and go."

"Any more?"

She shook her head. "Just use that. Get yourself a place. You don't ever have to come back here ag—"

In a flash he had his hand at her throat again. "Listen to me and hear me good. We're married, you and me, understand? You get used to the idea. You're my woman and I'm your lovin' husband. Anything you get from here out, it's mine—you got that? ... So, yeah, you go and stay here for now. I got to keep my head down for now. So you're going to have to be my eyes and ears."

"Sure, Deward. What're you thinking?"

"Thinking? Jail gives a man lots of time for that. The whole acting game was never meant for me. I'm more a producer. Yeah. I should be putting out my own plays."

"That's smart, Deward. You can start fresh. Just like me."

"Don't you worry. I've already got a part in mind for you." He fanned the stack of ten-dollar bills in her face. "There's more where this came from. They keep it somewhere. There's a safe, I bet."

"No, Deward. They use vouchers."

"They got to pay those vouchers, don't they? There has to be a safe. You sure you haven't seen it?"

"How could I?"

"Well, that's first. You find out where it is." Deward was calm and thoughtful again. He paced toward the bed. "You go take your bath. Next time I come, we'll have a nice long talk. We'll think things through, just you and me." He stopped to smile at what must have been her look of dread. "Don't worry, honey. I'll never be too far away."

FIFTEEN
"The Reckoning"

Their fathers were mortal enemies, though never on the same battle-field. By now the name of Major General George McClellan had risen from the ranks of history to command a nearly mythic post.

McClellan! How many times had he heard his father say the name? On occasions when he honored visitors with his account of the war, the old colonel would slow when he got to that name, savoring the juicy repetition of those double L's. It was like giving his own private tongue-lashing to the butcher of Antietam.

Those days spent on the porch alone with his bottle found him more likely to mash the three syllables together into one dismissive expletive. It was *McCle'n*, the pitiless despoiler of Southern honor; *McCle'n*, the general who had disrespected even his own commander-in-chief.

The man had a reputation for showing arrogance to authority long before President Lincoln appointed him first commander of the Army of the Potomac. He was just 35 years old, and he had expressed his contempt for Lincoln even then. Later it was Lincoln who famously mocked him with the comment, "If the general does not want to use the army, I would like to borrow it for a time." Then, after his strategic Union victory at Antietam, he refused to send his army to cut down what remained of General Lee's routed forces. His bloodthirsty fellow officers were greatly offended, and Lincoln was forced to remove him from command and sideline him to New Jersey for the remainder of the war.

Now it was a different McClellan who held the reins of power. Only months earlier, Mayor George B. McClellan Jr. had used his power to order the closing of all the nickelodeon theaters in Manhattan. The general's son had been a political force in New York City since 1892. And it was in his hands now that resided the fate of the entire Biograph Company.

Both of their fathers had tasted disaster at the end of the Civil War. Maybe he could use that to establish a bond between them. Old General McClellan, of course, had rebuilt a career for himself in European diplomatic circles and went on to getting himself elected governor of New Jersey. Old Colonel Jacob Griffith was not so lucky. He never got over the defeat of the South, and spent the rest of his days nursing his wounds with porch hounds and whiskey.

Those old soldiers had passed away long ago now. But they could still prove useful. It was a long shot, and Griffith knew he was being naïve to even think it, but wouldn't it be too perfect if their grown sons could rise together out of the shadows of history? Wouldn't it be delicious if those ancient divisions could become his ace in the hole?

The air itself brimmed with a sense of promise this morning. Nothing made him feel more alive than this city with spring on the wind. He stopped outside his building to take in the perfume of a million opening petals. This was no morning for train fumes and crowds of coffee drinkers. He got to the corner subway gates and kept going, setting a brisk pace toward midtown.

His life had come to another crossroads. There was nothing novel in that at all. He had made a good many course corrections in his thirty-four years. This somehow, though, felt different. It was coming to a head in this appointment with the mayor.

Something had changed since just that fall—maybe in only the past few weeks. It took a six-horse fire wagon to make him recognize it, but making these little "fillums" of his had come to mean much more than he imagined.

This was not just the latest unplanned detour. Something about the motion picture business had gotten in his blood. Telling stories with moving images was the greatest challenge he ever faced, and he was getting better at it with each production. It wasn't like he could just turn away now and walk away from it.

When Linda presented her ultimatum to him he knew he could never return to being an actor or even a playwright. He was a director now.

A street corner stop brought him back to the present. He caught the eye of an older, well-dressed lady waiting there for the signal beside him. When he offered her a brief, courtly bow she puffed up in offense and turned her eyes away. That was life in the north. It was rude and it was even hostile. But there were rewards as well.

The traffic cop tooted his whistle and Griffith melted back into the throng, trying to keep in step.

Had it only been eighteen months? At the beginning he had thought of motion pictures as simple abridgments of plays. That's what the picture studios seemed to be buying. He sensed he could pick up a little grocery money that way as well. Hadn't his favorite part of playwriting always been the creating of pretty stage pictures?

He wrote out a scenario from "Tosca," complete with stage directions, breaking it into simple scenes. Then he made an appointment at Vitagraph. That had only been last fall—hardly more than a year ago. He remembered because the sidewalk was covered in brittle leaves as he made his way to Mr. Edison's studio.

It was not Mr. Edison who met him, of course. It was the esteemed and ever-so-serious Edwin Porter, whose brushy mustache gave a tell-tale twitch whenever he was about to reject a suggestion. It twitched like crazy that day. The director of "The Great Train Robbery" did not want stories taken from the stage. He wanted action tales with "rescue" scenes that could be shot in the great outdoors.

"Tell me, Mr. Griffith," he said, scanning him from the top of his slouch hat to the toes of his imported Arizona boots, "have you ever tried acting in motion pictures?"

Later he had to cringe at the bluntness of his reply: "No, sir. I hope never to fall so low."

Porter brushed aside the insult. "I have a part in mind that you could play, if you are willing. It pays five dollars for the day's work."

Next thing he knew, there he was, leaping over clumps of weeds, running toward a line of sapling trees across the field, waving his arms in dismay. A giant eagle had swooped down at his cabin and stolen his infant right from under her mother's nose! Imagine the fright! And somehow he knew that bird had taken the baby to its mountaintop nest!

Soon he was dangling from a rope on the side of a cliff. Of course, there was no cliff. That was all staged back in Porter's studio. The mountain was no more than wet paint splashed on a backdrop. He was asked to pantomime a fight with that fearsome eagle, which summed up the picture business for him at the time: tussling with a feathered papier-mâché bird under warm lights, trying not to let the camera catch you laughing.

That night he told Linda the flickers would never amount to much. The people behind the camera had no grasp of character or theme, and he didn't like the way they shouted at the actors. They didn't have the artistic training to get honest performances. They were more like lighting engineers, always trying to illuminate things in better ways.

Linda wanted him to quit then and there. She had run into some theater colleagues that afternoon, and when they heard what he was doing they fell into an awkward silence. She knew what they were thinking. There was a word for people who did degrading things for money.

Ah, yes. Money. He was not unacquainted with that old wolf at his door. It came to stalk him sooner or later. It caused a lot of the friction in those early months of their marriage. After the fiasco with his play in Washington, it had followed them back to the city and taken up residence in their hallway. So he told Linda to give it a little time. He would stay with Porter and earn enough to feed them until the new theater season came around.

But before that happened there came the first audience showing of "Rescued from an Eagle's Nest." The crowd sat riveted at what they saw. The danger, the fight, the rescue—all of it more harrowing and immediate than anything ever seen on stage. Some viewers nearly fainted when that silly paper bird came swooping down on its wires. Later everyone stomped and cheered at Griffith's blurry likeness as he wrestled the beast to its death. People yelled "Hooray!" At that moment he forgot all about the humiliation of shooting in Porter's studio.

These shadow plays were like shafts drilled down into the viewer's mind. Audiences actually experienced what they were seeing like it was real. If only a filmmaker could harness that power to depict struggles of consequence. Instead of a stuffed eagle on wires, people could be shown the real wolves and hounds that beset civilization itself.

By the time he found work at Biograph he knew what he wanted. Arthur Marvin and Billy Bitzer did not exert such tyrannical control. They valued more of a give-and-take from their actors. Even Linda felt comfortable acting there and appeared in the last of their Mutoscope productions. Later they performed together in a handful of split-reel features as they packed their suitcases for Connecticut.

But before they could throw their names in a casting hamper for summer stock, fate intervened. At the eleventh hour word came that Biograph had just lost its latest director. The Marvins liked Griffith's air of competence and his way with actors. Would he like to try his hand at directing? Linda surprised him. Why not? she asked. It's better to be a captain than a passenger in steerage, no matter what the destination. So he agreed, but only if he could go back to acting if this directing racket was not to his liking.

For his first project he stole a page from Edwin Porter. His outdoor story would also center on an abducted infant, this time, though, by gypsies. They would hide the baby in a barrel that gets washed away downriver like Moses in the bulrushes. A search party forms as the mother grows frantic with worry. That would make a fine part for his Linda. Just in the nick of time, the barrel is pulled from the river and the child is saved. He gave this tale the whimsical title "The Adventures of Dollie."

Everyone liked what he showed them, including the Marvins. But he was sure he could do better. Before long he was taking on old favorite subjects, dramatizing U.S. history and social causes like the plight of Native Americans and poor Mexican migrants.

His "Edgar Allen Poe" may have been the turning point. Here he took on a subject that truly mattered to him, the treatment of artists by capitalist society. It could have spent years or even decades as a playwright before attaining any such level of control over his work. He was truly in a leadership position as an artist now. The only thing left for him to decide was what exactly did he wish to do with that power? Oh, and one other thing: Would he survive in the business long enough to do anything at all?

From the iron gate of a small corner park he could see New York's City Hall stretching out before him. It was magnificent, more imposing than ever because he had important business there.

Other buildings crowded close and vied for attention, but this one held the block with somber authority. He knew all its darker history, of course. That stone edifice which united fluted Greek columns and French windows beneath a colonial dome—it was also a symbol of bloody division. For over half a century it had stood facing the South as a taunting reminder of Union tyranny.

In 1861, a jubilant Abraham Lincoln had been honored there upon being elected president. Four years later a funeral train brought his corpse back to lie in state in the rotunda. New Yorkers filed past his coffin for two solid days, paying their respects before another train came to take him on his final journey to Springfield.

Lincoln had always been a great man to him. But his damned war—it never seemed to end. Forty-four years after Appomattox it was still exacting its measures of flesh. The fires of bitterness continued to burn in both camps, and if no one managed to put them out, the old passions might yet flare taller than ever, and this time they would bring America down with them.

The despised label "secessionist" and the scornful whisper of "sesesh traitor" were still heard far and wide at election time. No doubt even this young Mayor McClellan had felt the words "damned Yankee" fired at his back at least once for every vote he ever won.

Griffith pushed through the heavy glass doors and stopped to admire the grand rotunda. Its towering dome rose like a serpent over the wide, coiled slabs of marble. On both sides of the staircase was a rabbits' warren of polished hallways with dark, oil-rubbed doors and alcoves cradling the busts of noble thinkers.

The receptionist sat at a foyer table under the armed protection of a uniformed policeman. He recognized the blue woolen cloth and severe cut of the man's coat. It was not so distant a cousin of the ones once worn by government troops at Gettysburg and Shiloh.

"I have an appointment to see Mayor McClellan," he informed the freckle-handed man at the table.

The receptionist consulted his clipboard. "Your name?"

"Lawrence Griffith."

"Yes, sir. If you will wait one minute, sir."

Footsteps echoed down the hall and soon a young man appeared in a neat black business suit and tie. "Mr. Griffith? John McNamara. Pleased to meet you. The mayor is expecting you. Follow me, please."

They passed a series of closed doors in a long corridor hung with oil portraits. There was Alexander Hamilton and old Lieutenant General Ulysses S. Grant. Grant's body had also lain in state once in the rotunda. The procession of likenesses continued, all Northern heroes posed solemnly in their dress blues and chests crowded with ribbons. There was President James A. Garfield in all his wild-haired military glory. Griffith glanced quickly to read the names of those he did not recognize. Major General George Crook ... Major General James B. MacPherson ... Each set of eyes glowered back at him through the ages as he trod deeper behind enemy lines.

The assistant came to a stop before a thick wood door inset with a panel of frosted glass. Inside a male secretary rose to meet him and excused himself before returning to usher him to an inner office.

After passing all those whiskered, oppressive faces in the hall, Griffith was relieved to find a more friendly face waiting at his desk to greet him. He was clean-shaven and dressed in a black suit with a wing-tipped collar and a striped tie as flouncy as any gentleman's cravat. Though he looked every one of his forty-three years, he seemed both spry and collegial as he stepped around to offer his hand.

"Mr. *Griffin*."

"It is Griffith, sir. Do not apologize. Very nice to meet you. I thank you for seeing me."

"Please, have a seat. Can I have something brought to you? Coffee, perhaps?"

"No, thank you."

Whatever Griffith had expected of the ninety-third mayor of New York City, this was not it. He was far more handsome than the illustrations of his father in the history books. It was said that his features favored more those of his mother.

The mayor dismissed the secretary with a wave and settled back at his desk to scan down a typed page of notes. "I am trying to understand the facts that bring you here today. You are employed by the American Mutoscope and Biograph Company?"

"We go by the name American Biograph these days. Or just the Biograph Company."

"Indeed. And what is it you do there, exactly?"

"I'm a picture man. I make motion pictures."

"Ah, yes. Motion pictures."

"Yes, your honor."

McClellan winced slightly. "Please, I am not a judge. You can call me mayor. Better yet, call me George, as long as we're alone here. ... Says here your studio is on East 14th Street?"

"It is, yes."

"I know that area well. I lived on East 17th before I went to Congress. Had to uproot the whole family and move to Washington then. It was not easy on them."

Griffith fought to hold his smile. Leave it to a politician to remind you of all his great personal sacrifices.

"I also lived in D.C. for a time. They were producing my play there."

"Tell me, would I know any of your motion pictures?"

"You mean my own pictures, or the Biograph's?"

"Well, I couldn't tell one from another. 'The Great Train Robbery,' for instance. That was a good one. Was that yours?"

"No. That was from Mr. Edison's studio. Directed by a man named Porter. I have worked for him."

"Well, I enjoyed that one. Chasing down train robbers. On horseback. Quite a lark."

"Hard to believe, but that picture is already a half-dozen years old."

"Really?" McClellan reached out for a felt-lined humidor. "Well, I'm sure I've missed a lot of good ones." He opened the lid and offered a cigar to Griffith.

"No, thanks," he said, pulling a shiny tin case from his coat pocket. "I'll stick with my cigarettes."

"I smoke way too many of these," said the mayor. "At least, that's what Mrs. McClellan tells me." He picked out a fat one and began the rote process of rolling it between his palms before snipping the end.

Griffith lit a cigarette and held out his burning match to the tip of McClellan's cigar.

"Thank you. ... Of course, when I was a younger man, before I entered politics, I would hang around the arcades. They had those peep-show machines then."

"You can still find them around."

"I remember being taken with this one show in particular. It took place in a sultan's harem. All those harem girls, and big bare-chested guards with broad swords ..."

"Scimitars."

"Yes! And the girls lounging around on rugs between potted palms. All at once there's the sultan, coming through the drapes ... well, it was quite an eye-opener to a young fellow. Believe me. Made me wonder how I could get to be a sultan."

Griffith smiled. He decided not to point out that the mayor's office was large and rich enough for any Far East ruler. "Biograph has been working to raise the standards of our pictures."

"Oh?" said the mayor, his eyes betraying a glint of mischief. "Too bad."

They shared a quiet chuckle as both men took another draw on their tobacco.

There was a glass case over the bookshelves and inside it hung a polished military sword dangling on a braided yellow cord. Griffith wondered if it could be General McClellan's, perhaps even one he wore to his meetings with Lincoln. It was too soon to mention any of that.

"I just wanted you to know," the mayor went on between puffs, "I'm no prude. I'm a man of the world. Like yourself."

"That's why I was hoping to see you. I wanted to ask for your help in resolving … this problem."

McClellan paused and relaxed back in his chair before releasing his smoke. "I'll tell you straight off, I don't like getting dragged into business matters. Companies need to look after themselves. You know what happened with the Doull Ordinance?"

He had to stop and think a moment. He remembered it had something to do with the influx of immigrants and the old "blue laws" that prevented shop owners from doing business on Sundays. A politician by the name of "Little" Tim Sullivan had made a name for himself arguing that immigrants often only had Sundays as their day of leisure and deserved special considerations. The Doull Ordinance carved out exceptions to the blue laws, allowing the operation of certain small-staffed businesses, such as the German and Yiddish theaters, the Opera houses, ball parks and nickelodeons.

"Doull was good for everyone," said Griffith. "Immigrants are big supporters of the five-cent theaters."

McClellan nodded and then thought better of it. "Lots of my constituents would like the old laws back. Some even say Doull itself was the work of Lucifer."

"That's ridiculous."

"Maybe. But I am told there's nothing Satan loves better than seeing the nickelodeons opened on Sundays, filling up people's heads with lewd and unholy thoughts."

"No one could believe such talk."

"Many do. Decent folks, like Reverend Parkhurst. A real fighter, but a Christian gentleman. Others see it as an election issue. They hire lawyers and advocates, rile up certain self-righteous groups. Like these temperance people."

"Yes. They're the ones that got us closed."

"Did they now?" McClellan reached for his report again and read quietly a moment. "The fire commissioner filed an affidavit. It says a citation was issued by, um … the fire chief … Chief Mullendore." He looked up at Griffith. "Mullendore? Was he German?"

"I don't know. The man I met was Irish, I think. O'Brien."

"That's the fire captain." He looked again at his papers. "Oh, I see, it was Fire Chief Mullendore that ordered the closing."

"But there was no fire. Doesn't it say that?"

"No fire?"

"It was a false alarm."

"Oh, yes. Says right here: No fire detected."

"We think it was done out of spite. Someone wanted us shut down."

"I see. But the report indicates safety violations."

"Yes. We've already attended to those. We are eager to have the inspectors out so we can get back to business."

McClellan tapped the long ash off the end of his cigar. "These days, no one can afford any … mistakes. When it comes to public safety, a mayor is expected to act."

"Of course."

"Do you know our fire ladders do not even reach the top floors of these buildings nowadays? I'll tell you, modern cities are tinderboxes. There was a big fire down in Baltimore. 1904, not long after I was sworn in. Mayor down there had the devil to pay. Destroyed the whole downtown. And we have the same types of districts here. Manufacturing set right among the tenements. Tailors, tanners, shirtwaist factories." McClellan took another long draw on his cigar, watching the smoke curls in the air.

"That must be enough to keep a mayor awake at night."

"You have no idea. That license matter, last Christmas. The nickelodeons. *The Times* loved raking me over the coals for that one. 'The McClellan Massacre,' they called it. It's not like I have some vendetta against leisure entertainments. Mrs. McClellan and I, we love theater and museums and concerts of all kinds. These nickelodeons are popular right now. But many of them are set up in spaces not designed to handle crowds. I was being deluged with complaints, threats of legal suits, editorials on the fire risks. So, I made the rounds, maybe a dozen different theaters. And what I found … no emergency exits … no fire buckets or alarms … they were death traps. I couldn't in good conscience go away for the holiday without doing something. Could I? But I can tell you, none of the papers wrote about that."

"Mr. Mayor, we're on the same side here."

"Are we?"

"The safety hazards cited in that report concerned our wardrobe department. We've since moved it to the basement, posted 'no smoking' signs. We've done everything asked of us."

"Well, then, there should be no problem. You will pass inspection and be cleared to reopen."

"But we're told it could still take weeks, even a month. In my line it could be fatal. We would never catch up with the competition. Our business could close, our constitutional right to free speech taken away—all because of a false alarm set off by these protest groups."

McClellan took another long drag. "You sure about that?"

"What?"

"According to this, there was a phone call placed, giving your address. Report says it came from inside your building."

He could not believe what he heard. "I don't see how that's possible. Our only telephones are in private offices. Strangers have no access to them."

"Nevertheless." He looked again at his typed note. "Call was placed at 10:38 a.m. from 11 East 14th Street. That's *your* address, is it not?"

Griffith nodded.

"Could there be an enemy within?"

"I can't think of—who would do such a thing."

"Maybe someone afraid of something? Or someone seeking your attention? Whatever the case, this isn't anything for me anymore." Mayor McClellan rose to signal that the appointment was done, and started around the desk. "I'd like to help you, Mr. Griffith. I'm just not sure what the mayor's office can do."

Griffith rose to take McClellan's outstretched hand, knowing his purpose for coming was ending in failure. Oh, well, nothing left to lose, he thought. He might as well play his trump card now.

Griffith nodded to the sword in the glass case. "I have to ask you, sir. I've been admiring that sword. Was it your father's by any chance?"

"Yes. Yes, it was."

"May I have a closer look?"

McClellan gave a bow of consent.

The sword had a thin, slightly curved blade and was mounted

against bunting. Griffith bent close to read the engraving. "From the 112th. ... Would that be the Ohio militia?"

"Are you a student of the Civil War?"

"I know some. Mostly what I learned from my father."

"Oh?"

"Maybe you've heard of him? Colonel Jacob Wark Griffith."

"Sorry, can't say I have. Where did he serve?"

"He commanded the First Regiment of the Kentucky cavalry."

The mayor nodded. "Was he wounded?"

"Five times. Two serious. Once at Hewey's Bridge, then again at Charleston. They say he was too hurt to ride a horse. So he commandeered a farmer's horse and buggy and he led the charge in that. His men dubbed him *Roaring Jake*."

"They were a hearty breed, those men."

"I'd like to make a big picture out of it all some day. About the war, and what it meant to them."

"That's one I'd love to see."

The mayor led his visitor to the office door.

Griffith felt his last hope flicker and die. This was where it would end, then. "I'm sorry to bother you with this. It must seem a trivial matter, with all you have on your mind."

"It comes with the job."

"I guess I would not have come except—there are so many depending on me."

"Of course."

"I do hate to let down—the troops." He smiled sheepishly at the allusion.

McClellan opened the door for him and stopped. "Are you a student of President Lincoln as well?" he asked.

Griffith hesitated. McClellan's father had once snubbed Lincoln, leaving him waiting over an hour in his parlor and then going off to bed without a word to him. Lincoln had been a Republican and an abolitionist, while the mayor's father was a northern Democrat who saw a compromise on the issue of slavery as the only way to preserve the Union.

It would be unwise for him now to come out on a different side from the mayor. But, after all, he *was* asked his opinion. "Yes, I am very much an admirer of the Great Emancipator," he said.

The mayor nodded his approval. "Then perhaps you will remember what he said in regards to leadership?"

"Not at the moment."

"He said, 'Nearly all men can stand adversity, but if you want to test a man's character, give him power.'"

The mayor held out his hand. "I want to thank you for coming to me with your concerns, Mr. *Griffin*. I have a strong feeling that your studio's future is in capable hands. I will ask my German fire chief to look into your case again at his earliest opportunity. My best wishes for your future success, sir. And a good day to you."

SIXTEEN

"The Call of the Wild"

Borowski was late. Mack Sennett didn't know why, but that didn't matter. Griffith hated it when his schedule got thrown off, especially when there wasn't a damn good reason for it. So if Mack didn't know a damn good reason, he had better think of one and fast.

No matter what happened now the blame would be his. He was the one who enlisted Borowski and then vouched for him. It would all be his fault if that camera wasn't grinding soon.

The set—a bedroom in a mountain cabin—looked great and was as complex as any set they ever built at East 14th Street. A big window at the back gave the space definition, especially when its long white curtain was billowing in the breeze, courtesy of Nina's floor fan. Billy said the spatial sense was important because he would be working with low lighting. At center stage sat a double bed with a yellow bedspread, its headboard against an angled wall with an entry door that faced an open walk-in closet across from it.

Mack checked his watch. Quarter to nine. The sun had been up nearly two hours and Griffith had been pacing for a good deal of it. That meant it was time to see about borrowing the office telephone again.

Nine-fifteen now.

Mack had seen happier faces in a divorce court. Even actors with nothing important to do all day but relax were starting to twitch.

Nine thirty-five.

Griffith was over there in the dark, hopping around lightly from foot to foot, landing his punches on another invisible opponent. He stopped to check the production clock again. Then he looked at Mack across the stage, nailed him with one quick scowl. The look sent him reeling like an uppercut to his sense of security.

"I just called over there again, Mr. Griffith," he hollered.

"What in the Lord's good name could be holding him up?" All those within earshot knew the director was officially out of patience.

He didn't evoke the Lord's name unless he had reached a boil. Everyone on the set expected to see foam soon.

"I was told he had left. He can't be much longer."

"Mack, come over here, please. I want to hear that story again."

Mack felt like he had told it a half dozen times already. Griffith always gave it his full attention, listening intently as if trying to picture it clearly in his mind. Mack's secret fear was that he was still trying to figure out what was supposed to be funny about it.

"The couple—a husband and wife—this couple is having a row at bedtime. The wife caught him speaking with a young woman from another cabin. She's been nagging him about it ever since."

"How do we know that?"

"I'll write a title card."

"Something amusing?"

"Of course."

"Very well. Go on."

"The man tries to make peace, you know, snuggling up and such. But wifey will have none of it. She tosses him a pillow and says he should go sleep on the couch. So out he goes, like a chastened pet dog, and she turns the key in the lock behind him."

"All right. I've got that. Go on."

"Now wifey lights a candle next to the bed and switches off the lights. But she doesn't look mad anymore. She smiles like she's doing something naughty—you know, some mischief. She goes to the window and opens it up wide, pokes her head out, looking for something, then goes to her vanity. She splashes perfume water on her neck, telling us in the audience she is getting ready to receive her lover."

"How do we know that?"

"Another title card."

"Something funny?"

"Of course."

Griffith nodded. "Keep going."

"She pulls the ribbon on her—what's that thing they wear?"

"Her sheer nightgown?"

"Right. *That.* And then she heads for the closet to take it off. When she's out of the room this big gust of wind blows through. We see the curtain rise straight out, and there goes the candle flame. Now it's dark. The light from the closet falls across the bed. And next we see this big hairy body climbing in the window. It's our bear."

"But not you?"

"No, no. This is the real deal. We need to see it's real, moving, you know, like a bear. It goes straight over and climbs into the bed."

"Can we get it to do that?"

"This is a trained animal. Best one in vaudeville. A real trooper. Anyway, that's really all we need it for. Maybe get a clear shot of it growling or something, looking dangerous. That's what makes it funny."

"Why is that?"

"Because it's scary. People are saying to themselves, Wow, what if that scary beast came in my room?"

"And that's funny?"

"Of course. That and the reactions of the actors."

"Which are what?"

"Nothing yet. They haven't seen it. They don't know it's in the bed."

"Oh."

"So, next, the boyfriend comes climbing through the window."

"Wait," said Griffith. "Let's get the others in on this. ... Bobby! Where's Bobby?"

Bobby Harron came sliding down the sides of a tall ladder without touching a single step. "Right here, Griff!"

"Get me Mr. Cumpson and Miss Arvidson and Mr. Johnson, if you would."

"Sure thing." He ran off calling out the actors' names.

"Mr. Bitzer, have you been hearing all this?"

"Yes, Mr. *Griffitt*," said the cameraman. "Lots of darkness, and then the candle blows, too."

"Correct."

"And when no one sees nothing," deadpanned Bitzer, "Mr. Sennett can tell them on a title card what they're not seeing."

John Cumpson and Arthur Johnson strolled in from the shadows, followed momentarily by Linda Arvidson in a flowing white robe over a silk-paneled negligee.

Griffith signaled for Mack to continue.

"Okay, so the bear is in the bed and there at the window appears the boyfriend."

"That is you, Mr. Johnson," said the director with a nod to the leading man.

"Where am I now?" asked the portly John Cumpson.

"You have been banished to the couch in the next room."

"I have a question," said Arthur Johnson. "Do I really have to climb through the window?"

"Darn right," snapped Mack.

"Yes, you do," said Griffith.

"But I'll be in that heavy winter coat."

"Will that be a problem for you, Mr. Johnson?"

"Well, no. I'll work on it. It should be okay."

"Good," said the director.

"So lover boy sees this shape in the bed," continued Mack. "He goes to investigate but—suddenly there's a knock on the door. It's the husband, complaining that it's cold out on the couch. He wants another blanket. He tries the doorknob and finds it's locked. But Mr. Johnson doesn't know that."

"I don't?"

"No. How could you know it's locked?"

"So I go and open the door?"

"No. You're not supposed to be there."

"Like the bear?"

"Yes. So you panic and duck under the bed."

"Why do I do that?"

"Because you don't want to be seen."

"Don't worry, he won't be," grumbled Billy Bitzer.

Mack turned to the actress. "Now, Miss Arvidson—"

"Yes?" It was the first time she showed any interest in Mack's story.

"You come out of the closet in your nightgown, carrying a spare blanket, and you unlock the door and throw the blanket in your husband's face. Then you slam the door and lock it again."

"I am very angry with him?"

"No," said Mack. "But you are pretending to be."

"I get it. But why am I pretending?"

"You are clearing the way so you can be alone with Mr. Johnson."

"And I'm hiding under the bed," interjected Johnson.

"Yes, you are," said Griffith.

Linda looked confused. "Wouldn't it be more believable if the husband were the one having the affair?"

Mack moaned in exasperation. "I'm sorry. Was that me?"

Johnson appeared wounded. "I'm not climbing into any bed with Mr. Cumpson."

"No," said Mack. "It's always funnier when it's the man who is the cuckold."

"Is that what's funny about it?" asked Griffith. "Thank you for that. So, what happens next?"

"Well, Miss Arvidson turns and sees the shape under the sheets and smiles. She thinks it's her lover."

"Who is still under the bed," threw out Johnson.

"This is what worries me," said Griffith. "She is willing to sleep with this man who is not her husband?"

"Well, yes, that's the story," said Mack.

"I don't know, Mr. Sennett. This is not the way you told it originally. We talked about the husband climbing into bed with the bear."

"But it's funnier if it's the wife. It's her comeuppance for being unfaithful, see? She's getting her just desserts. That's how the audience will see it."

"I think it would be better if the husband got what he deserves," said Linda Arvidson.

"The husband didn't do anything wrong," argued Mack.

"I agree there," said Griffith.

Linda Arvidson grew huffy and withdrew, adding as an afterthought, "He *was* flirting with that woman."

"What woman?" asked Cumpson.

"The woman from the other cabin."

"Let's let Mr. Sennett tell us the rest of his story, shall we?" said the director.

"Right. Remember, this is a comedy. So wifey—Miss Arvidson— she slips into bed and starts cozying up to the body there until she sees it's a bear. She gives a scream and passes out, but her scream alerts the husband. He leaps off the couch and breaks down the door just in time to see the bear disappear out the window. He runs and grabs up his rifle from the closet, takes aim at the window and fires."

"What about me?" asked Arthur Johnson. "Am I still hiding under the bed?"

"That's the payoff, Arthur," said Mack. "You're the topper. When Mr. Cumpson fires his rifle, you jump out from under the bed, in fear for your life. And you go racing out the broken door. See how it all works?"

"Well, it's not the story we agreed on," said Griffith.

"It'll get roars. Belly laughs. Trust me," said Mack.

"I think I agree with Mr. Griffith," said Linda. "Adultery is not a fit subject for comedy."

"Well, the Greeks thought it was fit," replied Mack. "I'm told the French do, too."

The actress would have none of it. "Don't you think audiences in this century want something more sophisticated from their artists?"

"I must say I am concerned about the moral aspect," said Griffith. "I was just telling the mayor how we're elevating standards around here. Now what if he should see this?"

"Didn't you ever go see Weber and Fields?" asked Mack.

"In vaudeville?"

"Yes. That's the sort of comedy this is. It's not meant to be taken serious."

"I see Mack's point," said Arthur Johnson. "I think it might score a bull's-eye with audiences."

The discussion suddenly erupted into a free-for-all, with each actor determined to voice an opinion and shouting to be heard above the rest. In the midst of the melee, little Bobby landed with a thud at the center of the group as if hurled from a catapult.

"Hey, hey, everybody!" he yelled, causing one and all to stop talking and look at him. "There's a guy outside with a bear."

Mack wanted to squeal with delight at the news. "Mr. Borowski!" he exclaimed, glad for any excuse to escape from this madness.

It was indeed the man with the bear—a large rounded ball of black fur lying on its side and directing all its energies toward rotating its huge head around in a slow, continuous orbit inside a muzzle.

"Please excuse my extreme idiocy," said Borowski, who did not seem tall enough to have such a deep Russian accent. "I ask for a horse trailer, but it no arrive, and no arrive some more. It is in use elsewhere by the horses. Oh, well, this cannot be helped. Then I talk with a man with a truck for the catching of dogs."

Borowski had a flat face—a very Russian trait, thought Mack. Every Russian he had ever met had a face as flat as a dish and, likely as not, just as round. "A dog catcher?"

"Yes, is so. This truck have a big cage, too. But this opening is very, very small. For dogs."

"Because he's a dog catcher."

"Exactly. As you say. There is no way to get my Pavlovna in through that infinitesimal door."

He held up a golden chain and for the first time Mack noticed the beast was on a leash attached to the back of its muzzle. Mack wished he had seen the look on the picket ladies' faces when Borowski arrived and led his pet up the front steps. "That's a beautiful animal. Very big. … You sure she's safe?"

"Oh, yes, so safe. Very gentle, even fine for children to play."

"That's good, because we got a studio full of children right now," said Mack.

The Russian's flat face clouded with anxiety. "Listen, you promise Borowski you pay all expenses."

"Yes, within reason. I told you. Biograph will reimburse you."

"Okay. Because I must pay more for this truck."

"What did you wind up with?"

"Lucky for me, I know a man in the shop very next door. He has truck for business. He is very understanding. But we must agree on price. I say this, he says that. In the end, Borowski gets fair price."

"Good. What sort of truck?"

"My friend, he provide transportation … for the churches."

Mack struggled to understand. "Transportation?"

"For services, how you say? The big wagon with the back door open very wide. For drive to cemetery."

"A hearse?"

"Yes. That is the word. A hearse. My Pavlovna steps up, one, two three. She is inside, ready to be in the motion pictures. Am I very late?"

"No, Mr. Borowski. You would not believe how just in time you are," said Mack. "Let's go meet the kids."

Borowski gave a small yank on the chain and Pavlovna rolled once like a very large dog and was up on its massive paws. As the trainer tugged at his chain the great furred beast ambled ahead balancing its weight on what appeared to be four unfamiliar stilts.

Mack threw open the studio doors. "Everybody! Come meet Borowski and Pavlovna!"

Bobby let out a slow whistle and came running up for a closer look. The others held back, not entirely sure they shared his enthusiasm. Griffith approached with an excess of caution, followed by the others with various mixtures of curiosity and terror.

"Good morning. I am Lawrence Griffith, the director."

"Borowski."

"You are the bear's trainer?"

"And owner, yes."

"What is its name?"

"Pavlovna."

"How long have you and … Pavlovna been together?"

"Oh, two—no, three months now."

Griffith bit his lower lip but did not lose his smile as he tried to conceal his alarm from the others. "I see. Three months," he repeated, shooting a meaningful glance to Mack Sennett.

"I refuse to go anywhere near that thing," declared John Cumpson.

"She's a very gentle animal," Mack assured him.

"You won't have to go near it, Mr. Cumpson," said Griffith.

"Her," corrected Borowski, all at once a stickler for English grammar.

"I don't mind saying that I for one am deathly afraid of wild beasts," added Cumpson by way of explanation.

Griffith still sought to allay his fears. "We're merely using it for the entrance through the window."

"Using *her*," corrected Linda Arvidson.

"What?" asked Griffith.

"Pavlovna. She is … a she. I for one find it comforting having another lady on the set."

Cumpson continued to shake his head, speaking with an air of giving notice. "I don't think my agent would approve of this at all, not without some sort of hazard pay."

"No hazards, Mr. Cumpson," said Griffith. "Once we establish it as a bear, we will be finished with it. *Her*. Mack will then get in his rented bear costume and it will be his body in the bed after that. I trust there will be no bodily risk to either you or to Miss Arvidson. … Mack?"

"Yes, sir?"

"Why not go get dressed up so everyone can see there's no danger?"

"Sure. Right away," he said, and hurried off to locate Nina in the new wardrobe shop. On his way down he heard Linda Arvidson informing everyone on the proper way to approach a trained bear. She spoke to Pavlovna in a calming voice and edged ever closer to reach out and hug the animal's thick neck.

That was the last thing Mack saw. By the time he was properly situated inside his bear suit and Nina had him zipped in, a loud thumping was heard from up in the studio. It was quickly followed by screams and the sounds of a scuffle. Mack hurried up the steps as fast as possible on the leather pads of his paws. His wooden claws scraped against the handrail.

Through his eyeholes he saw Linda Arvidson sitting off by herself on the floor. She might have been sobbing but he didn't have time to check now. Across from her stood Borowski, yelling and struggling with his bear to let go of the terrified John Cumpson. Stagehands gathered timidly at the edges of the wrestling match as Pavlovna inched her forearms up around the rotund actor's frame.

All at once her muzzle became dislodged and dangled to one side. Her powerful jaws opened to reveal rows of gleaming, pointed fangs, and she let loose a gut-quaking roar that must have been bottled up for months.

GRR-RRLL!! ripped the air.

"Call her off!" screamed Griffith. "Pavlovna, down!" he commanded in his most stentorian stage delivery. "Borowski, do something."

Without stopping to think, Mack charged straight at the bear. To Pavlovna he could only have looked like a marauding rival, and her instinct was to guard her catch. Mack felt the powerful swipe of her paw and for a moment all he knew was that he was sliding somewhere across the floor and spinning on his belly.

When he slowed to a stop he struggled to swing around and look. Pavlovna had Cumpson in a limp heap across one paw. She let his body drop and gave out another fierce growl of defiance.

And then Mack watched Pavlovna spring up and charge straight for him.

She was on him in a few angry leaps. All he could do was flail about inside his suit, trying to break free of the animal's vicelike grip.

He felt a great clamping pressure on his upper arm and heard the canvas costume ripping somewhere below his shoulder. The enraged roars came at him louder than a Canadian thunderstorm, and just as he began to feel woozy and on the verge of passing out there came one sharp crack that ricocheted for an eternity off the dark inner walls.

The growls halted at once, and Mack felt a heavy weight fall across his lower body. It was all he could do to squirm backward and try to pull his legs out from under the crushing load.

He reached up to straighten his mask and when he got the eyeholes in place the first thing he saw was Borowski panting. His long coat stood opened to reveal an empty leather holster. His right arm was raised straight before him and it ended in the smoking metal barrel of a revolver.

"Holy Mother," said Griffith from somewhere off to the side, out of sight. "Is everyone all right?"

Mack looked down at the perfectly still body of the bear. Its mouth was open and its tongue was splayed across the floor like an uncooked salmon filet.

"You're hurt!" said Linda, which sounded more than reasonable to him at that moment. He tried to get a look at his arm and all he saw was a small amount of blood glistening near the gash in his sleeve.

Griffith had been checking on John Cumpson, who appeared stunned but unharmed. Now he was on his feet coming closer. He pointed to two of the immobilized stagehands. "Mr. Forrest, Mr. Alfreds, could you both please guard the doors and make sure no one gets in?" Then he was standing over Mack and Linda, shaking his head at the sight of the motionless carcass.

"Mr. Thomacello," he called to another passing stagehand. "Kindly fetch a tarp and cover the body."

"Yes, sir."

Griffith bent closer to Mack. "Are you hurt?"

"His arm's a little chewed up," said Linda Arvidson.

"Anything else?"

"I don't think so," said Mack. "It was so loud, I couldn't hear what he was doing."

They eased the bear mask off his head. The first thing he looked for was the Russian. Borowski was sitting off by himself on an upturned barrel, resting his forehead on his fingertips.

"Can you stand?"

"Not sure."

Griffith called for Arthur Johnson to help him and they got Mack up on his feet. He stopped to survey the scene. "Listen to me, everyone," he said. "Mr. Marvin must never know what happened here. Are we all agreed on that point?"

Mack stepped back to let the stagehands spread a tarp over the body of the beast. For that moment it dominated the room with an awful stillness. "Just looks like she's sleeping," he murmured.

Then the tall doors exploded and peeled back against the studio walls and in stomped Arthur Marvin. "Mr. Griffith! Now what's going on? What was that bang? I thought it was a backfire. They said it came from in here."

"There's nothing to worry about. An experiment went a little haywire. That's all."

"Sounded like a rifle shot."

"No, no. A set piece dropped. We're handling it."

The studio owner's eyes shifted to the mysterious bulge in the tarp at the center of the floor. His features relaxed, almost as if he decided it was better not to know. Then he spotted Mack. "Is that blood?"

Mack smiled and held up his arm. "Just a flesh wound. Nothing serious, Mr. Marvin."

"How'd it happen?"

Mack looked helplessly to Griffith.

"I think he's in a bit of shock," said the director.

"Mack? I asked what happened to you."

"Well, sir, I didn't want to say but—Miss Arvidson bit me."

Arthur Marvin looked at Griffith in amazement.

Griffith looked at Linda Arvidson and nodded. "Yes," he said soberly. "She bit him. Quite hard."

Arthur Marvin could not have appeared more bewildered. He looked back to Mack. "She bit you?"

Mack cast his eyes around the floor, letting his bottom lip quiver a bit as if he could make no sense at all out of what he was asked.

"Don't worry yourself, sir," said Griffith.

Mack gave a series of rapid nods. "She barely broke the skin."

"We have it under control."

Arthur Marvin failed again to comprehend the matter. "But—but why did she bite him?"

"It's never easy to know why these things happen," offered Griffith. "What do you think it was, Mack? Why did Miss Arvidson bite you?"

"I think," said Mack, "well, it could have been ... because I put my arm in her mouth."

"See," said Griffith, trying to force a smile. "Clears everything up. No mystery about it. Now, why don't you leave us so we can—"

"Why did the man have his arm in her mouth?" demanded the owner.

"It was to—to keep her from screaming."

"Why would she scream?"

"My guess is ..." began Mack, turning to Griffith and then to anyone else for help. He finally gave up when he could think no more. "... maybe she's afraid of bears?"

Griffith sighed, seeing that the game was up.

"Bears?" repeated Arthur Marvin with an uncertain chuckle. "That's balderdash. Where would she see a bear?"

Griffith bent and lifted one corner of the tarp, peeling it back with no further comment.

Arthur Marvin had not had a second to process it all when a stagehand came dashing through the studio door. "Psst!" he said in a stage whisper loud enough for all to hear. "It's the picket ladies! They want to speak with the owner."

"Tell them not now!" barked Arthur Marvin.

"It's all right," said Griffith. "I should see what they want. ... Mr. Johnson, would you kindly get a couple of the hands to bring around a stretcher and help our friend Borowski here remove his ... belongings?"

Borowski had not paid any attention to what was going on until he heard his name. Now he stood up straight and his jowls shook with indignation. "Mr. Griffith, I demand to be reimbursed for *theece*, my losses, everything!"

Griffith pivoted at the tall doors to take a few steps back toward the angry Russian. "Borowski, you brought a dangerous, wild animal into this studio and discharged a firearm. You will be lucky if Mr. Marvin does not decide to sue you for reckless endangerment. Pack up all your things at once and get out. You had better be gone when I return or I will be forced to notify the police."

With that, Griffith tugged at his suit jacket, straightened his tie, and pushed through the doors. To Mack he struck just the right dignified gait and posture for a Christian setting out on his date with lions.

Nina arrived with a first aid kit to attend to his wounds. He asked her to be quick as he didn't want to miss what was going on. She fashioned a large bandage and tied a sling of gauze around his neck so he could hurry on his way.

Griffith stood at the far front of the foyer, listening and nodding to his private lecture from three of the temperance ladies. From the doors Mack could only make out a phrase here and there. But it was enough to know they were informing the director they were calling an end to the boycott.

"Watch it, Mack," hollered a voice behind him. Two scruffy stage-hands stood holding the poles to a heavy stretcher. On top of it was a large, rounded heap covered by a black tarp. The stretcher hurried past, followed by the sullen flat face of the great Borowski.

Mack fell in line behind them, savoring the bewilderment of the temperance gals at the sight of such an odd procession. As if by divine will, just as the stretcher drew close to them a hairy, clawed arm dropped from under the tarp and went scraping along the marble floor all the way out the door.

This was turning into Mack's happiest day in years. Despite the pain of his wound, he could not keep from smiling. He stopped on the landing to watch the stretcher-bearers struggle to get their load down the steps to the waiting funeral car.

On the sidewalk the ladies stopped their collecting of banners and signs to watch the stretcher raised into the rear of the hearse. A few shook their heads as if to say they would never understand these motion picture folks.

Mack waited for Borowski to crank up his motor and climb into the driver's seat. The Russian stuck out a tiny hand and twisted his head for a last glance up. Mack gave him a wave of farewell and the hearse rattled and spat as it rolled off down the street.

One of the older brigade workers broke from the group to march up the steps and push past Mack without a look. He pegged her as possibly the senior leader of the whole shebang. When his curiosity overcame his sense of decorum he followed quietly inside.

Griffith had his back to him and did not see him enter. He was giving his full attention to this stately league officer as she delivered what seemed to be a prepared speech.

"We may no longer be a presence here, Mr. *Griffin*," she was saying, "but we are not abandoning our struggle."

"It is Griffith, Mrs. Kendall," he gently reminded her.

"We all recognize that books and plays have a place in society and influence a certain stratum. But these little windows you open on the world reach the broadest masses. We pray you appreciate that, and what a position of responsibility that places you in. Civilization hangs in the balance. What you produce will infect society with either good or evil."

"I do appreciate that," said the director.

"We shall keep an eye on you. We are dedicated to ensuring that this powerful medium of yours does not merely pander to uncouth instincts. It must never appeal to the appetites of the weak and defective—the braggarts and show-offs and those terminally depressed. We will remain vigilant for the sake of the future."

"Thank you, Mrs. Kendall," said Griffith. "The best of luck to you."

"Good day to you, *Mr. Griffin*," she responded with a pasted-on smile. Then the woman swiveled sharply and brushed past Mack again in her hurry out the door.

It was then that Griffith saw Mack there, standing with his arm dangling in Nina's makeshift sling.

Mack gave him a victory grin. "The picket line's gone," he said.

"Yes, I know. For now."

"Was it something we did?"

"I'm not sure. The front office did arrange a preview for them of 'Drunkard's Reformation.' They evidently liked it."

"That's good news."

"Is it? They want to sponsor showings all across the country. Part of their campaign, I take it."

"For what?"

"National prohibition."

"Oh." Mack moved closer, knowing he would have to think about that. "What was she talking about there at the end—about the future of civilization?"

Griffith glanced away momentarily before his thin lips formed a Puckish grin that Mack suspected might haunt him till his dying day. "Oh, that. She apparently wanted to warn me ... about people like you."

# PART III

SEVENTEEN
"The Lure of the Gown"

Throughout the long weekend Augusta listened closely to all the comings and goings on her floor. It wasn't until Sunday evening that she heard telltale movements at the end of the hall and peeked out in time to see her neighbor disappear in the washroom with her toiletries in hand.

Smart dresses and fresh modern outfits—that's what Griffith expected from her when she showed up for work in the morning. But Deward had taken all the money and left her with nothing, and she had been wracking her brain all week over what to do about it. Finally in the middle of the night on Friday her eyes popped open when she remembered the woman down the hall.

It only took a minute or so of chitchat with the pimple-faced bellboy to learn the woman's name. It was Gloria. From what she could tell, Gloria had been playing the most competitive game there was for a gal on her own in the big city. And she evidently excelled at it. It meant she had a good deal of money invested in keeping ahead of her competition. And the topper was that Gloria and she were about the same height and shared the same understated bust line.

She imagined whole steamer trunks and armoires bursting at their hinges from the weight of her wonderful apparel. All that was left for her to do was work up the courage to go and see for herself.

She gave it some time before scampering down the carpet to room 322, then took a deep breath and rapped twice on the door.

It cracked open a bit and a browless, bloodshot eye blinked out at her.

"Hi. Remember me? I live in three-ten?"

"*Shu-wah*," said Gloria. "What's the matter, sweetie? Lose your pussycat?"

"No. I mean, I don't have a cat."

The woman pulled back the door. "In that case, come on in."

Augusta could hardly believe this was part of the same hotel. There was color everywhere, broken up only by an intricately carved wooden screen or fans of peacock feathers sticking from floor vases. In place of her drab chintz curtains were windows trimmed in ecstatic bolts of red and yellow fabric. Each sofa pillow sparkled with rich Oriental thread, and the coffee table was covered in crystal orbs and small ivory figurines of ballerinas and prancing harlequins.

"Don't be shy, sweetie. Enter, enter," said Gloria.

"This is all so gorgeous," said Augusta, twirling to take it in. "I can't begin to imagine where you found so many wondrous things."

"Southern girl, hunh?" said Gloria matter-of-factly. "Well, we all have to start somewhere." She closed the door and was instantly hurrying away with her butterfly print kimono snapping at her heels. In a moment she returned holding out a bottle-nosed decanter and two stemmed glasses. "Wine?"

Augusta smiled. "Sounds perfect."

"*Parle-tu francais?*" she asked as she poured the glasses.

"No. But I've been to New Orleans many times. It was always one of my favorite cities."

"It's the only true American city," said Gloria, offering out a glass. "It decayed long before it was *au courant*." She raised her wine slightly in a silent toast then took a sip and folded gracefully onto the couch. "So what brings you to this little lily pad?"

She let Augusta prattle on a while about herself and her futile attempts at finding a job in the city. As she listened she opened a small wooden box on the table and brought out a rolled cigarette that fit nicely into the brass end of a glossy ebony holder.

Augusta knew it was no use avoiding her purpose any longer. "So, now I have this employer, and tomorrow will be my first day on the job."

"You were hired a week ago. But you're only starting tomorrow?"

"Well, they had the office closed down for a time. I mean, the fire department did. It was something to do with safety codes."

Gloria held a wooden match to her cigarette and took a puff. "You should have come to me. I know our firefighters." She shook out the match. "I'm a volunteer there in my spare time. Just like Mrs. Colt."

Augusta nodded and let it pass. She could not begin to picture the woman hanging from the side of a fire truck. "Anyway, it's settled now. And I so want to make a good impression my first day. I was hoping for some fashion advice. You New York girls are so much smarter about clothes and things."

"Bite your tongue, honey. I only know what I like. I adore the *fauvists* at present. André Derain is inspiration itself. And *cubism*. I hate complacency in art, don't you? The world has enough brown horses. Let's have some purple ones with filigree wings. And I have the biggest swoon on Jack Johnson—you know, the heavyweight champ? I think he's a great, sweaty dream. So please don't lump me with your New York gals."

Augusta was feeling totally lost. She had no idea what Gloria had just said, or even whether or not the woman was sane. All she could think was that she might have messed up her one chance with the only person who could solve her problem. She took a long sip before speaking again.

"I truly did not mean to offend you. I do apologize if I did. I was only seeking your opinion ... about what I should wear?"

Gloria let out a cloud of smoke and wiggled her holder as she gave Augusta's blue shift a long look. "Not that," she said finally.

"Oh, no, no. This would never do. I agree. Mr. Griffith said it must be something respectable but fun, maybe unexpected. Demure, but with a touch of the theatrical."

Now it was Gloria who appeared lost. "What kind of joint is this? I thought you said it was an office job."

As soon as she heard the words motion pictures, Gloria's eyes widened. She adored films, she announced, especially the magical ones by someone named Méliès, and she always loved stopping by at the arcade peep shows.

"You want to see why I keep this dump?" she asked, leaping up to take Augusta by the hand. "Come on."

At the very back of the sitting room was an unassuming door that Augusta expected to lead to guest quarters. Instead she found herself looking down a long walk-in storage pantry converted into a closet. Both sides were crammed to the end with racks of dresses two levels high, with row after row of shoes wedged underneath them. There were woven baskets on shelves filled with wraps and belts and fanciful headgear of every description.

Augusta had struck pay dirt.

"I originally came to this berg to be a showgirl," said Gloria. "All the producers I met had so much power and influence, right? Just not enough to get me anywhere. Anyway, that was a long time ago, so long ago I can't even remember."

The wine was getting to Augusta but she estimated Gloria to be no more than thirty-two or thirty-three. That meant she had packed a lot of forgetting into just a few years. In any case she could still pass for youthful, especially among her wealthier clientele. A few deep wrinkles at her neck and some popped veins on the back of her hands were all that gave away her age—not that she was too concerned about keeping things hidden. As she breezed through the racks of dresses her kimono parted and two whisper-smooth breasts took to the air from her fields of butterflies.

"Now, conservative businessmen such as your Mr. Griffith," she was saying, "they want the lady they are with to appear respectable. But you got to give 'em a splash of exuberance somewhere—a choker, maybe." To illustrate, she held a felt black ribbon to her neck, lifting her sculpted jawbone towards the ceiling with a pouty insouciance. "See? You got to give 'em a clue that other men don't even notice. But it lets your gentleman friend know that tonight you are his."

Augusta was feeling light-headed, and leaned against the doorway to let her body sink slowly to the thick carpet. "And other men don't notice?" she asked.

Gloria shrugged. "Men never notice much of anything, sweetie. All they look at is cigarette girls' fannies and whose hand is reaching for the check." She waved a sheer nightclub gown on its hanger so that Augusta could watch it shimmer.

"Do you have something maybe more innocent?"

"I've got a girly take on Gilbert and Sullivan. You want theatrical. ... Let's see." She pulled out a powder blue uniform with a strong nautical motif. It was cut to mimic a Victorian sailor's suit, with ankle-length pants and a billowy blouse with a blue slipknot neckerchief.

"Oh, I love that!"

"There's a sailor's hat to go with it. With a long red ribbon. I can find it if you like."

"I could do a whole series. Fun with the military!"

"You're welcome to try it on. I bet it'd look a sensation on that slim figure of yours."

Augusta rose halfway before growing dizzy again. She propped herself against the wall with a groan.

"Are you okay, dearie? You look pale."

"I'm not used to wine."

"You want a glass of water?"

"No, I'm better now. Funny, I never fainted in my entire life until I came to New York. I guess it's the northern climate."

Gloria went back to her browsing. "I know what you mean. I fainted a few times when I first got here. Then again, I was pregnant."

"Oh."

Gloria turned to her with stone-faced concern. "Have you seen anybody?"

"It's nothing like that. ... You have a child?"

She wagged her head. "False alarm. But remember, if you find out different—I know a woman who knows a woman who knows a doctor."

"I'm just overtired. I haven't been sleeping well lately. With all the excitement."

"Well, I can relieve some of your worry. How about I loan you a few outfits, just to get you going?"

"That is so incredibly sweet. I can't begin to tell you."

"Your service idea—I think it's adorable. I have riding jodhpurs, trim at the waist with puffy legs. There's a lovely woman's vest in a sort of russet brown. You could go for a cavalry look. Leather boots. A riding crop."

"I love it!"

"I have a female version of a Rough Rider's hat somewhere."

"Sounds too wonderful."

"We could pull together a soldier's tunic, as well, maybe add some braids."

"Standing watch over America in the new century!"

Gloria clapped her hands and they gave themselves over to giddiness. By the time Augusta gave her host a quick hug and headed down the hall she was carrying so many bags and hangers that she clattered along like a skeleton.

She cleared out space in her closet and as she sorted her bounty she absently started to hum an old tune from the river days. She was so preoccupied with wardrobe plans that she dismissed a faint metallic click at her doorknob. But it was quickly followed by a loud swish on the rug and Augusta spun about with the dread certainty of what she would see.

"Deward. I declare. … You're out so late."

He closed the door gently. "I came around earlier. Where were you?"

"Out. Visiting a friend."

He nodded as he pocketed the key, then loosened his tie with a finger. "What was that little tune you were humming?"

"Something from the river."

"Catchy. … You been shopping?"

"How could I go shopping, Deward? You took my money."

"So, where'd it come from? Boosted it, hunh?"

"No. A neighbor lady was kind enough to lend me a few things. I'm starting my new job tomorrow."

Deward slipped off his coat and went to hang it on the back of a kitchen chair. "Which neighbor?"

"Don't get yourself too comfortable," she said. "I'm about to turn in."

"What's the neighbor's name?"

"Gloria, if you must know. She was—"

"Not old Gloria!" Deward's face became a mask of unbounded delight. "Down the hall?" He gave a whoop and rocked back on his heels. "Well if that—" He stopped abruptly to stare at her. "You do know she's a whore?"

"Oh, Deward."

He laughed a bit more and shook his head. "The way you were going on, I thought a real lady had moved into this dump."

"Why should I even care what she does?"

"You don't care 'cause she had something you wanted." He laughed again. "That's rich. So, it's work clothes, is it?"

"That's right."

"What did you tell her?"

"I told her thank you."

"So she knows about you now. Where you live, where you work." Deward frowned and scratched his nose. "I thought you were smarter than that. She can finger you. She'll tell it's you by what you're wearing."

"I really don't have time for this, Deward."

He shifted his mouth around a bit while his brain whirred. "What did you find out for me—about that safe?"

"Safe?" Augusta paused, watching as he turned to pace. She sensed danger all at once. He was unpredictable when he got in a mood. All she wanted was for him to stay calm and leave. "Yes. I found out. He's got a safe. It's in his office. All right? It's in the wall behind a painting."

"His office, hunh? Tumbler or key?"

"Tumbler."

"You get the combination?"

"Of course not, Deward. What was I supposed to say? 'Excuse me, could you show me the combination?'" She had to stop herself. The wine was making it difficult to hold her tongue.

"That's first, then. You got to get that for me. Otherwise, things are going to get … messy." He gave her a challenging grin. "Does old *Kain-tuck* know about Owen?"

"Who?"

"Don't give me that. I heard about you two. He was all but moved in here for a time. Or did you forget that? Your new employer might be interested in the truth about his little missy sweet-britches."

Augusta pushed aside her fear as a flicker of temper swept over her. "You know, Deward, you're just bound and determined to make life harder on everyone." She forced herself to turn back to the closet and finish her reorganizing. "First you take all my clothes money," she sputtered as she shifted some hangers. "Did you leave me even a single dollar? No. Not you. What was I supposed to do? Wait for you to bring back my change?" She straightened a wrinkled seam and reached to close the door. "A girl could grow ancient sitting around waiting for that to—"

Deward was standing in the space behind the door, glowering at her with an icy fix to his eyes. His face moved closer until their noses almost touched. "I'm never going back to prison, you hear me?"

She caught a strong whiff of brandy and alarm bells began to sound. "Sure. No more prison. You're free now, Deward."

"Don't even think about crossing me again."

"What are you so worked up over? I said I'd help, didn't I? It's just right now, this new job's important to me. I got to be presentable, don't I? I mean, that's what you want, for me to fit in good there."

He backed off a bit and Augusta decided to try a firmer stance. "Look, Deward, why don't you sit and relax? Just be a good little boy and you go have a seat while I—"

In a flash his powerful fingers were clamped around her throat. He squeezed and pressed in tight with his thumb, forcing her head back sharply and cutting off her air pipe. She fought to pry his fingers loose but the room began to spin and grow darker. At the black fringes of her vision lightning bolts flashed, leaving a blood-red grid that blocked out everything. She felt an arm snake around behind her and heard the trunk scraping on the floor. He was bearing down on her body now, forcing her spine deeper into the open steamer.

"No! Deward!" she said with a last desperate struggle for air. "Stop! Stop it! Don't!"

She felt herself suffocating, sinking back into the stacks of old shirts and pants. Suddenly he relented and his grip on her loosened. He drew back as she struggled to sit up, coughing and hacking for air. She raised a hand before her, as if ready to fend off another attack.

But Deward had already slunk away like a wounded forest animal. He was sitting on his haunches back near the door, darting anxious looks around the room as if to spot whatever unseen power had taken hold of him.

Finally he gave a long whistle of pent up steam, and he settled his back on the wall and kicked out his legs in front of him. When he spoke, it was not to her at all. It was more like he was addressing himself. "Whew. Okay. Everything's fine. No real harm done."

Augusta eased herself off of the trunk and lowered herself down, scooting back to put more floor between them. She rotated her shoulders and then her neck, trying to determine if any serious damage had been done. After a while she stared at him with more pity than anger. "What happened, Deward?"

"I can't stand that—being talked to like that."

"Like what?"

"Your tone! Like I'm a little boy or something. My mother used to use that tone. It drives me nuts. Just never do it again, understand?"

"Sure. Okay, Deward. Sheesh."

His control was visibly returning to him in stages. Finally he shook his head and pushed himself up on his feet. "I got to get out of here," he said.

He collected his coat from the chair and took it to the vanity mirror. He slipped up the knot of his tie and ran his fingers through his tousled hair, then wiggled one arm after the other into his coat sleeves. "You get me that combination, you hear?" he said, smoothing out the collar. "You want to save yourself and Griffith and everyone a whole mess of pain ... you do what I say."

"How do you suggest I get it?"

"You're smart. You'll think of something. Nine times out of ten, a guy jots down numbers like that, in case he forgets. Get into his office and look around. Check the desk blotter, open ledgers, anything. There's got to be an address book. He's sure to have written it somewhere."

Deward stopped at the door and turned to her as if with a final thought.

"Yes?" she said, just wanting him to be gone.

He summoned an encouraging smile and pantomimed holding out a gun at her in his fist, dropping his thumb like a hammer and giving her a wink. "And, uh, good luck with your new job."

EIGHTEEN
"The Deception"

Judging by the way Griffith's eyes darted up and down her body when she arrived in her new outfit the next morning, Augusta was sure she had made the right decision.

He hurried to help her out of her heavy coat and then stepped back to admire how the tidy sailor suit accented every trim contour of her frame. "My dear," he said, "you look enchanting."

"Not too girlish?"

"That's its charm. Yes, it respects tradition but with a youthful zest. I think you've hit on something."

"I'm so relieved." She was suddenly aware that the whole studio had stopped to listen to them. "When you have a minute, maybe we can talk in private?"

"I have time now," he said, tossing her coat over his stool. "Everyone—ten minutes," he called, and nodded her toward the exit. "Let's go in my office."

As they walked he told her about his meeting with the head of advertising, a Mr. Drew, and how they had both wished to involve Nina in the wardrobe decisions. "But I'm sure they'll think this is a marvelous start."

"I was thinking of a whole line, perhaps. Biograph's girl-next-door does her duty."

"A patriotic theme? I like it."

Once inside his office Augusta went to the couch and waited for the door to close before beginning. "Mr. Griffith, may I speak frankly?"

"Always be frank with me, my dear. Have a seat."

She perched on the edge of the cushion and straightened both seams of her blue seaman's slacks. "Last night, I was so excited to start, I couldn't sleep. But then I had different thoughts. I began to worry."

Griffith pulled up a chair and sat facing her. "Is it about working … with me?"

"No, no. You've been very nice to me."

"You can say so, you know."

"No. This is solely to do with me. It's my own problem."

"You have second thoughts?"

"I do have, well, trepidations … about my qualifications."

"Come on. Out with it."

"It's just that the last thing I want is for you—you or the studio—to suffer if—that is, if it should come out that … I am not everything you advertise me to be."

"My dear, you are sweetness itself. You needn't worry over silly gossip."

"But we must. I mean, don't we?"

"If this is about Mr. Trawley—"

"Not entirely."

"Because you cannot be blamed for his character flaws, or for his crimes."

"It's more than that. … You may not know, but—I've secretly been seeing Owen Moore."

Griffith settled back a bit in his chair. "I see. No, no one told me about that."

"I assure you, it's over now."

"It is?"

"Yes. But we both know … how men talk."

"They do indeed."

"And the truth is, most men do not want … I mean, they prefer … their candy *unwrapped*, if you get my meaning."

"I know more of this old world than you may think, Miss Lee. Any artist's work must somehow reflect on the truth. And truth has a great many faces. It's not for us to say how others will judge us."

"Yes, Mr. Griffith, but as far as—"

"Audiences continually crave fresh examples of virtue and self-sac-rifice. Very few of us, though, can measure up one hundred percent to our ideals. Still, nobility lies quietly at the bottom of the mountain stream, glittering and shiny, calling out to us. Mankind's soul—"

"I'm not … so pure."

Griffith stopped abruptly and sat for a second at a loss. "Well. Miss Lee," he said slowly, "you have been frank with me, let me be the same. We men will always be attracted to candy. If it is sweet, we will want it—whether it is wrapped or unwrapped. Is that clear enough?"

"Yes."

"It's not half so crucial what a woman has done as the image she presents. It's how she feels about herself that matters. ... I hope that helps."

"Yes. Enormously. You have set my mind at ease. Thank you."

"So one question does remain to be discussed—brunette or blonde? I take it you still prefer not wearing a wig?"

"Yes, sir. No wig."

"All right," he said, taking both of her hands in his. "So Biograph's notion of fresh, unspoiled womanhood shall have all-American chestnut hair with a golden sparkle. She will walk in a haze of openness with a heart too pure to broach deceit or withhold a kindness." He leaned over to give her a kiss, but she turned at the last moment and his lips glanced lightly off her cheek.

She looked down as if to hide a blush and sensed him shifting to shake off the rebuff. It was time for her to turn to the other front. "Um, Mr. Griffith, about our poster series."

"Yes, my dear?"

"The little shop where I found this suit, they had something else I thought might be perfect. It was a riding vest with tailored breeches gathered below the calves. It all has a sort of cavalry look."

"Can you find this shop again?"

"Yes, I'm sure I can—"

"Then what's the problem?"

"Well, with this and the other things I found, I am over my budget. And it was a little bit expensive, and of course I would need boots and perhaps a riding crop."

"Say no more," he said, rising to go behind his desk. He swung the painting out from the wall. "How much will you need?"

She got to her feet and drifted casually closer. "It was somewhere ... let me think. It had a price tag of eighteen dollars. The boots are quite expensive, what with the price of leather now."

Augusta bent near to watch the tumbler spin in his hand. He slowed the knob to a halt when the engraved arrow pointed to the number fifty-four. Then with a quick spin to the right he brought the tumbler back around to number six.

He was slowly rotating it back to the left when a knock came behind them. The birdlike head of the receptionist darted in through the door. "Excuse me, Mr. Griffith," she said. "There's a gentleman here."

"Tell him to wait, please."

"He's not asking to see you, sir. He's asking for Miss Lee."

Griffith looked around at her. "Are you expecting anyone?"

"No," said Augusta. "Not a soul."

"Well, you go on," he said.

"Don't you think he'll wait?"

"Go on. I'll find you when I'm ready."

There was nothing she could do. Whoever was asking for her had just ruined her chance to get the combination. She was not in a forgiving mood as she went out to meet her caller.

She instantly recognized the stout figure standing by the front door. Assistant Fire Marshal Ellis Edwards was again quite nattily dressed in his chestnut-colored overcoat and dark suit and tie. She had barely given him a passing thought since their drive to Queens. It had all been pleasant enough and he was never less than a gentleman. But it became painfully clear they had little in common and she was in no position to make any more of it. So she had come away expecting never to hear from him again.

Now he waited with hat in hand, only breaking into a wide smile when he saw her coming. It surprised her to find how quickly her annoyance melted away. It was lovely to feel special to someone again.

"Mr. Edwards. How nice to see you."

"I had a little company business nearby," he said. "I hoped to find you here."

She offered him her hands but his eyes were now fixed entirely on her outfit. A frown appeared on his thick brow.

"Is something wrong?"

"No, ma'am. It's only—that suit."

"What is it? Don't you like it?"

"Oh, it's not that. It just took me back, is all. Puts me in mind of my time in the U.S. Navy."

"Why, Ellis, I didn't know you were a navy man."

"I don't talk about it much. I joined up at seventeen, you see. I guess it must have been back in '87. I was assigned to the USS *Newark*, the last American cruiser with a full mast."

"How interesting."

"Yes, ma'am."

"You should be proud."

"Yes, ma'am."

"I would love to hear about it some day. I am a little pressed for time—"

"I'll be quick. That's sort of what brings me here now. The truth is, that day ... the day of our drive up to Queens."

"Yes. Are you still driving around in that shiny automobile?"

"Yes, ma'am. I even stopped by here once or twice, after the building got reopened. They said they didn't know when you might return. I started to get worried."

"How sweet. Imagine worrying about me with all the important things on your mind."

"No, ma'am. I mean, it wasn't any trouble. I was worried because ... well, that day of our drive, I was so intent on safety and on my steering—keeping you from harm—well, I didn't say even half the things I should have. ... Where to start?""

"Well, you might have mentioned your service to our country."

"I did a lot of thinking about it later and, well, I hope you did not get the wrong impression." His nose twitched and he reached up quickly to smooth out the tips of his mustache.

"In what way?"

"Well, about my job, for one thing. I told you, didn't I, that I work for an insurance underwriter?"

"Yes. You said that."

"Passed my fifteen-year mark last December."

"I'm sure they know what a valuable employee they have."

"They do. I just didn't want you to think I'm in any way beholden to the crooks at Tammany Hall."

"I would never think that."

"There are other things I didn't mention. Like I'm a God-fearing Episcopalian. And a Republican. I like to go fishing and I enjoy dancing, when my flat feet cooperate."

Augusta held her smile but warning bells were sounding on every front. Why did he come here to tell her this? Was it all leading where it seemed to be headed? Just what impression had she given him that he could be anything other than a casual acquaintance? She had to interrupt him before he went any further and said anything to embarrass them both. "Well, it has been very nice seeing you again, Mr. Edw—"

"Because I have formed a very high regard for you, Miss Lee. Even in the short time I've known you, I can tell that you are a lady. I sincerely hope you appreciate, too, that I am a man of some character."

"Yes, I do," she muttered. It was hard for her not to see him still as her tower of strength after the basement incident. The kindness he showed by offering to take her home was heartfelt and touching. But there was no way on God's green Earth she could begin to fit some sort of courtship into the current mess of her life.

"Ever since you smiled at me and suggested that you and I should drive off to see Paris together—well, life has been very difficult for me. Alone, I mean."

She heard his voice go on but now it was in the distance. Her mind was spinning away from him, going off on its own tangents. There was an appeal in his boyish sincerity. He was asking her not to take him for anything other than what he was. He seemed very set on that. The promise of such a bedrock to life came over her like an elixir. Clearly she had to navigate with caution.

The fact that he valued his reputation and good name meant he had standards as well when it came to other people. And it was flattering to know he extended his trust to her. It was touching to think he might be ready to give even more of himself to her, but the thought horrified her.

Even putting aside matters of personal taste, a courtship right now was out of the question. How could she invite him into her life with Deward Trawley on the loose? The thought of those two crossing paths frightened her. Deward would predictably act as if he owned her. That was just who he was. And Ellis would almost certainly step forward to defend her honor. Sooner or later it would have to come to blows. Scrappy little Deward would pull out brass knuckles or resort to a hidden knife, though even then he wouldn't stand much chance. In the end his sense of ownership would be ground to dust under the might of the righteous Mr. Edwards.

And if Ellis did prevail, then what? His life would be ruined. Street fighting and manslaughter? His good name would be lost forever. He might even have to live years in prison. And it would all have happened because of some selfish choice made by her.

No, no matter how brave and responsible he might be, she could not do Mr. Edwards such a grave disservice.

When his voice returned to her again he appeared to be leading into his main point. "I am thirty-eight years old, Miss Lee. For the first time I am considering what it would mean to have ... someone in my life ... one single person to share it with, who depended on what I have to provide."

She realized she had been frowning and worked quickly to construct a smile. "Why, Mr. Edwards, I happen to know everyone from here to the borough of Queens depends on you each and every single day."

"No, ma'am. Not in the way I am speaking of. So, the truth is I would like to ask you one very important question."

"This is hardly the time for surveys," she joked. She moved away, treading the choppy waters around him, forcing him to follow her with his eyes as she threw panicky glances all around. "We must make a date for lunch very soon. I would like that."

"No, ma'am. I cannot wait on this. I won't have any peace at all until I get this matter settled. If I should—that is, if you would—"

If she did not come up with an excuse instantly she would be forced to lash out at the man, punish him for placing her in this position. It would be cruel, but at least it would be ended.

There was a loud crack at the rear of the foyer and the doors from the studio parted slightly. Out from the darkness slipped Owen Moore, no doubt about to sneak off for his first round of drinks of the day.

"Oh, Owen," she called out ecstatically, raising her arm. She hurried to him and grabbed him by the lapels with the desperation of a drowning victim. "There you are! I've been waiting and waiting."

Owen betrayed only a fleeting tinge of surprise. "Well, good morning, Augusta," he said, enfolding her in his arms and playing along. "I must have lost track of the time."

"Owen, darling, *please*. There's someone I would so like you to meet!" She looped her arm through his and rushed him across the marble. "Mr. Edwards is the sweetest man. I told you about him. He's the one who rescued me that day in the basement."

"Oh, the fire chief fellow."

"Assistant fire marshal," corrected Ellis, reaching out a mitt-sized palm.

Owen grabbed it and gave it a vigorous shake.

"Mr. Edwards, this is Owen Moore, a very respected actor and a leading man at this studio. And as of just a day or so ago ... *my fiancé.*"

Both men appeared to shrink a bit at her announcement. Owen, of course, was vastly better at hiding his feelings. He grinned and gave the burly stranger's hand a few additional hearty pumps.

Ellis Edwards stood stunned, finally rallying for a sportsmanlike nod. "Congratulations on your engagement," he said. "I wish you both all the happiness on Earth."

With nothing left to say, the well-dressed businessman pulled his hat on his head, muttered something about an inspection waiting, and made a fast exit out the door.

Owen waited a few beats before speaking. "Looks like your fireman just got his flame doused."

"I'm sorry. I couldn't warn you. I couldn't bear to let him make a fool of himself. Thank you for going along."

"I pride myself on never missing my cues. How about we go some-place to celebrate the new year?"

"It's only April."

"Not by my calendar."

"I would, Owen, but I can't leave now. I'm working today."

"Oh, I heard. Congratulations are in order, indeed. I always thought you could be a virgin if you put your mind to it."

"Don't be mean."

"It's a wonderful break for you. Steady pay, maybe a bonus at holi-days. I should take you up on that part you offered me."

"Part?"

"Fiancé. ... I could come by later tonight."

"No. It's not a good idea."

"Tomorrow, then. After work. Dinner and a drink?"

"Oh, Miss Lee," called Griffith at his office door. "If you're done with Mr. Moore, let's go and meet with Mr. Drew."

"Yes, sir," she answered, pushing Owen's hand away. "I'm ready."

"Tomorrow?" he whispered.

She smiled but said nothing before hurrying away.

All through that day's meetings with Biograph staff and execu-tives, Augusta could not shake the wounded eyes of Ellis Edwards. As soon as she would decide again that she had done the kindest thing for him his eyes would flash before her and her heart would ache.

So what if he was a bit oafish and would be absolutely no fun at parties? He would make someone a wonderful husband. It was just that he deserved someone better than her. He would get over this, just as she would certainly get over the sense he left her of feeling undeserving.

Oddly enough, that was one thing Owen never made her feel at all.

She took refuge in her new job and spent more and more time at Biograph as the week passed. It was great fun working with Nina and trying out the new outfits they came up with for her. By midweek she began some posing sessions with the studio's wisecracking still photographer, Tommy Janssen, a Swede with apparently no use for women at all.

Owen was not cast in any of Biograph's films at present, and he made no effort to stop around to see her. What had happened to her own self-respect, she wondered, if she took a cad like Owen as the best she could hope for?

Late Wednesday afternoon Mack invited her to dinner and to go with him to a Union Square showing of "Trying to Get Arrested." She had no real interest in seeing how the project had turned out, but Mack was persuasive. He met her outside her hotel and from there it was a short walk to the restaurant and the nickelodeon.

She worried that the sight of Rambo's and the Palisades would dredge up nasty feelings. But as the light from the projector cast a bright splotch at the center of the screen, it was all Augusta could do to keep her mind on the picture.

Friday would be her first payday. That meant she could expect Deward "Clang-Clang" Trawley to be dropping around again. He would be hungry for the lion's share of her salary, and that would leave her broke and feeling helpless.

How could she get rid of him? It was obvious her life would not get any better until he was out of the picture. There had to be a way. She managed it once, at least for a time. What she needed was an angle, a weakness of his she could bend to her advantage. He had mentioned old partners, and seemed to be afraid of them. Was there any way to find out where they were and get word to them?

For that matter, what exactly was Deward's legal status? Were there conditions on his release? Had all charges been dropped or was he merely out on bail? He would never tell her the truth, but maybe she could find out. His fear of the law was still a useful tool. If he threatened her again she could remind him how no judge would show mercy to an ex-jailbird who went around abusing respectable ladies with a job.

It made her smile to picture Deward stopping in and catching her in bed with Owen. It pleased her to think of those two fighting over her. They were more evenly matched and fully capable of resorting to their own underhanded tactics. She couldn't say who would win, but then again it wouldn't greatly matter.

No, this was really just between Deward and her. Owen should not get involved. She had brought this on herself and it was up to her to see it through. What would be so bad if she just stood up to him and let him go ahead and murder her?

Deward did not come at all on Friday, even after she spent the whole night expecting him at the door. She finally drifted to sleep thinking something must have come along and made him change his plans.

Then Owen showed up out of the blue on Saturday and asked to take her to lunch. She felt comfortable being with him again. Neither of them expected too much from the relationship anymore. When they parted, however, she worried a little about growing too fond again of her wild Irish lover.

By nine o'clock on Sunday evening the hotel was quiet except for an occasional passing car. Augusta shut her book and had just turned out the lamp when she heard a creaking in the hall and then a key twisting in her lock.

Deward stood silhouetted by the hall light, fumbling to extract his key.

"Deward!" She turned on the table lamp and reached for her robe.

"Ah, it's Mrs. Trawley," he slurred. He had been drinking and seemed a bit giddy. "You needn't have waited up."

"I didn't."

"Well, maybe you should have."

"Are you drunk?"

"Shh-hh." He freed his key and closed the door, then found his way to the kitchen table and plopped down on a chair. "Aren't you happy to see me?"

"I'll be happy to see the end of you."

"Aw, don't say such things. You remember, I'm your own darlin' husband?"

"You got any papers to prove that? Something that'll stand up *in court*?" She made sure to emphasize the last words.

"Maybe. I just might have some papers here somewhere." He patted his pockets before stopping to look at her. "How's that job?"

"Good. They like me."

"This your purse?" He picked it off the chair and opened the clasp.

"Leave me some this time," she said.

He pulled out a wad of paper bills and peeled off a top fiver to toss on the table. He grinned at her as he stuck the rest in his pocket.

"Fine," she said.

"Now, wifey, I've got to ask you a delicate question. Are you seeing another man?"

"No."

"Careful, now. I've got my spies."

"Why don't you call 'em to come take you home?"

"Okay. No more pleasantries. There's work to do. What did you find out?"

"About what?"

"Do we have to go through this again?" He smirked and shoved his right hand inside his lapel. "I told you once." He pulled out a folded manila envelope and slapped it down on the table. "I own you lock, stock and barrel."

"What is that?"

He drummed his fingers on the envelope. "My ownership papers."

"You get one of your shady friends to make up a phony marriage license? Is that it?"

He shook his head. "Better." He gave a superior grin and relaxed back in his seat. "That's a license that'll stand up to any judge or jury."

Augusta slipped her arms through her sleeves and slid off the bed. "What are you talking about?" In a few quick strides she was reaching out for the envelope.

SLAM! Down went his palm hard against the table. "Not so fast. I want to tell a little story first. It begins after our talk the other day. You know, you made me start to question your motivation. You said you wanted to help me, but I didn't feel it. And I had to ask myself, Why should she? She's got a good set-up here, good job, people to vouch for her. What about Deward Trawley? What has he got? Who's on his side?

"Then I remembered that tune you were humming. Where did I know it from? I thought and thought and finally it come to me."

"I was just making it up."

"No. It was something I heard in prison. An old cellblock buddy across the way—he'd play it on his harmonica at night."

"That's crazy."

Deward went back to drumming his fingertips on the envelope, speaking in rhythmic bursts. "One day I asked. 'What do ya call that?' He said 'It's a little romantic ballad. A piece called *Moonlight on the Monongahek*.'" Deward stopped his drumming to smile at her.

"You're bluffing."

"Am I? Jail's a sort of shadow world, you know? Everything going on outside those bars casts sad little shadows inside. One guy sees this, another sees something different. But in time you get the picture. This buddy, see, he did some time once with a fellow down south. Ever hear of a colored man name of Billy 'the Lamb' Jefferson? No? Well, he was putting out he used to be a stevedore on the riverboats."

"I remember him. Doesn't surprise me the least where he ended up."

"This fellow knew every crooked small-town player and dockside huckster on both sides of the river. He knew a guy doing a stretch for nothing more than taking pictures. At least, that's how he told it."

Augusta straightened up. "I don't believe you."

"Pretty pictures, he said they were. Nature studies. Flower vases. Maybe a few *dirty feet*. Anyway, after our last meeting I placed a call down there to someone who might know this Bill Jefferson. I let him know I'd sure like to see them pictures. I told him it'd be worth a hundred bucks to me. That's a goodly amount down south."

"Are you blackmailing me, Deward? Is that what you're saying?"

"I'm not saying a thing. Don't need to. These pictures are worth a thousand words. Want a peek?" He opened the clasp and slid out a half-dozen or so folded photographic prints, fanning them out just wide enough to show a portion of each.

Augusta recognized the surroundings, the backdrops, and her own naked body on a bed.

"I don't know what plans your Mr. Griffith has for you. But I don't imagine Arthur Marvin or his brother would be happy about these. Tell me I've got it wrong."

"What do you want, Deward?"

"What about that combination?"

"I got the first two numbers."

"Well, it's a start. Some guys could work with that."

"Good."

"But I'm not one of them guys. Time's running thin. We got to move ahead now. Next Thursday night there'll be the biggest payroll ever, from what I hear. That night, you'll get me inside. I'll lay low until everyone's gone. When it's just me and *Kain-tuck* alone, the rest'll be easy."

"How you going to get him to open the safe?"

"He'll do it. I'll sneak up behind him and throw a sack over his head. Then he either gives me the combination or—." Deward shrugged.

"What'll you do to him?"

"I saw a guy blind a racehorse once. Couple of quick slits. *Whtt whtt!* No noise. That's all it'll take to get him to—"

"That's horrible! How can you think such a thing? Mr. Griffith's an artist. He couldn't make moving pictures if he can't see."

"Don't go soft on me now. I won't kill him. Besides, blind men make lousy witnesses. Leaves a lot of room for juries to have a reasonable doubt."

"No one deserves something like that done to him, not on purpose."

"You put me away in a rat hole. That was on purpose. Did I deserve that? Why should *Kain-tuck* go on seeing the world and not me? ... You want to make it easier on him, get me those numbers. Otherwise, I'll take matters in my own hands."

Augusta returned to the bed and sat down drained of all will. Those photographs would get her fired quicker than the click of a shutter. They might set off a scandal that could reach who knew where? Something like that would shock the public. It would prove that motion pictures were hotbeds of lust and sin, and it would embolden censors throughout the land.

"All right, Deward," she said in a fallen seed of a voice that planted itself in the stillness. "Give me some time. I'll get what you want, one way or the other."

NINETEEN
"A Fool's Revenge"

Mack's arm would pound with pain from time to time and he was not the type to suffer in silence. By now the entire company had learned it was best just to avoid him.

A newer actor, though, might unintentionally cross him and face the brunt of his Irish temper. Inevitably the man would back off, mumbling something like, "Jeez, what's wrong with Sennett?" to which the favorite response became, "They killed his bear so now he's got to growl for two."

The mauling not only soured Mack's disposition, it played holy hell with his sense of proportions. The more his wound throbbed, the bigger the bear became.

One day after the dust settled Borowski came looking for his lost revolver. A green employee named Alfred was sent to help him scour the studio, and somewhere in the search Alfred told him an actor had nearly died there recently from an attack by "a ten-foot Alaskan grizzly." The Russian was horrified to learn of yet another bear attack at the studio. The laughter behind the scenes went on for days, although Mack himself did not share in the merriment.

On Monday the rains came and Mack's dark mood cut deeper to the bone than Pavlovna's jaws. After winding up the shooting of a crowded saloon scene on stage he managed something the other actors had thought almost not possible: He broke up the afternoon craps game and drove everyone fleeing from the men's dressing room.

"A lot they know about anything," Mack grumbled as he pulled a wobbly chair closer to the make-up mirror. "None of them knows what's really going on around here."

Raising a towel to the two somber eyes opposite him, he took a hard swipe that left a black smear down his cheek. Then he dug two fingers through a tub of cold cream and slathered it vigorously into his face.

A yelp ripped the silence and Mack sat cradling his arm like a baby. He studied that sad excuse for a human being seated before him. It was high time for a bit of soul-searching—but Mack was convinced his soul wasn't the problem so he called off the search.

No, his enemy was still on the loose. Someone had to be held accountable for the utter ruination of his life.

"The Drunkard's Reformation" had come at the absolute worst time. From the start he opposed it, telling anyone who would listen that it was a bad idea. The very nature of a "temperance lecture" had to be the farthest thing from anyone's notion of entertainment. It was sure to lay a giant egg at the box office. Oh, it might do some business out in the sticks, but never in a city as cosmopolitan as New York. It was far more likely to tip the scales against Griffith and bring about his early retirement from pictures.

But then the Temperance League announced its support of the film. By pure chance it was in the first batch of motion pictures submitted before the new state Board of Censorship, which had been set up in the wake of the McClellen debacle. "The Drunkard's Reformation" was certified and praised by members of the panel, making it newsworthy to gentlemen of the press.

Expectations built toward the first public showings, leading to good attendance. Most astonishing to Mack, the audience word of mouth was positive. Patrons packed the nickelodeons for a second and third viewing. Even viewers with limited English were moved by this stirring drama of a family suffering under the curse of alcoholism.

When the film's father, played by Arthur Johnson, vowed to his tearful daughter that he would give up drink forever the audience was bathed in emotion. The final scene of the family reunited around the hearth, illuminated from the side as if by Heaven's own kindling, evoked cries of "Hallelujah!" and hosannas of deliverance.

The Biograph Co. had hit a nerve. Patrons returned to theaters bringing their own straying fathers and sodden uncles as if it were a cut-rate trip to Lourdes. Men of the cloth such as Reverend Parkhurst and Canon William Sheafe Chase extolled it from the pulpit and thanked Biograph for spotlighting this urgent social need. For the first time anyone could recall, a motion picture was hailed as a positive moral influence on lucky nickelodeon ticket-holders.

Any public acrimony left from Griffith's Edgar Allan Poe disaster was cleansed and apparently forgiven.

But all of it just made Mack's arm throb harder. He felt blind-sided. "The Drunkard's Reformation" was going to be a much bigger hit than "The Curtain Pole," judging from early revenue earnings. No one would ever trust Mack's opinion about anything again.

Worse still, what if the Marvins swallowed the notion that audiences were hungry for more social problem films? Mack would only find it harder to push through his comedy projects.

His darkest fears crystallized one afternoon when the Marvins came out to address a general meeting in the foyer. Due to the great success of "The Drunkard's Reformation," they announced, their whole slate of spring releases was currently enjoying a surge of bookings. In addition to "The Road to the Heart," "A Rude Hostess" and "Confidence" they were rushing into production another temperance drama entitled "What Drink Did."

This was the opus Mack had spent all morning shooting. It was another moldy remnant of the past century, centering on a lush whose little girl comes to retrieve him from a saloon and ends up being fatally shot in a crossfire. All of Biograph's available male actors were enlisted for the big bar scene, and between camera takes they drowned their shame by passing around Owen Moore's never-empty flask.

The visit by the Marvins ended with Arthur Marvin mouthing the very words Mack most dreaded. He and his two senior partners were "looking ahead to the future," he said, and all three were "ecstatic to have the company name associated with meaningful subjects rather than the salacious peep show fare and burlesque farces of prior times."

Damn!

Mack slammed his towel down hard on the counter.

What a perfect beginning this has been to the next-to-last week of a perfectly ass-awkward excuse for a month!

"Is everyone decent?" called a female voice. A second later the sunny but reserved face of Linda Arvidson poked through the door. "Hello? Oh, Mr. Sennett. I thought I heard someone in here."

"Sorry to disappoint."

"I'm just wondering if you can tell me where to find Mr. Griffith?"

"He's finished shooting. Did you check the front offices?"

"Yes. Oh, well, I shall keep looking. Thank you," she trilled gaily and withdrew her head.

There was something very unsettling about that woman. She was always too polite and cheerful while keeping everyone at arm's length. He didn't know her any better now than the day they met almost a year ago.

Something was going on with her and Griffith. Yes, he knew that much. They tried to keep it hidden but it was hardly an accident that they always wound up with adjacent rooms on their overnight trips. If they wanted to keep their romance under wraps it was never any of his business.

But something was noticeably different lately. Since the day at the Palisades they were both more tight-lipped than usual. He hoped to learn more about it when he asked Augusta to go with him to a screening of "Trying to Get Arrested." All she could tell him was something everyone already knew—Linda had been responsible in some way for her role getting cut from the film.

It was almost criminal what they did to his simple hobo comedy. He knew Griffith was turning it into a commentary on the haves and have-nots of society. He accepted that. But after the urchin sidekick part was scrapped he never recaptured the comic spirit of the piece. If anything, he lost interest in the whole project.

The screening had been an embarrassment to all concerned. The audience seemed to know the story but could sense something missing. With Augusta's role no longer there it did not lead to a heart-tugging climax. What remained was an emotional mess with no proper right to be called either comedy or drama.

If Linda could influence Griffith like that, Mack shuddered to think what power she might exert on his future work. She had never been keen on making his mountain cabin comedy. She might have believed even less than Griffith that marital infidelity was a proper laughing matter. Maybe they were both just too much the old fuddy-duddy Methodists at heart.

But Griffith had been committed to it until the fiasco with Pavlovna. He could have still rallied the studio into production. That much was sure. The cabin set was built, the scenario ready. They could have done it with the bear suit in a day or two without the sacrifice of even a single additional forest animal.

But the incident left them both with a bitter taste. It became a good excuse for Griffith to pull the plug. And nothing could convince Mack that Linda didn't have a hand in that.

Both pet projects of his were in the ash heap now. And as long as the dreadful Miss Arvidson went about madly wielding her power at Biograph, Mack could only see his own role there withering up and blowing away.

Why did dressing rooms always feel smaller when they were empty? Where had everyone gone? Didn't they understand that misery craves companionship? Here he sat with the biggest pile of misery known to man burning a hole in his pocket. And there wasn't a soul around to help him spend it.

Where had Arthur Johnson gone to, that good-time Charlie? Did he have no time for a pal in his hour of need? Where was John Cumpson, or Owen Moore, the stingy Irish bastard? It was so like him to be nowhere to be found when for once it was somewhere he was needed!

To think that the grown son of the Sinnotts and the Foys had come to this. A long bloodline of fighters had left their long trail to the frozen wilds of Quebec. They had showed their backsides to all those hotheaded colonists spouting disloyalty to the king. They left New England with the honor of their name intact, founding the new burg of Danville with industry for all. What had he done?

He had followed their long trail back to New England, changed his name to something at odds with their legacy of bold initiatives. And now he sat on his own to face devious American betrayal from a place called California. She demanded that he bow to her and pay her tribute. This was not tolerable. It could not be allowed!

He kicked out his little chair and stretched to his full height. Enough already. He would venture forth and find a flame of sympathy to warm his soul or he would, in the name of all that was sacred, stamp it out beneath his boot!

The darkened floor in back of the stage was a jungle of slithering cables, ankle-cracking stage screws, boobytrapped buckets, and barricades—all of it put there to keep Mack Sennett from reaching the women's dressing room. Nevertheless, he persevered, stubbing his toes and stumbling along until a faint crack of light appeared in a doorway, showing the way to safety.

The door swung back only a foot or so before smacking hard against a wooden chair. "Watch it! Hold on!" cried Marion Leonard, jumping up to clear the way. "Oh, it's Mack," she announced to the others.

A squeal rose from the back and a tall blur of white-ribboned undergarments bolted behind a privacy screen. In the next instant Flora Finch's elongated face pushed out again to pitch a wastebasket at Mack's head.

"Hey! Look out!" he cried.

"You *cawn't* just barg in wherever you bloody please, you know," said Flora in her quirkiest British accent.

"Post more sentries," said Mack with a nod to Marion Leonard. The sight of Marion always helped boost his spirits. She was the one thing he liked about "Voice of the Violin," playing a young, love struck music student, even if she had been closer to thirty in reality. Marion got her start with Edison and acted opposite Griffith in some early Vitagraph pictures. She was truly a beauty and one of the first stars of theater to fully embrace the flickers. "Hello, my dear," he told her.

"Mr. Sennett," she said as she swung her leg over the back of the chair. "I heard you were eaten by a bear."

"It auditioned me. I wasn't to its taste."

"You might be more to everyone's taste if you respected a lady's modesty," groused Linda Arvidson.

Mack turned and saw the actress now, seated down at the end of the makeup table. He hoped she did not catch his momentary sneer. "We meet again," he said. "Did you find Mr. Griffith?"

"Yes," she snapped, saying nothing more about it.

"How's the arm, Mack?" came a female voice from the padded armchair opposite the mirrors. Florence Lawrence sat partly swallowed in fluffy pillows, thumbing through the pages of the latest *Theatre World Magazine.*

Mack raised his elbow to her. "It could stand a little kiss."

Florence did not look up from her magazine.

"I'll kiss it for you, honey," said Marion and pantomimed a pucker before twisting around to place her eye to the door crack.

"I thought Russians all knew how to handle bears," said Florence.

Mack shrugged. "No one told this bear."

"It was deeply irresponsible of Mr. Borowski to bring a wild beast," said Linda. "I spoke to Mr. Griffith and he agreed that no animals must ever be allowed in the studio again."

"What will we do with the men's dressing room?" quipped Marion from her station at the door.

Mack's curiosity now got the better of him. "What's so interesting out there?"

Florence flipped another page in her magazine. "Mr. Griffith has himself a new girl," she said.

"A new victim," hurled Marion over her shoulder.

"He had me once," said Florence. "But I got out on parole."

"As the oldest of the new girls," came Miss Finch's odd voice as she strolled out fastening the top buttons to her blouse, "it really ought to be my turn to be had." She had been a favorite in English varieties before coming to America, and now at forty-two she was indeed the oldest actress at the studio. Her tall, scrawny body made her the perfect comic foil on screen, and Mack had cast her in his jab at protest movements, "Schneider's Anti-Noise Crusade." Griffith had also used her as the leader of his more benign temperance group in "Mrs. Jones Entertains."

Marion gave a deep sigh and leaned away from the door. "I give up. I can't hear what the hell they're saying."

"May I have a look?" said Mack.

"Be my guest."

Marion climbed aside as Mack took her place, steadying his cheek against the door. His mind, though, was turning over what Linda had said about not allowing animals in the studio. It was the first time he ever heard her admit her influence with Griffith about policy. Was she not also acknowledging some part in the fatal axing of his cabin comedy?

Out on the bright platform stage, Griffith was talking to a tiny slip of a blonde. She looked like a child in her rolled-brim yellow hat and neat blue Easter suit. Even with the elevation of laced boots she appeared a full foot shorter than the director.

"She's a cutie," Mack reported back to the others.

"Told you," blurted Marion.

"How young is she, do you think?" asked Linda with an air of disinterest.

"I don't know," said Mack. "Maybe fifteen?"

"Or even fourteen," agreed Marion with a nod. "That's what I thought."

On the stage, Griffith was gently removing the girl's hat now. She shook her head and dozens of perfect corkscrew curls bounced and bobbed around her face.

"She seems very sure of herself," said Mack. "She's holding herself with the confidence of a pro." Abruptly he shot up a hand for silence and pushed his ear firmly to the crack.

"What is it?" asked Linda.

"I think he's asking her if she's free tomorrow."

"Really?" said Marion, hurrying around to take a new position above Mack.

"What can he be thinking?" asked Linda. "Our casting is complete."

Mack noted the tone of disapproval. Linda was growing more involved by the second in what was happening. He wondered how far he could push it. "Mr. Griffith seems to be taking an interest in this one."

"She's almost too perfect," said Marion.

"And petite," added Mack, beginning to enjoy himself. "I think she could be his new favorite."

Marion had been trying to hear what was being said on stage. Her mouth fell open and she looked down at Mack in disbelief. "Did he just call her *Mary*?"

Mack listened and nodded. "He just told her that that was also his mother's name." He turned back innocently to Linda. "Miss Arvidson, do you happen to know: Is Mary also his mother's name?"

"I—yes, I believe so."

"Shh! Shh!" cried Marion, still straining to hear. "He asked if he could call her 'Little Mary.'"

"That was fast," said Florence, scooting out of her chair and slapping down the magazine. She joined the others at the door, bending to have a peek. "My, she is pretty."

Mack now found it difficult to keep his delight hidden. The situation was just too good. He turned a quick eye to Linda and saw she was unraveling. "Would you like to take a quick look, Miss Arvidson?"

"No," she snapped with a wave of her hand. "As the author of 'Peter Pan' once wrote, 'All this has happened before.'"

"She still has a bit of baby fat on her, doesn't she?" said Florence. She took her eye away long enough to give Marion a suspicious glance and then winked at Mack.

If he wasn't sure before, he was now. Both leading ladies were having a ball making Linda squirm just as much as he was.

"How old do *you* think she is?" asked Marion again.

"Sixteen, tops," said Florence.

"My, my," said Linda. "She's getting older by the minute."

On stage Griffith was dragging a stool over and positioning it next to the girl. The stool was too high for her and it took a couple of attempts for her to seat herself on it.

Through the corner of his eye Mack saw Linda pacing like a caged tiger. Finally she flopped down into the overstuffed chair and picked up Florence's magazine. When he peeked out again Griffith was motioning for someone to join them.

"Who's he calling to?" muttered Marion.

"Can't tell."

"Is that ... Billy?"

A handsome, dark-haired man stepped into view. "No," said Florence. "It's Owen!"

Mack knew what that meant and what would come next. Griffith had his routine. He would throw the actors together in a spontaneous clutch and see if they would smooch. The old man didn't defer to his leading men much, but he sure enjoyed foisting them on the new girls. It satisfied him for some reason, getting them to do something he wouldn't dare dream of trying himself. It always made Mack uncomfortable.

He stood to leave and when he looked around at Linda she had slunk down in the pillows, dwindling away to next to nothing. Well, that was it. Time to move along. Maybe she would think twice now before going and messing with someone else's bear.

Then it struck him: The dark cloud had lifted and he might even have been grinning. For the first time in days he felt like singing an aria. And now that he thought about it—damned if his arm hadn't stopped throbbing as well.

TWENTY

"The Better Way"

All morning long she watched them step out in the foyer to sneak a sip from Owen's personal flask. In the beginning they were so amusingly discreet about it, casting quick looks about and grinning up at her before taking their swig and passing the flask to the next man. She doubted if any of them really craved a drink so early in the day. It was more that they enjoyed feeling like choirboys doing something naughty right under the minister's nose.

Griffith probably wouldn't have noticed anyway. He was busy inside shooting a saloon scene for his new temperance picture. All available actors had been called in to play lushes and barkeeps and beer hall habitués—roles they were all quite familiar with from real life.

By lunchtime there were no more guilty glances, no more grins at Augusta. No one even gave a thought to her anymore. They waved the flask about proudly and brayed like donkeys, unconcerned with how far the echoes carried.

It was typical male tomfoolery, the sort of behavior she had come to expect from all men. Whether her father's neglect or Deward's bullying or Owen's uselessness—it all really came down to the same thing: The bottle was first; then her if there was time.

In fairness, none of them knew what was going through her mind. All she could think was that if she didn't get that combination from Griffith's office, everyone's fun would be coming to an end soon enough.

At least working around the lobby allowed her to keep tabs on the studio comings and goings and watch for her opportunity.

Tommy had not shown up for work and the photographer she was given turned out to be unfriendly and rude. He made her do endless poses up and down the staircase, stopping only to let her use the powder room or change her outfit before starting again.

Griffith wandered out about midmorning to smoke his cigarette in peace. On his way back inside he noticed Augusta near the top of the stairs. "Oh, Miss Lee," he called up, "do you think you'll be ready for another Palisades trip? I've received permission for an outing this Friday. I'd like it if you came with us."

"What would you like me to wear?"

"Maybe your cavalry outfit, the one you told me about. I'd like some photos of you in the great outdoors. We'll discuss the details later."

"Uh, Mr. Griffith?"

"Yes?"

"Any chance ... I mean, I was hoping ... there might be an acting role."

"A role for you?" He thought a second and shook his head. "Not in this picture. But you know, tomorrow I'm shooting something here. A Jonesy comedy. 'Her First Biscuits.' You can play one of the young party guests. Have Nina find you something suitably frilly and girlish."

Suddenly the morning looked fully redeemed. It may have only been a good faith gesture, but at least he was open to working with her again.

The photographer insisted on one more series in a different outfit, keeping her working after everyone else was breaking for lunch. She watched Owen leave with Arthur Johnson, followed by three of the actresses escorted by John Cumpson and a few of the other men.

The photographer exposed a few final plates and announced he was finished with her at last. The officious Miss Bratt, however, continued to read at her front desk, keeping a sharp eye on the lobby. Augusta decided to hang back as long possible without arousing suspicions.

Soon there was a rustle at the front door and a petite female figure swept in from the rain. Augusta couldn't help staring. What was a child doing out all alone on a day like this?

The girl placed her bag down quite deliberately on the entry bench and began stripping off her rain gear. She simply had to be older than she appeared, thought Augusta. No mere child went about her business in such a methodical manner.

First she pulled off her rubber galoshes with a snap-snap and set them aside to dry. Then she jumped up to remove her rain slicker, rising on tiptoes to hook it over the coat rack. Under it she was dressed in an adorable blue Easter suit with a wide schoolgirl's sash. When she peeled back her rain hood, out fell a mass of blond ringlets that bounced and shimmied at her shoulders. Finally she rolled the hood, placed it on her galoshes, and marched off to have a word with Miss Bratt.

Augusta pretended to be brushing her hair as she bided her time.

When the girl was done she returned to the bench, lifted a yellow straw hat from her bag and pulled it evenly down on her head. She sat back, bolt upright, and folded her hands in her lap to wait.

Lawrence Griffith appeared minutes later, hurrying to his office.

"Oh, Mr. Griffith," called Miss Bratt. "I'm going to lunch now."

"Fine, fine," he said with a backward wave of his hand.

"And this young lady is asking to see you."

The director glanced over his shoulder but his expression did not change. He continued straight on to his office and shut the door. Only moments later he reappeared, this time walking up to the young stranger with a welcoming smile.

Augusta could not hear what was being said but she sensed her opportunity might be at hand. Once the photographer had packed up his equipment he carted the bags out to his car. Then Miss Bratt sashayed to the front door in her raincoat, stopping only long enough to open her umbrella with an explosive *SCHWACK!*

Griffith was wrapping up his interview with the young lady. He seemed quite happy with her and suddenly took her hand to lead her off to the studio.

The foyer was now empty and Augusta moved decisively. She had just reached the bottom step when there was the sound of stomping feet at the front door. Pinning herself back against the wall, she listened to the door swing open before risking a look.

It was Owen Moore again. What was he doing back now? He was by himself, shaking the rain off his hat and doffing his overcoat, dropping them both on the bench as he started across the marble floor. Just before pushing through the tall rear doors and disappearing, he reached a hand up to smooth back his damp, ruffled waves.

Griffith's office would have to wait. First she had to know what her Irishman was up to.

She felt deeply annoyed with herself all at once. What was it about the sight of him that still caused her stomach to do flips? She had put their brief fling behind her now, but still the sight of him aroused a longing within her. Couldn't some smart doctor come up with a medicine to help girls like her fight off the recurring infection of such a man?

Inside the studio Owen was standing on the platform stage, casting his shadow across the little girl in the blue dress. She was sitting on the same tall stool that Griffith had put her on just a few weeks before. She appeared so vulnerable and fragile next to the overpowering Owen.

At one point as they listened to the director's instructions, Owen placed his wide palm on the girl's shoulder. Augusta saw her nose twitch with dismay, as though she had picked up a very bad odor. She dropped her chin until she could manage a sincere smile, and then lifted it to his face with a flit of her lashes.

This girl was no novice! No matter how underage she appeared, she clearly knew the sensations she was stirring.

Owen took her small body in his arms and bent her back, lowering his face. They exchanged last words and then he brought his lips down and sealed them to hers.

The swine!

Augusta felt like a bucket of ice was dumped on her head. She heard herself gasp and dashed a look around to see if anyone was watching. She exaggerated a yawn and stretched her arms in manifest boredom just in case.

The girl's slim alabaster hand slipped from her lap and fell at her side, swinging like a drowsy pendulum there as the seconds ticked by.

She could not stand anymore. She spun on her heel and charged for the exit. How dare a grown man force such intimacy on a helpless girl! She would make him regret it some day if she ever got the chance.

The foyer remained silent and deserted. There was still time to go through with her plan. If she moved quickly she might get in and out before anyone was the wiser. The whole nasty business would be done with.

Pausing for a final look around, Augusta slipped through the office door and eased it to a close in back of her.

The desk was buried under the usual stacks of papers. They had to be lifted up one pile at a time to expose the desk pad. She moved along then to appointment calendars and desk drawers, scanning ledgers and notepads and handwritten invoices for any series of numbers that might be a combination jotted in the margin.

Finally she turned to the wall safe, swinging the painting out and spinning the tumbler first to the number fifty-four, then back to six and forward again. She advanced the dial slowly, holding her breath in the hope of hearing the faintest telltale click.

From outside came the sound of muffled voices. Miss Bratt had returned with her lunch and was speaking to someone. It was time for Augusta to put everything back as it had been and get away. Desperately she tried the handle at random stops, jiggling it and commanding it to yield to her will.

Now there was a man talking and the conversation was drawing closer. It was Griffith! Time was up! The clatter of boots stopped outside the office door and the knob turned. Slamming the painting back to the wall she took a quick leap to the desk as the door swung open.

"Oh, Miss Lee," said the director, startled to find someone there. For an instant he seemed sheepish, as though he was the guilty party. In his hands he was wringing the brim of a woman's yellow hat.

"I was … feeling dizzy," said Augusta. "I thought I might lie down here a minute. I didn't think you'd mind."

"You do look peaked," he said. "Would you like some water?" He moved haltingly forward and right behind him stood the girl Owen had kissed, frowning in distaste.

Griffith must have seen color draining from her cheeks. "Please, do sit yourself a moment."

"Yes, I think I will," she said, stepping to the couch to lower herself on its edge.

"Let me send someone—"

She cut him off with a raised hand. "No. Please. I think it has passed. I'm better now." Augusta ended with an open smile to the new girl.

"Well, I'm—uh, I'm glad you're here, Miss Lee. I want you to meet a new arrival." He summoned her forward. "This is … Miss Mary—?" He stopped. He had forgotten her last name.

"Pickford," said the girl.

"Yes, yes. Miss Mary Pickford. She comes to us from the Broadway stage. Miss Pickford, this is our Miss Augusta Lee, a very recent addition to our company."

"Very pleased to meet you," said the girl.

"The pleasure's mine."

Griffith looked down and realized he had been kneading the brim of her straw hat. He took it to the coat rack. "I've asked Miss Pickford to be in that little party scene tomorrow. So I won't need you after all."

"I understand."

There was a knock at the door and a middle-aged man from the front office had poked his head in. "Mr. Griffith. Mr. Forrester and Mr. Adams are asking if they can have you a minute to okay some invoices."

"What? Now?"

The clerk looked apologetic. "They need them in accounting."

"All right. Tell them I'll be right there." He shrugged as if perturbed, though to Augusta he was clearly grateful for the reprieve. "I'll only be a minute," he said to the new girl. At the door he paused to turn back to Augusta. "Oh, Miss Lee, I've invited Miss Pickford to accompany us to the Palisades Friday. Maybe you can answer any questions she has?" With that he was gone, pulling the door closed behind him.

Mary waited for the click before she abandoned her false smile. She was clearly distressed. "Miss Lee, I am in need of your advice."

"My advice?"

She nodded. "A worldly woman's advice. May I speak in confidence?"

Augusta suddenly felt protective toward the poor girl. It wasn't her fault that Owen had forced himself on her up there. "You can speak freely. Is there something wrong?"

"*Wrong* does not begin to describe it, I assure you. I really don't know where to turn." She slid the chair closer she could take a seat opposite her. "Are all motion picture people ... so forward?"

Augusta had to smile. "Surely you know how theater people are."

The girl waved a pouty frown back and forth. "I'm a Belasco actress, Miss Lee. That means everything in the world to me. Mr. Belasco personally asked me to be his Betty Warren in 'The Warrens of Virginia.' I acted on the Broadway stage for six full months. I was on tour with the company until just this March. I've played opposite many male actors and all manner of theater people. Some can be snobbish and others quite common. But never did any of them ever attempt ... liberties."

"May I call you Mary?"

"You may."

"How old are you, Mary?"

"Sixt—Seventeen," she corrected.

"You're not sure?"

"Mother says younger is always best when it comes to a lady's age. But I don't mind telling you. I had a birthday last week. I am officially seventeen now."

"Well, you still have your looks."

The girl did not laugh. "I know I cannot expect to play juveniles forever."

"You have a few more years."

"That's just it. I've been making the rounds since before the tour closed, and no one is casting. I have family responsibilities. I have a younger sister and brother dependent on me. Mother can't support us all."

"Where's your father?"

"Daddy passed when I was very young."

"Sorry. I know how it is to lose a father."

"Mother thought ... well, she heard that if one must act in pictures this was the best studio of its sort. She read all she could find about it. The Biograph Company is known for films of high morals. Their pictures have to pass a state board, like this latest one, 'A Drunkard's Reconstruction.'"

" 'Reformation,'" Augusta corrected.

"I would never disobey Mother. But if she knew what happened, how that man treated me, she would insist on dragging me away."

"You were never kissed on stage?"

The girl looked startled, and solemnly swiveled her head from side to side. "No, ma'am. I play younger daughters. If a script calls for a kiss, we would never truly kiss. Not on the mouth, anyway."

"Well, you have to understand. An actor has to think of his own reputation. Especially if he's a leading man, if you know what I mean."

"No. I don't know what you mean."

"Mr. Moore. ... Owen Moore. The man who just kissed you."

"I'm sorry. I was not speaking of Mr. Moore. When I spoke of taking liberties, I was referring to Mr. Griffith."

Augusta could not hide her astonishment. "Mr. Griffith?"

The girl's eyes grew more serious. "He led me by my hand. Then he put his arm around my waist in a most familiar manner."

"I see."

She sat back with a shudder. "I think he's a very old man. An old and an *ugly* man!" she said. Her hand shot up to her lips, as though ashamed at speaking so bluntly.

"He's younger than you might think."

Mary rose up from her chair in agitation. "No. He's old and he's ... very arrogant. He assumed I would be happy to be asked back tomorrow. He wants to put me in something about biscuits. I've never heard of such a play. It doesn't sound like a thing of high caliber at all."

"It's a comedy. It's meant to be amusing. It's about a woman who serves her guests a plate of awful biscuits."

"Why is that amusing? No, I don't know how I can agree to be associated with such a thing."

"Do you want me to tell you the truth, Miss Pickford?"

The actress stopped her pacing and gave a pouting affirmation.

"I think you might feel differently once you get to know him. Mr. Griffith is also an artist. He's a poet and a playwright. Yes, he can be arrogant and stubborn. But would you believe me if I told you he also has inner doubts?"

"About what?"

"Well, his looks mainly. You'll find he most often wears a hat, even indoors, because, you see, his hair is thinning. On sunny days you can see his scalp. Every day he finds himself surrounded by men much more handsome than himself. They must be, for the camera. And most of them have very thick hair—like Mr. Moore."

"Mr. Moore frightens me. The truth is, I've never even been out on a date with a *boy*. I never kissed a man until today. I did not want to do it. I did not wish to have anything to do with him. He referred to me in a crude and disrespectful manner."

"He did?"

She nodded. "I will never forget it. I heard him speak to Mr. Griffith, very quietly. He said, 'Who's the dame?' It's a slang expression, I believe."

Augusta wanted to laugh but managed to stop and sit back. "Yes."

"It means a woman of quite low character."

"I'm sure he did not mean that exactly."

"I think he had been drinking."

"Well, see, that explains it."

Tears were pooling in the girl's eyes. "Then Mr. Griffith insisted I accept him as my boyfriend. He said I must let him hold me, and make love to me! It was mortifying."

"I understand."

"But this is something you will not understand. I rather liked it. I think it excited me. I don't know. Can you tell me, is it always like this when you are acting for a camera? I mean, do make-believe kisses always leave a person with ... such private stirrings?"

"I'd put it out of my mind, if I was you."

"But I can't. I can't stop thinking about him. His lips. I find myself thinking—I would not mind if he kissed me some more."

This was awful. It was worse than she could have imagined. The priggish little stage brat was in love with Owen! There was a struggle going inside her now, a resistance to that overwhelming rush of first attraction. But it wouldn't last long. In the end she would surrender. No woman ever walked away from a thing like that. It might take her years to wake up and see her mistake, but for now the deal was as good as sealed.

What Owen was feeling was far less of a mystery. She saw how he came charging back to the studio from lunch. Someone must have tipped him about this little blond cutie who had come in looking for a tryout. Once she had flashed her lashes at him his goose was cooked. And the clincher was, he wouldn't even have to get her to wear any dumb wig. Those honey-gold waves and bouncing curls were natural. This "Little" Mary was the genuine goods.

Only it was more than that. She was the one Owen had warned her about—the virgin outsider, the game-changer who came out of nowhere and wielded unlimited power over king and queen.

Already she had caught Griffith in her spell and stolen away the part he had promised to her. What if he saw her as the ideal replacement for Florence Lawrence? What if he realized this Little Mary was the real perfect choice to serve as the new face of Biograph?

The little brat was a more direct threat to her than anything Deward Trawley could come up with. She was everything Augusta was not. There were almost certainly no scandals in her past. This Little Mary Pickford could well be on her way to being Biograph's uncontested star.

There must be a way to stop her. She had to be blocked before things could go any further. But Augusta knew she would need help. And the only one she could turn to for something like this was Deward himself. He wouldn't have any misgivings or second thoughts. Once she showed him the danger that the new actress posed, he would be a dependable ally through thick or thin, no matter what.

She didn't have to tell him about Owen Moore. No, he didn't need to know about any of that. She would just emphasize the girl's threat to her position. Deward would see that if he lost his one inside link at the studio the money spigot would be shut off for good. If they let Augusta go there would be no hope of getting to that office safe or managing a clean break-in. Even his hundred-dollar blackmail photos would be worthless.

He would know what they had to do. It would be easy to convince him. The power of this interloper had to be neutralized. And as soon as possible. Maybe this upcoming Palisades trip would provide the opportunity they needed. They would put their heads together and come up with something. Deward had the nerve necessary to see it through. He would never accept half-measures when it came to protecting what he had. That was his life motto, wasn't it?

All she needed was Deward's commitment and a quick, foolproof plan for the killing of Little Mary.

TWENTY-ONE
"The Planter's Wife"

"I appreciate experience, yes, of course. But these notices ..." E. D. Ebbett's jowls quivered with pessimism. "Most of them are ... from San Francisco? Before the quake?" He considered the problem while he took another puff on his cigar. "You know these theaters—many of 'em don't even exist anymore?"

Linda Arvidson scooted forward in the wooden chair. "Look to the back there. There are other clippings. From our East Coast tours."

"Oh?" He fanned through the pages, the weeks, the plays, all those grandiloquent establishments with their marbled steps and cement rustication.

The breeze from the pages dislodged his cigar ash and she watched it slowly topple and explode in a heap somewhere around 1906. It might as well have been fallout from Mount Vesuvius.

Mr. Ebbett wiped away the charred pile with his knuckles. "Let's see," he mumbled, hoisting the book and craning his head back to read through the bottom of his glasses.

Relax, she told herself. Have a little faith. ... Everything will resolve itself in time.

Her eyes roamed to his gallery of mementoes on the dark wood behind him. Mounted posters and yellowing handbills were hung around a good dozen framed publicity photographs.

Better not look too closely, she told herself. Too many smiling faces there she might know. Former colleagues, all of them happy and prosperous, living out the destiny that should have been hers.

A face leaped out at her. Carl! No, it only looked like Carl at first. The same dimpled grin, the handsome, playful eyes. ... But it wouldn't be him. He was still out in California, the last she had heard. He did not abandon the city in its hour of need. He stayed to help it get back on its feet. He would never have abandoned it for some vague promise of a new life out East.

Sweet Carl. It seemed an eternity ago he raised the possibility of an engagement. His was the first friendly face she saw in the lobby that morning. All the others looked dazed at being shaken from their sleep. Carl hurried to comfort her. He told her to stay close and they would get through this. He probably noticed her trembling and did not realize it was only that she was cold.

Poor Carl was always so sure she loved him and that she would marry him some day. But she knew the truth, and she had considered breaking the news to him then and there. It would free him to face what needed to be done. Maybe it would put his fairy tale hopes to rest along with all the other dreams that ended that morning.

But just as she opened her mouth to speak there was another massive jolt. It rumbled up through the foundation and lifted the lobby to a tympani of groaning oak and a glissandi of shattered glass. When she turned back to Carl he was was gone. Her brave protector had been among the first to dive headlong for an open window.

In the months to come she got big laughs with that story, from people who were not there—how that one aftershock sent Carl fleeing for his life without a thought to anyone else. Each time she told it the laughter increased. She embellished it and brought all of her talents to bear on the part of the abandoned coquette, robbed of her hapless hero. When she sensed the crowd about to turn on her for mocking the poor man, she would end it with the topper— that it had taken the same act of God to bring her together with the true love of her life, her one dear and ever-devoted husband, Lawrence "David" Griffith.

It had been more than a year now since she told that story. It was too hard to deliver that punchline without any trace of bitterness.

Anyway, Carl was not such a farcical figure anymore. He had the normal reaction and made an instinctive dash for life when danger struck. In truth, she was the cowardly one. She was really the one who had run away. This was her punishment. She had to sit before the judgment of an overfed dwarf in shirtsleeves and floral suspenders.

"Two years ago?" muttered E.D. Ebbett aloud again.

She watched him flip through a few final pages and then fold the back cover over. He lifted the scrapbook up and let it slap against his desk. He did not speak.

"Mr. Ebbett, don't my motion picture credits count for anything?"

"'Great Train Robbery,' maybe. ... Were you in that one?"

She swiveled her head from side to side. "No, but most recently I performed opposite Herbert Yost in 'Edgar Allen Poe.' I was his dying young bride."

"Really?" he said with a smile that instantly dropped. "Missed it."

" 'The Adventures of Dollie'? ... 'The Politician's Love Story'?"

"Afraid not."

" 'The Curtain Pole'? Everyone saw 'The Curtain Pole.'"

The agent leaned back to regard her through both of his smudged lenses. "Miss Arvidson, if I may speak to you frankly. You know, we have a standard bit of advice for all the actors who come to us. You know what that advice is?"

"I can't presume—"

"Don't get mixed up with these picture people."

Mixed up? How quaint, she thought. That's *exactly* what happened to her. She had gotten *mixed up*.

"There's no future there for any serious actor."

"Yes, I reached that same conclusion," she confessed softly.

Mr. Ebbett squeaked forward in his chair and adopted the demeanor of a kindly uncle. "These flickers—they open and they're gone. Poof. No notices, no playbills. Like nothing ever happened. Just a big fin someone spotted from their boat. Afterward, no one's even sure it was there."

"Like a dream," said Linda.

"That's right."

"And we know 'a dreamer is one who can only find his way by moonlight. His punishment is that he sees the dawn before the rest of the world.'"

"That's good. Who wrote that?"

"That was Mr. Oscar Wilde."

"The English guy?"

"He was Irish, actually."

"Ah, yes."

The silence threatened to go on too long. "Mr. Ebbett, my years on the stage were the most productive of my life," she said. "I am quite capable of playing a wide array of roles. With costume and makeup, there's no character I cannot become."

The theatrical agent looked frustrated. "Miss Arvidson, why are you here?" he said at last.

"I thought you understood. I am an artist. I want to share my art. I'm willing to travel for the right role. I might even agree to a reputable touring company. If it were headed west, all the better. I know that in San Francisco they remember me. I can still guarantee some audience draw. Or even farther to the south, I mean Los Angeles—"

"We're not a travel bureau."

She was stunned at his rudeness. "Of course not. I am trying to convey that I have much to contribute."

"What I'm asking, I guess, is why us? Why did you come to us?"

"I know you recently represented the interests of Miss Marion Leonard. You booked her last tour."

"Yes. I know Miss Leonard well. A wonderful actress. And a beauty."

"She recommended your agency to me personally."

"Is that right? Glad to hear it. Directors are always pleased to work with her." He took another puff on the wet end of his cigar butt. "Do you have a personal relationship with any directors?"

"Mr. Lawrence—David Griffith. He is one."

"Don't know him. Where does he work?"

"He is a playwright as well as a stage director. His last play was produced in Washington, D.C."

"Well, why don't you go down there and look him up? Maybe he's got something for you."

"I understand he has left the business."

"Oh. Too bad. I just don't think we can do anything for you, Miss Arvidson. Winter shows are on the boards. Casting won't get serious again until late summer. If you'd like to come back then—" Mr. Ebbett allowed the sentence to hang as he rose to signal the interview was over.

Linda Arvidson fidgeted a bit with her bag and pulled at her dress before rising.

The agent collected her scrapbook and again assumed the role of kindly uncle as he came around his desk. "Tell me, will you be seeing Miss Leonard again soon?"

"I believe so."

"Please tell her hello. From Edward."

"Yes, I will do that."

He walked her to the door. "Any other actors you see that I might know?"

"No. Well, that is, one of Mr. Belasco's younger actors joined us just the other day."

He opened the door and handed her the scrapbook. "Oh? Who was that?"

"A small blond girl. Mary Pickford."

A curtain rose and Mr. Ebbett's grin stood polished and gleaming at center stage. "Mary Pickford! You mean Gladys Smith?"

"Who?"

"The Pickford girl. That's Gladys Smith from Ontario. Oh, she's a go-getter, that gal. Wonderful, wonderful little actor. Why don't you tell her to drop by and see me? Her and her mother—Charlotte, I believe. I might find some work for a great little gal like her."

Linda Arvidson managed a gracious smile, thanked Mr. Ebbett for his time, and hurried out the door.

All the way to the subway she gave stern lectures to Mr. Ebbett. How dare he dismiss her like he did? What could someone like him know of the soul of an artist? He was a middleman, a mere ticket vendor. No matter how he objected, his office really was no more than a travel bureau. He might shuffle a lot of hungry actors off to the care of stage producers and managers, but he knew nothing about the new generation of performers and the growing allure of motion pictures.

That is where the competition truly became fierce. Those flurries of letters from fans proclaiming their undying devotion—they were only the tip of the iceberg. Every morning there was another handful of women waiting for an interview. They came from every imaginable corner of the continent, filled with their own big dreams. Most of them were not young enough for this business. To even have a chance in pictures these days a girl had better be in her early teens. The older ones, those whose figures might be filling out here and there, they found themselves despised before the camera. Most of them should be warned to stick to the legitimate stage.

How she wished she had been given that advice. Mr. Ebbett was not the first agent to remind her. None of them were at all impressed with her ancient stage clippings or her file of Biograph circulars.

The Earth had turned while she was not watching and it had rolled over everything she had ever done in life. All the people and plays she knew were flattened out and pasted between two covers easily carried under one's arm.

Odd that she had thought of Carl today after all this time. Where was he now? Why did she never hear from him again? He was so bright and talented. He could always manage to amuse her and lift her spirits with a witty conversational gambit about current people and events. Life would have been gayer if she had married Carl. Or was it just easier to believe then that life was ever gay because they were all so young?

What she wouldn't give to be a part of it again. The champagne laughter, the dancing at all those lovely, spontaneous cast parties—it only took a whisper after a performance to bring the crowd running. They would cram into her quarters to share whatever they had to offer, and there would be endless singing and storytelling. The camaraderie of real theater people did not exist here.

Even the most basic notion of a *curtain* was gone. There was none of the glamour of an opening night. And shows did not close, they were merely dismantled. Applause was heard only very weakly from the grateful stagehands at the end of a hot day. It would be two weeks or more before any actual audience saw a given performance. And who was this audience? None of them had any idea who the performers were, or seemed to care that what they were doing was something known as acting.

Even the idea of inviting fellow actors back to one's quarters under these circumstances was—

SCREE-EE-EECH!!

An automobile slid to a halt only a foot or two from her hip. She was astonished to find herself standing in the street. She did not know what to say, or if she should say anything to the driver at all, so she reacted impulsively. "Watch where you are steering that thing!"

"Here, let me help you," said a voice.

A young, thin man stepped off the curb. He reached out and gently lifted her free arm, guiding her back up on the sidewalk.

"Thank you," she said.

"You're safe now," he answered, with a squeeze to her arm.

How forward, she thought. Fending off an accident hardly negated the need for an introduction. She smiled anyway. "It seems they will sell an automobile to anyone today."

He was handsome and in his early twenties. Perhaps he was making a pass. He would not let go of her arm. There came a brief toot of a traffic cop's whistle.

"Let me help you across the street," said the young man.

Now she was offended. Did she really appear to him so decrepit? "That will not be necessary." She yanked her arm free of his fingers.

The stranger gave a tiny bow and went on his way.

Now she remembered why she loathed this city. It was so full of presumptuous young men. Something about the spring brought them out. God, to walk again in the steely Bay Area gloom and feel the briny spray of winds licked by countless tongues of foam. ... Manhattan packed its air with hidden moisture like a thug with a bludgeon.

By the time her husband came creeping in that night she had been in bed with the lights out for over an hour. She listened to him go through his predictable rituals, ending with those upper arm exercises and waist-bends.

She said nothing as he slipped in beside her, pretending to be asleep. Soon she heard nothing but the sound of his peaceful, rhythmic breathing. She envied his ability to fall asleep so quickly no matter what calamities the day had wrought.

As minutes built toward an hour she felt he did not deserve such rest. Sometime after two o'clock, she heard him snort and could not stop herself. She elbowed him sharply in the ribs.

"Humn? What?" he mumbled.

"You were having a nightmare."

"I was?"

"Yes. You woke me up."

"I don't remember it."

"You were groaning and you said 'Mary.'"

"I did?"

"Plain as day."

"Sorry."

She knew that would wake him. He would feel some guilt stirring now. He would lie there wondering if he had dreamed of the horrid Mrs. Mary Castle. He would never say her name again when he was awake. But it wasn't right that he should be allowed to forget it. He needed to be reminded every once in a while so he could regret what weakness had brought him to.

"I need some water," he said. "Can I bring you some?"

"Yes, please."

In a minute he was shuffling back across the floor with two half-full glasses. She sat up and he handed one to her. "I know what I was dreaming about," he said, taking a seat on the mattress. "I think I've found my Pippa."

So, that's what he wanted her to believe. She knew he was planning his Browning project, his filmed version of "Pippa Passes." All that was holding it up was the right young girl to play the lead.

"This new actress today. Mary Pickford. You met her."

"You mean Gladys? That's her real name."

"Is it?"

"I know you prefer to think of her as 'Little Mary.'"

"What do you think of her as Pippa? She looks the right age. She is wonderfully self-possessed. A little chubby, but she has a sweet face. Of course, I'll have to wait to see how she photographs. Anyway, that's probably what I was dreaming. Miss Pickford."

"But I distinctly heard you say 'Mary.' Only Mary. Quite familiar. And you pronounced it with … a sort of longing."

He set his glass on the nightstand and slipped his legs under the sheet. "You know what it might have been? I must have been reminded of an old schoolmate. That was her name, as well. Mary. Oh, my. Such a beautiful little thing. I must have told you about her."

"No. Never."

"I was young. My mother had just moved the family away. I had a new town, a new school. I didn't know a soul. She was in my class. She had golden curls and the sweetest little face. I would look for her after class and ask to walk her home. One day she said yes. She was my first friend. I think I might have asked her if she would marry me when we were a little older."

"What did she say?"

"I don't believe she made a commitment. I know she was more levelheaded than I was. Then one day she just chose not to see me. I tried to talk to her but it was as if I wasn't there. I couldn't understand what happened. I was mad and hurt about being snubbed. But I couldn't let it go.

"Weeks later I got her to speak. She admitted that her mother had put her up to it. I remember this thing she did with her finger. She couldn't look at me, so she kept tracing the swirls of the wood grain on her desk. It turned out her mother had forbidden her to spend time with me. She did not want her daughter hanging around 'that Griffith boy.' I was just a dreamer, someone who would never amount to anything in the world. She wanted better for her little girl."

"Why would you dream about her now?"

"Every time I face some failure in life, I remember that mother. I have to think how right she was … to protect her daughter from me."

"But you're not a failure."

"I don't think I ever feel like such a grand success." He snuggled into the covers and slid his body closer. "This Friday, what do you say we don't come back with the others?"

"Really?"

"Yes. Let's get a cozy room together somewhere. How would that be? A little mountain cabin."

"No bears," she said.

He chuckled. "No bears, I promise." He turned to hug her, but she did not welcome his touch and they both stiffened a bit.

"I have had something else on my mind lately," he said at last.

"What is that?"

"A strange thing that Mayor McClellan told me. He said he thought that the fire call—that it might have been placed by someone in the studio."

"Really?"

"Do you think it might have been a prank? An office girl, maybe?"

"I doubt it. Why would she?"

"Things do have a way of getting out of hand," he said. He gave a deep sigh. "Well, good night, dear."

She laid silently a moment before speaking out in her most matter-of-fact tone. "I'm thinking of leaving you, David." She waited but he did not respond. "Are you asleep?"

"No. I heard you. … Do you know when?"

"When the time is right." She waited again. "Do you wish to know why?"

"Oh, there are many sound reasons. I've given you plenty."

"So you won't discuss it?"

"I don't see how it would help. I just don't have the choices I did once upon a time." A while later he said, "I think I was always meant to end up alone."

She felt she could sleep now. At last she had addressed the thing and could put it aside. Let him be the one lying wide awake for a change.

TWENTY-TWO
"At the Altar"

This was Sixth Avenue and up ahead there, that was Third Street. So the smoke-charred cement building on the left, the one with no windows—that had to be Saint Joseph's. The only giveaway was a plain cross rising from the glistening slate of its roof.

Someone had told Augusta it was as old as Greenwich Village itself, and she could believe it. But no one said how spooky it might look on a drizzly night in the amber fuzz of streetlamps.

She stopped when she reached the corner and stepped under a doorway to wipe the mist from her face. That old sensation was back, the feeling she was being followed. The sidewalks were largely deserted. One lone couple in the distance was sharing an umbrella and strolling along like they had no place to be.

What was she hoping to do here, anyway? It was already too late to call things off, even if she decided she must. Tomorrow's trip to the Palisades provided the perfect cover for their plan. Deward was probably in place by now, waiting in that out-of-the-way traveler's lodge they had found. It was not a place used by picture people. No one there would give him a second glance or remember what he looked like later when the news came of an awful accident up at the cliffs.

A car turned up the street and its rubber tires splashed as it cruised slowly by.

She wanted to turn and run. But hiding wasn't much of an option anymore. It certainly wouldn't make her problems go away.

Another car was coming. She waited for it to pass and then hurried to the corner and stepped off the curb.

Across the street a low iron fence stretched around the turn to a front gate and a cement walkway. It led to a broad cascade of steps up to a pair of wide stone pillars.

Churches still held a deep mystery for her. As a girl she was intrigued by the sight of the land folks pulling up in front, the women in their starched dresses and bonnets, the men in silken cravats and coats with tails. The minister would more often than not greet them at the doors, holding tightly to his Bible to stop its priceless secrets from spilling out.

Sunday services were quite the dramatic affairs. There was music and maybe an organ with a booming voice, and robed choirs looking as angelic as could be. She thought she would like to join a church like that some day, though that pretty much ended when she found out what they did with their dead.

One morning she got there real early and found herself a comfortable crook in a tree. She couldn't hear what was said but it was impressive nonetheless. They would rehearse just like any production, and there might be a fiddler or harpist playing as the mourners arrived. When the preacher finished they would lower the casket into a hole, and after everyone was gone a couple of men would roll up the grass and pull down the tent. Next time her boat came through there would be no real grave to look at. Maybe she would find a small concrete marker where the remains were supposed to be.

Her mother was in a mud hole like that. And her father, too, not long afterwards. They were a hundred miles apart, waiting for some future Mississippi flood to resurrect their bodies and wash them down to some backwater eddy. A hole in the mud too close to a riverbank didn't seem up to the long haul of eternity.

"Psst!" came a call from the top of the landing. Someone was wedged back in the shadows behind a pillar.

"It's me," whispered a high voice.

Augusta gave a sigh of relief. "Bobby!"

"Yeah."

She hurried toward him up the steps. "Bobby, you been following me?"

He stepped into the light looking frightened and cold. "I won't make no bones about it. I been keepin' an eye on you."

"Spying on me, Bobby?"

"I promised, didn't I?"

"Well thanks for scaring me half to death."

"You here to see Father Bill?"

"I was thinking I might."

"Smart." Bobby's brow wrinkled. "I know what's got you spooked."

"What do you mean?"

"I seen him."

"Who?"

"Mr. Trawley. He must've got sprung. I saw him hanging outside your building. He was watching—watching you come and go. Yesterday, he went inside."

"You shouldn't have been spying, Bobby. It could be dangerous."

"Did he hurt you?"

Augusta swiveled this way and that, searching quickly up and down the street before dragging Bobby back with her into the alcove. "Bobby," she said in breathy bursts, "did you tell anyone else about Mr. Trawley? About seeing him, I mean?"

"No."

"Bobby, tell me the truth."

"I didn't say nothing."

"You've got to promise me now. You listening?"

"Sure."

"You can never tell no one. You got to swear it."

"What?"

"That you saw him. ... Mr. Trawley. Understand?"

"If you say so."

"Bobby, you've got to promise. If anyone ever, *ever* asks you about him, you gotta say you used to see him at the studio. But you haven't seen him in over a month. Swear to me."

"If it's what you want."

"It's got to be that way, Bobby. I have my reasons."

"He threatened you, didn't he?"

She hesitated before nodding.

"That's what I thought. Well, you don't have to worry no more."

"What do you mean?"

The boy gave guilty looks around before reaching down and gathering up the waist of his sweater. He boosted it high enough so she could see his belt and, poking from it, the polished wood grip of a hand gun. "I didn't forget."

"Where'd you get that thing?"

"It belonged to that big dumb Russian. Borowski. He just dropped it and left it there."

"In the studio?"

Bobby nodded. "No one saw. I was careful. No one saw me grab it."

"I'm surprised at you," she scolded. "A good Catholic boy."

"I know. But the Lord helps those who help themselves. ... Here, take it. It's a lot heavier than it looks."

"No."

"It's got a kind of beauty to it. You know how to work it?"

"I don't think—"

"It's simple. You just make sure this safety thing is off. See here?"

"I'm not going to need it now."

"What?"

"Bobby, I can handle Mr. Trawley in my own way. I don't need a gun."

"You sure?"

"Please, just do what I said. Never mention a word about him. To anyone. Understand? No one can know a thing about Mr. Trawley coming to visit me. Please swear it."

"Yes. Okay. I swear."

"And get rid of that horrid thing. Give it to Mack. Tell him you found it. Okay?"

Bobby looked hopeless all at once. "You sure there's nothing I can do ... to help?"

"You've been a huge help, Bobby. More than I can tell you. If anything happens—" She stopped. She didn't want to give him cause to worry.

But it was too late. A drop of moisture glistened in his eye from the light of the streetlamp.

"Oh, Bobby, dear, listen. I'm going to be fine."

"I got this feeling ... I won't ever see you again."

"You mustn't worry. Go on home to your family. They need you."

"I'm afraid ... somethin' bad's going to happen."

"I'll look after myself, okay? Like it or not, it's up to me. So go on home now. Scoot."

A black man in a heavy coat and neck scarf stood just inside the carved doors. He was dragging a mop across the cement, expanding the wet patch around his ragged shoes. Augusta saw his breath and realized it was somehow colder here than it was outside.

"Excuse me," she said, gathering her collar at her neck.

The man stopped mopping to look at her.

"Could I speak to Father Bill?"

Without a word in reply he propped his mop handle against the wall and held up a pink palm for her to wait.

The stiff wooden backs of pews trailed down to a front table covered with burning candles. Caught in their glow were the half-naked figures of saints and martyrs with their eyes fixed mournfully on the empty upper galleries.

"Yes, can I help you?"

A slender, dark-haired priest in a white collar was pulling on his wool coat as he came closer. She felt disappointment. He couldn't have been much older than she was.

"You're not Father Bill."

"You're right. I'm not."

"I was hoping to see Father Bill."

"He's left for the day. I'm Father McConagher."

"Oh."

"You could request an appointment, if you like. Of course, I don't know his schedule."

"No. I mean, that will be too late."

"I can try to help. You can call me Father Hank."

She smiled but she was at a loss. "Thank you. I'm sorry to have bothered you." She turned to leave.

He must have sensed her hopelessness. "Are you a member of our parish?"

"No."

"Perhaps you are thinking of joining?"

"I just wanted ... to talk. What do you call it?"

"A confession?"

"No. Not exactly."

"Let's start again," he said. "Are you Catholic?"

"No. Just ... looking for some advice."

"And only Father Bill will do?"

"Bobby told me he was a kind man."

"Bobby? Bobby Harron?"

"Yes."

"I thought so. Something told me you might be a friend of Bobby's."

Augusta was alarmed that she might have already said too much. Father Hank would remember her coming in now. He might tell others that she had come in, clearly bothered about something.

"Look, I better go. I can see you're busy. I understand."

He smiled to himself.

"Was that funny?"

"I just imagined saying that to the guard at the Pearly Gates: 'I see you're too busy. I understand.' Look, you're in luck. I do have some time I can spare. Let's have a seat."

Their footsteps echoed down the aisle as he motioned her toward an empty pew. She slid in and watched as he slipped in after her.

"It's cold," she said.

"Yes. These old buildings. It's a problem. ... Where do you know Bobby from?"

"The studio."

"Then you're an actor too?"

She nodded.

"I thought so. And I think I know what this is about."

"You do?"

"You're getting ready for something. Am I right?"

"Yes."

"You're preparing for a new role. A Catholic. You are looking for some insight."

"Yes."

"Go ahead. Ask away."

"Is it possible for a person to confess a crime ... before it has happened?"

Father Hank looked puzzled. "I've never been asked that. It sounds like premeditation, which is in a different category. Tell me more."

"Well, I'm not sure my director ... would want me to reveal too much."

"Speak generally, then. I assure you, I do understand show business. I am a huge theater-lover, you know. I acted a bit myself in grade school. That was down in Baltimore, years and years ago. But once it's in your blood."

"Well, maybe you can understand."

"Trust me. I have a small confession of my own." He bent closer to her and lowered his voice. "I love motion pictures even more. Especially the action ones. 'The Great Train Robbery.' Horse chases. Sword fights. ... What's your play about?"

"Well, there's a ... blackmailer."

"Ah. I am intrigued already."

"I have made mistakes."

"Your character, you mean. She is only too human. With human weaknesses."

"Exactly. I don't want to do anyone harm. But I am caught in a bad position."

"Yes, yes. You would like to reform but you cannot because you're trapped. I love this. Tell me, what mistake have you made?"

"I was alone."

"Yes?"

"And hungry. I … I stole something. A box of jams."

He waited but she did not say more. "Is that all?"

"Well, a store detective stopped me. And he said—"

"He threatened you with jail unless you do precisely what he tells you."

"Exactly."

Father Hank smiled. "Knew it. I've heard of such things. But why can't she go to the police?"

"She can't, you see, because… she can't let her father find out what she did."

"I thought she was alone?"

"Well, she is, because she is in hiding … from her family. Her father is very rich, and she had to run away because … he was forcing her to marry a man she does not love."

"I see. And a scandalous headline like a shoplifting episode, that might hurt them both?"

"You really do understand."

"I told you, I love shows like this. So, what will she do?"

"Well, she knows she has to get out of this thing by herself."

"Naturally. That is the nature of guilt. It wants to stay hidden from others. What does she come up with?"

"Murder."

"Really? … Murder? I don't know if I understand. She goes from lifting a box of jams to arranging a murder?"

"The blackmailer is a killer, you see. He will kill her, too, in a second if she backs out. And her father. And her little brother as well."

"I don't know. … But I think I want to see this play. How does she propose to … knock him off?"

"I can't tell you that."

"What?"

"I mean, the director hasn't told me. I don't think he has fully worked that part out."

"How about a gunshot?"

She shook her head. "No. Too loud. There will be people around. And it mustn't appear like a murder."

"It could be made to look like ... part of a robbery."

"Yes. But she doesn't want to get the police involved."

"No investigations?"

"That's right."

"Well, then, it has to be made to look like an accident."

"That's exactly what I was thinking, Father! I'm going to tell the director what you said."

"I knew a young man in divinity school. He died in a fall off a horse."

"Was that an accident?"

"Oh, goodness, I hope so. We all thought so at the time. ... Drowning is good, too. A person can hit his head and fall in a bathtub. Bathrooms are very dangerous places."

"Yes, that's true."

"So what is it your character is looking for specifically ... from me?"

"I guess the question for her, Father, and for me, is to be able to play this part with sympathy ... it involves this matter of conscience. You said it before. Premeditation. She needs to know ... Can murder be forgiven if it's for a good cause?"

"From what you've told me, I'm not too sure about the cause."

"His death will save the lives of a number of other innocent people."

"Murder is a mortal sin, of course. I don't know that the number of people who benefit is really pertinent."

"Will God forgive me? I mean ... *her*?"

"That is a thorny question there. Catholic theologians since the Middle Ages have raised no basic objection to capital punishment, for example. There is some talk that the Pope is going to address the issue again in light of our modern age. But it is certainly consonant with Scripture and tradition. It recognizes God's hand in the law of nature. Since the Enlightenment, Christian churches have supported the judicious application of capital punishment. Those who are more resistant to the belief in a Divinity and an afterlife—they often oppose the idea. It's the finality of death they object to. But the Holy Scripture does not see death as the end at all. Capital punishment can under the right circumstances be a wholly appropriate way of dealing with those who pose a threat. ... Does that help?"

"It does. I want—I mean, my character—I know she wants to do the right thing."

"Of course she does. Let me ask this: Has she considered, perhaps, pushing the blackmailer under a subway train? That would make a very strong impression on the audience."

Augusta slipped forward off the bench and onto her knees. "I think I better pray for guidance."

"That's always a good place to begin."

"Dear God, I am asking for help. I need help. I need courage and strength."

"God is listening."

"My soul is in need. I need healing. My sins are many, Lord. Please send me strength to overcome my fear and indecision. Give me strength. Guide my way. Help me do what I must to save others."

"That's good. You even had me believing it."

"I feel better."

"You should."

Augusta smiled and wiped a blur from her eyes. "I think I can do this now."

"I know you can."

"Thank you, Father."

"Delighted to help. ... Are you sure now?"

"Yes, I am."

"Because I have more ideas."

She rose to leave, and he stood to give her space to pass by.

"Thank you again," she said.

"God bless and keep you," he said.

As she listened to her shoes click up the aisle and out to the door, she heard Father Hank call out suddenly from behind her. "Burial alive! That's another good one! Very dramatic. ... Think about it!"

TWENTY-THREE
"The Fatal Hour"

A ribbon!

Little pretty golden one. … Now that's a good omen!

"Come to Papa," muttered Deward, snatching it up from a thicket of vines.

Just a shiny little snippet—but she tells the tale. … It's the true and proper path we've found, Deward, my boy. Shut my mouth and call me the next Natty Bumppo!

He stopped for a quick appraisal of the forest ahead of him. There was a name for those trees. Maples, maybe. They had to have shallow roots up here because the topsoil was not deep. Bedrock, mostly. Any strong wind comes along and … well, just gaze about at all those exposed roots. Over there was a small white ash—a goner for sure. Talk about your tough childhoods.

Yeah, know exactly what you're going through, gents and ladies. But thank you all for showing me the path to redemption. Just passing through myself. I ask your indulgence a wee bit longer. Soon I shall be out of your forest for good and for all.

Yes, sir. After a lifetime of bad leads and dead ends he was about to see his ship come in at last. His whole sorry history was a castoff treasure map marked over with red X's where the treasure was not found. This time, however, his fortunes were going to change.

Just beyond the next rise and around the coming turn a clearing waited for him, filled with promises of silver and stacks of green. A reckoning with some road managers and a token for the troll beneath the bridge, and off he would fly. The future was a succession of paydays for Deward Trawley. There would be daring wagers and drinks on the house for all those absent pals who would have rather seen him dead.

Another there! Yes, a pretty purple—hard to miss even half-hidden in the underbrush. *You're a fresh and silky one on your face, aren't you? Come to Papa.*

He slipped it inside his vest with the other. Everything was happening as she said. One, two, three. First, the deskman with a call up the stairs about a phone call for a "Mr. Beaverbrook." That was the name she picked for some reason. It was his signal that the company had arrived and was heading up to the Palisades by caravan.

He took his time packing and getting out to his rented car. No reason to hurry at this stage. It was just a jaunt up the winding road, keeping one eye peeled for the posted turnout. She had picked out the perfect spot for him and described where he should park in the minutest detail. Follow the colored ribbons, she said, and they would lead to an unprotected bluff overlooking the channel.

That Augusta was a pip. For a dame, she was quite the treasure herself.

Didn't she think of everything? "Be careful to pick up the ribbons as you go," she told him. "We don't want anyone finding them there later." That was good thinking. Even a copper would have his suspicions aroused by a marked trail to the accident site. A thing such as that might make him wonder if there was an accomplice and if it could have all been planned. No, it all had to appear like an accident. A ribbon left lying on the trail wouldn't jibe with Augusta's story about her and her young friend setting off on a spontaneous stroll upon the cliffs.

Something landed on the rim of his ear and he swatted it away. A swarm of small flying insects surrounded a nearby tree. Mosquitoes! A doozy of a cloud of the things! He threw up a hand and stirred the air, slapping at a sudden prick to the back of his neck. He ducked his head and beat a hasty zigzag to the left, not stopping until he was sure he was clear of them.

Ah! A bit of pink over there under that old uprooted stump. Is it—? Yes! Another shiny little souvenir for his collection. This ribbon was a little worse for wear, beginning to unravel at the edges. *Watch out for those frayed ends!* He snickered at the thought, then stuffed it in his pocket with the other two.

He was on the right path. Any moment now he would break out of the trees. He would spot the clearing and the flat rock stretching off to the edge, just like she described. That's where he would find his patient Little Mary. Augusta would have brought her there so she could see the very best spot for admiring the view. She would offer some excuse for leaving her alone, and the girl would never expect that anyone else could be around. She would not hear him sneak out of the brush and come springing at her from behind.

Augusta would be safely back with the others by the time they heard the scream. She would stall them as long as she could, leading them on a detour or two before bringing them to the cliff. That would be all the time he needed to get away. Long before someone spotted the body down on the rocks he would be turning his car toward home.

Old *Kain-tuck* would have to file a report with the local constable. It would be an hour or more until they could leave. He would be back in the city by 11 a.m., establishing his alibi just in case his movements were ever questioned.

Her plan was smart all right, but maybe not entirely foolproof. There were some unknowns in the action—enough to give a cautious man the opening night jitters. By and large, though, it was a dandy plan and the show they were putting on was a guaranteed humdinger.

Glowing notices, my boy, that's what the future holds for us! Box office to beat the band. Interviews in the trades. And long seasons of nothing but low women and high living.

What could go wrong? ... Well, something was there in the back of his mind, nagging at him. Maybe he should run through it one more time.

He stopped to look behind to where he had been. The clumps of brush, those vine-covered trunks and twisted boughs—all of them looked pretty much the same. Which way was the path back? He had already walked so far from the road he couldn't hear any passing motors. Was he supposed to follow that narrow footpath to the right, or was it that beaten down opening in the brush near the skinny hemlock tree?

This could pose a problem. What if when the deed was done he took a wrong turn? It would be a disaster if the police found him wandering around lost after some poor wretch had just fallen to her death. That kind of odd coincidence would raise some doubts.

Hold on. Why not leave the ribbons where they were? Yes. Then there would be no question of finding his way out. He could bend down and swoop them up as he left. That shouldn't take him any longer.

Devil with it, then.

His mind was made up. He would not pick up any more of her damned ribbons. He pulled the latest one from his vest pocket to put it back where he found it. It was the shiny pink one. "Pink," he scoffed. It figured.

Pink had always been a bad omen. That was his sister's favorite color, the color of that stupid dress she finally outgrew and then passed it along to him. Mother said there was some use left in it, and boys were tough on summer clothes. So she pulled it over his head and tied it at his waist before she sent him out to play. What did he know? It flapped in the breeze and felt cool on a sweaty summer's day.

He never counted on those vicious Duncan brothers. They didn't see the economy of it. It led to his first real beating, and the sight of that dark red blood flowing freely down his sister's prized dress scared the bejeezus out of him. All he could think was to run. At times he could still hear the jeers and hooting of his pals as he slipped through a loose board in the fence. Not until he was safely out of sight did he yank off the dress and stomp it in the mud. He ran the whole way home in nothing but his underpants, sobbing like a hungry brat.

To this day, pink fabrics made him think of his mother and that hand-me-down dress. It was the day the world learned what a sniveling coward he was.

Something had landed on his left brow, and now he felt the itch. He slapped at his forehead but the culprit was gone. A new cloud of insects swooped down around his head. He batted at them with open palms and ducked his head, hurrying along through the trees.

Where did that trail go now? Not a ribbon in sight. Maybe he had strayed too far. He searched the bases of trees and used the toe of his boot to sift through small piles of fallen branches.

Most men weren't much better than dumb bitches when a fellow really got down to it. A few had some brains and played their cards right. But almost all of them were suckers when it came to dames. Yeah, men were patsies who couldn't help but lose their way from time to time. It was a stacked game.

Up to now he thought Augusta and him made a pretty good team. Now he was wondering how he could trust her. That oversight with the ribbons was telling. Maybe the most he could count on was her doing only what was in her own self-interest. That meant she could be outfoxed and even made to—

Wait! There it is, the next ribbon. Just a tiny bit of blue shining through the tangled growth. Blue can sure catch a man's eye under a pile of sticks and vines and—*Hold on! Yikes! That's poison ivy! A big patch of it! The dumb bitch! Doesn't she know what poison ivy looks like? Just like a dumb bitch to put down a trail marker in a mass of red roots!*

What was that girl thinking, anyway? She sure as hell didn't always have her mind on things. Mosquitoes, markers, now this. Well, that was it. That blue ribbon could just stay where it was and rot, for all he cared. He might not even bother plucking that one out on his way back!

Why couldn't she just stop and consider it from his side one time? Did she want him to get lost? Didn't she care if he was in danger of not finding his way back?

Wait a second. Maybe she was planning on that. That might have been her plan from the start. Get him to take the rap for the whole killing? Sure, she had her alibi. She wouldn't be anywhere near the cliff when it happened. Then she could point to the ribbons as evidence that he was marking his path back. He might have used her hair ribbons thinking it would further throw suspicion off himself.

The dumb bitch! Was that her plan? How stupid did she think he was?

Wait a second. She might say it was all his idea, but he still had the photographs. She couldn't paint herself as a total innocent in all this. He could prove she had the motive. She was the one who had everything to gain from getting Little Mary out of the picture. He never even met the little bitch!

Guilt and the fear of being exposed for what she was—that would keep her in line. As long as she valued her job with Biograph she would do whatever he told her. And if the business did happen to go belly-up, the pictures wouldn't be enough. He couldn't use them as a bargaining chip anymore. That's why he had insisted she marry him. They would drive down to Jersey as soon as this thing was over. Marriage would be better than photographs for keeping her in line. It would give him legal access to her earnings and a say in everything she did. To top it off, if they ever found themselves in court for some reason she wouldn't be able to take the stand and testify against him.

Augusta didn't see that one coming. But what could she say? If she wanted his help she had to agree. She was no smarter than any of the others, really. Most bitches couldn't see more than two feet ahead of them. Wave a new pair of shoes under their noses and they would forget everything else.

But hold on. If Augusta wasn't as smart as he used to think, what did that say about her so-called "foolproof" scheme? There could be other little flaws in her thinking. Maybe there was something there neither of them thought of!

You best stay on your toes, Deward Trawley. Could be more sides to this than a bigamists' convention.

The forlorn blast of a steamship sounded in the channel and his nostrils flared with the smell of salt water. Yes, the cliffs were just ahead now. The foliage was thinning out and more sunlight was falling on the path. He better pay attention to where he was stepping and not alert anyone to the danger.

A rustling of fabric was brought on the breeze. He tiptoed cautiously to behind the next fat trunk and risked a peek around. There was a clearing and then a wide flat rock that stretched to the edge. A lone female figure stood silhouetted by the sky. She wore a woolen coat with a bright neck scarf, and was absently dropping bits of twigs over the cliff. With each toss her blond curls bounced below the brim of her floppy hat. Off to her right lay Augusta's red winter coat, folded in a pile on a rock as their signal that things were going according to plan.

Everything depended on him now. He must not lose the advantage of surprise. He stepped softly around the tree, placing one foot ahead of the next. In four full strides he was across the open ground and at the edge of the rock. He could be upon her in a split second now.

The girl continued tearing at her branch, letting the pieces fall from the tips of her delicate fingers.

Deward lowered his foot and got set to spring. But something caught his eye. There in the leaves was something black and smooth as a snake. But when he looked closer he saw tiny, frazzled bits of fiber sticking from its shiny hide. He poked his toe at it and when it didn't move he lifted up a section. It was part of a cord that ran off around the rock to a larger coil and then wrapped itself around a three-foot piece of log at cliff's edge.

"Well," he said aloud, pulling back his foot. "What have we here?"

The shoulders of the girl bobbed a bit and she turned by degrees to face him.

Now things were starting to make sense. "Hello, Dirty Feet," he said.

"Hello, Deward."

"Change of plans?"

"I'm sorry."

"You could've died, you know?"

"I don't care."

"I could've pushed you over by mistake."

"It honestly doesn't matter. If I went through with this, I couldn't live with myself."

"Well, that's just plain stupid. You're the one who wanted this."

"At the start, maybe. But it turned out I just wasn't the person I thought I was."

"And where's that leave me?"

"I don't know. All I know is I'm not doing what you say anymore, Deward. If that's what you want, you might as well just throw me over the side."

He bent down and pulled up the black rope. "Looks like you went to a lot of trouble here." He looped the cord around his palm and caught it under his thumb, reeling in some slack and following where it led around the rock.

"At first, " she said, "when you were talking about a robbery, I thought I could do that. But then you were talking about killing him, or leaving him blinded. Awful things. I could never let you do that, Deward."

"What's he to you all at once?"

"He was nice to me."

"Is that so?"

"I do believe he's an artist."

"There you go again. Artist!" he exploded, making another couple of loops around his hand. "You had me fooled for a time. I was thinking you might be more than another dizzy dame."

Augusta watched him gather up the cord, tucking the loops under a thumb.

"You think that stuck-up Southerner gives one thought to people like us? It was that damn Confederacy of his that almost brought down the whole country."

"You surprise me, Deward. Here I was thinking you just wanted money."

He was at the log now and he looked closely to see how it was wrapped and tied around the bark with a thick knot. The thought of her laying a trap for him touched off a wave of anger. Without looking up he spoke very low now, hardly caring whether she heard him or not. "I don't deny I got a need for money," he said. Then with a sudden flick of his forearm the whole coil of rope shot from his hand and hurtled out over the precipice. It spiraled and unwound as it dropped out of view. "But I got an even bigger problem with disloyalty."

He stepped up and put his boot on the log. "You know what's a damn pity, though?" he asked.

"What's that, Deward?"

"You and me. I thought we were a good team. God forbid they ever give you bitches the right to vote." With a grunt he gave a forceful shove and straightened his leg, sending the log skidding over the edge. He listened to the splintering of branches as it fell, ending with a dull, far-off thud below.

The Palisades grew hushed, and Deward couldn't help flashing a little victory grin.

Augusta's eyes lowered almost seductively and she unstrapped the flaps of her overcoat. Was she going to offer herself in surrender, he wondered. It might be fun letting her think that she could still put things square between them. He had some time now. It would really be sweet to end things between them the same way they started.

But when she opened her coat all he saw was more black coils of rope in crisscrossing strands around her body. In a flash it occurred to him that he had been tricked. She set up a fake snare to hide the real one. Now with a yank to one loose end the rope fell free and she grabbed it in both fists for one swift, hard yank as she dove back across the rock.

Any slack in the rope vanished with a snap and it stretched taut as a loop leapt up around Deward's ankle and caught him by the foot. He kicked and stomped to break free as Augusta plunged both hands into the folds of her red coat and set another small log tumbling toward the ledge. It teetered on the brink an instant as Augusta drew back her boot and aimed a fast sure kick it its center, sending it plunging over the side.

Deward made a desperate lunge at her legs, grabbing hold of one and then fumbling for the other as she kicked and thrashed about blindly. The rope zipped past, whistling as it scraped against bedrock until the loop tightened around his ankle and his body jerked and he went sliding toward the chasm.

He fought for a firmer grip of Augusta's legs. Suddenly his tangled foot was floundering out in the open. He jammed his elbows against the hard rock but nothing could slow his slide now. In an instant his body had plummeted over the edge and fell free.

Something stopped their fall. He hugged tightly to Augusta's legs, his whole body weighted down by his left ankle. The rope dug into his flesh and muscle. With his free foot he kicked and flailed for something he could push against.

The only sound was a gentle wind and a lulling creak of the rope. He bent his neck as far back as he dared and tried to see above them. Augusta was apparently unconscious, hanging over the side on a single strand of rope. She had one end wrapped around her waist. The other was probably tied to a tree. It was bearing the load of both of them now, the only thing that was keeping them alive.

He tried to adjust his grip, see if somehow he could shimmy up her body. But it was no use. The weight of the log holding him was too great. He would need leverage, some toehold. The face of the cliff was possibly within reach. He might get them swinging a bit and be able to reach it. But it was hardly more than eroded roots and sand and an exposed matting of moss.

He kicked his free boot toward the vegetation and stretched out his leg. The sound of the rope sawing against the rock made him stop. He dared a quick look down across his right shoulder to the peaceful, implacable surface of the Hudson.

"Help," he heard Augusta mutter. She did not have the air in her lungs for a proper yell. He heard her draw a deeper breath. "Help!" she said slightly louder.

There she goes! Someone'll hear for sure.

"Shut up!" he shouted to her.

She tried to look down at him below her. Her eyes did not seem to focus and he could tell she was on the verge of passing out again.

Gotta get myself out of here! Gotta pull myself up!

Then he felt a warm trickle on his arms. Pink droplets splattered against his cheeks. He tasted salt and saw a watery red dye streaming down her naked legs.

Blood!

Bleeding! … The dumb bitch … is … bleeding … on …

He felt himself slip. Her blood pooled around his arms and seeped into his hands and fingers. He could easily lose his grip. He lifted an arm to let the blood flow through and raised it a bit for a higher grip.

The blood was richer now, coming at him faster. It was falling in his face. His eyes. Blinding him. He tried to move a shoulder, bring it close enough to rub an eye clear. His grip was giving.

Help! Save me. … Oh, Mother, no!

His fingers unlaced and his arms slid down. He dropped lower and lower, first to her ankles, then her feet. There was just enough breath left for a fast, horrified groan as he gave up his struggle and let himself fall free. The air rushed past his ears and he thought of the wind and the sun and all the lovely smells of the sea.

TWENTY-FOUR
"Love Finds a Way"

"You're awake."

"Yes."

"You need anything?"

"Water. Please."

The nurse filled Augusta's glass from a pitcher and held it close over her chest. She helped her raise her head from the pillow and waited for her to finish.

"Thank you."

"You've got one of these." The nurse lifted a metal bedpan with a little flip toward the ceiling. "Let me know when and I'll help you." She slipped it back on a shelf under the nightstand. "You'll have to stay off your feet another day or so."

"All right."

"Anything else you need?"

"No. I was looking out the window. … It's so peaceful."

The nurse nodded. "I'll let them know you're awake."

The doctor had waves of black hair shot with white, and a goatee that had overrun his chin. He could hardly have been more than forty but he looked haggard, certainly too tired to attend to his grooming.

She did not hear him come in, but all at once he said, "Miss Lee?" and he was standing there at the side of her bed, rifling through the sheets of paper on his clipboard.

"How are you feeling?"

"Groggy."

"Can you tell me where it hurts?"

"Sides. … Stomach."

"Uh-huh. Well, you have three broken ribs. One quite serious. We might need to operate. Your abdomen—that will mend by itself. You had a miscarriage."

She did not reply.

"Did you know you were pregnant?"

"I thought I might be."

"Oh? Why is that?"

"I was getting ... faint. Light-headed. Quite a bit."

"Did you see anyone about it?"

She turned her head back and forth on the pillow.

The doctor's goatee lifted as he pursed his lips. "Well, you're not anymore."

"I understand."

"Is the father ... in the picture?"

"What do you mean?"

"Do you know the father?"

She rolled her head back and forth. "No father."

"Virgin birth, huh?"

"If you like."

"Except for the birth, of course." He grinned and scribbled something on his clipboard. "Is there anyone you wish notified?"

"No." She watched him scribble some more. "What will they do ... with the baby?"

"It'll be buried."

"No!"

"What?"

"No mud holes. I want the body. I will bury her."

"Very well. We'll store the remains until you can make the arrangements. I'll leave word."

"Thank you. And thank you ... for all this."

He looked up from his writing, quite surprised. "For what?"

She lifted her hand in a weak circle. "This. A private room. I feel very special."

"It's policy in these cases. Until the police are through."

"Police?"

"They're outside. They're waiting to ask you some questions."

"Oh."

"After that you'll be transferred to a ward."

"All right."

"Don't worry. We'll have you good as new in no time." He opened the door and paused in the doorway to look back at her. "They said they found you hanging by a rope?"

"Yes."

The doctor shook his head and let the door close behind him.

Augusta drifted, opening her eyes from time to time. She was in an engine room, all snug and warm. She wondered what had happened to the vibration. It was too smooth. We must have docked, she decided. Any minute now there will be men coming ... along ...

When she opened her eyes again there were two policemen staring down at her from the foot of the bed. They introduced themselves but she hardly heard their names. The shorter one was going to do all the talking, and the taller one flipped open a notebook and held a pencil stub at the ready.

"Ma'am, we understand from the Fort Lee constabulary—his report stated it was an accidental falling. The victim—uh, Mr. Trawley—fell to his death. Did you see it?"

"I was there."

"So you two knew each other?"

"Yes."

"Where did you meet?"

"He helped me with my luggage. At the train station. When I first got to the city."

"When was that?"

"February."

"Did you have any further association with the deceased?"

"He helped me find lodgings."

"Why would he do that?"

"He became a sort of ... theatrical agent."

"And he arranged your meeting with, uh ... Mr. Griffiths?"

"Mr. Griffith. No 'S.' ... Yes, that's right."

"And afterward?"

"What do you mean?"

"Did your professional relationship get ... more personal?"

"I think he might have wanted that. I didn't."

"Did you know Mr. Trawley had a police record?"

"I knew he was arrested, yes."

"Yes, ma'am. And after he was released, did he contact you?"

"No."

"Are you sure?"

"I never saw him."

"What do you think he was doing on the Palisades that morning?"

"He must have heard something. He must have known where we

were going. It was no secret. We were going to make a picture. He sometimes acted … at the same studio."

"Did anyone but you notice him there?"

"I don't know."

"How do you think he found you there on the cliffs?"

"Maybe he followed me. Or someone else told him. I couldn't say."

"What do you know about the ribbons?"

"Ribbons?"

"Colored ribbons. Little pieces. We found some in Mr. Trawley's vest pocket. There were others, too … up on the bluffs, under the trees."

"I'm afraid I don't know about that."

"What about the ropes?"

"Ropes?"

"There were three. The one tied around your waist and to a tree. We found one tied to a small log down below. And a third might have been attached to him. His ankle, perhaps. There were severe abrasions to his leg."

"He must have had the ropes with him. I was hanging there. I thought I would fall. He threw down a loop and told me to put it around me. He must have tied it to a tree. That's the only rope I know about. That's all I remember. … I heard a scream. I didn't see him fall."

"What about the logs. How do you explain them?"

"I can't recall any logs."

"So, Mr. Trawley was attempting to save you?"

"Yes."

"He fell trying to rescue you?"

She lifted her shoulders in uncertainty. "That's what it seemed like."

"Is there anything else you can add? For the record?"

"No. I mean, I'm feeling very tired all at once. Maybe I'll think of something … later."

The next time she opened her eyes the sun was sunk below the window. A harsh overhead light made her squint as she tried to make out a figure standing in the glare. It was a thin, beaked man holding out a bouquet of red summer roses.

"Mr. Griffith—" she muttered.

"My dear. How do you feel now?"

"I didn't recognize you … without a hat."

He seemed to smile at her.

"How long were you there?"

"Only a minute or two. You looked so restful."

"You brought me flowers?"

"From Biograph. From all of us. You had us worried."

"I'm feeling better."

"What an awful thing to go through."

"Are the police—?"

"They're gone. I think they have what they needed."

"Really?"

"Bobby set them straight."

"Our Bobby? Why? What did he tell them?"

"There was some question about the ropes. It turns out Bobby knew all about them. He evidently saw them among Mr. Trawley's possessions. In a trunk, I believe. He positively identified them as belonging to Clang—*Mr. Trawley*."

"Bless little Bobby."

"We all suspected that fellow was up to no good. Bobby told me he was following you. It must have been terrifying. Why did you never tell me?"

"It was only a suspicion. What could anyone do?"

"I would have filed a complaint. That's what police are there for. They're certainly not paid to go bothering poor girls in the hospital."

"So, you think they're finished with me?"

"I told the detectives they should classify the whole thing for what it was, attempted murder. But they want the official record to show it as an accident. Less paperwork for them, I suspect."

"I can't believe it's over. What a nightmare."

"You can put it all behind you, my dear. Your whole life awaits."

"My job, too?"

Griffith's smile vanished and his gaze fell to the bouquet in his hands. "Unfortunately, no. The police reports, the medical records— they are being splashed all over the newspapers. Yellow journalism."

"Oh."

"Better prepare yourself for a patch of rough water."

"Is it because of … the baby?"

Griffith's eyes avoided hers. "Maybe … if you had been married. I am truly sorry. I can't ask Mr. Marvin to let you represent Biograph now. When you're stronger, I can help you find a position elsewhere."

"I understand."

"You know, Miss Lawrence has given me notice that she will be leaving. Perhaps Miss Arvidson will be next."

"Oh. ... I am sorry to hear that."

"Sometimes I have to wonder—all the fighting, the risks, the broken relationships—are these little stories we tell on film worth it all?"

"I heard a wise man say once, 'There are no sad outcomes in art.'"

He smiled. "Who said that?"

"It was you. Up in Nina's costume shop."

"I forgot that."

"Just before ... the accident, I met a young priest. He also thought that what you do has value."

"Oh. Well, if a priest said that, maybe I'm on the right track." He smiled. "I've been hearing good things from companies out on the West Coast. They say California is ideal for picture-makers. Constant sun. Billy and I are talking about taking a group out there for the winter."

"I'd love to see California. Some day."

"The older I get, the more I return to the words of that old church hymn: 'This world is not my home. I am bound across the river.'" He looked suddenly self-conscious and gave a small snort. "Or maybe California."

He talked a bit more about his plans but her energy began to ebb and he must have noticed. "I'll ask the nurse to find a vase for these," he said, raising the bouquet a final time.

"Thank everybody for me."

"Is there anything else I can do?"

"If you run into Owen Moore, it would be nice to see him."

"Of course."

Then he was gone. After a time the nurse reappeared with the summer roses fluffed out in a pottery vase and set them on Augusta's nightstand.

She did not really expect Owen to come rushing to her with concern. He was probably too busy with the new girl and those natural blond curls. But she wished he would come because she really wanted to tell him something. She wanted to say he had gotten it all wrong. Virginity wasn't as important as he made out. It didn't have all that much value at all. Everyone came into the world with virginity. There was no extra cost for it. It was free with delivery. All it meant was the absence of experience, and that was fleeting and temporary. The thing that really turned out to have value was a clean conscience. That only came with experience and over time. It made life not only enjoyable, but worth living. And a clear conscience had to be earned bit by bit, minute by minute, choice by choice. That's what she wanted to tell him.

Sometime after breakfast the next morning Augusta got another caller. Her head was clearer and she was daydreaming about mornings on the showboat when there came a light rap at the door. It opened slowly and in poked a flushed cheek and a groomed mustache followed by the round head of Assistant Fire Marshal Ellis Edwards.

"Are you feeling fit for a visitor?" he asked. He stepped in with his arms around a tall bouquet of lilies and white tulips.

"Yes. Please, come in."

"My most sincere condolences to you, Miss Lee."

"Oh. ... Then you read the newspapers?"

"I did."

"And about ... ?"

"Your baby, yes. I am terribly grieved by your loss."

"Thank you. That's generous of you. It's just that, right now, I am not in a particularly apologetic mood."

"You have nothing to apologize to me for."

"Good. Because I no longer have my job at Biograph."

"I am sorry."

"But, you know, I will be out of here soon and I will find another one."

"I'm sure you can do whatever you set your aim on."

"You see, I like earning my own way. I like doing a job like no one else can do it, and to know I am good at it. I'm as smart as the next person, smarter than some. I like having a salary and fixing up my own place to live. I don't need a man to tell me where to live or where to work. And when women get the vote I will be at the front of the line telling them, 'Don't you dare waste it, don't you—'" Her voice was taken over by a sudden hacking cough.

"Here, let me," he said, crushing the flowers against his chest as he lunged for the water glass. He held it under her lips, just as he had that first day back in Griffith's office.

"Slowly, slowly," he coached as she swallowed. Then he set the glass aside as she settled back on the pillow.

"I know you are a woman of her word," he said. "There's not a doubt of that in my body. And I am a man of my word, as well. I would never stand in the way of someone becoming her own person, standing on her own feet. It's a blessing in this life. I know I was not put on this Earth to be anyone's judge—nor anyone's warden, either."

"Thank you. For the flowers," she said at the end of an awkward silence.

"And this, too." From behind the bundle of long stems he brought forth a thin package wrapped in butcher paper and tied with string.

"For me? What is it?"

"Open it, if you like."

She was not prepared for its weight and it fell against her stomach. She pulled the string and peeled back the wrapping and in her hands laid a gold-painted statue about eight inches tall, cast in metal. At first she took it for a model of an oil derrick or a new electrical tower.

He saw she was bewildered. "You know what it is?"

"A paperweight?"

"It's the Eiffel Tower. ... In Paris."

"Oh."

"You remember?"

"Yes."

"You know what I'm asking?"

"Yes."

"You have an answer?"

She gazed down at her prize and the hint it carried. The small twist of a smile formed on her lips.

"Of course," she said.

EPILOGUE
September 1920

"He-ere," said Billy Bitzer. "Let me *luke* at you."

"It doesn't feel right, that's all," he said, turning to face Billy. "They must've gotten the measurements wrong."

"Bond Street? Never would they make such an error."

He tugged on the sleeves and looked again in the gold-framed mirror above the serving tray. "We're all human," he said, stretching each arm across his chest to find the source of the pull. "Human beings are known to make mistakes now and then."

"Not when they are dealing with the world-famous D.W. *Griffitt,*" said Billy. "Turn to me again."

"Anyway, there isn't time to have it fixed."

"I think you look splendid."

He attempted a smile but it would not stick. It was such a petty thing to care about one's appearance on a day like this. The problem was that everyone would want a good long look at him. "I've always hated black suits," he said. "They make me look like a small 'i.' ... A small 'i' with a large nose."

"Well, you *luke* like a capital 'I' to me," said Billy.

It was a shame Mack wouldn't be there. Sennett had a knack for slicing through pretenses. He might have turned the whole thing into one of his "slapsticks."

There's this vain man, he would say. *Someone with too much dignity for his own good—make him a symphony conductor. So this celebrated maestro is away on tour when his valet fails to show up one morning. It turns out he passed away in his sleep. The maestro wants to attend the services but all he has with him are his long tails. He needs a proper black suit, so he hurries up and down Main Street, checking every men's shop but there's nothing in his size.*

Now Mack would do one of his trademark pauses before adding, *He's a very small maestro.*

Anyway, time is running out when he spots this magicians' novelty shop and there's a mannequin in the window dressed in the perfect dark suit. It's cut small even for him but he's desperate. So he rents it and hurries off to the funeral parlor—tossing away metal hoops and live pigeons and pulling out endless streams of colored scarves as he runs.

Of course, Sennett would have to have his cops. *So the maestro arouses suspicions of the cop on the beat. He phones in a report from the street box to a cross-eyed desk sergeant who, it turns out, has just gotten word of a nearby bank robbery. The desk sergeant rings the alarm and all of Mack's beloved Keystone Kops come piling into their rickety old Model-T and go racing off down the street. They jump out in front of the funeral parlor and fall all over one another to get inside, only to find the place is filled with dignified little men all in black suits.*

As an idea it wouldn't work. Not even the fabulously rich and famous Mack Sennett could whip up laughs in a convention of mourners.

"Are you ill?" asked Billy.

He had forgotten he was not alone and his features had taken on a brooding air. He plunged a finger inside his collar. "It's this shirt," he said. "The thing is strangling me. It's how they make them these days. I swear, the whole modern age has it in for me."

Billy chuckled softly. "Sounds like someone could use a drink."

"Last night I would have sold my grandmother to General Sherman for a nightcap. I was about to dial up room service when it hit me. The appalling truth of it. Talk about being made to feel like a child again."

"If you wanted a nightcap I'm sure the front desk could have helped."

"So that's it? We must all surrender to being outlaws now?"

"We have no one to blame but ourselves," said Billy. "Remember 'The Drunkard's Reformation' and the others? We gave those temperance people what they wanted."

"But we got to continue making our pictures."

"And they got their Prohibition."

He stopped fiddling with the collar and let his arms fall at his sides. "It's no use. The suit wins," he said. With a final shrug he turned to Billy as if to apologize. "Everything seems a little overwhelming today."

Billy nodded in sympathy and then lifted up a finger to him. "Hold on," he said with an impish twinkle. "Wait here." He turned and trotted toward the door.

Griffith checked his wristwatch. "It's nearly ten."

But Billy had already twisted the knob and pulled the door toward him. "I'm just going down the—" There was a loud slam.

Silence dropped over him like a net. The suite was too high for the city noise. He felt isolated, paralyzed. Soon he would run out of air.

In desperation he returned to the mirror, bending toward it to study the grayish folds under his eyes. These restless nights had done him no favors. There would be so many of his colleagues there from the Biograph days, some he had not seen in a decade. They would tell him he hardly looked a day older. They would be lying.

Linda, of course, had always been a wonder at these things. She could talk to anyone and it always sounded effortless. All he needed to do was stand by, express his condolences whenever attention turned his way, maybe mutter a word or two to cover his awkwardness. After that he would be free to wander off and find someone to talk a little business.

But it was at least a year since he and Linda had even traded nods at some work function. And Miss Lillian had flatly told him no, she didn't care to come in so early with him. It was a waste booking another suite in the city, she said. She would leave Mamaroneck in the morning along with the others. She wanted the hour on the train to watch the buildings pass by and be with her own thoughts. It was such a Lillian thing to say.

Why did the women in his life always seem to come up missing in his hour of need?

Damn! Why wouldn't that hair stay down? Didn't it understand that he had forgotten to bring his own comb?

He stomped off to the bedroom and snatched the metal comb from the vanity set there. The sharp, cutting pain of its teeth across his scalp was small penance for his failures. Lord only knew how his hair would look when he went to remove his hat in church. Maybe hotel management wouldn't care if he just borrowed their comb for the morning.

He slipped it in an upper coat pocket and patted the lapel for comfort.

Anyway, it wasn't Miss Lillian's absence that bothered him. And he never blamed Linda for walking out, not even for an instant. He knew he was no one's picture of a romantic hero. With Mary, though, he had wanted it to be different. She was his ideal in so many ways.

He forced himself to accept that she did not feel the same. Early on he decided it was better to keep her close as a friend than to lose her altogether to jealousy.

Through the darkest hours of her divorce and all her fears of a career-ending scandal, he had been there for her. So how could she have turned her back on him now? How was it possible that she hadn't moved Heaven and Earth if that's what it took to be here for him today?

Maybe he could have done more to warn her about Owen. It would have saved her from so much grief. But she didn't ask his opinion. And no one expected her to just up and run off with the man like she did. She never even told her own mother until after they were wed.

Later, when she said it was time to quit Biograph, he did not try to talk her out of it. It would be their "trial separation," he joked, never once betraying his sense of abandonment. And he did take her back later without a word of reproach, only to see her turn and run out on him again.

As things went downhill with Owen he made himself available in case she needed him. He knew how alarmed she was by Owen's need of alcohol and how she blamed Owen for her own drinking problem.

Dashing Doug Fairbanks was one of the first of the new crop of picture stars to sign a public sobriety pledge—a truly divisive thing in the polarized years leading up to Prohibition. Many in the industry called him "stick-in-the-mud Doug." But liquor had caused such a chasm between Mary Pickford and most others in Hollywood that only a genuine teetotaling athlete like Fairbanks could have made the leap across.

One day without warning there he was leaping around on her tennis court, looking as entitled as any owner. Anyone could see something was up. He flashed his famous teeth—they always looked whiter than anyone else's teeth because his skin held such a deep sun-browned glow—and raised his racket over his head like a Hottentot with a battlefield trophy.

Naturally, Mary was her own woman and she never asked his opinion of Douglas any more than of Owen. If she had he would have called the man an over-active showoff.

But the newspapers sure ate it up. Douglas and Mary. Might as well have been *Sir* Douglas and *Princess* Mary. Was that notorious flirtation, that Hollywood courtship, really as important *as a world war*? That's how the headlines made it seem. Joe Public woke up one day demanding romance for breakfast and decided to devour theirs. Poor Mary was the only one in the world who did not get to enjoy the storybook thrill of it.

She might have looked like royalty in her tailored suits and million-dollar smiles on all those Liberty Loan drives together. But he knew how unhappy she was. When the war news was bleak, it was his shoulder she came to cry on. He knew the strains on her. He never once chastised her for those empty bottles outside her door each morning.

Owen had made Mary's life miserable for so long. In the end, even one hundred thousand dollars was not too big a price for her to pay to be rid of the man. After a "quickie" Nevada divorce she and Douglas were finally free to pursue their own happiness together.

But he knew the path was far from clear. Marriage was best, after all, when limited to two parties. Theirs had a third: Doug's jealousy. It was embarrassing to watch, really. He could be so juvenile. What sort of husband insisted his wife never even *dance* with another man?

If her marriage failed again, he vowed to be there for her. He didn't place too much faith in the whole United Artists enterprise. A business like this one had to have a strong person in charge to make the decisions. It couldn't be managed via shares and ballots. But one thing United Artists gave him was a very good reason to be close at hand. If she and Douglas didn't last, he darned well wouldn't let her get away from him again.

Through all of the weary bond drives and divorce hearings and threats of a public scandal he had been at her side. That's what hurt him so much about her not being with him today. Romance was famous for being fickle, but being jilted by a friend felt more like betrayal.

A faint rattling in the front room drew him out in time to see Billy's smiling face poking around the door. "It's your genie with a bottle!" teased the cameraman. He lifted up a silver hip flask and started toward him.

"Why, what have you there, Mr. Bitzer?"

Billy was making small circles in the air like a priest spreading incense. "Your wish is my command," he said. "Have you something to pour it in?"

"I do." He took the glass by a pitcher on the serving table. "I must say, I am a little surprised at you."

"Desperate times," came the reply.

With a metallic clink the flask found the rim and Griffith watched silver reflections of the room dance on its polished surface. When the trickle came to a halt he held his glass to eye level and waited for Billy to give the toast.

"To Bobby," said the cameraman.

He let himself savor the sharp bite of the rye, then smacked his lips with satisfaction. "Let's sit," he said, motioning Billy toward the sitting area.

He settled himself back on a sand-colored settee with wide, curved arms, making sure to straighten the crease of his trousers. Billy perched across from him on the edge of a leather wingback chair.

After one more sip he was beginning to feel back in control again. "We Southerners like to think we know a few things about whiskey," he said. "That, sir, is not moonshine."

"No. Everyone's much more sophisticated now. Even the bootleg hooch is better."

"It was said that Owen provided some of the best."

"Owen Moore?" Billy's nose wrinkled. "Why did you have to mention him?"

"Tell me the truth, Billy. What do you think Mary saw in that man?"

"She was very young."

"Even at seventeen Mary was nobody's fool."

The cameraman puckered his lips and his bushy eyebrows dipped in thought. "Long ago I reached the conclusion there's no logic to much of what we do in life."

"How do you mean that?"

"We have no rational control over the important things. Who we love, who we hate—it's not of our choosing. Why look for explanations? The heart is not a matter of science." He held out his flask. "More?"

"Thank you."

Billy held the neck over Griffith's glass and poured. "She was her family's sole support. Maybe marriage was her escape from a grownup's responsibility. Maybe if her father hadn't been gone it would not have happened."

Griffith raised his glass in a toast. "To missing fathers."

Billy dipped his flask and took a drink.

"You should be a father, Billy."

"At my age?"

"You're not too old."

"Nora's ten years older than I am. Don't tell her I told you. No. It's not in the cards. And what about you?"

"Me? A father?" He waved a hand and scoffed. "I'd have been terrible at it."

"So, you learn," said Billy.

"Mine never did. You know, that man never once told any of us kids that he loved us. It wasn't his way. I remember standing on the porch with him one morning—it's such a clear memory. He put his hand on my head and looked down at me with a smile. 'Son, how are you this day?' That's all he said. To me it was like Moses parting the Red Sea."

Billy raised his flask somberly. "To missing fathers," he said.

Griffith tipped his glass back for its final drops.

"A little more?"

"What time is it?"

"Ten-twenty."

"No. They'll be coming now. I'll have to talk to people. They're all going to ask me how I feel."

"So?"

"I might tell them."

"Then do."

"No. No, thank you. I'd rather just save all my feelings for my pictures from here out."

"Pictures can't love you back."

He stared a moment into his empty glass. "Do you know what they called him?"

" 'Roaring Jake'?"

"No. Not him. I meant ... *Bobby*."

Billy drew back a little in his chair. "Oh."

"They called him 'Griffith's Boy.'"

"Who called him that?"

"Some magazine. I can't remember which now. It was a profile. The headline was, 'Griffith's Boy.' It was just so demeaning. Not to me, mind you. To Robert. He had really grown into such a fine young actor."

"I will always think of him as a boy. Taking a dive off the ferry dock."

"Into the ice!"

"Yes," said Billy, his face illuminated with a smile.

"If there was a scene he couldn't play, I never found it. He was as good as any actor I ever worked with." He shook his head. "'Griffith's Boy,'" he repeated. "I never thought of him like that."

"You spent a lot of time at the hospital."

"Yes. If it hadn't been for the premiere I would have spent more. But there were so many others depending on me. I had interviews, appointments."

"Did he ever tell you about … that night?"

"I spoke to Heerman about it. You know Victor Heerman?"

"No."

"He's a comedy director. Worked at Keystone for a time."

"With Mr. Sennett?"

Griffith nodded. "Yes, and afterwards. Victor and Bobby came out from Los Angeles together on the train. They were sharing that room at the Seymour. Victor told me how he went off that night for a script meeting. He left Bobby in good spirits. They were both looking forward to the premiere of 'Way Down East.' Somehow they got his number. When they said Bobby was in the hospital, he just couldn't believe it."

"I still can't."

"I hardly had a moment to think until the premiere was over. On Friday I went straight there."

"How was he?"

"In a fog. The doctors were giving him something for the pain. He asked about the premiere, how the audience liked the picture. On Saturday he was more like himself. He was propped up in bed, doing a crossword puzzle, kidding the nurses."

"Did you ask him about the gun?"

"No. I knew what he told the police."

"That it fell out of his bag?"

"Wrapped in a pair of trousers, yes. It was a .38. He was unpacking a suitcase and it fell out and went off. The bullet caught him right here." He touched the soft patch under his ribs. "On his left side."

"But he didn't think it was serious?"

"No. He even tried to talk them out of calling an ambulance. He was just embarrassed. He kept apologizing to the hotel staff for causing such a fuss."

"Who brings a gun across country? Do you think he was feeling threatened or something?"

"He told police he needed it for a role."

"But he didn't come back here to make a movie."

"I know. And carrying a gun without a permit is a violation in this city. The Sullivan Act, or something. It's a felony."

"Terrible."

Griffith checked his wristwatch again, feeling agitated. "What time do you have?"

Billy pulled on a gold fob. "Ten-thirty-five."

"They should he here."

"So that's why they wanted to take Bobby to jail."

"I don't think it would've come to that. But changing his story made things worse. He tried to convince them a panhandler sold him the gun."

Billy shook his head. "Bobby, Bobby."

"He said he wanted to do the man a kindness."

"Bobby always tried to do the right thing."

"Well, the police didn't really care. Whether he brought it with him or acquired it illegally, it was still a felony."

"He would never intentionally break any laws."

"When I went to see him Sunday he had taken a turn for the worse. He was mentally confused. He wanted to tell me something but he was weak and couldn't get it out. I could barely hear his voice. There were tears. I know … I know he wanted to say something."

Billy was hanging on every word now, waiting for the ones that would fall into the right combination to unlock the mystery of why it had happened.

"I shouldn't have left him, but there were things that still needed my attention. His doctor assured he was getting stronger. He had the best care, the medicine was working. When I got back, Father Bill was there, standing by Bobby's bed, reading him the Last Rites."

There were muffled footsteps in the hall then a tapping at the door.

"Yes?" answered both men at once.

Someone from the hotel said, "Mr. Griffith? Your driver's here with your car, sir."

"Fine, fine. Thank you."

Billy was looking again at his watch. "That means mine will be here too," he said, rising to his feet.

"Please reconsider. Come ride with me."

"No. My Nora has been beside herself since all this happened. Crying night and day. I promised her it would be the two of us together. Just her and me … saying our farewells to Bobby."

He saw a bit of embarrassment and a new brittleness in the older man's eyes. If the unflappable Billy Bitzer were to fell apart now there was no guarantee he would not follow. "I understand," he said. "Give Nora my love."

He went off to find his favorite butternut overcoat and his brushed fedora. When he looked back, Billy had slipped away into the hall.

With a last look in the mirror he patted his coat pocket to make sure he had the comb. Yes, it was there. Good. If he lost that he wouldn't have a prayer of getting through what was to come.

"We still have time," said D.W. Griffith, scooting in through the rear door and settling back on the seat. "Can we make a short detour?"

The man in the chauffeur's cap adjusted his rear view mirror. "Any direction in particular, sir?"

"Yes. Cross-town. Union Square and East 14th. That neighborhood."

The cap gave a small dip and then turned as the driver waited for a break in the flow of cars.

No reason to get there early. Socializing and what was called "small talk" were difficult under the best of circumstances.

How could he face Mrs. Harron now? Time after time he had assured her on the phone that her son would be fine. He said God would hear their prayers. Then she booked the first train out from Los Angeles. But no train would have been fast enough. Today he had no words of comfort left in him for Bobby's mother.

Besides, mothers had an instinct for the truth. They knew when their sons' hearts had been broken. It wouldn't mean a thing to her to hear what an ordeal they had all gone through up in Vermont. She probably knew how Bobby felt about being passed over for "Way Down East."

"Turning on East 14th now," announced the driver.

Really? It all looked so very different. The row of brownstones had shaken off a century of coal soot and smoke, and the natural reddish-orange tone of the brick was beginning to show through. Basement coal chutes were sealed off or converted into flower boxes.

Most of the old canvas awnings were pulled down and carted away, and the flow of traffic was much more orderly and sane despite the marked increase in cars.

Number 11 was apparently a private residence again. The walk-down tailor shop next door still remained. "That's where we were," he said in an urgent rush. "That's where it all started."

The driver's head did not turn. "Would you like me to pull over here?"

"No. It's all right. Drive on."

It was not his world anymore. He often felt that, even at his new studio. He would meet former colleagues or come upon a table full of actors at lunch and their attempts to recapture the past always rang hollow. They spoke of scenes from the early films as though they were real experiences, and got actors mixed up with the roles they had played.

The sense that he was hardly more than a ghost already would come over him. He thought if he accidently bumped a piece of scenery or lifted a prop the only ones he would excite were spiritualists.

The driver steered around a stalled taxi near the park at Union Square and stuck out an arm to make a left turn.

Spiritualists. Now there was a word from his youth. It was a dated name for the charlatans of a more innocent time. When the twentieth century was still naive enough to believe in séances, the spiritualists would swindle widows out of their estates. Today the ones running a similar scam were known as the Hollywood press. They bilked the gullible out of their pocket change with magazines that claimed to put them in touch with the immortal apparitions known as *movie stars*.

He would never support a word they wrote again—not after what they had done to Bobby. His heart had been set on that role of David in "Way Down East." He knew he was the right age and he let it be known to the press that he was most anxious to play it. But David had to be a strong romantic hero with a virile mystique. Bobby was best suited for playing naïve young men with a "killer slouch"— clean-cut college boys with attitude.

No, the one most suited for the role of David was young Richard Barthelmess. He had a sensitive but commanding masculine quality on screen. Besides, the studio needed a guarantee for its investment. Barthelmess had proven a hit with ticket-buyers in "Broken Blossoms."

Marketing said the drama needed all the help it could get, and Barthelmess would attract the bulge in post-war female ticket-buyers.

Bobby had to be told he was out, but in person and with great tact and sensitivity. No one but his longtime director could do that. He knew what he would have to say to soften the boy's disappointment and allay his fears. He would remind him of the value to all of making practical business decisions. He would make a vow that they would be working together again soon.

But before he had the chance to have that private meeting, the story was out there in hard newsprint. The press jackals had picked up on the gossip that Barthelmess was in and Harron was out. Bobby read all the "inside" accounts in the trades. Barthelmess had more sex appeal than he did. Harron was washed up. He was too old to play juveniles and was loaned out to Metro Pictures because no one wanted to work with him any longer, especially his longtime protector, the cold and aloof D.W. Griffith.

He had left shortly after that for Vermont and didn't speak directly to Bobby again. When "Way Down East" finished shooting, it was Lillian Gish who invited him to come to New York as her guest for the premiere.

That last cross-country train ride must have given him plenty of time to sit and brood about being passed over for the movie. All the planted advance word in the press was what a big splash the drama was about to make. The stories probably opened old wounds and stirred thoughts of how he had been betrayed by the ones he counted on. In his pain he might have considered taking the easy way out. Perhaps in a moment of weakness—that night before the premiere, alone in his hotel room—he had attempted to follow through.

The mystery surrounding his gun just underscored people's doubts. Even Bobby knew how bad it looked for him. "You don't think I did this on purpose, do you?" was often his first anguished question to bedside visitors. He swore on the Bible to Father Bill that it was nothing but a horrible freak accident.

No one wanted to suggest otherwise. His mother and sister were still dependent on his earnings, for one thing. Suicide would put a quick end to Bobby's remaining marquee draw. And as with any devout Catholic, the one thing that mattered above all else was being laid to rest in hallowed ground. Just the suspicion that he might have taken his own life would threaten that. The only thing left now for those who loved Bobby was to see that he got his last, most cherished desire.

The driver pulled up behind a line of limousines waiting outside St. Joseph's. Streams of mourners dawdled as they climbed out of backseats and headed up the steps to the wide wooden doors.

Near the top landing by a pillar was Lillian Gish. She stood anonymously behind her dark veils until her head turned to the light and he caught a glimpse of that telltale drooping of her mouth. The frail, draped woman leaning against her was almost certainly Mrs. Harron. She had not regained her strength from the long trip yet, and she probably never would.

Lillian's younger sister Dorothy had meant to be there but she was still eight or nine days from home. She had been off traveling in Europe when the news came. Dorothy and Bobby had become romantically linked in the past few months, and many expected them to announce their engagement when she returned. Now there was no reason for her to rush home. She was going to miss her final chance to say goodbye.

The whole thing was just too damned heartbreaking.

Watching Bobby slip away under that thin hospital blanket—it was sadder than he could have ever imagined. He had sat at bedsides when his relatives passed. He always found the sense of peace and ultimate release profoundly moving. Whenever he staged such scenes in his films he tried to respect the human intimacy of those last moments, filming them from a distance. But Bobby's passing had played out before him as if in one merciless, unrelenting close-up.

Whatever Bobby's personal trials, the traces were all there on display in his final hours. He had directed Bobby so many times he recognized each emotion. Bewilderment, confusion, dread, regret—there was hardly a flicker of feeling he did not read in those soft, expressive eyes. When his struggles ceased and his doubts disappeared, the only thing they left was the smooth, lineless face of a young and innocent man. *Griffith's Boy.*

Two attendants appeared at the cathedral doors and went to help Lillian and the frail Mrs. Harron inside. Oh, good, all the others were now pulling away from their private clusters to head up the steps.

In another minute or two his way would be clear. He could dash inside and find space for himself in a back pew. He wouldn't have to speak to anyone until after everything was over.

"I'll get out now," he told the driver, and waited for him to come and open the rear door.

He hurried around some stragglers and was starting up the steps when a tall, scruffy-bearded man moved from the railing as if he intended to tackle him.

"Excuse me," he said, stepping close to block the way.

He was only a panhandler, he thought. He pushed a hand down in his pocket to find the poor fellow a spare bill or two. But the pants were not his and the pockets were sewn shut. "Sorry. I have nothing for you today," he said, patting his hips.

"You're Mr. Griffith."

"Why ... yes." He looked closer to see if the man was someone he might have known. He was dressed in a heavy wool turtleneck and work trousers stained with various dried textures of clay and mud. Still, he was too hale and hearty to be a hobo. "Have we met?"

"I thought I recognized that nose. Meaning no offense."

"We've learned to live with one another."

"You don't know me," said the stranger. "I'm from New Orleans. Originally, anyway. By trade I'm a sculptor."

"Is that so?"

"I studied with Daniel Chester French. Maybe you heard of him?"

"Indeed. The Lincoln Memorial statue. You learned from the best."

"My limitations—that's what I learned. Blocks of stone and figures for library steps. Sometimes a headstone frieze, or a cornice with an angel. From time to time someone recommends me for a commission."

"Yes, I see. Is there something you want?"

"That's how I met Augusta Lee," he said.

"Who did you say? Augusta Lee?"

"Yes. You know her. She says she worked for you."

"I remember a girl by that name. It's been a number of years."

"Eleven."

"Yes. Where is she now?"

"Couldn't tell you. It's been some years for me, too. I was hoping she might show up here today."

Both men stopped to scan the few faces still hurrying toward the church.

"She was quite a beauty," said the man.

"Yes, she was."

"I tried to catch her likeness in my angels. Never did pull it off, though. Maybe Mr. French could have. But not me."

"Well, pity she didn't come. I would've loved to see her again."

"Rich ladies can disappear on a whim."

"Rich ladies? No, not Augusta Lee, surely. She was a simple working girl."

"Rich enough to pay me for some months of work."

"Well, good for her. I'd like to talk, but right now I really should—"

The man had been studying his face as he spoke. "Your nose gave me a lot of trouble."

"Excuse me?"

"All I had was a couple of photos to work from. No real profiles. But I could see its shape. Maybe not its length."

"You made a study of me?"

"Not a full sculpture. But Miss Lee insisted. She wanted you in there."

"Where can I see this creation?"

"I can't tell you that either."

"You can't?"

"Don't even know if the place has a name. Most of my work I do in a studio. I went up to the site, once or twice. To supervise, you know? Off a bus stop in Queens. Peaceful little place. Couple miles from the river. Behind an old warehouse."

"You mean it's in some park?"

He shook his head. "A cemetery."

A choir had begun to sing a hymn inside and now a somber attendant was hurrying down the steps at them. "Excuse me," he said. "The service has begun."

Griffith looked around, surprised to see everyone else had moved inside. "Thank you." He turned back to the stranger. "I really must go."

"Good, then. Just wanted to meet you and say hello."

He mumbled good morning and hurried away up the steps, regretting at once that he had not asked more questions. The man said his work was in a cemetery. What could that mean? A decoration at a gate? If it was for a grave, whose grave was it? And why the expense of commissioning a sculptor?

He removed his hat and tried to pat down his hair, unbuttoning his coat as he slipped into an empty pew. It was the same Augusta, that was clear. Why didn't he get the sculptor's name? It would have been a pleasure looking up Augusta again.

The choir ended its final offering and a communion prayer was shared, and then a priest stepped forward to speak of Robert Harron. Even at a distance he recognized the dark-framed glasses and could tell it was Father Bill. The handsome middle-aged man remembered Bobby as a frisky and mischievous young boy with a grown man's sense of responsibility to his family.

Many of his stories were funny and others quite touching. Still, somewhere in the course of his speech his words became just a jumble of background noise. This mystery of Augusta Lee now occupied Griffith's mind, whipping his imagination this way and that. It was as if a lost, broken-off piece of his life suddenly loomed on the horizon like an iceberg, a menace to navigation.

Eventually Father Bill commended Robert Harron to God's merciful love, and ended with a quotation from St. Paul to the Corinthians: "What eye has not seen, and ear has not heard … this God has revealed to us through the Spirit. For the Spirit scrutinizes everything, even the depths of God."

It was over. He grabbed up his hat from the bench and held onto his coat as he went shooting outside to find the shaggy sculptor. The only ones waiting there were the expected handful of drivers standing by their cars.

It was easy enough to lose himself at Mamaroneck. From time to time he would make a casual inquiry of former colleagues. Did he or she recall a charming young actress named Augusta Lee? Had anyone heard what had become of her? Someone who had talked to Mary Pickford by telephone asked if she knew anything about the young woman's fate. Mary claimed not to remember any such person. Miss Lillian, of course, had not come along until a year or two after Augusta vanished.

One assistant thought Owen Moore might know something about her, but there was nothing that could move him to speak to that man again. He had corrupted Mary's underage brother Jack Pickford, introducing him to alcohol at thirteen years old. He had gotten Jack mixed up with some of the sleaziest elements in the business, which led to him losing his virginity in a bordello at the tender age of fourteen.

All that might have remained ancient history except for the tragic consequences it sowed. All reports were that Jack had turned into a lost alcoholic degenerate. He even infected his lovely young bride, a promising actress and former Ziegfeld girl named Olive Thomas, with the sins and ravages of his hedonism. No sooner was Bobby Harron laid to rest than the word arrived from Europe that twenty-one-year-old Olive Thomas had fallen victim to her own mad descent into alcohol and drugs. Whether confused or on purpose, she had swallowed a bottle of poison in a fit of despondency.

Owen Moore had a lot to answer for. Now that he and Mary Pickford were legally divorced he never expected to have to talk to the man again.

There was one other person who might have more personal knowledge of Augusta Lee. He knew she had been buddies with Mack Sennett back in the early days. It was possible that they had remained in contact. So, late one Wednesday afternoon he initiated a cross-country phone call to Los Angeles. Moments later he was connected to the world-famous "king of comedy."

Sennett had been the hottest producer in the business since 1912 when he left to found his Keystone Studios. By 1917, though, he wanted out of the full-time grind of running a studio. He opted for the less stressful pace of making two-reelers for Paramount Pictures under the Triangle banner.

The trade advertisement for Mack's fresh start managed to offend Griffith all over again. It was a new jab at their "artistic" differences. A top-panel cartoon showed a crowd lined up for a Sennett program. "Laugh and the world laughs with you," it said. Below it was a cartoon of a deserted theater offering something titled "A Mother's Sorrow." The words below it seemed aimed at Griffith's last few releases: "Weep and you weep alone."

Mack Sennett sounded touched to hear from him. "So sorry to miss the funeral and all. Hope you got my letter."

"Sure. I wrote you back."

"It just came at a really awkward time. I couldn't leave. Hope everyone understood."

"Next time I come out I want you to take me deep-sea fishing."

"Let's do it. Maybe we can work in a boxing match, too. You seen Dempsey? He's got killer style."

"I've heard that. ... Listen, I ran into a man back here."

"I hope you weren't in a car at the time." Mack gave a loud laugh. Even across three thousand miles of phone cable his bray of a laugh sent shivers up Griffith's spine.

"What's that? No. He was asking about a girl you might remember. … Augusta Lee?"

"Who is that? I didn't hear."

"Augusta Lee."

"Augusta Lee! Sure, I remember her. Southern gal. Sweet. Quite a looker."

"This fellow I was talking to, he did some business for her and he was trying to find her. I couldn't tell him a thing. Said I'd ask around. I know you see a lot of actors out there."

"I do, yes."

"I thought there was a chance … maybe you heard something about her?"

"No. If I did, I'd throw her some work. I can always use a sharp gal like that."

"So you don't know what happened to her?"

"She got married, didn't she? A big fella, worked in insurance."

"That's right. This man out here, said he did some work for her. Said she had lots of money."

"Don't surprise me."

"But she was just a working gal. How do you suppose she came into money?"

"I don't know. Maybe that husband of hers left her set up."

"I guess."

"Hey, old man, I'm sorry, I got to run. No rest for the wicked. Call me some Sunday next time. Love to catch up."

"All right, Mack."

"I hear that 'Way Down East' is goin' great guns."

Mack was either joking or he was just being kind. They both knew that box office for serious drama was as flat as Kansas now. Ticket-buyers wanted adventure serials and chases and matinee getaways. To hear Joe Public tell it, Mack Sennett had practically invented their kind of movies.

"We're doing all right back here, Mack. You take care of yourself, you hear?"

At the end of each busy day now he shut his eyes on the mystery of Augusta Lee, and every morning it was the first thing he thought of. On impulse he dispatched his driver to make a proscribed run around the easternmost part of Queens. He told him only to keep an eye out for any abandoned warehouse or a possible out-of-the-way property that might include a cemetery. The driver returned before lunch asking for more details on what he was supposed to be looking for.

Late one morning, however, the driver came back with a different report. He had happened upon an old gravel and cement factory that backed onto a neglected tract of land. Off beyond a wrought iron gate he could make out what appeared to be the tops of crosses.

Griffith cleared his afternoon schedule and when his last production meeting ended he had the driver take him back to the place he had found. The cement factory sat boarded up off the road behind rusted wire fencing with a padlocked gate.

"Wait here," he told the man and went off on foot down a worn dirt path that weaved around the building.

The back lot was overrun with weed clumps and strewn with the broken rubble and gravel of quarried stone. The stiff paper of torn sacks of sand flapped in the wind. Across a gentle swell he came upon a valley of wild grasses bounded by hickory trees and a distant grove of birches. Down at the sagging center of it all was a patch of scuttled crosses and rows of sunken markers leading to taller memorial headstones and crypts.

With no sales office in sight and not a soul anywhere to ask, he headed down the slope. What on Earth was he doing here? How could anything he found in a place like this ever satisfy his questions?

The rows pointed him toward a marble sarcophagus that he decided to use as a landmark for a systematic sweep. The sarcophagus appeared larger than the others, with three distinct tiers to it and a frieze in front of carved figures.

As he got closer he realized he had found what he came for.

The male figure to the right bore an unmistakable likeness. That was his chiseled form rising from the stone with an opened script cascading from his hand. To his right crouched a man whose face was hidden behind a camera on a tripod, and in back of him stood a round-faced man, alert and watching. It was possibly meant to be Mack Sennett, though the carved figure was less hulking and more graceful than its model.

Other figures in the frieze appeared to be society ladies in puffed-out skirts and parasols standing near elegant, top-hatted gentlemen. The way they stood listening suggested they might be actors in costumes, awaiting directions for their next scene.

The stepped tiers were etched with a crisscrossing latticework like the rails of a riverboat. On top was the suggestion of a pilothouse and beyond that two barrel-like projections like the nubs of smokestacks. This was no simple grave marker. It was Augusta's life history set in stone.

There were three engraved shields across the block's base. Each was inscribed with a name and dates. *Elzaphen Walter Lee, 1868 – 1908*, read the first. *Jemima Thompson Lee, 1871 – 1907*, read the second. Judging from the dates, the first could have been Augusta's father and the second her mother. The final shield held a simpler name in quotation marks: *"Baby Lee,"* and the single date, *May 7, 1909*. That would have been the day of the tragedy at the Palisades, the day that poor fellow—what was his name?—plunged to his death. This must have been the infant she had lost that sad day. There was no mention of Augusta's husband.

She had brought the remains of her family here. It hardly seemed possible. She never struck him as the foolishly romantic sort, and this went well beyond the sentimental. What could be the point of it?

He took a final walk around the stone, marveling at the eye of the sculptor, the skill and care of the carving. There was a pleasing beauty to it all. Despite that, there was also something futile and pathetic about it in some way.

Visitors might glance up as they passed, but they would never know the story it told. Nothing achieved by man or woman in this life was destined to last. Bobby was gone just as surely as Linda had left him. All of their movies would disappear as well, and the last drops of their devotion and purpose would bleed back into the earth, forgotten.

He had spent too much time here. He should get back to his driver, back to all the pointless activity that remained to be done that day.

He looked off at the footpath and was startled to find he was no longer alone. Sitting quietly there nearby him was a large dog with a dusty yellow coat. It had crept up without making a sound, and was sitting on its haunches with its head cocked curiously, a foot-long stick gripped in its jaws.

"Well, hello. Where'd you come from?"

The dog lowered its snout to the ground and dropped the stick on the path at his feet. It never took its watery brown eyes off of his.

"My, you are a pretty fellow, aren't you?" he said. He started to give the animal a pat on its neck but it scooted back out of reach.

"Where do you belong?" He looked around at the sloping hills for any trace of an owner. "You know, I had a pretty fellow just like you once. He got too old, and my father had to come take him away."

The dog's head tilted to the side and its alert eyes brimmed with impatience. It lowered its wet nose again to nudge the stick toward his boot.

"No one to play with you, hunh? Me neither." He bent for the stick, then put one foot behind him and twisted his spine as he pulled back an arm. "Okay, boy. Here it goes!" He pitched the stick as hard and far as he could manage.

The dog was off in a flash, moving at full speed through the rippling wildgrass. It pounced and disappeared a second, then came leaping up again with its prize. The black wings of its nostrils flared as it dropped the stick at his feet and fixed him again in its sight.

"Once more? Okay, pretty boy." He picked it up again, feeling it damp with saliva. "Fetch!" The stick hurtled end over end into the sky before dropping.

In no time at all the dog was back, prancing at his feet with excitement for another throw.

"Okay. Once more, but then I must go." He tossed it higher this time into the glare of the sun. The dog seemed to lose it for a moment and ran blindly in a circle until the stick came down and bounced upon the grass. Instantly he had it and was on its way back.

"Good boy!"

He tried one more throw, and then another.

It felt so good to be out in the air with the warmth of the sun and the breeze buzzing with life. He was reminded of a day long ago with Edwin Porter when he went chasing after a papier-mâché eagle that had swooped from the sky and carried away a stuffed baby doll.

Today he had been the one swooping. He came here hungry for explanations or perhaps justifications. What he found was a charming gesture left by one sweet, unloved orphan girl who desired a bit more permanence in this confoundingly unstable existence.

Where would he have to go to find a better answer than hers?

Now as he waited for the stick to return he was a schoolboy again. He bobbed on his toes like a boxing ring god, jabbing at nothing, guarding his chin, dodging invisible fists.

THE END

An Interview with the Author

What is your book about?

It's an historical novel about the first battle over motion picture censorship. This happened long before there was a Hays office or a production code. The action takes place in Manhattan in 1909, at a time when most film production was centered in New York. It's an invitation to readers to step inside one of the earliest movie studios in America.

What were those first studios like?

They were wild and lively places, filled with the fumes and freedoms of the industrial boom. Their rooftops and brownstone quarters attracted all manner of bohemian actors and crazy inventors—young people with fresh ideas who had not been corrupted by riches or a desire for fame. They were like the "garage bands" of their day. Everyone was busy making it up as they went along. They railed against Edwardian conformity and social injustices. They were working in a medium already known for deplorable excesses. My novel centers on one not-so-innocent young actress who is chosen to help reform that sleazy reputation.

Is that the meaning of the title?

"The Designated Virgin" is actually an old show business tradition stretching back to renaissance Europe. But it was adopted in America sometime in the 1800s when New York stage companies began visiting frontier towns and ran afoul of local "community standards." The managers might dispatch their sweetest, most innocent-looking young actresses to private meetings with the opposition in hopes of winning them over. In the new century movie-makers also confronted threats of censorship and set up their own "designated virgins" to improve their image.

How did movies acquire a sleazy image?

Don't forget, the public's first exposure to moving pictures was via hand-cranked machines in penny arcades. Pioneering cameraman Billy Bitzer wrote about making them for American Biograph at the turn of the century. They were literally "peep shows" featuring dancers like Little Egypt and subjects like "How Girls Undress" and "The Sultan and His Harem." They had to have a midway exploitation angle. Even Thomas Edison targeted the lowest denominator with his Vitagraph recreations of shoot-outs and historical beheadings.

There were also the newsreels, of course, what Bitzer called "news happenings." He shot footage for Biograph of the Spanish-American War, the sinking of the U.S.S. Maine in Havana Harbor, and the aftermath of natural catastrophes. Boxing matches were always popular with the men. But we forget today that boxing matches were banned in 19th century America. The studios that filmed them and distributed the footage risked big fines and even jail time. They were pretty much the pornographers of their day.

When did movies become scandalous?

That happened with the first projected films. The big screen turned those guilty pleasures into very public events. Even something as innocuous as Edison's 1896 short "The Kiss" incited controversy at a summer fair in Louisiana. It was just a medium close-up of two stage actors—May Irwin and John Rice from the New York stage comedy "The Widow Jones"—sitting and sharing a kiss. But public displays of emotion were frowned upon in Edwardian society. And journalists of that time were quick to champion modesty and civic virtue.

One newspaper published an editorial against the outrage of showing such a thing to unsuspecting families. That just guaranteed everyone would want to see it. Producers learned there was money to be made from those public outcries. By the time Edison's company released Edwin Porter's "The Great Train Robbery" in 1903 there was a demand for more theaters that could handle the crowds.

So projection itself reshaped the business?

Yes. And the speed at which the five-cent theaters spread caught elected officials off-guard. By 1908 there were thousands of those nickelodeons in small towns across the country. Over three million Americans attended movies on a weekly basis. Moralists worried about them glorifying sex and criminal behavior and alcoholism— all potential problems for cities in the industrial revolution.

Politicians also had to contend with the crowding in those unregulated storefront spaces converted into theaters. The nickelodeons were denounced as firetraps and breeding grounds for vermin and contagious diseases. A lot of it was just fearmongering by those who hoped to kill off the new movie industry. But the public safety issues were real enough.

Who wished to see motion pictures fail?

Legitimate theater owners, for one. Broadway producers had monopolized the American stage and established nationwide circuits for their touring productions. Movie houses offered a whole evening's entertainment for a nickel. At the other end of the spectrum were the vaudeville owners. They couldn't compete with the nickelodeons. But they soon decided "if you can't beat 'em join 'em," and began putting split-reel comedies and newsreels on their live bills.

The staunchest enemies of movies, though, were the civic watchdog groups. There was a clamoring across America for someone to regulate what was being shown in the movie houses. In Manhattan, reformers like Canon William Chase and Reverend Charles Parkhurst joined forces with the Women's Christian Temperance Union and the Anti-Saloon League to form a potent lobby. If a governor or mayor wouldn't recognize the moral threat posed by motion pictures, the reformers would offer to support his political rivals. The opposition party could always make some hay by occupying the moral high ground and condemning motion pictures. Suddenly, those making little filmed entertainments found themselves in the fight of their lives.

And that led to the "McClellan Massacre?"

Yes. In 1908, New York City Mayor George B. McClellan bowed to political pressures from the Tammany Hall bosses. Using the excuse of public safety and existing "blue laws," he revoked the business licenses of all the nickelodeons in New York City.

This was right at the start of the lucrative Christmas holiday, when the whole industry depended on the added revenue from the family trade. Insiders dubbed the action "the McClellan Massacre." Fortunately, it did not last long. The Edison Trust lawyers won an injunction in court to halt it. But the repercussions were dramatic.

What were the consequences for producers?

All the affiliated studios of the Edison Trust agreed to the establishing of New York's first Board of Censorship. They agreed to submit their latest feature films to the board for advance certification. It put motion picture makers and their exchanges on notice. They had to be able to defend their releases in light of undefined "community standards." It did not stop producers from exploiting sin and human weakness on screen, but it did challenge picture makers to package them in more sophisticated ways.

"The Designated Virgin" is set in that crucial period of early 1909, in the wake of the McClellan Massacre. It dramatizes the pressures that came to bear on picture studios in the days before the industry was even considered newsworthy by *The New York Times* and other journals.

Why did you choose to write it as a novel rather than non-fiction?

A good work of historical fiction will honor the known facts while providing a human framework for them. It can clarify complex issues and make them more understandable.

Of course, film historians and researchers wade through a lot of gossip and nonsense in show business periodicals and biographies. Their problem is always separating fact from fantasy, which places us at odds. *Who do we novelists think we are, coming in and twisting the facts and traipsing across their neat historical carpets with our muddy lies?*

But it's not as black-and-white as that, is it? Historians could never have all the facts. They are often left to speculate and guess at the most inopportune junctures. *Why did so-and-so do thus? What was truly behind the decision to incite such-and-such an event?* Even when the facts are clearly documented, motives are often open to interpretation. Different historians measure "reality" by their own lights and standards, fitting it into the theoretical templates they prefer. Good historical novelists can illuminate the past in ways non-fiction authors cannot. They dramatize issues and reveal characters that make them pertinent to human beings today.

What drew you to this particular era?

The rise of nickelodeons and a motion picture industry marked the arrival of the whole transformative glacier known as pop culture. Movies literally showed society its own reflection for the first time, creating new markets for the leisure classes.

I wanted to take readers back to 1909 and the first great American film studio—The American Biograph Co. When I began to lay out the time frame and saw who was actually on the scene at the time, I knew that D.W. Griffith would have to be a defining presence. He had only just gotten his start as a film director, bringing his stage experience to bear on the problem of telling stories without dialogue. What sort of pressures were on him to produce two films a week, what job insecurities could he have faced?

Suddenly the name Mack Sennett jumped out at me. I wanted to shout, "Eureka! I have a comedian!" My novel wouldn't just be about infidelities and crumbling marriages. I was able to add a wonderful slapstick sequence about a studio encounter with a live bear, as well as some of Sennett's famous subversive wit. No matter what sort of terror Sennett became when he was head of his own studio, in the early days he was a sweetheart, a gangly, socially awkward burlesque clown who thought he wanted to be an opera singer until he found himself relating more to the hooligans on the Bowery. He had a distrust of social hierarchies and rigid codes of conduct. That's how he came up with the Keystone Cops. To him it was always more amusing to watch society's pretentions bruised and deflated.

Together, Sennett and Griffith were central to what American movies were to become. They were worlds apart psychologically, but as a team they trail-blazed all the major commercial genres, from gangster films and situation comedies to slapstick farce and chase thrillers.

I wrote a blog about it on my author's site—"When the Movies Were of Two Minds." They complemented one another at the beginning, but in just four short years they went in separate ways to run their own studios according to their own tastes. They served as the prototype for all future "artistic differences" in the new Hollywood.

What would you like your movie history novels to achieve?

There's an idea out there that the European immigrants who ran the first Hollywood studios imposed their values on the American movie-goer. It was actually quite the opposite. What Hollywood represented reshaped the immigrant view of the world in profound ways. Those studio heads were obsessed with fitting into the great democratic experiment of America. They didn't fill their stories with Old World values about class distinctions. They did not accept that their destiny was limited to whatever station their parents had inherited. The whole edifice of a "dream factory" was built on the optimism of breaking free from the chains of the past.

I want to fit the whole sweep of America's cinema history into that broader context. A Conestoga wagon meant much more to the early film directors than a prop for a Western. It represented the pioneering urge to explore a limitless horizon. The American revolution and all it represented still hung in the dry California air. For the first time, ordinary citizens could decide what they might make of their lives.

D.W. Griffith would go on to direct the polarizing "Birth of a Nation." Why humanize such a racist?

That's not a simple question to answer. I gave it a lot of thought. Of course, "Birth of a Nation" offends everyone today, and rightly so. At the end of his life, even Griffith voiced regrets over the racial discord it sowed. He recommended that it be withheld permanently from public exhibition and shown only to film students and scholars. He told an interviewer in the 1940s, "The Negro race has had more than enough of its share of injustice, oppression, tragedy, and sorrow."

I did a good deal of research while writing my book. I read Griffith's original notes and hand-typed manuscripts at the Library of Congress, pored through the various drafts of his "autobiography" and other biographies. I'm convinced Griffith was what I would describe today as a "collateral racist." He was infected by all the racial assumptions of his day. He and his peers knew very little about the new science of genetics. Interracial marriage was a serious crime prosecuted by law in most states. But I'm also sure Griffith was not himself a bigot. Hatred simply was not a defining component in his psyche.

Even though his father eventually died of war wounds he suffered as a Confederate officer, Griffith did not identify with the South at all. He always felt apart from those he grew up with and did not think of himself as a regional writer. He wanted to follow in the footsteps of Shakespeare, which is why he became an actor with the goal of playwriting. He grew up idolizing Abraham Lincoln and would eventually depict "The Great Emancipator" as a tragic hero in a number of his films. Lincoln's assassination inside Ford's Theatre is the emotional heart of "Birth of a Nation."

Fifteen years before that, Griffith appeared on stage as an actor in a 1900 revival of Harriet Beecher Stowe's "Uncle Tom's Cabin." He played two roles—both the good husband George and the slave-owning villain, Simon Legree. He got good notices in both roles, which means he had grappled with the issues raised by Stowe's book and struggled with the question of what made George "good" and what made Simon Legree so despicable. Slavery was abolished a decade and a half before Griffith was born in 1878. But he had come to terms with how dehumanizing slavery was, both for the slave and the slave-holding family.

When he got to the point as a filmmaker of being able to make an epic, he used the Civil War as his subject because he wanted to thrill audiences with the grandest, most emotion-packed canvas he could imagine. In almost all ways, "Birth of a Nation" stands apart from Griffith's career output. In his first years at Biograph he chose social outcasts as his heroes. He celebrated Mexican vaqueros in California and Zulus in Africa. His 1910 version of "Ramona" contained the subtitle "A Story of the White Man's Injustice to the Indian." Four years before "Birth of a Nation" he made a two-reeler titled "The Rose of Kentucky," a story about evil Klansmen attacking a white plantation owner for refusing to join their ranks. When "Broken Blossoms" was released, Griffith was castigated by the Ku Klux Klan for questioning white supremacy.

None of this can excuse "Birth of a Nation" for its racist propaganda. Even when it debuted in 1915 it was indefensible. Audiences had no immunity to the powerful illusion of moving images. The fact is that Griffith had the opportunity to set America on its ear with an epic that spoke to the improvement of race relations and promoted human understanding. Instead, "Birth of a Nation" inflamed passions against the most innocent bystanders of the Civil War, people with almost no voice in their own destiny. The film now will stand forever as a billboard for Griffith's personal failure to seize his opportunity to make the case for racial tolerance.

My novel portrays Griffith in all his limited idealism and in his fallibility. Fiction is a magnificent vehicle for shedding light on human imperfection. Luckily for authors, world history has no shortage of what Mark Twain called "illustrative examples."

What message would you share as a historical novelist?

I know it's common today to categorize everyone who came before us as either victim or oppressor. But I see that as a grave disservice. It forces one to exist in a sad world. Isn't it gloomy to see all past generations as flawed and exploited? It's a lazy way to view history, I think. All people have limitations imposed on them by the times they live in. All of us face oppression and injustice in some form or another, whether it's due to skin color or birthright or the government we live under or the economic system we inherit. Who escapes all that without suffering indignities and slights? We might be tempted to lash out at others. But all religions teach us to be bigger than that and rise above our worst instincts.

The choices we make define us. Those who carry on with their dignity intact deserve respect. Our ancestors were much more than beaten-down, sorrowful victims. To understand that is to never again view history as dull or sad.

It sounds like you are no fan of the trend toward removing statues or erasing names from monuments.

Any official act of historical desecration should be taken very seriously. It's what totalitarian governments do, isn't it? I see the attempt to whitewash the past as an assault on the minds of our grandchildren and of future generations. It's like mental ethnic cleansing. It seeks to rob them of tools they might need to clearly see the world. It's often the case that the very things that make yesterday's causes and heroes politically incorrect are what they have to teach us today.

Today's heroes are those who will stand up for preserving a complete record of the past, not just a version of it. You can criticize your father's opinions and still love him. It's no stretch to only love and honor the people who agree with us. Even the ancestors who fought for a cause we hate were human beings first and foremost. Bulldozing a swath through history does not demonstrate a heightened grasp of social justice, only a diminished capacity for benevolence. We shouldn't forget that at the end of the Civil War President Abraham Lincoln asked that his Northern band play "Dixie" for the crowd. It's never too soon or too late to heal divisions.

About the Author

Born and raised in Los Angeles, John W. Harding grew up amid all the magic and drama of movie-making in the 20th century. For 20 years he covered the film industry as a writer and award-winning editor with the Tribune Company, leaving journalism in 2012 to re-explore the lost era through his own historical novels.

As he puts it, "The movies always saw world history as fair game for dramatic interpretation. It was time that someone turned the same fictional lens on them."

His first published novel was *The Ben-Hur Murders: Inside the 1925 'Hollywood Games'*, a look at the way Prohibition twisted and transformed the growing studio system.

He currently lives in Maryland with his wife.